Hunting Grounds

Maddie Castle
Book 3

L.T. Ryan

with
C.R. Gray

LIQUID MIND MEDIA

For information contact:
contact@ltryan.com
https://LTRyan.com
https://www.instagram.com/ltryanauthor/
https://www.facebook.com/LTRyanAuthor

The Maddie Castle Series

The Handler

Tracking Justice

Hunting Grounds

Vanished Trails (Coming Soon)

Want a free copy of the Maddie Castle prequel novella? Sign up for my newsletter and download a copy today:

https://liquidmind.media/maddie-castle-newsletter-signup-1/

Love Maddie? Jack Noble? Rachel Hatch? Get your very own L.T. Ryan merchandise today! Click the link below to find coffee mugs, t-shirts, and even signed copies of your favorite thrillers! https://ltryan.ink/EvG_

Acknowledgments

A special thanks to LaNell Strietzel for providing her insights into the inner workings of police K9 operations and for her service to community and country. Her rescue and recovery efforts conducted have helped countless people.

Also, I'd like to thank Brian Shea for sharing his extensive law enforcement experience in the creation of this series.

It's heroes like LaNell and Brian that have served to inspire the Maddie Castle series. We hope these books serve to honor those unique officers and their four-legged partners.

And to all of my early/beta readers for their feedback and assistance finding those lingering typos that always seem to make their way into a manuscript.

Chapter 1

SO PRETTY.

Maddie Castle was so pretty like this.

Fisting a bound up pink paisley blanket to her face. That blond hair like an ocean wave composed of golden thread on the purple pillow-case. The way her supple cheeks flushed in her sleep, the rosy glow illuminated by the moonlight.

So pretty. So feminine. So dainty.

That growling and snarling bitch in the crate by the closet was closer to how he'd remembered Maddie Castle. Beautiful, yes, but lethal enough to rip a limb off. She almost had.

His grandfather used to say that about women. That's why they called them bitches. They were like dogs. When looking at one, the body flooded with an urge to touch. To run fingers through their hair. To hold them close. To find comfort in their embrace.

That was precisely what made them so dangerous. Evolution had programmed them to seem harmless. To be inviting. To make you want to get closer. But when you did, they'd snap and snarl and scar you forever.

That was why, like dogs, they needed to be kept in crates or on a leash.

He found it so hard to accept that this woman—so pretty, feminine, dainty—had held the gun that put a bullet through him. Massaging the pain that pulsed harder at the memory in his left bicep, his jaw tightened. This one tiny woman ruined him in a way no other person ever had.

Clenching the blade tighter, he debated if he should do it now.

He could. In a heartbeat, he could slice her throat just like he had all the others. He could end her. She'd be gone forever.

But what fun would that be?

The kill was fine, but the fun part was watching them squirm. Like a mouse to his cat. Of course, the cat could kill the mouse before the mouse realized what was happening, just like he could now. But cats loved tossing the mouse in the air and watching it fall to the ground with a broken leg. They loved to let the mouse go, only to snatch it up in its claws again and listen to it squeal. That squeal, that cry for help, it was the cat's favorite part. Sure, cats needed to eat, but that wasn't why they did it. They played with their food because it was fun. Watching them suffer was the best part.

Much like how, for all this time, he had watched Maddie suffer. He watched her relearn to walk. He watched her lose her fiancé. He watched her battle a little orange bottle. He watched her fight to keep her lights on.

Now, she wasn't struggling. She spent much of tonight smiling. She was excited about the future. Her car was paid off, as was her trailer. She had a blossoming, fairytale romance. Almost every night, she was out with Bentley, or Alex, or Grace, and what fun was that?

No, no, no. It was time to make her squirm again.

Stepping closer to the bed, he leaned down. Shutting his eyes, he took in a long whiff of her hair. Again, he was shocked, maybe a bit excited, by the floral, dainty scent.

There came that urge. The lethal one. The aching yearning to touch. He knew he shouldn't, but he had to.

Peeling off one glove, he trailed a finger down those golden waves. Yes, that was it. Excitement. Excitement rushed through him like adrenaline from a pounding heart. The urge may've been dangerous, but that only strengthened the excitement.

It was exactly how he'd imagined it'd feel. So soft, so delicate. He could spend the rest of his life trailing his fingers through that silky, smooth gold.

Metal rattled.

Thump!

He jolted back.

The crate was on its side. The dog, Maddie's new dog, must've seen him touch her. She snapped and snarled behind the bars, warning him.

But there was nothing she could do behind those metal bars.

Smirking, he slid his glove back on and leaned close to Maddie once more. Much like a gardener would hold the bud of a flower as they assembled a bouquet, he grasped the lock of hair with gentle fingers and chiseled away at it with the blade in his hand.

As he straightened, he found the red string in his pocket. Carefully, he tied a neat bow around the golden lock. Making sure to be gentle, he tucked it neatly in the breast pocket of his black jacket.

Giving the dog in the crate a smirk on his way past, he stopped in the bathroom. Just as carefully, he wrapped a red ribbon around the faucet handle, tying it into a neat bow.

When she woke up, she would come here, see her lock of missing hair, the red ribbon on the faucet, and she would know.

The Red Ribbon Killer was back.

Soon enough, that bitch would be in a cage of her own.

Chapter 2

TEMPEST RARELY CRIED IN HER CRATE. IT WAS HER FAVORITE place in the house. That's where she got her meals, where she got to enjoy her lick mat. In the mornings, she waited for me to wake up and go to the bathroom. When I'd come back, she'd patiently wait for me to tell her it was time to come out.

Not today.

Today, sun barely peeking through the curtains, Tempest whined and cried. The clock on the nightstand read 6:05, meaning she wanted me to wake up two hours before my alarm. But I'd had dogs long enough to know that if I didn't get up on her command, I'd have a disaster to attend to when I woke up on mine. The last time Bear had woken me before my alarm, it was because the night prior, he'd gotten into the garbage while in the yard. He had one nasty bout of pancreatitis, which resulted in a mural of feces on my wall.

So, with an exhausted whine of my own, I sat up. Stifling a yawn, rubbing the crust from my eyes, I said, "What is it, Tempy? What's the matter?"

Only now that I had blinked hard enough could I see her, crouching awkwardly in her crate. The crate that was turned on its side.

4

Fumbling to my feet, everything blurred around the edges. I didn't know if it was the morning fog or if I was dizzy at the thought of another mural of feces on my wall.

The moment I opened the crate door, she barreled out. But she didn't run to the door. Knocking me backward, Tempest licked me all over. My face, my neck, my hair. *Specifically* my hair. She wouldn't stop sniffing my hair.

"How'd you do that?" I roughed up her ears, voice soft. "Are you sick? Do you need to go outside?"

Typically when I said "outside," she bolted to the door. But this time, she kept licking and sniffing my hair.

Glancing out the window, mostly covered by my yellow curtains, I checked for signs of a storm. That, she would cry and whine about. She'd never knocked over her crate before, but if there'd been thunder, I could see it. Thunder was Tempy's arch nemesis.

The sky was blue, though, and even if it had stormed, why hadn't it awoken me?

"What's the matter, baby?" Looking her all over, I patted her body, expecting her to yelp that something hurt. She didn't. All hundred pounds of her climbed into my lap instead.

Weird.

If she was still acting like this by the time the vet opened, that's where we were going.

After a few moments of puppy cuddles that calmed her down, and nearly lulled me back to sleep, my stomach started churning. The taste of acid and rotten food burned my mouth.

Struggling to my feet, I hurried to the bathroom and bent over the toilet. What happened there wasn't pretty, and I certainly didn't need a crowd for it. I had one, however. Tempest's big brown eyes guarded me in the bathroom doorway with every lurch.

"I'm okay, Tempy," I said when my stomach stopped spasming. Standing and walking to the sink, I kept eye contact with her in the mirror. "I'm just coming down with something. Everything's okay."

Then I reached for the faucet.

It wasn't only metal beneath my touch, but silky fabric.

A red ribbon was tied between the handles, meeting at a bow atop the spigot.

My heart dropped into my stomach.

Instinctively, I reached for the gun on my hip. The one that was tucked below my bed. I kept it there because if anyone came in my room while I was sleeping, I could grab it and defend myself in a heartbeat.

But now I was in the bathroom, and the only weapon I had was Tempest in the doorway.

I didn't have my phone.

Watch. I had my smartwatch.

Calling Tempest into the room, I shoved the bathroom door shut and hurried every heavy object I had in here in front of it. Wasn't much, just my laundry basket and my cane. I didn't use it often, but it came in handy when I was getting out of the shower, so this was where it stayed. I rushed to extend the bar and shoved it beneath the handle, barricading the laundry basket in front of it.

Scrolling through my watch to my phone app with shaking fingers, I reminded myself how stupid that was. The window was too small for me to fit through, meaning I had no escape route. Walls and doors in trailers were far too easy to break through. One glance at the holes my mom had punched through them was reminder enough of that.

Should I have run to the bedroom? Probably. But if he was in the house, was I better off behind a barricaded door?

No. I wasn't. I should've run to the bedroom. Why didn't I run to the bedroom? In every horror movie I'd ever watched, I screamed a million things that the heroine should've done differently. Now that I was in her position, all thought escaped me.

Thought escaped me altogether. Putting it into words, forming words at all, was harder than it'd ever been. I'd chalked the dizziness up to sickness, but something wasn't right. My thoughts weren't right. Was I hallucinating? The walls weren't breathing, and nothing else in here seemed out of place. But I couldn't remember the last time I'd been this flustered.

Come to think of it, I wasn't sure what I remembered at all.

What happened last night? Why did no thoughts come when I pictured last night?

What did he do to me?

The dial tone on my watch rang three times before it went to voicemail.

I didn't even know who I called. But I sure as hell knew who I was calling next.

He answered on the second ring. "Hey, Mad dog. How have—"

"He was in my house." Voice trembling, staring at the barricaded door, I walked backwards. Something touched my ass.

With an embarrassing shriek, I spun around.

The bathroom vanity. That's what touched my ass. Because I walked into it in my groggy stupor.

"Maddie, what the hell are you talking about?" Derek asked.

I heard him, but I forgot how to form words.

Because now that I faced the mirror, I looked at myself for the first time.

My hair was long. Too long, reaching the middle of my back. The side bangs had grown out, and I kept telling myself I needed to get it cut, but now, I was gonna have to.

A chunk on the right was gone. A hacked, jagged cut, directly beside my face, now only reaching my collar bone.

He cut my hair.

He was close enough to touch me.

He came into my house while I was sleeping and cut my hair.

He could've killed me.

"Madison Castle, if you don't start talking right now, I'm sending everybody."

"Do that. Send everybody."

He spoke into his radio, but all of it was gibberish, like he pulled the phone away from his face.

Staring at that chunk of hair in the mirror, I gripped the counter for stability. Lightheaded again, dizzy, I held that Formica countertop so tight that it hurt. Tempest was at my side, licking my fingers as I slowly lowered myself to the floor.

"Alright, talk to me, Maddie." Derek's voice was somehow strict and concerned at once. "What's going on?"

"He's back," was all that came out. My breathing wasn't right. I wasn't hyperventilating, but my breaths were short, slow. Just speaking was a challenge.

"You gotta tell me more than that, kid." Derek's sirens blared in the background, distracting me from his voice. "Are you okay? Are you hurt?"

"No. No, I don't think so, but he was here. He was in my house. The Country Killer. The Country Killer was in my house. He-he might still be in my house. I don't know. I don't know what to do. I'm trained for this, and I don't know what the hell to—"

"Breathe, kid. Come on, breathe with me." Derek told me to hold my breath for four seconds, exhale for four, and inhale for four on a loop. Four, four, four. The most effective breathing technique to calm the nervous system. He'd shown it to me when I was a kid, and I'd shown it to a few dozen of my own.

It did the trick well enough to soothe my slamming heart, but my breaths were too slow then, nearly lulling me to sleep on the bathroom floor. Like I was stoned. I felt like I was high, but I hadn't taken a damn thing, and that only scared me more.

Derek was walking me through another round of *four, four, four*, but I cut him off with, "What's the ETA? I don't feel right, and he could still be here, and-and—"

"I'm two minutes from your house. I'll be there soon. Tempest isn't going crazy, is she? Because if somebody's in your house, and you let her out of her crate, she'd go after them. Right? Isn't that how she is?"

It was. That made sense. I listened to that again in my mind, stroking my fingers down Tempest's head. Her big brown eyes were concerned, focused entirely on me.

If someone were here, she wouldn't have run to me. She would've run to the attacker. That suggested he was gone, gone long enough for her to calm down and refocus her energy on my safety.

"Yeah, she's in my lap. Maybe I should go to my room and get my gun—"

"No, you stay exactly where you are. I'm on your road. I can see your park now. You stay exactly where you are until I get there." At least he had a rational mind, because I absolutely did not. Not right now. "Talk to me, Maddie. Tell me what happened."

I rehashed it quickly, grasping that chopped lock of hair between my quivering fingers. Somewhere during it, I got myself worked up again. "He cut my hair. He–he took my hair. That's his signature. That's his trophy. He took my hair, and—"

"Alright. Alright, I'm here. I just pulled into your driveway. You're in the bathroom, right?" I nodded in answer, as though he could see me. "If your front door's locked, I'm gonna break it."

What was one more broken thing around this place?

"Okay. Okay, just be careful. If he's here, he'll shoot."

Derek said he understood, then kept talking to me about useless things I couldn't remember if someone held a gun to my head as he walked through my house. His heavy footsteps were almost as loud as my pounding heart.

So many times, I had been the cop who'd walked into the aftermath of situations like this with a level mind. I knew how to handle things like this. The last time I had been this terrified, I was in the exact same spot. I vowed that I'd never be this scared again. That's why I became a cop. So I didn't end up here, rolled into a ball on the bathroom floor with the door shut, petrified of my mom breaking it down. So I could *be there* for the person rolled into a ball on the bathroom floor.

Derek was that person today. "It's clear, Maddie. No one's here."

I'd never stood so quickly in my life.

The moment I flung the door open, I reached out and held that wall of a man just as tightly as I had when he'd arrested my mom.

9

Returning the hug, Derek patted my back a few times. "It's alright. It's all alright, Mad dog."

Stepping back, pounding heart leveling, I pointed to the ribbon on the sink. "That's him. It has to be him."

Derek didn't respond, only brushed past me into the bathroom.

My watch buzzed, and *Ox* lit up the screen.

Apparently, he was who I'd called in my frenzy.

Chapter 3

WITHIN AN HOUR, THERE WERE HALF A DOZEN PATROL CARS AND almost twice as many police lined up around my trailer. Ox had made it here within thirty minutes, record time given how far away he lived. EMS came too, and my vitals were in the normal range. But I disagreed. My heart rate may have been 65 beats per minute, but it felt like it was twice that.

A walk-through of my house made it clear how he'd gotten in. As per his MO, the window behind my table in the kitchen was broken. It wasn't always the *kitchen* window, but that was always his method. A broken window. Because the trailer was situated on a weird hill, he didn't need a ladder to snake his way inside. All he needed was a cinderblock from the pile beside my back door that I used as a staircase.

While they looked around, searching for more evidence, I sat on the grass and hugged my knees. Tempest was at my side the whole time, snarling at anyone who approached too quickly.

One of Derek's guys, a state police officer, said to another a few minutes earlier, "Couldn't it have been a prank? Everybody knows she's the one who shot him."

I would've agreed, if not for the fact that I had no recollection of last night.

My brain was like a web with a series of bugs trapped within it. One of them was a memory from yesterday morning. I had taken Tempest on her walk with Bentley. We had breakfast at his house, and then... And then I had no idea.

I remembered flashes of Bentley's face. I remembered laughing. I remembered feeling sick. But I couldn't attach visuals to all those memories. I couldn't remember where I had gone or what I had done. I didn't remember putting these clothes on—a pretty red blouse that I only wore on special occasions, and my dark washed blue jeans. Yesterday morning, I wore sweatpants and a hoodie on my walk, like I always did. Now I was in a nice red blouse and a pair of jeans.

And it was terrifying.

As someone who'd grown up with an abusive parent, as a cop, and then as a P.I., I'd been involved in life-threatening situations more times than I had fingers and toes to count with. But nothing scared me more than not knowing how these clothes ended up on my skin.

Squatting in front of me, Ox pulled my attention from my scrambled, racing thoughts. Those usually cold blue eyes were the warmest I'd ever seen them. "Did you hear me, Mads?"

Rubbing my hands up and down my arms, I cleared my throat. "No. I'm sorry. What'd you say?"

"Has anyone looked at your cameras yet?" He gestured to the corner of the trailer where the wall met the roof. "They work, don't they?"

Why hadn't I thought of that? Why did it feel like someone had put an emulsifying blender into my brain and pressed pulse until it was mush?

"Right. Yeah, they work."

I fumbled for my phone in my jeans pocket, then swiped it on. Things didn't even look right. Flipping through the applications, trying to get to the one that controlled my cameras, my head pounded. It was like I was drunk, like I was spinning. I kept flicking for a few more heartbeats, before it slipped through my sweaty fingers and landed on the dewy grass.

Ox got it before I could. Coming a little closer, he put a hand on my shoulder. "Are you okay?"

Out of instinct, I nodded.

"You don't look it." Any other time, I would've made a joke about that, but I couldn't think of one. "You didn't relapse, did you?"

Chills swept over my entire body, and my stomach ached. "I don't think so."

He furrowed his brows. "What do you mean, you don't *think* so?"

"I don't remember." Swallowing hard, that ache in my stomach intensified. "I don't remember much after yesterday morning." I opened my mouth to continue, but I wasn't sure I wanted to voice it aloud. I wasn't sure I wanted to voice it to him, at least.

"What do you remember?"

It was such a muddy mess; all I could do was shake my head.

Rather than pressure me to say more, as I would've expected from Ox, he sat beside me. Close, but not so close that it was uncomfortable. It was soothing, in fact. No matter how things had gone between us, we had spent a decade together. Just his familiar presence was enough to dull the terror that locked up my limbs.

Flipping into my cameras, he scrolled back to yesterday. The cameras only recorded when there was movement, which there was when I'd left to go on my walk with Bentley, and then again when I returned. I looked my usual self, laughing and smiling with my best friend. Ox tensed at that, but he didn't say anything. He flicked to the next recorded movement, which was around 5 PM.

It was me, walking out of the front door. Wearing the red shirt and dark washed jeans.

A wave of relief crashed through me.

Especially so when I walked to the driveway and met Bentley at his car. We talked for a few minutes, then he got in his, I got in mine, and I followed him out of view.

I didn't remember it, but there were few people I trusted more than Bentley. If I was with him, I'd been safe. And that meant that he would know something. He could tell me where we had gone and what we had done. I desperately needed that right now. I needed someone to tether me back to reality, because I was stuck in the cobweb, and I didn't know how to get out.

The next clip Ox clicked on was around 11 PM. It was Bentley's car pulling into the driveway beside mine. My car didn't come up next, however. Instead, I stumbled from the passenger seat. Grace got out behind me and helped me stay steady. I must've said something to her, because she laughed. But then I hurled.

Bentley took Grace's place, holding me around my waist to keep me upright. He walked me to the door and then inside. The next piece of footage was inside my entryway, then in my kitchen.

There was audio for those.

"I really don't like this, Maddie," Bentley said, bearing almost all of my weight as he carried me through the living room. "You should come to my place so I can keep an eye on you."

I said, "I just need to sleep."

"You need a banana bag." He spoke under his breath, shaking his head slightly. Usually, he was softer. In this video, though, he looked annoyed. "Are you sure I don't need to go get the naloxone?"

"I'm not high, Bentley." I sounded equally annoyed. But in the position I was in now, I didn't blame him for believing I was high. I looked all too much like my strung-out mother in this clip, clutching his shirt just to stay on my feet. "It's the flu or something. It has to be."

He didn't say anything, only continued walking me through the house. As he got closer to the camera, though, I saw the look on his face. The look I knew far better than I wished I did. It was the same expression he gave his father when he came home drunk.

Had I relapsed? Nothing had happened. My pain wasn't even bad yesterday. There were no drugs in this house, and I didn't even know where I could get more.

Actually, I did. Simeon Gunn. I made a mental note to check my texts and calls after Ox finished going through them. But even if that were so, even if I had relapsed, why was my hair cut? Why was my window broken? Why was there a ribbon around my faucet? Why was Tempest's crate knocked over?

The only places I didn't have cameras were the bedrooms and bathroom. The one in the kitchen faced down the hall, toward my room. It picked up on mine and Bentley's movement in that part of the house. Although barely more than blobs, it looked like Bentley helped me into my bed and covered me up.

He didn't say anything to me before he returned to the doorway.

Then, hardly audible, I heard my strained, stoned voice say, "Are you mad at me?"

Facing the camera now, I got a look at Bentley's face. His jaw clenched for half of a second. Blowing out a deep breath, it softened. He looked at me again, meaning that I couldn't see his face. "No, Maddie. I'm not mad at you."

"I didn't relapse," I said again. "I'm sick. I'm just sick."

He said nothing for a few seconds, then he nodded. "Okay."

"I didn't. I swear I didn't."

His shoulders rose and fell with a deep breath. "I believe you."

But when he turned around, his face said otherwise.

God, that hurt. The disappointment. The heartache. It practically poured out of him, and I didn't blame him. *Couldn't* blame him. I looked like I was high, I sounded like I was high, and I couldn't even walk on my own.

The next few clips were Bentley letting Tempest out of her crate, taking her outside to do her business, bringing her back in, and feeding her. He asked me one more time if I was sure I didn't want him to take me to the hospital, and I confirmed that I didn't. In usual Maddie fashion.

And then, at 2:06 AM, all of my cameras began recording at once.

Ox clicked the first one. But it wasn't a video.

Just a black screen with a red ribbon strewn across it, tied in a pretty bow.

Each and every camera recorded a black screen with a red ribbon from 2:06 to 2:53 AM.

15

Then, the only recordings were of stray cats leaping through my yard.

"How is that even possible?" It could have been the haze, or maybe the trauma of knowing that a serial rapist and murderer had been in my house for almost an hour last night while I slept, but my brain still felt like mush. "I don't understand. Can somebody just hack a security camera like this?"

Ox didn't answer me. He stood and started toward Bentley's trailer at a pace that made my heart feel like it was going to break my ribs.

Chapter 4

QUESTIONING BENTLEY MADE SENSE. OX RUNNING TO HIS PORCH and slamming on his door as though he was the killer did not.

Ox pounded on it so hard that the curtain on the other side, held up by a magnetic rod, fell to the floor. That wasn't a rare occasion. That damn curtain fell all the time, but it did say something about Ox's fury.

Grabbing his arm, I attempted to pull him back. Which was just about fruitless. Ox was over six feet tall with the body of a linebacker. Even if I were at my best, I couldn't pull him away from much of anything.

"He took me home and got me to bed," I said, still trying to pull him back. "He didn't hurt me, Ox."

"You were sober when you left, and you came back higher than a god damn kite." Jaw taut, he pounded on the door again. "He better have a good explanation."

"And you better behave like a cop and not like a jealous ex," I snapped.

He shot me a look for that.

I hadn't said it to be dramatic. If Ox was in his right mind, he would recognize the conflict of interest here. This wasn't because he thought Bentley was The Country Killer.

This was because he knew I loved Bentley, and Ox didn't think he was good enough for me. Ox saw those videos, knew that monster had been in my house, and knew that Bentley had left me vulnerable. If Ox had found me in that state, he would've hog-tied me and carried me to the hospital if he had to. He would've made me take a drug test when I'd insisted I hadn't relapsed. Had I refused, he would've held me down and shoved the naloxone up my nose.

That was how Ox showed care. Tough love. To hell with what I thought. Ox knew best.

Bentley showed care like a gentle parent. He was disappointed in me. Angry that he thought I'd gotten high. But he knew I wasn't in a place to talk rationally, so he breathed through his frustration, did his best to make sure I was safe, and walked away to calm down.

To me, that was emotional maturity. But to the hard ass detective, that was weakness.

Yes, I was defensive of Bentley because I cared about him, but I cared about Ox too. I didn't want to see his temper derail this investigation or his career.

"Do you even have your badge on you?" I gestured to his baggie gray sweatpants, wrinkled T-shirt, and hoodie. "Question him, fine, but watch how you do it."

"You're the victim here, not my superior. Don't tell me how to do my job."

Nothing got my gears grinding more than being called a victim. While it was true, he knew I found that insulting.

I opened my mouth to rebut something smart, but the door swinging open cut me off.

Bentley's sleepy brown eyes grew to discs the moment the door was wide open. He looked at me, then at Ox, and then at the dozens of officers scattered about. Before he had time to say anything, Ox began.

"Were you with Maddie last night?"

Blinking hard, he said, "What's going—"

"I asked you a question. Were you with Maddie last night?"

I said, "Ox, you know—"

"I'm not talking to you. I'm talking to him." His gaze stayed on Bentley. "Were you with Maddie last night?"

"Yeah, we went out with my daughter." Still flustered, Bentley stepped closer to me. "What's going on?"

Ox stepped between us. "Where were you?"

"We went to my daughter's chorus concert." Bentley's tone was just as annoyed with Ox as it'd been with me last night. Awkwardly craning around Ox to see me better, his eyes were concerned. "Are you okay, Mads?"

The chorus concert. I did remember that. I remembered that last week, Grace had asked me to go. It was patchy, but vague memories floated back of searching for her face among the few dozen kids on stage. Grace introduced us to a few of her teachers. I sat beside Bentley in the crowd. We made jokes about how the music teacher had worn the same cardigan as when she'd taught our chorus class back in the day.

Then after the chorus concert, we went... somewhere. I had bought her flowers, and I'd handed them to her when she walked off the stage, but I didn't remember much after that. Vaguely, I remembered getting in my car and following Bentley again, but it was all a blur.

"I am." I wasn't, but I was okay enough to pretend that I was. "And I'm sorry about him. He's worked up but—"

"I *will* charge you with obstruction of justice." Ox shot me one of those icy glares over his shoulder again. "Stand here if you want to, but I have the right to question a witness."

Bentley shook his head in disbelief. I didn't know if he was wondering what I had done, or why the hell I had ever agreed to marry this man. I was kicking myself for the same thing.

Pressing my mouth to a line, I stepped back and leaned against the railing. Ox gave me another look, as if to ask if I was going to behave myself now. With a glare, I pinched my thumb and forefinger before my lips and spun them to the side to signify locking them shut.

"Did Maddie seem intoxicated at this chorus concert?" Ox asked.

"No, she was fine." Bentley looked at me again, the same look he'd given me when he knew I'd done something my mom would beat my ass for. Brows slightly raised, head tilted the smallest bit. Trying to determine if he needed to cover my ass.

"I don't remember last night," I said.

"Do you think I'm kidding?" Ox gave me that look again. "Because I—"

"Then charge me with obstruction of justice, Ox. He sees all these cops here, surrounding my house, and he's worried I did something wrong. He doesn't want to snitch me out and confirm that I was high last night if you're gonna arrest me for a DUI or something." I turned to Bentley. "I'm the victim, not the criminal. Tell him the truth."

"Victim of what?" Bentley asked, still craning awkwardly around Ox, trying to see me better.

Ox looked between us, then huffed. Apparently just catching up. While it was foreign territory to him, this was how it worked for people like us. If the cops showed up asking questions about someone you loved, you answered none of them until you knew what you were allowed to say. Snitches and stitches and all that.

"Is that true?" Ox asked. "Was she sober at the concert?"

"Yeah. She was completely herself." The color slowly drained from Bentley's face. "You don't remember this?"

Frowning, I shook my head.

"Did she appear intoxicated at all last night?" Ox asked.

Could've just asked when I'd started acting weird, but he was trying to trap him in a lie so he could arrest him for the rapes and murders of nearly a dozen women.

Bentley looked at me again, as if to ask if I was certain I should tell him. Likely knowing that if there was proof I had a drug problem, I could lose my private investigation license. He didn't know Ox well enough to admit to information like that. The guy was my ex. What if he was just trying to ruin my life?

I gave a nod of approval, mouthing, "Tell the truth."

"Yeah. I thought she relapsed," Bentley said. "After the concert,

Grace wanted to go out to dinner. Maddie followed us to the restaurant. We were halfway through dinner when she started nodding off."

Grace had seen that.

My stomach ached at the thought. Bentley did everything right by his daughter. He was determined to protect her from all the things that haunted us.

Now, whatever I'd done last night would haunt her.

No wonder he was pissed at me in those clips.

"Did you put something in her drink?" Ox asked.

Simultaneously, mine and Bentley's mouths fell open in disbelief.

"Are you insane?" I asked. "He took care of me. He—"

"Answer the question," Ox persisted. "Did you put something in Maddie's drink?"

"Of course not. I was with my kid." Bentley waved inside. With every word he spoke, his voice heightened in intensity. "Maddie got sick, we left early, and I brought her home. I told her that I should take her to the hospital, and she said no because she doesn't have insurance. I offered to let her stay at my house too, and she said no because she didn't want me to have to clean up after her all night. I didn't like it, but you know her. Which is a conflict of interest, by the way." Looking past Ox at me, Bentley's expression softened, as did his voice. "Do you think I drugged you?"

"God, no. You were just the last person who saw me last night, and then—"

"Did you hear anything last night?" Ox asked.

I clamped my jaw shut. Apparently, I wasn't gonna get a word in until he was done.

"Hear what?" Bentley asked, eyes growing more and more concerned. "Did something happen to you? Did someone hurt you?"

"Noise." Ox gestured to Tempest at my feet. "Barking. Maybe a window breaking."

"Wait, someone broke in?" Bentley glanced past me at my trailer. His eyes were wide when they met mine again. "You think they drugged you and waited for you to go home so they could..."

"You still haven't answered my question," Ox said, stepping closer to Bentley. "Did you hear anything last night, Mr. Roycroft?"

"I went to sleep half an hour after I got her into her bed." Bentley's shoulders squared, and his tone was just as deep as Ox's. "So no, Detective, I didn't hear anything last night."

"You got any proof of that?"

"Proof of *what*? That I was asleep? Does the data from my watch count?" Bentley held up his forearm, gesturing to his smart watch. "How else can I prove that I was asleep, man?"

"Sure. Show it to me."

I scoffed. I doubted that'd fly in court as a defense. Ox knew the same thing. Also knew there was no crime in sleeping. He was just trying to make Bentley's life difficult.

Ox paid me no mind, just waited for Bentley to pull out his phone and open his health app. After a few heartbeats, Ox handed him his phone back. "You're not planning on leaving town anytime soon, are you?"

Another scoff.

Bentley only held his gaze for a moment, brows furrowed. "No. No plans on leaving town."

"Good. Until I say otherwise, don't." Ox looked past him into the house. "Mind if I use your bathroom?"

"Yeah, I gotta pee too," I said, knowing that Ox would use the opportunity to look through all of Bentley's belongings unless I walked in with him.

"No, you hold it because you're about to piss in a cup for Alex." Ox pointed inside. "Down the hall?"

With a half laugh, Bentley lifted his hands at his sides. "Look at whatever you want to. My daughter's sleeping, so I'd appreciate if you stayed out of her room. Bring a dog in here and have them look for whatever it is you think I drugged her with."

"Appreciate your cooperation." Ox turned my way and snatched Tempest's leash from my hand. "Same commands as always?"

Licking my teeth, I nodded.

Yes, the commands were the same. No, I had no idea why I had ever agreed to marry this man.

When I didn't respond, he called for Tempest to follow him and gave her the command to search for narcotics.

Standing in the doorway, Bentley let out another one of those annoyed half laughs. "What the hell's going on?"

With a deep breath, I gestured to the lawn chairs. "Probably better if we just sit."

* * *

GENTLY LIFTING OUT MY PIECE OF HACKED HAIR, BENTLEY'S EYES filled with concern. A dozen emotions crossed his face while I brought him up to speed, but that one was the most prevalent. Concern. Fear wasn't far behind. "Did he hurt you?"

The second time he'd asked. Both times had given me butterflies. "No, I don't think so."

"Have you gone to the hospital yet?" Releasing the lock of hair, he found my hand instead. "Do you want me to go with you?"

"No, Alex'll take care of me." While she was the coroner, she was also the medical examiner, meaning that she was a qualified doctor. "I'm okay."

"No. You're not. No one would be after that." He held my hand a little tighter, soothing his thumb along the back of mine. "Do you need anything? Can I help?"

That was what I loved about Bentley. Everyone else asked if I was okay. Bentley knew I wasn't but didn't pressure me to say it.

Giving a smile, I shook my head. "I don't think so. But thank you."

Biting his lip, his gaze fell to the grass under our feet. "It had to have been someone at the restaurant, right? Because you didn't take anything when you got in your car, right?"

That was a good theory. One I hadn't thought of. "I guess. I don't know. It feels like somebody put my head in a blender. I'm not thinking right." Rubbing my temples, my stomach did that spinning thing again.

Not the good kind Bentley gave me, but the awful kind that had me bent over the toilet before realizing the murderer had given me a chop shop haircut. "Kind of like I'm hungover, but not the same? And I know opiates. This is not an opiate comedown."

"It sounds like roofies." Touching my chin, he brought my gaze to his. Wasn't the first time, doubted it would be the last time, but each time he did that, I felt a little safer. "I'm so sorry. You've been clean for a while now. I should've known something else was wrong. Even if you'd relapsed, you wouldn't have done it in front of Grace. I'm so sorry. If I would've just used my head, none of this would've happened, and—"

"I saw the video. My cameras." Forcing another smile, I pointed to them. "I don't blame you. We both know addicts. We get high, and we lie. You tried to take me to the hospital. You put me to bed and locked the door. You did everything you could. And I'm okay, anyway. You don't have anything to apologize for."

He kept holding my hand, but he lowered the one on my face to his lap. "But I know you. I know you wouldn't have done that, and I shouldn't have thought the worst. You deserve better."

"I'm actually glad that's where your head went. You'll keep me accountable if I do relapse." The smile wasn't forced this time. "It was better this way. If I would've been at your house, or if you would've been with me, he might've... Grace..."

A shudder coursed through me. The hair on Bentley's arms raised.

"This was to mess with me. He wants me to know that I'm not in control. He can get in my house and—"

I cut myself off before I could go farther. I didn't want to say it aloud. Why was it so different to speak it than to think it?

He wants me to know that he can get into my house, rape, and kill me before I realize what's happening.

It had been a long time since I'd felt like a victim, and I didn't like it, damn it.

"They're not gonna let you be alone now, right?" Bentley asked. "Is Derek gonna leave some guys here to watch over you tonight?"

"If Ox doesn't cuff me and put me in a cell."

He almost laughed at that, then glanced at the door as Ox walked out with Tempest. "Well, now that I know the story, I can't say I blame him. I'm sure I'd be doing the same thing if I were where he is."

"Looking at you? The guy who didn't even live in this state when the killer was last active?" I shook my head. "You and I are close, and he's jealous. That's what that was."

"You got a script for the pills in the container in the bathroom, don't you?" Ox called.

Bentley stood. "Yeah, they're Grace's."

"You got the bottle they came in?"

Oh, yes. I had definitely lost a night of my life, nodded off on a preteen's low dose birth control used to treat her acne.

"Sure, let me go grab it." Bentley gave my hand one last squeeze before he let go. "Let me know what happens, okay? And call me if you need me."

Smiling, I nodded.

As Bentley went up the steps, Ox handed me Tempest's leash and crossed his arms.

My smile turned to a glower. "What?"

"You say I'm biased. Like your glasses aren't rose-tinted."

Chapter 5

"I'm not annoyed with you because I'm biased." I struggled to get comfortable in Ox's passenger seat, stomach still bubbly. How fast he was flying down the highway didn't help. "I'm annoyed with you because you're being illogical. Why would Bentley be the killer? Why would he have waited until now to attack me if he was going to?"

"Why would anyone rape and kill innocent women, Maddie?" Ox's gaze stayed on the highway, pressing harder on the gas. "Why do people wait until several years into a relationship to assault their partners? It doesn't make sense to me either, but that doesn't mean it's not possible. That doesn't mean it isn't a pattern."

"If it were Bentley, don't you think that he would've given himself a concrete alibi? We know how smart this guy is. Apparently, he has some experience in tech. Which Bentley doesn't have. He types with his pointer fingers."

"I think a narcissist is exactly the kind of person who'd convince you he was innocent. That he was just a sweet trailer park kid. That he—"

"*Sweet trailer park kid?* Trailer trash is more common, but hey, I like it. It's got a nice ring to it."

Ox rolled his eyes. "That wasn't a jab."

"No? What was it then? What'd you mean by that?"

"That's who you are. You're the first person to come to the defense of people like Bentley. You know society looks down on people like you guys. You know there's a stigma around people who grew up like you guys did. So you'll be the first to go to bat for him. You've got pull with every local P.D. because of what you did, because you're a hero. And how better to keep people off your tail than to have the hero defend you? The best way to keep anyone from looking at him is to have someone like you on his side."

Laughing ironically, I shook my head. "He isn't Vanzant, Ox."

"This has nothing to do with Vanzant. This is a narcissist, and—"

"This is about the profile?" I asked, turning to face him better in my seat. "Alright. Let's talk about the profile. He's too intelligent to work in the service field. That's what the FBI said. Bentley is a paramedic, and was a massage therapist prior to that. Both are service fields. Both are healthcare. You can't care for people day in and day out and be a narcissist with antisocial personality disorder."

"He stalks his victims for long periods of time before he attacks them. He goes inside their homes. Bentley has a clear view from his bedroom window into yours. He can see your entire yard, every time you walk in and out of the house, from most of the windows in his house. And you think that's a coincidence, Maddie? That he moves into the house right next door to yours a few months after you move in?"

"We grew up together in that trailer park. So yeah, makes perfect sense that he'd come home at some point. Almost a year after I moved back, to clarify," I snapped. "The FBI said that this killer is the kind of person who'd be likable if you met him, but only on a superficial level. That isn't Bentley. He makes friends with everyone, everywhere he goes, because he is a genuinely decent person. They said that this guy wouldn't be able to hold personal relationships, and Bentley has. He's close with his mom, his sister, his sister-in-law, his daughter, his nephew... me. That's the opposite of antisocial."

"People find him charismatic and entertaining. That's how you describe Bentley."

"You're leaving out the part of the profile confirming that people who met the killer *casually* find him charismatic and entertaining. People close to him are afraid of him. No one I have ever met is afraid of Bentley Roycroft. He doesn't have a violent record either. The FBI said the killer would."

"Bentley does have a violent record."

I wasn't sure if it was the scent of Ox's obnoxious, pine air fresheners, or if it was the strobing effect of the sun between the trees along the highway, but for a moment, I thought that I would hurl again. "What the hell are you talking about?"

"You let this guy in your house how many times, and you didn't do your homework?" His voice had an edge, but his eyes were soft when he looked at me. "2020. He was arrested on a domestic violence call."

That urge to hurl returned, stronger than it had been all day. "That's not possible. You can't have a record like that and be a paramedic."

"The charges were dropped. Took a lot of digging to find it. But I'll get you the paperwork. You can see it yourself."

I shook my head. This wasn't something Ox would lie about, but that couldn't be true. Bentley wasn't the kind of guy who'd hurt someone he loved. He wasn't the kind of guy who'd hurt anyone.

"If the charges were dropped, it couldn't have been that bad. The cops would've filed if the other person didn't. It has to be a misunderstanding."

Ox sighed, but otherwise stayed quiet.

"What? What else do you know?"

"Just what I told you."

"Then what was that sigh about?"

"Listen to yourself." He glanced at me again, expression unusually gentle. "'It has to be a misunderstanding?' That's what defenders of abusers say, Maddie."

"Don't."

"Don't what?"

"Act like you understand abuse and its cycles better than I do. I'm not a victim blamer. The justice system defended my abuser, and I would never do that to someone else. I'm just saying that if all you know is that he was arrested on a D.V. call, but no charges were filed, there's more to the story."

Again, he huffed.

"What about that is unreasonable, Ox?"

"I didn't say it was unreasonable."

"Your huffing and sighing says otherwise."

"You're right, Maddie. The justice system isn't designed for victims. It's innocent until tangible proof says you're guilty." I hated how kind his eyes looked when they met mine. "Technicalities let abusers get away all the time. They intimidate their victims, their only witnesses, into saying, 'it was all a misunderstanding.' No proof, no charges. Especially if you're a likeable guy with connections. The kind of connections that someone who interacts with law enforcement, like a paramedic, would have. That's all I'm saying. Maybe you should have your guard up a bit higher when you learn that the guy you opened up your life to isn't the 'nice guy' he's made you think he is."

Maybe I did need to have my guard up higher. Maybe I had gotten lost in an idyllic vision of who Bentley was. Maybe my glasses were rose-tinted, to some degree.

Regardless, he still didn't fit the profile. "The profile also said he'd suffered some type of abuse from a female figure in his life. Bentley didn't. His dad was a drunk, but his mom was, and still is, a saint in his life."

"Saints don't let their husbands abuse their children. Your dad may not've hit you but tell me you don't blame him for what your mom did to you."

And that was where I drew the line. Say my glasses were rose-tinted? Fine. But use my trauma to manipulate the facts to fit his narrative? No, that wasn't gonna fly. "You keep talking about trauma like you understand it, Ox. You're not a psychologist, and your life has been pretty damn cushy. You're taking bits and pieces from that profile and molding them to fit Bentley."

"I'm calling it as I see it."

"They said that he would be single with no children. And ask Grace how great of a father he is. That little girl has an amazing relationship with him. That isn't possible with a narcissist with antisocial personality disorder. They said that he would come from a well-off family. Bentley did not. They said that he would be an experienced hunter. Bentley once cried because there was a dead deer at our bus stop."

"They told us this guy would do everything in his power to look good during the investigation. As soon as he realized we were onto him, he would be calm and cooperative. Kinda like how he just let me in his house this morning." I was about to rebut that being cooperative was a good sign, but Ox continued before I could. "They said he's a sexual sadist too. You know anything about that?"

My eyes narrowed to slits. "He's my friend. I'm not screwing him."

"You talk about sex with your friends. Has it ever come up, Maddie?"

About to snap that it hadn't, I remembered a case I worked a few months ago. The one where a nineteen-year-old girl was killed by her stepfather while bound in her own bondage equipment. Bentley had told me that those types of restraints wouldn't have left marks on her body. He said he knew that because of a romance book Grace wanted to read, but he'd read first.

Guess I didn't respond fast enough, because Ox arched a brow. "And you don't see why my head has gone where it's gone?"

"I didn't say he was a sadist."

"Then what are you saying?"

The thought process was enough to make me raise my brows, but it wasn't enough for me to condemn Bentley as a serial rapist and murderer. Even if he had lied about where his knowledge had come from, that didn't mean anything. There was an entire community around BDSM, and they weren't murderers. Many of them were upstanding, respectable people.

"That you're looking for a reason to blame him for this, even though there's no evidence. Even though he didn't live in this state while the murders took place. I get how badly you want to catch this guy." I waved angrily at my knee. "I get it a hell of a lot more than you do. There's nothing I want more than to lock this guy up for the rest of his life. Or put another bullet through him. I'd prefer the latter. But I don't want a good, innocent man to go down for this just because you're jealous of him."

"I'm not jealous of anyone." His tone said otherwise. "But I'll tell you what. He gets me records proving that he has an alibi for every murder that took place, and I'll never mention it again."

"Shouldn't be a problem." Swiping my phone from my pocket and typing Bentley a message, I said, "And when he gets you those alibis, you owe him an apology."

He sighed and kept a sad gaze on the road. "I hope you're right, Mads. I really do."

Chapter 6

Ox walked me into Alex's office. No, *dragged me in*. He had an ironclad hold on my wrist like I was a toddler digging in my heels the moment we got out of the car. I'd told him I was fine, but he'd insisted on sticking close to me. Considering how controlling he was, I wouldn't be surprised if *he* was the killer.

Unlike him, however, I could look at this objectively. While he fit far more of the characteristics in the profile than Bentley did, he was an ass, not a narcissist. He didn't care what anyone thought of him. Everyone thought Ox was a shit head, and he liked it that way. That was not narcissistic. He checked off the antisocial box, though.

When Alex said that she needed to ask me personal questions, it was the first time Ox had left my side in hours. The relief was unimaginable. Of course, before she asked me anything, Alex embraced me in the tightest hug, then patted me all over, searching for injuries.

I told her I was okay, peed in the cup, then walked her through the bits and pieces I could recall from last night as she drew my blood. At the tail end of it, she shook her head in disbelief. "I can't believe he's back. This isn't normal, is it? Serial killers like him, they don't just stop. Right?"

"BTK committed ten murders over twenty years before he was caught." Holding the piece of gauze to the spot of blood on my arm, I raised a shoulder. "It isn't unheard of. But this guy, he was devolving. His cooling-off period went from a week down to a couple days. It was practically back to back when he stopped."

"Do you think it was because you shot him?" Alex sat in the armchair before her desk, facing me. "You think he wasn't physically capable?"

Inhaling deeply, I nodded. "That would make the most sense."

Apparently, I looked as bad as I felt, because she reached out for my hands. Not uncommon for Alex. She was an affectionate person, even if I wasn't. I found her touch comforting today, though. "Have you talked to anyone yet? Other than the cops, I mean. You've gotta be scared."

Giving a half smile, I narrowed my eyes. "Are *you* not scared?"

"For myself? No. He likes white women. I'm safe." She gave me the same teasing smile, attempting to lighten the mood. When I chuckled, she did too. As it faded, the air thickened. She rubbed her thumbs against my palms. "I'm scared for you. He was in your house. He drugged you. He could've killed you. If you're right, and he did stop killing because of you, that means he blames you. A guy like that, he's gotta hate women already. Then you stopped him, so that makes you enemy number one."

My stomach did that rumbling thing again. "It's a good thing you work with dead people, because you're really not good with the living ones."

I expected a laugh for that, but she didn't give me one. "If you're not scared, then what's on your mind?"

"Ox." I gestured to him through the blinds into the hall. "He's got it in his head that Bentley did this."

"Bentley? What the hell does Bentley have to do with the murders?"

Bentley and Alex had met a few months prior. She called me one night, Bentley was with me, she wanted to hang out, and one thing led to the next. Grace was at a friend's, so the three of us went to dinner. Since then, we've all gotten together several times.

Both in the medical field, they had commonalities to discuss that were above my head. She said that he was kind, a good dad, the type of person who I should give a chance. Suffice it to say, she'd given her blessing.

So, I wasn't surprised by her shock at Ox's accusation.

I explained what had transpired on the car ride here, and Alex dropped her chin to her hand in thought. Then she shook her head. "If Ox knew Bentley had a domestic violence charge on his record, why is he just now telling you about it?"

"The charge isn't on his record. He was arrested, but no charges were filed, according to Ox." Biting my lip, that feeling in my stomach intensified. "I think I need to eat something."

Walking to the other side of her desk, Alex frowned at Ox on the other side of the window. He'd been on the phone since we got here and didn't seem to notice. "You're not letting this mess with you, are you? Before you even talk to Bentley about it?"

Was I? No. Yes. Maybe. I didn't know.

I didn't think Bentley was The Country Killer. I couldn't see him drugging me, not when I considered everything he had done to help me maintain my sobriety. Not when I thought about all the history we had.

But I felt like we didn't know one another suddenly. I hadn't thought about his story. Why he'd come home in the first place. What he'd left behind in Ohio. He'd said he hadn't dated since the death of his wife, Bella, but he was arrested for a domestic dispute? He'd said he came back to Pennsylvania because his mom was getting older, and he wanted Grace to know her. That had made sense at the time, but now I felt like there were gaps.

It wasn't like I'd expected him to tell me everything. I certainly hadn't told him every detail of my life. He didn't even know the whole story with The Country Killer, how his story connected to mine. But a domestic dispute that resulted in his arrest felt like a big thing not to tell your best friend. Especially since we seemed to be heading for more than that.

"Talk to him, Maddie." Handing me a pack of crackers and a pop, Alex gave me a mothering look. She didn't use her seniority over me often—she was approaching forty while I was going on thirty-three—but when she did, she meant it. "It got dropped for a reason. You're a P.I. Find out what happened."

Tearing open the crackers and shoveling a few down, I nodded. My thoughts weren't as fuzzy now, the effects of the drugs finally wearing off. "This doesn't count as a relapse, does it?"

Brown eyes growing sympathetic, Alex joined me at the catty-cornered armchair again. She took my hands and squeezed. "Absolutely not. You didn't do this."

"I thought so." A dry laugh left me. "Sounds like such a dumb thing to be worried about, doesn't it? Like my clean date should be the biggest priority right now."

"It's not dumb. You're proud of your clean date, and you should be. *I'm* proud of your clean date. You've worked hard. Nobody gets to take that away from you."

Covering my smiling lips between chews, I said, "Thanks, Mom."

Returning my playful smile, she opened her mouth to speak, but a knock on the door cut her off. Ox called, "Can I come in?"

"I guess," I said under my breath.

Alex chuckled and headed to the rapid urine test on the counter in the corner. "Hold your horses. I still have to wait for this to finish up."

"What's it say?" Ox shut the door behind him and crossed his arms. "And how long before the blood work comes back?"

"I'll rush those and get them to you by dinner, but the rapid urine's done." Alex stopped abruptly, looking at me. "Are you okay with him knowing your medical information?"

"He's just gonna steal the file if you don't tell him. Then subpoena it." Standing, I cracked open the can of pop. "Go for it."

Alex nodded and said, "It's positive for Rohypnol, as we expected. Explains the nausea, memory loss, confusion."

After a few gulps, I wiped my lip. "Yeah, that's what Bentley thought too."

"Of course he did," Ox muttered, rolling his eyes.

"He's a paramedic," I said. "I'm sure he's helped a lot of college girls who were dosed with it, Ox. Having knowledge of medicine doesn't make him a murderer."

He didn't respond to that, turning to Alex instead. "When will you have the results of the rape kit?"

I almost choked on my drink.

Alex's mouth fell open. "Oh my God. You didn't tell me—"

"Because I wasn't."

"You have no recollection of last night, and he was in your house." As they had been earlier, Ox's eyes were softer than usual. "He cut your hair. He was with you for almost an hour. Do you think he just watched you sleep the whole time? If there is any bit of his DNA on your body, we can use it against him. You have to get one."

"I know my body. If anything had happened to me, I would feel it." It had been almost two years since anything went on down there. Pretty sure I would have noticed a change in that region since yesterday morning. "This was psychological torture. And yes, I do think that he would've stood there for an hour and watched me sleep. Stalkers do shit like that. And it'd explain why Tempest knocked her crate over."

"Maybe so. All the more reason you should get the test done to find out for sure."

"I understand you're concerned," Alex said, "but Maddie gets to say whether or not she wants that. That's also the sorta thing that gets done at the hospital. Not in my office."

"If there is evidence on your body, and it could help us find him, why wouldn't you say yes to a simple test?" Ox insisted, brows furrowed. His eyes were still warm, kinder than usual, but he seemed genuinely surprised. Like it was no big deal to have that type of testing done. "If you don't, and we could've found something, you're not going to forgive yourself for that."

I wasn't angry. Until now, I wasn't angry. I nearly crumpled the half-full pop can in my hand. "I lost a night of my life. I have no recollection of what happened to me. A chunk of my hair is gone, I haven't gotten to go through all my belongings, and I don't know if he hurt my dog last night the way he killed Bear. Do you know how violating that feels already? Do you have any idea how invasive a rape kit is? It's not just a blood draw, Ox.

"And, either way, this isn't about sexual gratification. It's about power. Rape always comes down to power. In his case, it's the fear that he gets off on. So he didn't need to rape me. He's torturing me enough. I'm not gonna put myself through more, only for the results to say what I already *know* they would say. I may have been assaulted last night, but I wasn't sexually assaulted. Even the rape kits they did on the victims came back with nothing. He wore condoms. All those rape kits told us was that it was brutal. Which is how I *know* that he didn't do it to me. And aside from that, if he rapes, he kills. I'm alive. So this conversation is over. It's not happening."

Ever so slightly, Ox's jaw clenched. "Fine. You think I should advise Rachel to follow your example?"

"Who?" I asked.

"Rachel Emerson."

At the mention of her last name, the warmth drained from my face. His last victim. The one who had lived only a few miles from my house. The teenager I'd lost my knee for.

"What happened to her?" My voice came out sheepish. "Is she okay?"

"She's alive, if that's what you mean," Ox said. "She woke up disoriented this morning with a chunk of her hair missing. Called nine-one-one in hysterics. A team of techs are on their way to sweep her apartment now. I'm gonna get her statement later because she's gonna be at the hospital all day. Since she *wanted* the rape kit to be sure. Just in case there's any chance it could help us catch this guy. Which is why I thought you'd get one too. But I guess not."

"If Rachel wants to do that, it's her right," Alex said, moving in between the two of us. "Maddie has the right to make her own choices too."

"Don't I know," Ox muttered. "Are we done here then? Can we go check out that restaurant you went to last night?"

Chapter 7

RACHEL CALLED OX ON OUR WAY TO BISTRO BANTER, THE LITTLE restaurant that Bentley and I had eaten at last night. Unimaginable relief flooded through me when she said the rape kit came back with no signs of sexual assault. I wasn't happy to hear that she'd also tested positive for Rohypnol, apparently after having gone out for drinks with friends from school. Ignored the fact that she wasn't of age to go out for drinks with friends, but that was beside the point. At least she felt safe enough with both of us to be honest about it.

Her story was the same as mine. There were only two differences. The first was that I had gotten home mid-evening, while she got home after midnight. It added up though. He drugged me first, Rachel after.

The second was much more sinister. Alongside the dosing, he had cut Rachel. She didn't specify where, only indicating that the injuries were where he'd held the knife to her the day he attempted to kill her. The day I'd stopped him.

It made sense. Light torture had been a part of his MO before I got him. All that changed was that he hadn't raped, and he hadn't killed.

Not immediately.

The only conversation Ox and I had on the hour and a half drive was him asking, "Why didn't he sexually assault either of you? I could see him doing it to one but not the other to scare you guys, but why not do it to either of you?"

"The answer's in the question," I said. "To scare us. All of this was to remind us he's still out there, and we aren't safe."

Silence followed. Silence I was grateful for.

I was frustrated with him. I was frustrated altogether. In his position, yes, I would look at Bentley. It was a rational, reasonable thought process, albeit Ox's reasoning to go there still seemed out of jealousy.

But damn it, I was angry that I didn't trust Bentley anymore. I was angry that I was picturing Bentley slicing that comatose young girl for the thrill of it. I was angry that I thought I knew Bentley Roycroft, and I didn't. I was angry that The Country Killer had been in my house. I was angry that Rachel would have scars because I hadn't put the bullet where I should've that night.

Seeing my car in the lot didn't put me in a good mood either, because I didn't remember parking it there. But there it sat. My pretty flower and butterfly decals looked a hell of a lot darker in the dimness from the gray clouds, sprinkled in raindrops.

Just as he shifted the car into park, Ox's phone dinged. It was a text, and his fingers were going a mile a minute as he answered.

"What is it?" I asked.

"They got a partial print at Rachel's apartment." He typed and typed a bit faster. "I'm telling him to run it against Theodore Tyler."

Theodore Tyler. The convicted murderer who'd supposedly died decades prior whose DNA somehow showed at the crime scene the night I was shot in 2020. We'd had no idea how that was possible then. Now, I had a good idea.

The killer was a computer nerd of some kind. That was how he'd hacked my security cameras. He must've hacked into the National DNA Index System. The database that kept track of every criminal's DNA throughout the country for reasons exactly like this.

How? I didn't know. I knew next to nothing about computer programming. But I knew enough about technology to know that no firewall was foolproof. If teenagers were able to hack into government files and dox Supreme Court judges, was it all that shocking to learn that a genius hacked into a government database and swapped a dead man's DNA for his own?

"What does it matter if it matches?"

"Proves that he hacked into the NDIS. Which is going to make it easier to get a warrant when we can tie a guy who works in tech to these murders." Tucking his phone into his pocket, Ox nodded toward the restaurant. "You ready to go find out what you did last night?"

Unbuckling my seatbelt, I sighed deeply. "As I'll ever be."

Tempy's paws clicked in the back seat. My chest warmed as I looked her way.

She was behind Ox on the driver's side, looking from me to him with her head slightly tilted. He slid a hand back there and roughed up her scruff. "We'll be back. You be good."

She shook his hand away and looked at me, confused.

"No, she's okay." Reaching behind the passenger seat where I sat, I snapped my fingers. She rushed to my hand and tucked her head beneath it. "Good girl."

Straining awkwardly to the rear handle, I pulled. The angle didn't allow me to push it open, but that was okay. She knew what I needed and pushed her head against it, wedging the door open a foot or two. Then, as I'd trained her, she waited.

Out of the corner of my eye, I saw Ox squint at us. Despite the rest of the chaos today had been, pride bubbled through me as I opened my door. Showing off Tempy's skills was my favorite hobby.

"Stand assist," I said.

She hopped from the backseat and came to my side. Pushing her head my way, she waited patiently. My knee pain wasn't too bad today —probably an adrenal response—but I was showing off.

With one hand, I grabbed the handle above the window, and with the other, I grasped the handle of Tempy's harness. I needed her support after all, though, because I was typically the driver, so my left leg, my good leg, went out first. On the passenger side, my bad leg came out first.

Relying on Tempest's strength with my arm put less pressure on my right leg. There was still pain as I straightened, but I may've tumbled without her.

"New trick, huh?" Ox asked, shutting the door as he stood.

I smiled. "She's got more where that came from."

He *almost* smiled back. "That right?"

I untied my jacket from my waist and dropped it to the ground. "Retrieve."

She picked it up between her jaws and angled it up to me.

"Good girl." Collecting it and stepping away from the door, I gave her the smile this time. She just panted up at me, waiting for her next command. "Close door." Tempy nudged it with her nose. When it didn't click, she got onto her hind legs and pressed her weight on it, then did the same to the rear door before swiftly returning to my side.

Ox chuckled. "Damn."

My smile stretched a little wider. "She just passed her Public Access Test last week. She's officially a service dog to assist with my mobility."

"Congrats, Tempy."

She didn't so much as look at him. Just as I'd trained her.

"We confused her. I'm usually the driver. That's why she went to your door. She knows I need her when I'm getting out of the car. And she loves it." I gave her a pat on the head and wrapped her lead around my hand. "This was what she needed. A job."

"Looks like you needed her, too." Ox tucked his hands into his pockets, looking from me to Tempy. "Glad you took in the stray after all, huh?"

That was putting it mildly.

* * *

"OH MY GOD, THAT'S INSANE." SOPHIA—MY SERVER FROM LAST night, apparently—pressed a hand over her heart. "You think somebody *here* drugged you?"

"We don't have any reason to believe it was anyone on your staff," Ox told her. "But we are trying to understand how someone would've gotten drugs into her drink."

Maybe he was, but I had already put it together.

Straight ahead was the bar. U-shaped, the focal point of the dining room. As Ox spoke with Sophia, I watched a waitress pour a few drinks from the soda hose. Directly in front of the soda hose sat a man enjoying a burger for lunch. When the bartender turned around to cash someone out at the register on the other side of the bar, that man had plenty of time to reach forward, dump something into one of the cups on the tray and look completely normal by the time she turned back around.

"Was there anyone at the bar who struck you as odd?" I asked, interrupting Ox. "Charismatic. Nice. Maybe a little too nice?"

Gradually, her full cheeks paled. "There was a guy, actually. He walked in a few minutes after you. Diana, our bartender, she made a comment about how he kept looking at someone in the mirror." She pointed to the bar and the mirror that faced the seats. "He didn't turn around, but she thought he was watching me. I guess he was watching my section, where you were. When you got sick, everybody was kind of looking at you, him too, but..." Slowly, she lifted her hand before her face. "I thought you were fine. You were with that big guy, and the way that you were falling on him, I just assumed he was your husband or something."

"Was the guy watching me sitting right there?" I pointed to the man with the burger.

She nodded.

"When you poured their drinks," Ox said, gesturing to me, "did you set them down on the bar at any point? Right in front of the guy who kept looking in the mirror?"

A swallow bobbed her throat. She looked from me to him, then opened and closed her mouth a few times.

"No one's putting you on trial." I managed a smile. "We're just trying to figure out if it was possible for him to have put something in

43

my drink at all. That only could have happened if you'd set the drinks down before you brought them to the table."

Her breathing quickened and her eyes darted between us.

Ox cut in before she could run. "I'm not going to arrest you," he said, in his usual tone. Cold. "We're just trying to figure out if it was possible."

After another hard swallow, she gave a nod. "He spilled his drink. He asked if I could get him some napkins. I had just poured yours, and I turned around to grab them, and..."

He saw his opportunity and took it.

"Does that work?" Ox pointed to the security camera above the register.

"Yeah, I can't access it, but I can call, my GM. She's supposed to come in soon anyway."

"Appreciate it." Ox put a hand on my back and led me to the booth Sophia said I had sat at last night. "We'll be here."

Chapter 8

WHEN WE SAT IN THE BOOTH, I HOPED SOMETHING, SOME memory, would come flooding back. But nothing did. No memory sparked when I touched the leather cushion. Even that server's face did nothing to jog my memory. Nothing could get me to pick her out of a lineup.

Which was terrifying.

Tempy's panting smile helped in that regard.

"How would he have known which drink was yours?" Ox squinted from the table to the bar, at least a good fifteen feet apart. "She said it was busy in here last night, so he wouldn't have been able to hear you order it. And he came in after you, so how did he know which one was yours, and which one was Bentley's?"

"Bentley and Grace always get Sprite." Massaging my hands up and down my biceps, I stared at the glass that sat before me. "I always get root beer."

It took Ox a moment to process the point I was making. I knew it'd resonated when his jaw hardened. "If it wasn't Bentley who put it in your drink, that would mean that this guy is aware of your preferences."

"It'd mean he's been following me long enough to realize that I

45

drink dark pop, and they drink clear pop." Looking around the restaurant, I nibbled my lip. "Yep."

"And you really think that's possible?" Ox propped his elbows on the wooden table and leaned in. "That a stranger paid that much attention to your preferences."

"You mean, that a *stalker* paid that much attention to my preferences? Yeah, I do. Just like how he learns the precise layout of his victim's homes. He doesn't go after people he knows. Never has." Crossing my arms, I leaned back in the booth. "The only reason he's after me and Rachel now is because we're the ones who got away."

"Alright. Fair enough. But look at this from where I'm sitting. Really think about it." I couldn't recall the last time Ox's eyes looked so warm. "Imagine you were the cop. Imagine you were where I am right now. You think it's more likely that somebody sitting at the bar, rather than the guy sitting right beside you, spiked your drink?"

"No. I don't think it's more likely."

Narrowing his eyes, he squinted me over. "So you think it's Bentley?"

"I think if the guy's been stalking me, he's banking on *you* wanting it to be Bentley. If he's been watching me, he's been watching you. He sent you a letter when he was active. He's well aware of who you are, and he's tied together who I am to you. He knew you would look at Bentley. More than likely, that's why he did it last night. While I was out and about with Bentley, so that you would have a reason to dig into *him*, and not suspect someone else. Which reminds me, actually. You said it was hard to find that file on Bentley. So how did you?"

Ox traced his tongue along his teeth.

"Did it just show up in your mailbox?" I asked. "Just like the letter where he called himself The Red Ribbon Killer instead of The Country Killer? Better yet, if you knew Bentley had a domestic violence record, why didn't you tell me sooner? I know you and I aren't as close as we used to be, but that seems like the type of thing that you would've told me if you'd known about it for any length of time."

Jaw tightening, Ox leaned back in his seat as well.

"When? When did that file show up, Ox?"

"It didn't." His tone was sharp again. Ox dared not admit when his logic was faulty. "Alex was talking about him at work yesterday. Something about how great of a guy he is."

"And you wanted to prove her wrong?"

He glared. "No one's as great of a guy as Alex was making him out to be."

So he had wanted to prove her wrong. "How'd you find it then?"

He sighed deeply.

"Nefarious means?"

"I didn't do anything illegal."

"'Course not. You'd never break the law."

Another glare. "Why am I your villain, Maddie?"

He wasn't. A villain was an enemy, and Ox wasn't.

But I was a mess. The last few hours, the whole day, had been a raging fiasco. Then he hit me with that line about Bentley, and it hurt. For the first time in a long time—maybe in forever—I felt like I was where I was meant to be with Bentley. I was happy, fantasizing about a future together, and I wanted to hold on to that.

Knowing that Ox was digging into Bentley's past to prove 'no one was such a great guy,' hurt. Watching my fantasy shatter, trying to accept that a serial killer had been stalking me, drugged me, broke into my house, and could've killed me last night, all *hurt*. My head was all over the place, I still didn't feel like myself, and Ox was closest to the damage—he was taking the brunt of the fallout.

Aside from that, I'd just healed from the shattered fantasy I'd built with Ox. Now he was trying to convince me that my newfound hope in Bentley was fruitless?

"You're not my villain. But when someone's been through as much as I have today, telling them you think their best friend's a serial killer doesn't exactly help, Ox."

Ever so slightly, his jaw softened.

"I'm sorry. Alright? I'm not trying to be a bitch to you. I'm just not myself right now. But can you please tell me what you know about Bentley's arrest?"

A long moment of silence stretched on. He finally broke it with, "It was expunged."

Meaning there was close to no paper trail detailing what happened. "Then how did you find it?"

"His past addresses." Crossing his arms, he leaned back in his seat. "There's nothing on file. I left a message with the arresting officer so that I could get more, but that's all I know. He was arrested at his own house on a domestic dispute call. And until I hear back from the arresting officer, I'd appreciate if you didn't mention it to him. I don't want him coming up with an alibi beforehand."

"When did you call?"

"While I was in his house."

I tried with all my might not to glower. "You had literally just learned this before you spewed it to me?"

"I would've waited until I had more if he hadn't been present right before a serial killer broke into your house."

That was fair. I didn't like it, but it was fair.

"You're right, okay? I'm sorry." His tone was just as cold, but his eyes were warmer. "I shouldn't have dumped this on you right now. But I didn't do it because I wanted to ruin... whatever is going on between you guys. I was just worried about you. I saw you sitting there in the grass, and then I saw that footage, and all I could think was, 'he's manipulating her.' And maybe I'm wrong. Maybe he is the great guy that Alex and you think he is." Frowning, he raised a shoulder. "But I don't believe in white knights, and he's too close to one. People who look as innocent and perfect as he looks always have skeletons in their closets. You know that as well as I do.

"You've been dealt one shitty hand after the other, and you deserve better. I want you to get what you want out of life. And if it's him, if he's as perfect as you guys think he is, then good. But I'm afraid he isn't." He folded his hands in his lap and looked down, taking a deep breath. "I'm sorry I made your bad day worse, and I'm sorry this isn't what you want to hear right now, and I'm sorry that I'm coming off as the jealous ex, but that's not why I investigated him. That's not why I told you about the record. I told you because I'm afraid for you. There are only a handful of people in the world who matter as much to me as you do, and I don't want you to get hurt. That's all."

Damn it. He sounded a hell of a lot more like a friend than an ex all of a sudden. It was a rare occurrence to see this sort of compassion in Ox's eyes, but he meant every word he'd just said. He wasn't trying to paint Bentley as someone he wasn't. He just wanted me to take off the rose-tinted glasses.

"Thank you. For looking out for me, I mean. I appreciate that."

He didn't smile, but his eyes glittered as though he wanted to. "I'll let you know as soon as I know more, alright?"

"Thanks." That was, if I didn't find out more first. "By the way, have you contacted the FBI yet?"

"They're flying in tomorrow."

"Good. That's good." I opened my mouth to ask if he thought I was sober enough now to drive my car home when we left, but a woman in a button-down and black slacks approached the table.

"Detective Taylor?" she asked, extending a hand across the table. "I'm Lois Thompson, the general manager. I was told you wanted to speak with me?"

"We do." Ox stood and shook her hand. "We were hoping we could look at your security footage from last night."

SURE ENOUGH, AS I HAD ALREADY SUSPECTED, THE FOOTAGE HAD been wiped. Lois gasped, saying she had no idea how that was possible. Neither did I. But tech wasn't my specialty. Navigating social media was where my understanding of technology stopped.

I knew it could be done though. Even more so when she explained that their cameras weren't managed by a security system. Security companies had a lot to lose if a customer's system was hacked. Better encryption or something like that. I only used cheap cameras because I was too poor to pay a hundred bucks a month for the maintenance fee. They were hardly the safest option.

Regardless, the server agreed to give the description to the sketch artist, but the artist would take an hour to get here from the city. So, I told Ox I would go for a walk in the meantime.

He objected, until I shut off my phone, left my smart watch in my purse inside his car, and gestured to the gas station half a mile down the road. "We need phones we can search shit on without him knowing. Let's go grab a few."

Ox agreed and paid for both phones since he had cash and I didn't.

By the time we got back, the sketch artist was working on the image. Ox and I got drinks and a plate of French fries—which I immediately regretted eating—while the other servers critiqued the image. More input, a better-rounded rendition of the prick.

When the artist finished, showing the image to me and Ox, Ox said, "Does he look familiar to you?"

Not a bit.

Anywhere between mid-forties to mid-fifties. Dark hair, trimmed at ear-length. Blue eyes. Attractive, but not exactly a head turner. Boring, honestly. The kind of face your eyes would graze over in a crowd. Just a slightly above-average mediocre white man.

Which would make catching him that much harder. He looked so normal, so typical, that no one would think to equate the sketch to someone they knew in real life unless they were looking at them side by side.

Chapter 9

When we made it back to my trailer, Ox asked if I had a ladder. I did not, but I said I could go ask Bentley. Greg was outside, however, so Ox wanted to go ask him. I asked why he wanted the ladder at all, and as he was jogging away, he called, "This guy has been stalking you. You think it's smart to leave your cameras up?"

Which was fair enough.

Much to my dismay, Grace was just walking out the front door when Ox said that. I could practically see her skin crawl.

As uncomfortable and terrifying as all of this had been for me, I didn't want her to feel the same way. Giving a smile, I started toward her with Tempest at my side. "Hey, kid."

"Are you okay?" All but sprinting down the steps, her big brown eyes were wide with concern. "Dad said you weren't hurt. You're not, right? You're okay?"

"Yeah, I'm okay." Before I could say another word, she tossed her arms around me, nearly pummeling me. I still wasn't a hugger, but Grace had grown on me. Laughing, I patted her back. "Are *you* okay?"

Tugging back enough to look at me, she kept her arms around my waist and shook her head. "He was right there. Just a few feet away. And I knew something wasn't right. Last night at dinner, I knew it. Dad was so mad at you, but I knew that you didn't do anything. We should've taken you to the hospital. Next time, I don't care what you say. You're going to the hospital."

Was it really possible? Could Bentley really have hidden some dark part of himself when he'd raised this little girl to be such a kind, compassionate person?

"Did you hear me?" Grace tugged back and propped her hands on her hips. "If something like that happens again, I don't care what you say. You're going to the hospital."

"Fingers crossed something like this doesn't happen again."

"There have been about a thousand times when you should've gone to the hospital, and you didn't, so next time, you are *going* to the hospital. Deal?"

Had to agree to disagree there. While, yes, last night I should've gone to the hospital, the many other times that I had refused to, I was fine. But to ease her mind, I said, "Deal."

"Good. Do you know these guys?" Lowering her voice, Grace glanced around at the two remaining police cars. One was a state officer, and the other was an undercover from the city, likely brought here by Ox. "Can we trust them? You don't think they're in on it, do you?"

I laughed. "We all go through phases, but I think you're spending too much time looking at conspiracy theories."

"No, I was doing research today." She leaned closer. "I found out about that drug thing that was going on. That cop? The one who was selling drugs to dealers? He was with the Pittsburgh P.D., and that's who's here. I checked their badge numbers."

If only she knew that cop had also been my drug dealer. "You gonna be a private investigator too one day?"

"I'm serious, Maddie. We should've looked into things before we moved here. This place has got a serial killer on the loose, corrupt cops, and what else? Demogorgons? Because it wouldn't surprise me."

While no one knew better than me how maddening the last few years had been in this area, I could ease her worries a bit.

"See that guy?" I pointed to the state police cruiser and the man who stood outside it talking on a cell phone. Grace nodded. "That's Derek Ames. I've known him since I was a kid, so has your dad. You can trust him. And that lady?" I pointed to the officer in the unmarked vehicle and lied my ass off. "She's Candace Jones. When I was a cop, we worked together. She's one of the best people you'll ever meet, and I promise, not a Demogorgon."

Laughing, she shoved my shoulder. "You're not funny."

"I'm *hilarious*." I grinned. "Don't worry about this stuff. Worry about your finals. You finished them up today, didn't you? How do you think you did?"

"They were easy. I already have a ninety or higher in every class, so I could've bombed them and still passed." She shrugged. "I kinda wish I had. We got our home room assignments for next year today, and apparently my teacher's a total ass."

Tossing an arm around her shoulder, I tapped my hip for Tempest to join us and started toward her front door. "Mr. Walsh? I had him in middle school. Meanest teacher I ever had."

"No, Mr. Oakley. Dad said he must be new. But I've heard about Mr. Walsh too." She laughed. "Dad said if I got Mr. Walsh, he'd call the school and get me moved out of his class because he'd have a grudge against me because of what Aunt Phoebe did to him."

I snorted a laugh. "Did he *tell you* what Phoebe did to him?"

Eyes lighting up, excited to hear the story, she shook her head.

"Mention the words 'chocolate laxative' to any teacher at that school, and you'll watch them fall into a PTSD flashback."

Grace's mouth dropped. "No!"

"Yup."

She pinched her lips together to push down her smile. "That's awful."

"It was awful of him to push thirteen-year-old girls' pencils off their desks so he could watch them bend over to pick them up."

Grace wrinkled her nose. "Valid."

"Hey, you," Bentley called, dragging my attention to the shed at the rear of his trailer. "You okay?"

Yesterday, my stomach would've been full of butterflies. He stood just outside the door shirtless, glistening with sweat, shoving those dampened brown curls away from his face. Bentley was no body-builder, more of a dad bod physique with strong arms and a soft tummy, but whew. What a view.

Only, today, I didn't get butterflies. More of an anxious swirl. I didn't know if it was because I was afraid Ox was right, or if I just felt guilty for telling Ox I would keep the arrest quiet until he had more information.

Tempy looked at him, then at me. Her tail wagged. Like she was waiting for me to give her permission to go say hello.

With that sweet, boyish smile, Bentley squatted and opened his arms for her.

Releasing her leash, I said, "Go see him."

Tempest barreled across the yard and leaped into his arms. Laughing, he embraced the puppy kisses and petted her all over.

Ox got in my head. He was wrong. He had to be wrong. There was more to the story with that arrest, but Bentley wasn't involved in this. He couldn't have been. Dogs were the best judge of character, and even Tempest adored him.

Stop being paranoid, I told myself. *He's the same guy he was yester-day. He's the same guy he's been for the last six months. Nothing's changed.*

Walking over to him, I ignored that spinning sensation in my gut. My gut was rarely wrong, but it couldn't be trusted today. It'd hurled I didn't even know how many times.

"Have you eaten?" Bentley asked when I was closer, only a yard or two apart. "I was going to go fry some chicken in a few minutes. You want to come over?"

"Or we could eat at Maddie's," Grace said. "The cops probably want you close so they can watch you, huh?"

"Yeah, I should probably eat." Leaning against the edge of the shed, I said, "Did you get my text this morning?"

"I did, yeah." Squinting to see through the evening sun, he gave

Tempest one more scratch as he straightened. "Could you go and get that chicken out of the freezer for me, kid? Defrost it in the microwave?"

"I guess. Ooh, Maddie, do you want those kitchen sink cookies for dessert? I think we have everything. That might help get your mind off what happened."

"Sure. Thanks, hon." I gave her a smile, which she returned before bounding into the house.

Once she was out of sight, Bentley's expression changed. No longer wearing that boyish, heartwarming smile, he scratched the side of his head. "About your text."

The one where I asked him to get records of his alibi for Ox? "What about it?"

"What counts as a concrete alibi?" Wiping some sweat from his forehead, he leaned against something under a tarp inside the shed. "Is that, like, credit card statements? Or security camera footage?"

My stomach wasn't spinning anymore. Now it felt like someone had kicked a hole through it. "Credit card statements, security camera footage, a manager who will vouch for your presence at work that day. Things like that. Why do you ask?"

"For most of the days you told me I needed an alibi for, I'm good. I was working overnights in Ohio, and for all except two of them, I have pay stubs to prove it. I did talk to my manager, and she has it all on record."

So why did it still feel like there was a hole in my stomach? "That should be good. Do you have a concrete alibi for the days you weren't working?"

Swallowing, Bentley rubbed a hand down his beard. He was already sweaty and flushed from working in the humid, early summer heat, but I swore his cheeks got redder. "I mean, yeah? Kind of?"

"Kind of?"

"I was at my mom's house during two of the murders." Meeting my gaze, he nibbled his lip. "Does that count? I mean, I know that can't look good, right? But I was sleeping on my mom's couch. She can vouch for that, but she doesn't have security cameras. My credit card statements are gonna show me getting gas here, and Grace wasn't with me that weekend. I don't think that exactly looks good either."

That hole in my stomach stretched and stretched. "Which two?"

"Uh, let me check." Sliding his phone from his pocket, I got a glimpse of his arm, and somebody may as well have hit me with a truck.

Around the back of his left bicep was a scar. A scar I didn't realize had existed until this moment. A scar I knew well, because it looked a lot like my own. The one on my knee.

I was no doctor, but I knew a scar from a bullet.

Beyond any doubt, Bentley had been shot in his left bicep.

Which was the same spot where I had hit The Country Killer the night he'd attacked Rachel. The night I'd lost my knee. The night I'd lost Bear.

"November 14th and 28th Bentley tucked the phone back into his pocket and leaned back on his palms. "But, I mean, I have solid alibis for every other night. Those were the only two nights when I was here. And they know that this is all the same guy, right?"

It took everything I had to swallow down the urge to vomit.

November 14th. I remembered that kill specifically. It was the day the FBI had arrived. They'd been delivering the profile to us when the call came in.

When we'd arrived at the scene, the house was burning. The victim was unrecognizable. She was out of his demographic as well, twenty-six, while all of his prior victims had been middle-aged or elderly. I'd found the change so jarring that I'd suspected we had a copycat killer.

November 28th. The night my life had changed forever.

He had the scar. He was here, in this town, only a few minutes down the street from where we'd grown up, the night the victimology had changed, and the night I'd lost everything.

"Maddie?" Bentley tilted his head to the side. "You okay? You just got really pale."

"Why were you here?"

He'd already looked a bit puzzled, but now, his face screwed up in confusion. "Wait. You don't think I did this, do you?"

"Why were you here, Bentley?" I repeated.

"I was visiting my mom. I told you that." He still looked confused, but his tone softened. Like he was hurt. "I know it was weird that you were with me last night, and then this happened, but you know me. You know I wouldn't do what this guy's done. Especially not to a kid. And that's what happened that night, right? The last girl, wasn't she in high school?"

I never knew that he'd been shot either, yet he had a scar from a bullet in the same spot where I had hit the killer. "Why were you here, Bentley? And why wasn't Grace with you? You were so anxious when she had a sleepover with a friend, but you didn't even have family in Ohio."

"She was with Phoebe." Still, his face was screwed up in confusion. "I was trying to figure out how to move back here, so I stayed with my mom for a few nights." Straightening up to approach me, his foot brushed against the tarp. And I got a glimpse of what was underneath. A quad. "Maddie, you can talk to my mom. She'll tell you. I was at her house."

His mom's house was a fifteen-minute walk from Rachel's. A walk I knew firsthand was accessible through the woods. A walk we had taken regularly as teenagers. In those same woods, we'd smoked weed for the first time. On a quad, ironically.

I had been the one to teach Bentley how to ride a quad. He was petrified of it. Some distant relative of his had cracked their skull open and suffered permanent spinal cord damage, so Bentley had been terrified of riding one.

Now he had one? The same vehicle that the murderer had used to escape on after I shot him?

His mom would vouch for him? Of course she would. Even if she knew he'd murdered people, she would vouch for him. That was how it worked for people like us. We kept our mouths shut. We covered for our friends, for our family. Obviously Bentley's mom would. She'd covered for her abusive husband all throughout Bentley's childhood.

As he approached me, stepping closer and closer, my heart slammed against my ribs like a drum at a concert. He was the right height. He wasn't the right weight. Bentley was on the heavier side, and the killer had been relatively thin.

But that was a year and a half ago. Weight was easy enough to put on. Especially if you were healing from a gunshot wound that would impede physical activity.

"Okay, hang on." Only a foot or two before me, Bentley opened his arms at the sides. "Maddie, just think for a second, okay? How could I have committed murders that I wasn't even here for? It was the same guy. All the reports say that it was all the same killer. That would mean—"

"Why did you move back here?"

Still, his face was screwed up in confusion. "I had no family left in Ohio. I wanted Grace to know my family. You know this—"

"But Bella died years ago. You've only been back here for about six months. So why, Bentley? What changed?"

He opened his mouth to speak, then snapped his jaw shut. While most of him looked confused, maybe even hurt, suddenly, he had nothing to say? When I asked what changed, we both knew something had. The woman involved in the domestic dispute. That was what changed.

Yet, he said, "I don't know."

There it was. I gave him a golden opportunity to tell me what happened. Whatever the story was with that woman, he could've told me. He could've explained it right then, right there. But he didn't. He was hiding it, just like he was hiding that quad below the tarp.

"Maddie, we've known each other all our lives." Brown eyes looking so soft, so hurt, Ox's words bounced between my ears. *He's manipulating her.* "I wouldn't do this. You know I wouldn't do this."

Desperately, I wished I could believe that. But the quad, the scar, that change in MO, and the arrest he'd kept from me, all paired with the fact that he *had* sat beside me while I drank that spiked root beer...

"I know." Lifting my shaking fingers into my hair, I took a step back. Not only to put distance between us, but to get out of the shed. I was just inside the door. No killer was bold enough to kill when there were two cops stationed in front of our houses, but I wanted someone to see me there. Just in case. "I'm sorry. I'm not accusing you of anything. I'm tired, and antsy, and paranoid. But you're right. You were only in town for two of them. We know this is all the same guy, so it couldn't have been you."

He didn't exhale with relief. Those sad, mopey brown eyes looked exactly as they had a moment prior. "Do you want to call my mom? We can. I'll call her right—"

"No, that's okay. I just need to get some sleep. It's been a long day. I need to lie down."

"You don't want to have dinner?" So sad. He looked so damned sad. "I can bring it over to you. Or I can send Grace over with it? And the cookies too, I guess?"

Forcing a smile, I shook my head. "I think I'm just gonna go pass out. I'll text you tomorrow, okay?"

"Are you sure?" Those eyes. I couldn't keep looking at those sad, mopey brown eyes.

Turning away, grabbing Tempest's leash, I said, "Yeah, I don't think I could eat, anyway. I'm still kinda nauseous."

"Okay. Sure, but—"

I didn't hear another word. I was too busy power walking around the trailer while battling with all my might to swallow the vomit running up my esophagus.

Chapter 10

I DIDN'T TELL HIM.

When I got back to the trailer, and Ox was still on the ladder taking down my cameras, I didn't tell him.

Why? Because he was already convinced that Bentley had everything to do with this. I wasn't. Not yet.

If I had seen that quad yesterday, I would've thought little of it. I may have asked why he had one now when he'd hated them as kids, but it wouldn't have convinced me that he was the killer. If I had seen that scar yesterday, I would've asked about it. I would've asked why he'd never mentioned it in all the many times we'd talked about my scar, and it wouldn't have made me think he was The Country Killer. If I would've known he was in town during those murders, I wouldn't have assumed he was the one responsible.

Since the day he'd showed up in town, he'd taken care of me. As kids, he'd taken care of me. He'd *always* taken care of me. When I looked at my life, and I looked at all the men who'd been in it, he was the only one who hadn't hurt me. When I said things like, *I hate men,* Bentley was always the exception. He was good. Kind, loving, compassionate. All the traits he'd been bullied for as a teenager were things that I loved most about him.

I couldn't believe that he was a villain on a few droplets of circumstantial evidence. I was terrified that he was, but I couldn't *believe* he was. All I was convinced of, beyond any doubt, was that he was lying to me about something. I had to find out why and what about before I brought this to Ox.

So, when I got into the trailer, I snatched up my laptop, ran to my bedroom, and got to work.

Had Bentley gained weight in the last year? That was the first thing I needed to figure out.

I wasn't active on social media. I only had one to spy on Grace. Okay, maybe *spy* wasn't the right word. She had convinced me to get an Instagram so that I could see the pictures she posted of Tempest. They were cute pictures, a few of which I had framed around my house now.

But, in typical gen alpha fashion, Grace posted every day, usually several times a day. Whether it was a selfie, or a picture of Tempest, or a picture of her lunch, or a picture of a pretty tree she saw while walking, there was always something. It took a lot of scrolling before I made it back a year.

Eventually, though, I did. There were a fair number of photos of Bentley throughout the hundreds, but July 4, 2020, Grace shared a photo of Bentley without a shirt on. He was much thinner then. His shoulders had always been big, even when he'd weighed a dozen or two pounds less than he did now, but the rest of him was rather limber. I couldn't say scrawny. He had muscle. But so did the killer. Was it similar *enough* to the man who had shot me?

I couldn't be sure. It had been dark that night. It was always dark at night where I lived. There were few streetlights on country roads, if any at all, and the killer had worn black from head to toe. He blended right in with his surroundings. All I had been able to make out were the whites of his eyes when he lay on the gravel after I shot him.

Could it have been Bentley? There was no way to say yes for certain, but no way to say no either.

Again, though, it was circumstantial.

In that photo, the one where he was shirtless on the Fourth of July, he didn't have the scar. So it came after. Which fit the timeline with the killer. At some point between July 2020 and now, June 2022, he had been shot. Why? Just to give him the benefit of the doubt, if he wasn't the killer, who the hell shot him? What had he done? What had he been involved in?

I had to find out.

I kept scrolling. I scrolled, and I scrolled, looking for anything that would point to a girlfriend. Why? Because that was all I had. The police had been called to his home for a *domestic* dispute. That was an important detail. He wasn't at someone else's. He was at his own home when he was arrested, and it couldn't have been about Grace. That, I had no doubt about.

Last month, Bentley had asked if I could keep an eye on Grace because he'd had to work late. I had, of course. We'd gone out to grab a pizza, and I let her control the music. She played the song *Teenage Dirtbag* by Wheatus. I'd been shocked she knew it, since it came out in 2000. Grace said it was a trending song on TikTok, and she thought it was catchy. That'd sparked a conversation about the cryptic origin of the song, which then led to me mentioning a movie with the same name. A very dark, sad movie inspired by a true story about a teenage boy with an abusive father.

Despite my initial protests, she'd persuaded me to let her watch it. During the grimmest of scenes, while I sighed with a cathartic frown, Grace said, "This can't be based on a true story," and, "This is so unrealistic. Nobody would do that to their kid."

There was no way Bentley ever hit his daughter. Grace was too well-rounded, too normal, too dumbfounded at a movie that featured child abuse, to have been abused.

So if someone had called the cops for a domestic dispute, it had to have been a girlfriend. I supposed a friend was possible, but a girlfriend seemed more probable. After all, the title of domestic dispute meant that two or more people living in the same household were involved in the altercation. Unless he had a roommate, which I doubted considering how protective he was of Grace, girlfriend was the obvious conclusion.

Alongside that, considering how many pictures Grace posted, it stood to reason that if Bentley had had a girlfriend who was living with them, Grace would've posted her at some point. She posted photos of literally everything else. Yours truly included. It just made sense.

Having scrolled almost four years back, certain that this was useless, I found a photo. Christmas 2018. Standing before the pine tree covered in twinkling white lights, Grace smiled at the camera. On either side of her crouched two people. Bentley on the right, kissing Grace's cheek, and a woman on the left, smiling at the camera with her chin on Grace's shoulder.

A young woman. I could tell she was young because of her figure, but she looked older. It was a difficult thing to describe, but the sort of thing anyone with my life experience would know from a quick glance.

Incredibly petite. I didn't like to use the word skinny, it often came with a negative connotation, but it fit here. She wasn't just thin. Her cheeks were slightly hollowed. Her collarbone protruded through her baggy T-shirt. The bags under her big eyes. The scars and scabs on her cheeks from picking, although she had no acne. The yellowing teeth, and the missing one on the bottom when I zoomed in. I knew the look.

The photo didn't prove that Bentley was in a relationship with her, even though it looked like a family photo. But I had no doubt when I saw that girl. She was probably around 18 and likely addicted to crystal meth.

The caption read, *Merry Christmas!*

That girl, whoever she was, wasn't tagged in the photo, so I couldn't click over to her profile. I was just about ready to run Bentley's name through one of my many database apps to find his old address, then cross-reference and figure out who'd also lived with him when a knock sounded at the door.

Chapter 11

SNAPPING THE LAPTOP SHUT, I PULLED MY BLANKETS IN CLOSER. "Yeah?"

"Are you decent?" Ox called.

Huh. He was considerate enough to ask before barging in. Wasn't giving him a gold star for it, but I appreciated it. "Yeah, I'm good. Come in."

The door swung in, and Ox walked through with a red pizza box. Dropping it onto my bed, he gave Tempest a scratch below her scruff. "All the cameras are down. Turned off, disconnected, so inaccessible to the guy." He nodded to my laptop. "You cover the camera?"

I held up my phone. "Put tape over both cameras."

"The son of the bitch is probably listening to your conversations anyway." Meaning, more than likely, he was also watching me search the Internet. Yeah, I'd already thought of that. "But I guess it's better if he can't see you."

"I guess." Holding open the lid of the pizza box, I grabbed a piece out. "Thanks. For this, and everything else today."

"Don't thank me. Derek had me bring that in for you." Leaning against the doorframe, Ox crossed his arms. "How are you feeling?"

Scared. Betrayed, maybe? Confused. Uncertain. "It's been a few hours since I puked, so I guess I'm doing better."

"That's a lot of guesses for Maddie Castle."

"That's all I've got today." Managing a smile, I shrugged. "You get any word on those fingerprints yet?"

"They don't match Theodore Tyler." Running a hand through his hair, he grabbed a fistful at the back. "Doesn't make sense. Why change the DNA, but not the fingerprints? They didn't match anything in the database, so he doesn't have a record."

"Beats me," I muttered. "But I'm not exactly on my game today, so probably not the best person to ask for input."

"Yeah, sorry." There was the slightest change in Ox's expression. It was hard to catch, but it was there. "I know you don't want to talk about this, so I'm sorry for bringing it up, but do you think I need a warrant to get your boyfriend's prints?"

"Not my boyfriend." I nodded to my nightstand. "But you don't need one. When he was helping me into bed last night, on the video, I saw him put his hand right here." I gestured to the dust that I wish I hadn't let collect, but now, I was glad I had. His handprint on top of it was perfect. "Collect them from there. Run it against the partial. If it matches, a judge will sign off on the warrant."

Squinting at me, he arched a brow. "You *want* me to do that?"

"I want you to be wrong." Which was true. "I don't want him to be who you think he is. But I do want the possibility of it out of my head."

Expression softening again, he exhaled. "I want to rule it out too. But we swept for prints today. I'm pretty sure they're logged already, and forensics would've called me if it was a match."

"Yeah, but did they run them against the print from Rachel's apartment? Because they might've gotten logged into the system at different times, right? So, unless they specifically run them against each other, you may not have gotten a hit."

"I'll call." Again, he squinted at me. "Did something happen?"

"You mean, aside from a raping murderer breaking into my house?"

"With Bentley. You were quick to defend him today, but now you're suspicious of him."

"I'm suspicious of everyone and everything today."

Still, he leaned against the doorframe and kept his eyes narrowed on me.

"What, Ox?"

"What changed?"

"You. You got in my head, and now I'm paranoid."

"You weren't paranoid until you went over there."

The unfortunate side effect of having been in a relationship with the detective who was investigating murders your best friend may or may not have committed. Almost a decade together made it pretty easy to tell when the other was lying. Or rather, it was easy for him to tell when *I* was lying. Ox only lied about cheating on me with my best friend. Aside from that, he spared no one's feelings. Why lie when facts mattered more to you than anything else?

"You told him about the arrest, didn't you?" His eyes weren't narrowed in focus anymore, but annoyance. "I told you I didn't want you to bring that up to until I knew more—"

"I didn't mention the arrest."

"Then what happened?"

I opened my mouth to speak, but nothing came out. It wasn't like I considered myself to be the best liar on earth, but I was usually better at it than I was today. My brain was lagging like an ethernet Internet connection.

Pushing that damn chunk of hair from my face, I swallowed and prayed Ox didn't notice my hesitation. "I kept thinking about it while I was over there, and then Grace went in the house, and I just started getting worried. Because what if you're right? What if that little girl is over there with a murderer right now? And I don't want to think that, but she isn't that much younger than Rachel, and..."

Breaths picking up in his chest, his expression became solid as stone. He straightened in the doorway, no longer leaning against it. "Did she say something that made you think you needed to worry?"

Bad lie. Stupid, *stupid* lie. My attempt to avert the crisis just made it so much worse. "No. Of course not. If she'd given me any reason to think that he'd done something to her, I would be the first one to turn him in. You know that." That much was true. Snitches get stitches didn't apply to pedophiles and incest. People like me may've looked the other way when it came to drug dealers, but never pedophiles. "Child abuse just hits close to home for me. I'm not thinking right, and the possibilities started rapid firing through my head, and I don't know. I feel awful for even thinking it. I *wouldn't* have even thought it if you hadn't put it in my head, but now it is, and I'm just stressed the hell out."

Ox frowned. "I'm sorry." Crisis averted. "I shouldn't have brought that up to you today."

From an emotional standpoint, no, he shouldn't have. But I'd learned long ago not to expect emotional intelligence from Ox. "It's alright. The arrest was something I should've known about. I'm glad I do now. And that reminds me, actually. Do you have the name of the arresting officer? In the file you found, it didn't mention who the dispute was with, did it?"

"Yeah, I'll send you his information. But no, the report didn't mention who the dispute was with. I did check for CPS reports, and there aren't any. So it wasn't about the kid."

A relief. Only a tiny smidgen of relief, but a relief all the same. "Thank you."

"But you better tell me if you find anything." Rather than a wag of his finger like most people would do in that situation, he only pointed it in my direction. "People like you better than me, so he might tell you something he won't tell me. And if he does, you better tell me, Maddie."

"Oh, of course. You'll charge me with obstruction of justice if I don't."

Another glare. This time, with an almost undetectable smile. "You bet your ass I will."

He wouldn't. But to Ox, this was banter. Flirting. I used to find it charming. Now? I preferred Bentley's awkward blushing.

And I hated that that sweet, awkward, blushing, boyish smile was the same one that parted only to lie today. I hated that even the sweet guy, the nice guy, opposed to the brash, overtly masculine man, couldn't be trusted.

But who was I to judge? I'd just spent the last several minutes lying to Ox's face.

"Anyway." Ox glanced around my room. "You got any pillows?"

"Laying around here somewhere. Why?"

"The throw pillows suck." Stepping into my room, he headed to the closet. "I need a blanket, too."

"Um. Excuse me." Bringing myself to my feet, too quickly apparently, because I had to grasp the bed frame to stay standing when pain shot up my thigh. "I'm pretty sure you have blankets and pillows at your own house."

"Obviously. But I'm not driving all the way to Pittsburgh and back for a few pillows and a blanket."

Having already slid the closet door open, Ox fished around on the top shelf. When we'd lived together, that had always been where I kept the blankets. He'd hated it—said to put them under the bed so that we could use the shelves in the closet for underwear and socks since you couldn't hang those. I always argued that I'd rather use the nightstand for underwear and socks, because unlike him, I was not a giant who could reach the top shelf every day.

"You're not staying here, Ox."

"Are you twelve?" Pulling the pile of blankets from the top shelf, he held out my *Rick and Morty* comforter. "You really need a blanket with a cartoon on it?"

Glaring as I waddled across the room, I snatched it from his arms. "*Rick and Morty* is not a children's show. It's actually incredibly complex. There's commentary on addiction and social justice. And you watch *Family Guy,* so I don't want to hear it."

"There's watching a show, and then there's decorating your house like the show." He reached further onto the top shelf. "Is everything you own designed for a kid?"

"Let me get this straight. You come into my bedroom, state—you don't ask, you *state*—that you're sleeping here, and then mock everything I own?"

"Ah, I take it back." Holding another blanket out now, this one a pale floral print, I swore there was a twitch of a smile at the edge of his lips. "You're not twelve. You're a grandma."

"Fine. I'm a grandma, and you're an asshole." Tucking my blanket against my chest and crossing my arms around it, I nodded to the door. "Go home. There are four cops stationed outside. I'm fine."

"None I trust." He bundled the *grandma* blanket to his chest. "So I'm sleeping on your couch, and you're gonna deal with it."

"You've got some nerve."

"That I do. And I'm not sorry for getting on yours. You need someone to protect you right now, whether you like it or not, so I'm staying here. I'm not gonna bother you, but you're not gonna get me to leave."

"PA is a stand your ground state. I've got a gun, and I'll use it."

"Go for it. Maybe the killer will leave you alone if he thinks you're cold enough to kill me."

Damn it. I was enjoying this banter more than I should have. "I'm serious, Ox. I don't need you here. I want to be alone. Please go home."

"I appreciate that you asked nicely. But no." He reached past me into the closet, showed me the pillow he was taking, and started to the door. "Sleep tight. I'll text you that info."

"Lennox Taylor." Limping after him, I bit back a wince with each step. "I'll call your mom. She'll make you leave."

"She's the one who told me to stay." A smirk over his shoulder. "Night."

Chapter 12

THERE WAS NO WAY TO FALL ASLEEP. EVEN THOUGH I FOUND SOME solace in the fact that Ox was sleeping a few steps away, and that there were cops right outside my windows, I couldn't sleep.

Partially because, no matter how painful it was to admit, I was afraid. Afraid that he'd find a way in and finish what he'd started a year and a half ago. Afraid that I would lose Tempest like I had lost Bear. Afraid that the phone would ring, and it would be Rachel telling me he'd come back again and finished what he hadn't last night. Afraid that he was Bentley.

Fear didn't serve me. Sure, fear was a good thing from an evolutionary standpoint. It was developed as a safety measure. It reminded us there was danger nearby and told us how to protect ourselves. But after the day I'd had, the exhaustion seeping through my bones, sleep would've served me better far more than fear ever could.

Having concluded hours ago that tonight, my body would disagree with me, I'd decided to stay bundled beneath my blankets with a loaded gun under my pillow. Tempest curled up in the crook of my knees, and I was three years deep in Grace's Instagram page.

Pictures during holidays featured Grace and Bentley with many others. Grace's friends from school, Phoebe and Julia, neighbors—Bentley's sister and mom. Hell, there was even a picture from Memorial Day last year with Greg, the landlord of our trailer park.

But that girl never showed up again. I didn't understand why. She was there on Christmas—Christmas that Grace and Bentley had spent in Ohio, away from his family—furthering my theory that she was an important person in their lives. Yet, she didn't show up again. If she'd been around on Christmas, it stood to reason that she would've been featured in at least a few other holiday posts. If she had been, Grace couldn't have deleted them. Or rather, she couldn't have deleted the pictures with just the girl without deleting the rest of the pictures posted with it.

So I didn't understand. Maybe I was wrong entirely. Maybe the girl in that photo had nothing to do with the domestic dispute call. I prayed she didn't, because the last thing I wanted to envision was Bentley in a relationship with someone Rachel's age. But every time I scrolled back to that photo, something in my gut screamed that I was right.

Was it logic or paranoia? I didn't know. Logic told me there was no reason a girl like that would be with Bentley and Grace. Not because she was an addict, and not because I was judging her. Bentley allowed me around his daughter, knowing I was a recovering addict.

Maybe it was the pose of the photo, which was eerily similar to a photo of Grace, Bentley, Tempest, and me from last month. It wasn't identical. The one with the four of us had both me and Bentley resting our chins on Grace's shoulders.

That was just it, though. The photo was almost intimate. I wouldn't have posed with Grace that way if I hadn't been involved in her life the way I was. If she'd been just a friend, though, why was there only one photo with her? And why wasn't she tagged? The photo was taken inside their home. Maybe it seemed like a small thing to get hung up on, but that was the only Christmas photo, meaning their celebration that year was a small, intimate gathering. There *had* to be more to the story.

Should I have just asked Bentley? I would've, if I hadn't been worried that he might be a murderer. That was the same reason I couldn't ask Grace. Or maybe I *could* ask Grace.

Flipping out of the app, I went to my texts. The clock in the corner read 2:53 AM. A message from her that I hadn't opened said, *Are you sure you don't want me to bring you over some cookies? They'll make you feel better. You know they will!*

She'd sent that at 8:30 PM. I should've opened it then, but I didn't know how. Lying to Bentley was one thing. Lying to Grace was a complete other.

He had texted me, too. I swiped the bar down to read it again, but in a sneaky manner so that I could see what he'd said, but it wouldn't display a Read receipt on his end. *Hey, I'm sorry to bother you. I just wanted to see if you were okay. It's weird not seeing you at dinner.*

Three sentences that gave me butterflies and made my stomach hurt at the same time. Was I being unfair? Was this all paranoia? What if he did have a good explanation? Would I believe him if he offered me one?

I had given him the opportunity, and he stayed silent. So why did I feel guilty? Why did I feel like I was the one betraying him? I hadn't. Even when Ox sent me that arresting officer's contact information, the message I left said something like, "Hi, my name's Maddie Castle. I don't know if you'll be able to help me, but I'm a private investigator, and I was hoping you might be able to tell me a little about an arrest you made in 2020."

I hadn't said that Bentley was connected to anything illegal. In no way did I tarnish his good guy, family man, single dad persona. I could've said that I'd suspected he was involved in the rape and murder of a twenty-eight-year-old and attempted rape and murder of a seventeen-year-old. But I hadn't. That sure as shit would've gotten me a quick callback from the arresting officer. But I hadn't done it. So why did I feel like—

The phone rang.

Not my phone. Ox's. It wasn't the fact that it rang that made my stomach sink, but the ring tone. Jones. Ox's Sergeant. I'd hated when that ring tone went off in the middle of the night throughout the decade we'd spent together, but I hated it so much more tonight.

Since the walls were made of paper, I heard his voice answer the call. While I couldn't make out what he was saying, I knew the tone.

Stomach swirling, I brought myself to my feet and used the bed frame to help me to the door. With the chaos of yesterday, I had missed my daily pain-managing walks and workout routine, but I would be damned before I lay uselessly in bed. Tempest's paws clicked behind me as I headed through the doorway. By the time I made it to the living room, Ox was stepping into his shoes.

"What happened?"

He jumped, then saw me and quickly recovered. "Get some sleep, Mads."

"I can't. My body thinks I got enough when I was tranquilized last night." Leaning against the doorway, I did my best to put on my calmest cool and collected face. "What happened?"

Ox frowned. "It's an ongoing investigation. You know I can't discuss it."

"Is it Rachel?" While I knew he couldn't by technicality, I also knew that I could get it out of him. "Is she okay?"

"To my knowledge." Standing, he grabbed his jacket off the recliner. "I'll be back. Get some rest."

"I wish I could, but now that I know something happened, something that got you out of bed in the middle of the night, that means it was bad. Whatever the call was about, it was bad, and I need to know. Because if you don't tell me, my head is just gonna go in circles. And now I'm gonna be worried about you too."

Still frowning, he looked me over for a moment. That expression, it was such a difficult thing to describe. The frown was obvious, but his eyes were so focused. Like he knew that I felt something, whether from my words or the look on my face, and he wasn't sure how to deal with it.

He understood reason and logic. That was why he loved being a detective. It was simple. There were laws, and the people who didn't follow them needed to face a penalty. It was his duty to bring them in.

His job was to right wrongs, to fix a problem, because those were things he understood. Murder, drug dealing, these things hurt other people, and finding those responsible for them was how he helped people who were hurt.

That was the irony. He didn't understand emotions, but he wanted to fix them.

Ultimately, the only thing that would fix any of this was putting The Country Killer away for good. He knew that, and he wanted to do that, but he didn't know how to help *me*.

So I gave him the face I always gave him when I saw him struggling like this. I took the wall down. I let the tears bud in my eyes. I hated being perceived as weak, but tears made sense to Ox. As much as I hated to cry, if I let my eyes get glassy, he'd know how much I needed this.

"He killed a woman." Although his voice was flat, a hint of compassion reflected in his eyes from the dim glow of the lamp. "Not even five minutes from here."

That swirling in my stomach took over again.

"I'm going to go check it out. I'll be back."

"Can I come?"

His frown deepened. "You're not a cop anymore, Maddie."

"Because of him." I didn't intend for my voice to crack, but it did. "I'm a P.I. If you need me to fill out some paperwork, I will, but I'm not a civilian. You *can* let me come. I really don't want to be alone right now. Please. Please let me come."

It was a rare occasion that I said please, especially to him, but it did the trick. Frown deepening, he nodded to the door. "Take Tempest out first."

* * *

I THOUGHT I WAS PREPARED FOR WHAT WE WERE WALKING INTO. I was not.

When we arrived, Officer Dave Moore was outside. He and I were never the best of friends, but we spoke frequently enough back when I was a cop. The moment he saw me step out of the car, he stepped in front of the door. While Ox and I began dressing in our protective gear, he said, "What are you doing here, Maddie?"

"Consult?" I asked. "Is that the technical term for this?"

Shaking his head slightly, he gave me a look that I didn't understand. Fear? Discomfort? "You don't want to go in there."

I told him I'd be fine. This wasn't my first crime scene. It was no big deal.

Turned out, Moore was right. I should not have come in here.

When I walked through the threshold, it was what I expected. Upper-middle-class home, on a desolate back road, with a quaint wraparound porch and foyer to match. It had a sort of mid-century modern vibe with dark mahogany floors, a pretty handrail that lined the wraparound stairs, and cozy brown walls painted with wet crimson. A bloody handprint stretched from the top of the stairs all the way to the landing. More bloody footprints lined every step.

That much, I was prepared for. Gruesome as it may have been, it wasn't the first time I'd seen it. This was his MO. The Country Killer turned the home of every woman he murdered into his personal hunting grounds, and those hunting grounds resembled the goriest parts of his mind.

He made this place look like a horror movie so that even the officers investigating would be afraid. So that when the journalists wrote about the victim, no one cared about her. In a way, it was genius. Genius for a narcissistic, attention-hungry sociopath, at least.

By making his kills look so treacherous, he got to feed off the fear of the entire community. Not only my town, but all the neighboring ones, stretching all the way to the city. He attacked in three rural and suburban counties east of Pittsburgh, and the fear that came with each volatile murder rippled outward in all directions like a bomb.

What came as a surprise was the victim and the wall above her bed.

He always tortured. That wasn't new. His cuts in the past, however, had been superficial. A few thin slices on the arm, perhaps on the breast, enough to hurt, to make her afraid.

To spare the details, it was far worse this time. Rather than a puddle of blood beneath her neck, the bed was drenched in more than liquids. Overkill was putting it lightly. She was hardly more than a hunk of butchered meat.

The Country Killer'd had an almost gingerly approach to his attacks. While everything else in the house was a massacre, the victim never was. She always looked at peace. Her hands bound together in a red ribbon, her eyes either shut or hardly open. Without having seen the rest of the home, minus the red on the sheets, a glance at her would've made you think she was sleeping.

But it wasn't until I was directly beside her that I could even make out who she was. I could, though, and I had to swallow down vomit when I realized.

Amber Robinson.

She was a sophomore when I was a freshman. We rode the same bus all through school. Different cliques, I hung out with the burnouts and stoners while she hung out with the jocks and other cheerleaders, but we'd spoken a time or two back then. We even had a class together.

"Shit," Ox said, glancing from Amber to myself. "It's almost scary how much she—"

"I know."

When The Country Killer had begun, he only attacked older women in their homes. Gradually, with each kill, the victims got younger. There were only a few things tying the murders together initially, primarily their violent nature. Once he had progressed to younger women, he had a clear preference for brunettes.

Amber was blonde. The same golden blonde as me.

But it wasn't only our hair color. We had the same blue eyes, the same petite figure, even similar facial features. A small nose. Thick lips. A pixie-like face shape. We looked so similar that our bus driver mixed us up regularly.

I didn't know if it was any more jarring than his initial change from older victims to young victims, but it was for me. He had hand-picked her, not because she was his preference, but because she had a personal connection to me, and because she looked like me.

"You think that's Latin or something?" Moore asked at the door.

Although I should've looked at the blood on the wall sooner, I'd only spared it a half glance. I was more concerned with observing the victim than the show the killer liked to put on.

When I looked up though, I only felt worse.

Recontrez-moi, Chloé.

"Maybe," Ox said. Peeling off his glove, he dug in his pocket. "Let me Google it."

"It's not Latin," I said, shocked when my voice came out evenly.

"No?" Ox asked. "What is it then?"

My chest was so tight, it was hard to form the words. "French." Approaching the writing on the wall, it took a minute to conjure up memories from freshman year French. That last word, though, was the one that stood out. "It says, 'Meet me, Chloé.'"

"The victim's name is Amber," Ox said.

"It is."

"Then why the hell would he say that?" Ox asked. "What's it supposed to mean? This guy has never played mind games before. He doesn't want us to find him. He wants attention."

"It's not supposed to mean anything to you."

"I don't wanna play mind games with you either. Just tell me what the hell it means, Maddie."

If I could form words, I would. It wasn't that I was trying to keep anything from him. I was just trying to make sense of this. For a long moment, I just stared at her blood pearling down the red splattered wall.

And then, the obvious hit me.

It was exactly as I'd said yesterday. Yes, he was getting off on the psychological torture. That much was obvious. I just hadn't realized the extent of it until now.

Swallowing to make sure my voice didn't crack, I turned back to

Ox. "Me and Amber Robinson knew each other. We weren't friends, but we went to the same high school. I was a year younger than her. She failed her junior year semester of French class, so she had to take it again with the sophomores. I took French. And at the beginning of the semester, the teacher made us pick our own French names." I pointed to the writing on the wall. "I picked Chloé."

Chapter 13

WE WERE ON THE HIGHWAY AGAIN, DRIVING SO FAST THAT I WAS certain my internal organs were a few miles back. Couldn't say I minded. If I was going to die, I'd prefer it be in Ox's car rather than at The Country Killer's hand.

The chance of that was highly unlikely though. No one was on the roads at this hour, and Ox was almost thirty-five without a single accident on his driving record, even though he drove like this.

It didn't matter much to me either way. Whether it was sleep deprivation or the lingering effects of the Rohypnol, it would've felt like we were going ninety even if he was going twenty-five.

In the driver's seat, I heard him on the phone. Not a word of his conversation registered. It was all chatter, noise. The only thing that made sense, the only thing that felt right, was Tempest's fur between my fingertips. Her front paws were perched on the center console, head as close to me as the seats allowed.

But even Tempest felt a bit unreal. Like I was dreaming.

Such a common phrase. *Like I was dreaming*. Maybe even a cliché. That was the only way I could describe it though. I couldn't even call it a nightmare. In a nightmare, my heart would've been ready to burst through my ribs. I would've been warring with the sheets to free my legs so I could run.

This wasn't like that. I wasn't inside of my own body. I was in a simulation of some kind. Everything even looked pixilated. I believed the technical term for it was derealization, maybe disassociation. I had never felt it until this moment. Despite all the drugs I'd had in me at one point or another, the ones that were supposed to cause derealization and disassociation, didn't. Not until I saw that writing on the wall.

It was for me. He had killed Amber to get to me. Not even to get to me, but to *mess* with me. To terrify me. To coax me out.

At first, it hadn't made sense, but just a few moments of thought made it all line up. Sure, he could've killed me last night. But why do that when he could hurt me in the worst way imaginable? Why rape and murder me when I was powerless, under the effects of a drug that I hadn't taken, when he could do this?

Attacking Rachel in her home wasn't to hurt Rachel. He was done with Rachel. He'd gotten nothing from terrorizing her last night. It had nothing to do with hurting or torturing her. It was about me.

Rachel was the person I had given everything for. I'd lost Bear, my knee, my career, and later my fiancé, by saving Rachel that night. Killing her would hurt me but making me wonder every moment of every day if he would kill her. *That* was torture.

This, all of this, was torture for me.

Of course, the joke was on him, because my brain decided that I didn't have it in me to feel pain. It would rather gaslight me into believing that the world around me was a simulation than convince me that this was my fault. It was shutting down, trying to preserve something. My sanity, maybe.

"Castle." Ox tapped my arm. It was more like a smack, but I assumed he intended it as a tap. "Anybody in there?"

"Sorry, did you say something?" I asked.

"A lot of things." Out of the corner of my eye, I saw him glance at me, but I kept my gaze out the window. "Were you sleeping?"

"I dozed off for a second." I hadn't. Saying I had was just easier than saying the truth. "What's up? Who was that?"

"Derek Ames. I had him check on your boyfriend."

"Again. Not my boyfriend."

He waved me off.

"He was at home, right?"

"Yup. Hasn't left all night, so he's off the suspect list."

Maybe Ox's. But I wasn't convinced. I didn't know if there were two killers, but until this guy confessed to all of them, Bentley was still in the running.

"Good thing he's your neighbor," Ox said, "because if he wasn't, I'd be bringing him in right now."

"Good thing," I murmured.

"You aren't happy about this?"

Face screwing up in confusion, I finally met his gaze. "Why the hell would I be happy that Amber was murdered, Ox?"

"I didn't mean that you would be happy about that. I just meant that now we know it's not Bentley."

I snorted.

"Oh, so you do think it's Bentley?" Now, there was an edge to his voice. "What the hell's going on with him, Maddie? What aren't you telling—"

"I didn't say that I think it's Bentley," I snapped. "It's annoying that you think I could be happy right now. I knew her. He knew that I knew her, and he knew that I would see that, and he knew that I would understand it, and he did it just to hurt me. He *killed her* just to hurt me, and you think I can be happy about anything right now? Would you be happy? If you were where I am, would you be *happy?*"

Silence set in as understanding crept into Ox's expression.

How had I done it before? We were together for ten years, and I'd found his brash demeanor so charming then. For whatever reason, I thought it was sexy.

Was it because when we'd met, I had been so starved for attention and affection that it was easier to believe he loved me even when he'd shown no signs of it? Then, for the last six months, I'd had Bentley who was the polar opposite, who gave me friendship and kindness without thought. Did the contrast accentuate the resentment that I already had for Ox?

I didn't know. But damn it, I really wished he had just an ounce of emotional intelligence right about now.

"This wasn't your fault." His tone didn't match the words. "You have a heart. He doesn't. That's why you think this was your fault. Anybody with two brain cells knows this wasn't your fault."

"If that was you trying to make me feel better, I think you just called me dumb."

Ox made a noise in his throat that resembled a growl. "I'm not calling you dumb. I'm saying that it's irrational to blame yourself for this."

"Irrational, less than two brain cells. God, you're so good at pep talks."

"I'm not trying to give you a pep talk. I'm telling you a fact. You didn't do this. You weren't holding the knife that killed her. So you didn't kill her. That's a fact. You aren't to blame for this."

With a careful inhale, I shut my eyes and blew out slowly. Obviously, that was true. I didn't kill her. I had done nothing wrong. But that didn't change that I had failed a year and a half ago, and if I hadn't, Amber Robinson would be alive. Which was a rational conclusion to come to and *did* suggest that I had more than two brain cells.

For the rest of my life, I would hate myself for failing that day. There was no changing that. My life changed forever because I didn't act fast enough, and because my aim was off.

Some of the changes weren't bad. I liked being a P.I., and if I would've never lost Bear, I wouldn't have had Tempest. It was best, in a way, that I had lost Ox too, because one way or the other, we weren't meant for each other. And Rachel had survived. I'd saved someone that night. The things I'd lost that night were worth it, because, even if only for a while, he hadn't taken another life.

But now there was a body. An innocent woman was dead. No, she wasn't Rachel, but she was an innocent woman, and she was gone.

"Was Bentley in that French class?" Ox broke the silence.

"No. He took Spanish."

"But he knew you knew Amber from that French class. And he knew the name you chose was Chloé."

"Hell if I know, Ox. I barely remembered that was my French name. But sure, I guess he could've. Now good luck getting a warrant for his arrest when Derek is going to vouch for the fact that he was in bed all night."

Silence again.

When I looked over, Ox was frowning deeply at me.

"Well, that's where you were going with that, isn't it?"

"No. That *wasn't* where I was going with that." Flicking on his turn signal, he slid into the right lane. It was only then that I realized we were several miles past the exit to return to my house. "You need coffee. You're a bitch when you're tired."

"You want to see me be a bitch, and I will show you a bitch." He scoffed at that, and I continued, "Where are we going? Our exit was five miles back."

"I just told you. Coffee. And food. You still smell like throw up."

"Thanks. But what about after coffee and food? Pretty sure you wouldn't have driven out here just for coffee and food."

"Oh, I wouldn't have? There's no food at your house. What the hell do you eat?"

"Take out and frozen waffles. Now answer the question."

"To the city. I just got a text from Gayton. They're landing in twenty minutes." Gayton was one of the FBI agents who assisted on the investigation when The Country Killer first began. "Figured you wanted to come. But if you want me to take you home, just say so. I would be more than happy to get rid of you if you're gonna be like this all day."

"You know, two years ago, if you would've said that to me, I would've giggled and thought, 'Oh, he's just joking.' But you're not. You really do want to get rid of me."

"I don't want to, but I wouldn't mind. And you can't get mad at me for that. You know I don't joke. The fact that you thought I was joking when I was just being the same asshole I've always been is a problem you need to work through. Not me."

"You're right. I do need to work through that."

Squinting slightly, unsure of what I meant, he glanced at me as he turned into the McDonald's parking lot. "No rebuttal?"

"What is there to rebut? You're right. I need to work through the fact that you were a raging ass to me for ten years, and I found it adorable. That's not normal. No normal person hears the man they love being mean to them all the time and thinks that it's cute. The red flags were just pouring out of you, and I was like a bull. Just charged headfirst."

He was still squinting, likely trying to determine if I was teasing or still being a bitch. In fairness, I wasn't sure which one I was doing either.

Eventually, he said, "You want me to take you home or not?"

"Not. And I want two McGriddles. And you're paying, because you make more money than I do, with good health insurance, and the pension that son of a bitch took away from me."

Easing onto the gas once the person ahead of us in line moved up, Ox huffed. "I thought you didn't like to play the charity card."

"Fine. It's payback for you screwing my best friend. Is that better?"

"Bitchier, but touché." Stretching upward to reach his back pocket, Ox dug around for his wallet. "And I don't want to hear about the pension, because I told you I would pay for the lawyer so you could fight for that pension."

He had. After he had slept with my best friend. Which was why I didn't take him up on it.

I should've though. It was bullshit that I didn't get a pension after having lost my knee on the job. All because of a technicality. I had worked for the P.D. for nine years, and I would've had to have worked for the P.D. for ten to qualify for a lifetime pension post injury. And because, while I lived with chronic pain, I wasn't *technically* disabled. Not according to the social security office. I hadn't lost a limb, after all. The P.D. covered my knee replacement surgery and physical therapy that should have cured me. How was it *their* fault that I couldn't pass the Police Physical Abilities Test?

If I would've taken it to court, I was sure I would've won. But I was petty and refused to accept help from anyone, especially Ox.

"It is what it is now," I said. "But what point were you trying to make? When you brought up Bentley, I mean."

"I wasn't trying to make a point. I was trying to ask a question."

"Which was?"

"That your high school was small. So anyone who went to your high school would've known you had the French name Chloé in class, right?"

Oh. That was a good question to ask. And yet again, I was being petty rather than thinking. "Yeah, it wasn't a secret or anything."

"So this guy must've gone to school with you. That helps us narrow down the pool."

"Kind of? That's still hundreds, maybe a couple thousand, students."

"True. But—"

"Or, he didn't go to school with me, but he got hold of my high school records, or maybe just a yearbook, and looked for girls who looked like me that I would've known when I saw their faces."

"Maybe. But maybe not. Gives me a good reason to look into Simeon Gunn."

It was me who scoffed that time.

"Oh, you protective of him too? He your other boyfriend?"

"Not gonna lie, part of me wishes he were."

Ox arched a brow. "You wish your boyfriend were the leader of a drug cartel?"

"Drug cartel is a bit dramatic. He just works with people who are part of the drug cartel. Mafia is a better descriptor." That almost got a laugh out of Ox. "And not because of that. Because then my life would be a Wattpad novel. A small-town girl caught in a love triangle between the big city, broody detective, and a hot Mafia lord from her hometown. I got a busted knee, a dog, a falling apart trailer, and a drug problem. Why wouldn't I want to be that small-town girl?"

He shot me a look.

I returned it with a smile. Okay, this was why. This was why I found Ox's brash demeanor charming. Because he poked my buttons, and I poked his back without feeling an ounce of guilt.

"Simeon saved your life." Now that the air was a bit thinner, I needed to be as candid as possible. "Leave him alone, Ox."

"Whether he saved my life or not, the guy needs to go to prison. And he fits the profile, doesn't he? Well off financially, narcissistic psychopath."

"Just because he's a drug dealer doesn't mean that he's a psychopath."

"What drug dealer do you know who isn't a psychopath?"

"Lots, actually. Most drug dealers are just businessmen and women. I know in your fancy little suburb, it's easy to paint them all like villains, but you're just wrong. You don't know them."

"Oh, and Simeon Gunn is a perfect little angel?"

"No, I'm pretty sure he's a murderer. But he isn't the murderer we're looking for."

I couldn't tell if he scoffed or laughed. "You think that he's capable of taking a life, but you don't think he's The Country Killer?"

"Lots of people are capable of taking a life. Including the two of us, in case you forgot."

"Why do you like him? What makes you think that he's innocent?"

By no means was Simeon Gunn innocent. I was sure he had committed a thousand felonies. But I could guarantee none of them were rape. "I was at a party in high school. He beat the shit out of this guy who tried to take a drunk girl to his room. Not once, never, have I seen him so much as disrespect a woman. Matter of fact, he has given small business loans to every woman who has come to him and asked for one. He doesn't do that for men. But every single woman who owns a business in town, he has helped them get there. And The Country Killer hates women. You have to hate women to do to them what he has. And if you hate women, you wouldn't go around giving them small business loans so that they can get their family out of the trailer park and off of food stamps."

He huffed again.

"And if you like the whole, you know, breathing thing, leave the Gunns alone."

"You think they'd kill me?"

Wouldn't be the first time they killed a cop. Might be the first time they did it without my help, though. "Yep."

"Will you investigate it?" He almost sounded playful. "Avenge my death?"

"Apparently unlike you, I do like the whole breathing thing."

Chapter 14

Emily Gayton, Nora Martin, and Mason Phillips. The FBI agents assigned to The Country Killer case.

They were a good looking group. Gayton was in her early fifties, a Black woman with pretty brown eyes and tight black curls pulled into a tidy puff at the back of her head. Martin was around the same age, likely of Irish descent, judging by her gray streaked auburn hair and freckles. Phillips was younger than the others, somewhere in his late thirties or early forties. He was light-skinned with dark hair, and much to my surprise, more attractive without his beard.

We met them at Ox's office. All three were kind enough, just as they had been the last time we met. They were concerned, however, about my presence after Ox informed them that I was no longer an officer but a private investigator.

Which came as no surprise. Almost every case I had worked since I became a P.I. came with some type of resistance from the authorities. While I was a bit of a hero to a lot of the local police departments, and that helped in some regard, those who didn't know me weren't a fan of me.

There were two reasons cops didn't like P.I.s. The first one, I understood.

Often times, P.I.s were hired to exonerate the person the police were investigating. They would stand on the sidelines of the scene that I had been first to arrive at and watch my every move. P.I.s all had some law experience, whether as a detective or a cop like I had been, and far too frequently, they were the ones who caught us making a small error that would derail the case the police were attempting to build. That was how the justice system in America worked. In a courtroom, it didn't matter what was right and what was wrong. It mattered what could be proven beyond any doubt to a jury. That was the very reason that so many rich, powerful people got off scot-free on technicalities. And yes, P.I.s often played a part in that, whether hired by the perpetrator of the crime, or the perpetrator's lawyer.

The other reason, which seemed more likely here, was a point of pride. What could a private investigator bring that those with a badge couldn't? Not that they thought we were incompetent. They just thought they were better than us.

Story of my life.

Ox stammered his way through explaining that I still had all my clearances before I cut him off.

"All due respect," I said, standing from the chair before Ox's desk. "If I hadn't been at the crime scene this morning, Detective Taylor would've been scrambling to figure out that message on the wall. And no one knows this case better than I do. Just because I'm not a cop anymore doesn't mean I don't have some insight to lend. This guy's murdering people in my hometown. He may or may not have gone to my high school. He snuck into my house while I was sleeping and cut a chunk of my hair off."

"I never said that your insight wasn't valuable." Phillips lowered himself to the small sofa tucked before the window. "None of us did."

"We're all on the same page then."

"I don't think we are, Ms. Castle." Gayton frowned at me. "You shouldn't be involved in this investigation. Not past a consultation."

"You should be at home, in your bed, with officers around you on guard." Martin nodded to Ox. "You two were engaged. I don't know the details of why you aren't anymore, but I do know that's an obvious conflict of interest. You are the detective here, Mr. Taylor. You are not a patrolman. That's who should be guarding her."

That much, I couldn't argue with.

"I can do my job with her close by." Contrary to the stuttering he'd done a moment prior, Ox's tone was flat, and his shoulders were square. He may have gotten nervous at the mention of the legalities that came with bringing me on a case. But question his ability as a detective? That, he would go to war over. "She's not distracting me."

"While I doubt that's true, that's still not the point." Phillips propped his elbows on his knees and leaned forward. "Bringing her to the crime scene, letting her be involved in this, is giving him exactly what he wants."

"You said it yourself." Gayton leaned against the window beside the sofa, gray wisps in her hair now visible in the sunrise peeking through the glass. "We wouldn't have known what that writing on the wall meant if you weren't there. And now that we know he's skilled enough to hack into the NDIS, I have no doubt he was watching you when you found that woman's body. I guarantee you, he was getting off on the look on your face when you realized you knew her."

Although the hair on my arms raised, I didn't regret that I had been present. Because while, yes, she was probably right, I imagined this sick bastard was getting off on everything I had said and done since yesterday morning. What difference did it make if I had been at the scene, or if Ox told me about it later? No matter what, he was watching me. Now that there was a body, it was just a matter of time until the news stations got wind of it and tied together that I had half my county's police officers parked around my house. Then, he'd be getting off on the fact that I locked myself inside my trailer. If he wasn't Bentley, he'd be getting off on the fact that he and I weren't talking.

No matter what I did, he was getting off on my misery, so wasn't it best if I was just as involved in the investigation as they were?

"This is your investigation, Detective Taylor," Martin told him.

"But, if you would like our advice, it would be to keep this investigation within the department."

Ox's face was still flat, emotionless. Which was fine. If he decided he agreed with them, I would just flip him back to my team.

"I do appreciate the insight, Agent." Considering the lack of inflection in Ox's tone, and emotion on his face, it was hard to tell if that was earnest or sarcastic. "But either way, you want to interview her, don't you?"

"As well as Rachel Emerson, and the family of Amber Robinson," Phillips said. He gave me a smile as he looked my way. "But since you're here, sure. We can start with you."

* * *

So, I told them. I was sure that Ox already had, but I told them again. I told them what I remembered from the night he shot me. I told them everything I had gathered in the last twenty-four hours. I told them everything, aside from what I had gathered about Bentley.

If new information came forward about his involvement, I would give it to them. But all I had was circumstantial. It was useless to involve him, especially considering he had an alibi for last night's murder.

When we got to the tail end of that, Gayton said, "Let's talk about your high school then. Is there anyone from that French class, or any of your other classes, who'd match the profile?"

"Off the top of my head? Not really, no."

"Then not off the top of your head." Phillips swiped around on the tablet he had been taking notes in and turned it my way. A digital version of my class yearbook. "Flip through it. Tell us about anyone who might match the profile."

It was hard not to laugh, but I managed. Guesswork at its finest. I knew the FBI used behavioral analysis to build profiles, to find criminals, and I knew it worked. But until now, I had been on the receiving end of it. From a rational perspective, I could understand why it might be effective. But telling me to flip through my high school yearbook and point out the people I had deemed as psychopaths as a teenager felt unfair at best.

Martin must've caught the laugh I tried to swallow, because she smiled. "I know. Who isn't a psychopath as a teenager? This might be useless. He may have just done enough digging on his own to realize that you and Amber had a connection, and that killing her would impact you in a way that killing a stranger wouldn't. But there is a possibility he's in that book. Maybe a face will jog a memory."

So, with a sigh, I did.

What Martin, Gayton, and Phillips didn't understand was that while I had attended the high school, I had never gotten a gold star for attendance. More times than I had fingers and toes to count with, I was under the bleachers getting high. The clique I'd been part of had vast knowledge of botany and the difference between indica and sativa, but next to nothing about the rumors circulating through our community.

Or at least, that was what I thought. Until Phillips flipped, and I flipped, and distant chatter floated back. Robbie Davis. The jock who had raped his long-term girlfriend and been found not guilty because they were *both* drunk, despite the fact that she had no recollection of what had happened the following day. He'd gone on to college some-where out west with a full ride.

Matthew Brown. A theater kid who I had once sold weed to. While he didn't strike me as a rapist then, I remembered him being arrested for arson in our freshman year. He came from money, judging by the Jaguar he'd driven when he turned sixteen. Considering The Country Killer had used fire twice to dispose of evidence he may or may not have left behind, he was worth putting on the list.

Andrew Clark. Not a guy I had known well, but we'd met in passing at parties. He wasn't as into the drug scene as I had been, more of a drinker, so we hung out on different sides of the beer pong table. He was worth mentioning, though, because he also came from money, was a strict evangelical, felt women belonged in the kitchen, and beat the hell out of his girlfriend right before we graduated. I knew about it, not because he had been arrested, but because the girlfriend was Phoebe's best friend.

Hannah Wright. Neither a cheerleader nor a burnout, a girl who'd fallen somewhere in the middle. We were never friends, had never even spoken, but she'd been labeled a slut for having had sex with a group of guys in the same night. She'd stopped coming to school after that. Back then, I'd thought little of it. Now? I was fairly certain they had raped her, and she'd been shunned and ostracized into dropping out.

Ryan Nelson. The kid who'd brought a gun to school in sophomore year and boasted about it at lunch. Claimed he was going to shoot the place up. He was arrested, went to juvie if memory served, and never returned to my high school.

Ben Lewis. One of the cool guys. He had found a stray Pitbull puppy and used it as a punching bag. That wasn't so much a rumor as it'd been one of the few clear memories I had of my school. Me, Bentley, a few other friends—including Simeon Gunn—were hanging out at the park after school, getting high in the woods, heard a dog yelp, ran toward the sound, and caught him hurting her. No use in going into the specifics. But we'd all beaten the shit out of him. He never got a dog again, and one guy in our group took the puppy home. It was a sad story with a happy ending in my book.

I mentioned it for the same reason that they had me flipping through this book. If they would've asked me if anybody from my high school was an obvious murderer from my memories, I would've told them no. But by the time I made it to the end of the book, there were at least ten men I could see becoming The Country Killer. Turned out that there was far more scandal in my small town than I'd remembered off the top of my head.

None of them were Bentley.

Torturing animals was a classic sign that someone would progress to killing people. Violence against women then may have suggested violence against women later in life. While The Country Killer didn't seem to be an arsonist, he was when it served him. Someone who'd committed sexual assault as a teenager was likely to do it again as an adult.

"We'll crosscheck these names with anyone who graduated with a degree in IT," Phillips said, typing around on the tablet again. "Fingers crossed writing you that message on the wall was the clue we needed."

"Fingers crossed," I murmured. "I never realized how messed up my school was."

"Every school has stories like that," Ox said. "You put a bunch of hormonal, obnoxious teenagers into a room together for eight hours a day, five days a week, and crazy shit is gonna happen."

"My school had a stabbing," Phillips said. "Just one among many scandals."

"Really is every school," Martin murmured. "Now, Maddie, have you gotten an additional cell phone?"

"Yeah, but I've just been using it when I'm not home so he can't trace my location when I'm away from the patrolmen." But I wasn't surprised she was bringing this up since she had both me and Ox leave our cell phones and Ox's laptop in the hallway outside his office. "I know he's probably watching my location and monitoring what I'm doing on the Internet, but I'm sure he's been doing that for the last year and a half. Do you guys think that's the safest route?"

"Yes, so long as you keep your regular phone off when you go somewhere you don't want him to know about or discuss something you don't want him to hear. Use these exclusively to communicate with us." Gayton tossed Ox a flip phone and handed me one. "Continue to use your regular phones as normal, but when you communicate with each other and us, use these. If you're going somewhere you don't want him to know about, turn yours off."

"But keep yours available," Phillips said. "He'll be making contact with you soon. Call us on that when he does so we can try to trace it. If he hasn't contacted already, of course."

"He hasn't." Martin's arched brow told me this was a question.

"I would've told you if he had," I said.

Ironically enough, no sooner had I spoken that sentence than Ox's phone rang in the hall.

He glanced between the agents, as if to ask for permission. How strange that was. I couldn't remember the last time I had seen Ox ask permission for anything.

"Go ahead," Gayton said. As Ox started toward the door, her eyes turned on me. They were soft, compassionate. "When he does make contact, do you know what to say to him?"

"'I hope you rot in hell?'"

"Yes. Just like that," Martin said.

Laughing, I looked her way. She didn't laugh. Neither did Phillips. "Wait, really?"

"Really," Gayton said. "Be the biggest bitch you have ever been."

Well. That wouldn't be difficult. All I had to do was look down. There was my omnipresent reminder of why he deserved anything but respect.

"You have made him feel weak. That's what he's trying to do to you." Phillips shook his head. "Don't let him."

"Not like I was planning on stroking his ego or anything, but sure. I can be a bitch."

"No matter what," Martin said, eyes and tone becoming incredibly serious. Far too much like the mothering look Alex had given me yesterday morning. "Do not let him know you're afraid, Maddie. Do not beg him for anything. Ever."

Although it had taken a moment to realize they weren't joking, I understood the point they were making. "Right. Because that's what he thrives on. Pain. Whether physical or emotional, that's what he wants. He wants to see other people suffer. So long as I don't give him mine, he loses."

"He'll keep you alive," Gayton clarified. "As long as he doesn't see you suffering, he's going to keep *trying* to make you suffer. So you'll remain alive until he gets that out of you."

"I've moped plenty in the last year and a half. I'll make sure he doesn't see me do it again."

"Did something change recently for you?" Phillips asked.

95

"Something like...?"

"Some circumstance in your life that made you happy." Phillips scrutinized me for a few heartbeats. "Maybe a surgery on your knee that improved your pain?"

Oh. Shit. "I guess a few things have changed. I worked a really profitable case recently. Made twenty grand, paid off my trailer and got a free car. Mentally, I've been doing better. After my knee, and then everything with Ox, I wasn't in the greatest place, and I've started climbing out of that. My knee has been doing better too. I started this exercise regimen with—" Bentley. I cut myself off before I could say it because I didn't want to make Bentley's life anymore difficult until I had a reason to. "With a massage therapist. And I had a few appointments with the physical therapist I saw after the surgery. Those have helped with pain management."

"Could be what set him off," Martin said, squinting at me as well. "But that's it? Just gradual improvement?"

"Pretty much, yeah. Why? Do you think something in my life was his trigger?"

"Possibly, if something big happened," Gayton said. "Like if you had gotten married, or if you'd had a baby, I could see that being his trigger."

Obviously, neither of those things had occurred. But something had. Or at least, it would've *seemed* like something had to someone who was watching me through my cameras alone.

Last week, Bentley and I had gone out to see a movie in the park with Grace, got dinner after, and then we took her to her Aunt Phoebe's. Grace had become good friends with her next-door neighbor, and they had frequent sleepovers at Phoebe's.

After we dropped her off, we went back to Bentley's and ate ice cream. I fell asleep on his couch. Completely innocent. Nothing had happened. But both of our phones had been shut off at the movie, and we didn't turn them back on. Tempest was our alarm clock the next morning.

It wasn't the first time I had slept at Bentley's house, but it was the first time that I slept at his house under those circumstances. When Grace wasn't home, and I wasn't working a case that had me injured and required his medical attention in the middle of the night, and I'd been dressed in what some might call date attire. I'd done my makeup, I'd worn a new outfit, and my phone hadn't been on. Meaning that if he had been listening to me through the microphone on my phone, or on Bentley's, he couldn't have listened to our conversations that night. Which may have led him to believe that Bentley and I had taken the next step that night.

That had happened the weekend prior.

The color must've left my face, because Phillips said, "Did you think of something?"

With a hard swallow, I reiterated what I had just thought.

When I finished, Martin sighed deeply. "That'll do it."

"We really are just friends," I said. "If he's been watching me, he would know that."

"If he's seen you together, he thinks you're more than friends," Ox said in the doorway. "Just like everybody else with eyes."

I shot him a look that I expected him to return.

He didn't. There wasn't an ounce of annoyance. Not an aggressive tease either. He just looked at me like he had the last time his phone rang.

Heart suddenly falling through my chest, I stood and was amazed that my voice stayed steady. "What is it?"

"A blonde, thirty-one-year-old woman from Somerset County was just abducted from a walking trail not far from your house."

My heart was all the way in my gut now.

"That was fast." Gayton grabbed her briefcase off Ox's desk. "Decide quickly if you're going to stay away from this case or not, Ms. Castle."

He made this about me for a reason. I didn't have a choice. There was no walking away.

Tapping my thigh for Tempest who lay in the corner of the room, I grabbed my jacket off the back of the chair. "Let's go."

Chapter 15

Hemlock Trail.

About a twenty minute drive from my trailer, located just inside Laurel Hill State Park. Several times a month, I walked this trail with Tempy.

Almost everyone in my area did. Everyone knew it. There were few things to do for fun around here, but this was one of them. On the weekends, in the evenings, the only options you had for entertainment were going to the bar built on the second floor of the local fire hall, whatever picnics the local churches organized, or the hiking trails.

It wasn't significant that he knew this place. Every local did. But it *was* the sort of place that you would only know if you were a local.

When we stepped from the car, with Tempest on our side and the agents at our flank, Ox and I approached the man with his head in his hands who sat on a log just before the trail's entrance. That expression told me he was the husband who had reported the abduction.

Ox showed him his badge, then asked for what he knew.

Voice crackling, tears bubbled in his brown eyes. "I was on the phone with Josey while she was on her morning walk. That's what we do every day. She works from home, so she goes on her walk while I drive to work. We just talk while she does. I hadn't seen the news yet, so I didn't know he was back, she didn't either, but-but this can't be the same guy, can it? The Country Killer, he doesn't kidnap. Right?"

No, The Country Killer had never kidnapped anyone before. But the fact that a woman who looked like me, from my town, had gone missing on the same morning that The Country Killer had murdered someone else, led to an obvious conclusion.

"We're not sure yet," Gayton said. "But how about you tell us what happened? You were on the phone with her when it occurred?"

Nodding, the man swept his tears away. "We were just talking about how many butterflies there are this year. Stupid things, you know? And then she said she heard something."

"Did she see anyone?" Phillips asked. "Someone following her?"

"No, it happened so fast. One second, we were talking about the butterflies, and the next, she said she heard something, then she screamed." His lips quivered, and the tears rained from his eyes. "She screamed for help."

"Did the phone cut out after that?" Martin asked. "Did you hear anything else?"

"Screaming. I heard screaming, and then she was crying, and then the call ended." Cupping a hand over his mouth to trap in the sob, he shut his eyes and took a few calming breaths before continuing. "I called her back I don't even know many times, but I knew where she was, so when she didn't pick up, I called nine-one-one. I was on the highway, so I turned around and flew back here. A few of the police were already here. They found her phone when I kept calling it." Tears overwhelming him again, he gestured down the trail. "They wouldn't let me go back there. She isn't back there, is she?"

"No. We haven't found her," Ox said. "But we're gonna do everything we can to find her."

Sniffling, he nodded again.

In any other context, I might have considered him a suspect. Knowing exactly where she was, arriving at the scene just after the police. But if this was The Country Killer, it came as no surprise. He was moving fast. Because this time, he had an end goal.

Me.

It was all making sense now.

At the root of all the other awful attributes he possessed, The Country Killer was a misogynist. He attacked women who were alone in their homes, starting with older women then widening his horizons to younger women, women my age, because he thought we were easy targets. Weaker than him, worth less than him. He used our bodies for his pleasure, a power trip, then discarded us when he was finished.

To be a misogynistic narcissistic serial killer, only to have his spree of torment halted by a lone female officer, was the biggest hit his ego could've taken. This wasn't about the thrill of the kill anymore. It was about me. And he would do *anything* to get to me.

Yes, he could've killed me yesterday. He chose not to so he could psychologically torture me, but more than inciting fear within me, he wanted me to willingly hand myself over to him.

He knew that if he took a woman hostage, he could use her against me. When he contacted me, as Gayton, Martin, and Phillips suspected he would, this was how he would get what he wanted. He would tell me that if I turned myself over to him, he would let her go. This wasn't a change in MO. It was a change in motive.

It wasn't about the kill anymore. This was about proving that he was right. That women were weak. Less than him. Convincing me to walk into his arms would do just that.

Now I understood what Gayton, Martin, and Phillips had meant back at Ox's office. This was why I had to show no fear. This was why I needed to be a bitch. The moment I was no longer a challenge to him, the moment he broke me, would be the moment I kissed my life goodbye.

While Phillips collected Josey's husband's information, the rest of us started down the walking trail. Beside me, looking ahead, Gayton said, "You know he's going to use her to get to you, don't you?"

"Yep."

"You know she's going to die unless you give him what he wants?"

I swallowed the lump that formed in my throat. A nod was my response.

"You know if he gets what he wants, you'll be gone, and he will keep killing. He won't stop after you."

Another nod.

"So you know that you can't give him what he wants, no matter what he says or does."

Yes. I knew that.

I just didn't want to think about how bad it was all about to get.

AN EARLY SUMMER WALK IN THE WOODS WAS A LOVELY experience. Relaxing, almost euphoric. But as I walked the moss-coated soil littered with boulders, framed by vibrant wildflowers, canopied by thick green trees, I knew I would never see this hiking trail the same again. Every time I drove past the gravel road leading to it, each time a friend suggested walking it, I would think of this day. The day that Josephine Hall was kidnapped to bait me into the hands of The Country Killer.

When we made it to the abduction site, it was easy enough to tell what happened. Beside the flattened brush, a few officers squatted to the soil with little flags to stake the crimson droplets.

He came up behind her, attempted to grab her, then hit her on the head with some type of blunt object so that he could get her to his car.

Along the path, I'd yet to notice any tire tracks. There were no drag marks near that flattened brush either.

"He had to have carried her," I murmured, scanning the area a moment longer. Surrounding us, the early summer blooms were between my knee and hip height in all directions, aside from that flattened area of foliage. While the ground was mostly dry, there still would've been some evidence of a vehicle if he had used one. "At least a short distance."

"Couldn't have gotten her body out of here any other way," Ox said. "Where's the trail lead?"

"It wraps around to another parking lot," I said. "We should walk the whole thing. Look for any other signs he went through the woods. It might lead us to his car or tire tracks of the quad he used."

"I'll do you one better." An officer I'd met in passing stood holding an evidence bag. Inside it was a pink jacket. He nodded to Tempest. "She was a cop dog before she was a service dog, right?"

"She was. Is that Josephine's?"

"Yep. Found it in her car. Her husband said she wore it this morning."

Taking the glove Ox offered me, I grabbed the evidence bag and thanked Young. After carefully pulling it out, I held it out to Tempest. "Track."

She sniffed and sniffed a moment longer, then dropped her head to the ground and began her job. Rarely were canines trained in multiple areas, but rarely did a canine have a dog trainer as an owner.

Chapter 16

TEMPY WALKED FASTER WHEN SHE TRACKED, WHICH MY KNEE wasn't a fan of, but I managed. Ox was close to my tail, quiet so Tempy could focus. Or maybe he was quiet because neither of us knew what to say. What *was* there to say?

Luckily, it was a warm, sunny day. While there was some dew on the ground, no rain had washed away the trail. She didn't even need a second sniff to hold on to it.

We trekked somewhere near a quarter mile before she attempted to lead us off the trail and into the woods. Here, it was easy to tell that the ground had been disturbed. A person of decent size, like the man I had battled the night Rachel was attacked, easily could have done the damage.

Ox called for more officers before giving me the okay to continue with Tempest off the trail. We had made it another ten feet or so before she lay flat on her belly. She found something.

Squinting at the ground, ignoring the bugs that buzzed around my legs, I looked for something obvious, like another article of the victim's or blood. Hell, maybe a body. But there was nothing I could see from this height.

This was about the time that I needed my service dog. She had done her job, however, and now I had to do mine. Holding a dangling tree branch from overhead to keep me steady, I lowered myself to a squat and cursed under my breath at the pain that soared up my thigh. There, tucked below a bush, laid an orange syringe cap.

Those were common enough to find in the woods. Plenty of addicts got high in private, which the dense foliage allowed for. But this one was fresh. It wasn't dirty, as though it had been here for days or weeks. And Tempy smelled Josephine on it.

"We got something," I called. "Gonna want to get some pictures back here."

"What is it?" Ox called.

I told him, followed by, "I don't see tire tracks yet. I'm gonna flag it and have her keep going."

"Just don't go too far. You got your gun, don't you?"

"Always." After praising Tempest, I held out Josephine's sweater again. "Track."

With a wagging tail, she got back to work.

Two dozen more strides or so, and there it was. Early summer greenery flattened by the tracks of a small vehicle. Smaller than a car, at least, but not as small as the quad I had gotten a glimpse of in Bentley's shed. It seemed so at a glance, anyway.

I called to Ox once more, telling him we'd found the quad tracks, that I was going to flag it and keep going. Again, he expressed his understanding, reminded me not to go too far, and I gave Tempest the command. She tried, but I couldn't say I was surprised when she sniffed the article and began leading me back to the syringe cap. He'd probably learned his lesson and gotten a quad with doors and windows.

Now that we had the tracks, however, I could see the exact direction he had taken. They led to a quad trail. Problem there was, there were dozens of different tire marks along the trail. Since all I could tell from the flattened brush was that there had been a vehicle of some kind here today, I fought the urge to stomp my feet. A tire track may or may not have led us to the killer, but proving he had those tires would sure as shit help with the conviction.

Not like this guy deserved a trial.

Just as I was ready to return to Ox at the last flag, I saw it. A perfect tire print between the flattened foliage and the quad trail. It was no more than six inches long, tires roughly eight inches in width, but it was, beyond any doubt, freshly imprinted into the damp soil.

Again, I called for Ox. But this was something I could use in my own investigation. So kneeling with Tempest's assistance, I snapped a few photos, using my forearm as a size reference to compare to Bentley's tires. It could have been the same size, but maybe they were a bit bigger? I didn't know. I had to compare in person to say for sure.

"We bagged the syringe cap," Ox said, panting as he got closer. "What do you got there?"

As I showed it to him, the FBI team approached, and I explained what I had just gathered.

"Let's get some guys down here to follow the trail," Ox said.

"If the dog lost it, doubt they're gonna find much," Martin said.

"I still might bring some blood hounds in to check things out. Tempy's specialty is narcotics, not search and rescue," I said. "But I'm guessing she lost it for one of two reasons. Either, he concealed her in blankets and a poncho that contained the shedding of her skin cells, or —more than likely—the ATV is enclosed. Just like when someone gets into a car and drives off, the skin cells are contained. Once she was inside, the skin cells Josey was shedding were trapped inside, so there's nothing for the dogs to follow. Someone might be able to identify the tire tracks and follow them though."

"Maybe. Doesn't hurt to check." Biting his lip, Ox shook his head slightly. "How much you want to bet that there will be trace amounts of Rohypnol on the syringe?"

"I don't think any of us are betting against that," Gayton said. "But I'm more concerned with the fact that he carried that woman—What? Half a mile?"

"We thought that he started on older victims because they were easier to subdue," Phillips said. "But I'm not a small guy, and I have a hell of a time carrying my two-year-old for half a mile."

"It's been a year and a half." Martin pulled her hair back and tied it in a ponytail. "He could've spent that time working on his fitness."

"I'm sure he did," Gayton said. "A woman almost managed to take him down. I bet he's going to be significantly stronger and larger than he was when he began, if for nothing else than to prove that he's stronger than Maddie."

Like Bentley had grown stronger and larger over the last year and a half.

"Maybe. But if that's the case, why use the Rohypnol?" Ox asked. "Against Maddie and Rachel, I understand. It was more about inciting fear than needing to subdue them. But hitting Josey over the head did the trick. So why use the Rohypnol? Because it's easily accessible? Because he works in a medical field?"

"Rohypnol isn't easily accessible, even to the medical field," I said. Whether or not I liked it, drugs were sort of my area of expertise. "It's illegal in the US. The FDA and DEA considered it a schedule five controlled substance in the seventies because of its potential for abuse and addiction. And because it's so easy to use exactly how this guy is using it."

"It's not easy to get on the streets either, because everybody knows why you're getting it. Most drug dealers don't want to help rapists," Martin said. "In my experience, anyway. When I worked with CIs, and I caught dealers, they were concerned with making money, but not helping people hurt other people."

That was my experience as well.

"Well, he's getting it somewhere," Ox said.

"This is definitely his comfort zone," Gayton said. "Do you have any CIs in this area?"

"Not out this way, no," Ox said.

"I do," I said. "Well, not exactly CIs, but I know the local dealers. Give me an afternoon with no cops nearby, and I can find everyone in the area who sells Rohypnol. Probably who they sold it to for the last several months too."

Ox's expression was hard as stone again. "Absolutely not."

There was no stopping my eye roll. As previously established, the dealers around here were not villains. They were my old friends from high school.

Maybe not a statement to announce with pride.

"No one's gonna hurt me," I said. "I won't go for any lonesome walks in the woods, and I'll have my gun on me at all times."

"No. This guy has almost a dozen bodies under his belt," Ox snapped. "And he's looking for you. You're not going anywhere without a cop until we find him."

"And how do you suppose we find him if we don't explore every lead we have?"

"I'll talk to the locals. I'm sure somebody has a CI who's willing to help with this."

"None of those CIs have the connections that I have." I shrugged. "Sorry. That's the truth."

And it was. People didn't snitch on Simeon Gunn. He ran his shit like a business that gave out more than pizza on staff appreciation days. As long as his guys kept their mouths shut with the cops, he took care of them. He paid their lawyer fees if they got busted. Once the lawyer got them off, he'd give them a bonus, so to speak, for keeping their mouth shut about him. Very much operated by the, *You catch more bees with honey than vinegar*, motto.

"Tough shit," Ox said. "You're not leaving police custody. We'll find the information that we need elsewhere."

"CIs don't become CIs because they know dealers who are moving Rohypnol, Ox," I said. "CIs are CIs because they're involved with heroin and meth. Heavy shit. My connection knows everybody and what everybody is selling."

"'Course he does. Wouldn't stay in business if he didn't," Ox said. "All the more reason that you are not going."

"The killer won't come after me the moment you guys aren't around," I insisted. "That's not what he wants. He wants to torture me. He'll keep doing that, until I turn myself over to him. He wants to break me. If it was just about killing me, he would've done it when he cut my hair."

"Maybe. But that's not a chance I'm willing to take."

"All due respect, Detective," Phillips began, "but this was what I meant. What we *all* meant."

"Conflict of interest." Gayton frowned as she looked between us. "Maddie makes good points here. If she has connections you don't, she should use them."

Ox opened his mouth as if he was about to rebut something, then snapped it shut. Hands balled to fist at his sides, his jaw tightened. A long moment of silence stretched on before he broke it with, "Fine. But you call me every five minutes, and you share your location with me. If you don't answer, I'm coming after you."

Raising my hands at my sides in mock defeat, I said, "Yes, sir."

Chapter 17

The last time I was here, I was seventeen, drunker than a sailor, spending time with a guy upstairs whose name I couldn't tell you if my life depended on it. A lot had changed since then, but this house hadn't.

House. That was a lie. This place was no house.

Mansion was more like it. After they let me past the gate, it took me another five minutes to get to the wraparound driveway with a fountain in the center. The building almost resembled the White House. For the color, obviously, but also the decorative pillars lining the porch. Tack on the million windows all framed by high-end, luxury curtains, the Mercedes in the driveway, and the flatscreen TV that was probably larger than my car shining from the living room, and it was exactly what you would expect from a drug kingpin.

Tempest waited at my side as I trudged the seemingly never-ending staircase. Every step was like its own torture device. It was my fault that the pain was so bad today, having not done my exercises or gone for my usual walk.

Actually, it wasn't my fault. It was The Country Killer's fault.

I was so damn tired of blaming myself for my pain as though I'd been the one who caused it, who kept causing it. Take my addiction for contrast. Definitely my fault, in tandem with genetics.

All I had done that night was my job. Even so, knee replacement surgery wasn't supposed to continue to cause pain almost two years after the trauma. Maybe it was the surgeon's fault. And maybe if I ever got around to buying health insurance, I could get a second opinion to prove it.

I was about halfway up the stairs when the big red door creaked open. Leaning against its frame, Simeon arched a brow at me. "There's a ramp around back if you need it."

Glaring, I shot him a universally inappropriate hand signal.

He gave a half smile. "Do you need help?"

"I need there to be less damn stairs," I said under my breath, forcing my pace to pick up. "What is it with rich people? Why do you all need so many stairs?"

"Symbolic of the corporate ladder, maybe?"

"And what corporate ladder did you climb?"

"I was born at the top." He nodded to Tempest. "She's not gonna shit on my floors, is she?"

Nearly at the top of the stairs now, I narrowed my eyes further. "Not unless I tell her to."

That devilish, half smile stretched wider. "You're not going to tell her to, are you?"

"Depends on if you make another shitty comment about my limited mobility." Finally atop the stairs, I returned the devilish smirk. "It's a low blow, you know. I could say worse things about you."

"Oh, yeah?" Still, he leaned against the doorframe. "Like what?"

"Like the heroin you sold is probably what killed my mom."

That wiped the smirk right off his lips. Rather than a playful glower, his shoulders broadened ever so slightly. Today he wore a pair of jeans and a button-down shirt that tugged with his movement, opposed to the usual suit and tie he wore since he had become an adult and inherited his father's family business. He carefully scrutinized what I was wearing. A pair of sweatpants, a baggy T-shirt, and my hair spun into a bun atop my head.

Then he looked back up at my face, his expression genuine. "What's this about, Castle?"

"I need your help."

"With?"

"Finding The Country Killer."

For a few seconds, he processed. Then he snorted a laugh. "I know it's been a long time, but that is a much different business than the one I run. I don't know shit about that guy."

"I think you know more than you realize."

Another scoff that almost resembled a laugh. I didn't return it. Slowly, his face screwed up in confusion. "You think I'm him?"

"No. I think you or one of your guys has sold to him."

There was still confusion in his brown eyes, but his breath all but stopped in his chest. He looked behind me, as if expecting sirens to come blaring down the driveway.

"I'm not trying to bust you," I said. "But the drugs he's using aren't easy to come by. You run every county from here to—What? Lancaster? I just need—"

"You need to shut your mouth and get inside."

There were few things I hated more than being told what to do. One of them was a serial killer I desperately needed to put away.

So, I shut my mouth and got inside.

"Look, I'm sorry to just barge in," I began once he shut the over-sized front door. "I didn't know where else to go. I know you keep tabs on all your guys, and I know you know what goes in and out of this county, and—"

"Give me your phone." He held out his hand. When my face screwed up, and I opened my mouth to rebut something, his eyes darkened. "For all I know, you're recording this, so give me your goddamned phone, Castle."

Hackles rising, Tempest growled low and edged toward him. I told her to sit and rewarded her with a pat on the head when she did. I dug in my hoodie pocket and passed it to him.

Just to be sure he knew I wasn't setting him up, I also handed him the burner phone that the FBI agents had given me this morning. "This guy's stalking me, and he's a hacker, so that's the one I'm talking to the cops and FBI with."

With a snort, he traced his tongue along his teeth. "You're working with the FBI?"

"To find a serial killer. Not to get you busted for trafficking."

His jaw tightened. He looked me over for a moment, then nodded at my chest. "Take your shirt off."

Now it was me who snorted. "Hell no."

"You show up at my house, ask me if I know people dealing illegal substances, then tell me you're working with the FBI. And you think I'm gonna tell you a damn thing until you prove you're not wearing a wire?" He shook his head. "Take off your shirt or get out of my house."

Fair enough point, but I still had no interest in removing my clothing. "Is it enough if I just admit that I helped you kidnap a man who was never seen again?"

He glared. "Hypothetically, if you *had* done that, there's no way I could know you hadn't made a deal when evidence surfaced in that investigation and came here to get me to confess to it on tape."

Growling my annoyance, I laid Tempest's leash on the ground. "We've known each other since we were kids. Have I ever struck you as a snitch?" I ripped my hoodie off and handed it to him. Underneath, I wore a T-shirt and a sports bra beneath that. Lifting up my shirt was enough to prove that there was no wire. I may not have been entirely flat, but there was nowhere to hide in there. "I know you. If I snitched on you, you'd kill me. I'm not stupid, Simeon."

"Turn around," he said.

Still cursing under my breath, I held my shirt up as high as I could as I spun in a circle. "Satisfied?"

He nodded toward my pants. "Empty your pockets."

With another grumble, I did so. "Happy yet?"

"They're baggie. Pull them down. Prove there's nothing strapped to your legs."

"If this is some elaborate ruse to see me naked, just know that I wear granny panties and haven't shaved my legs in at least a month." But I pulled them down, as violating as it felt. "Is that enough for you? Or do you want to do a cavity search too?"

That, he gave me a half smile for. "The granny panties are plenty."

I shot him another hand signal, which he laughed at. "Are you gonna answer my questions now?"

With a billowing sigh, he sat in the armchair beside the entry table and tossed me my hoodie. "Hypothetically, what kind of drugs are you looking for?"

"Rohypnol." I yanked it back over my frame. "Roofies."

"Below my pay grade. I don't move that shit."

"Pot is below your pay grade too, but I know you move it."

"There's money in pot. There is no money in roofies." Propping his elbows on his knees, he leaned toward me. The next bit, he spoke almost as a threat. "But, hypothetically, if I knew some people who dealt it, and I told you their names, that would stay between the two of us."

"The only person I'm trying to get put behind bars is The Country Killer. He's back, and he won't stop until he's dead or in prison. I don't care about dealers, Simeon."

"That's not what I said." His tone sharpened. "Hypothetically, anything I tell you, is going to stay between us, is it not?"

"I just told you." My tone sharpened as well. "I don't want to end up on your hit list."

"Who says I have a hit list?"

Damn it, I'd had enough. "Cut the shit. Cut the hypotheticals, and the ifs, and the maybes. We both know you're a drug dealer. We both know you keep tabs on every other dealer, big and small, in every direction for at least a hundred miles. I don't care about the heroin you're moving, or the meth you're making, or the coke you sell, or the weed you grow. I could give a shit less about all of it. The only thing I care about is that an eighteen-year-old girl was drugged and tortured in her home two nights ago. I care that Amber Robinson was murdered last night because she looks like me and went to our high school. I care that Josey Hall was just kidnapped by him to try to lure me into giving myself over to him. I care that he drugged me, broke into my house, and cut my hair in my sleep to keep as a trophy."

Judging by his silence, I'd rendered Simeon Gunn speechless. I took this as my cue to continue, and let my tone soften.

"This guy is local. He is killing innocent women from our town, our home, and he is using *your* dealers' drugs to do it. I know he is, because Rohypnol isn't legal in the US, meaning he has to have gotten it on the streets, and you run these streets. I don't think you're the devil. You're a businessman, even if what you sell is morally questionable. I don't think you advocate for the ruthless murder of innocent people. I'm not going to give your name, or any of your guys' names, to the cops. I just want to find The Country Killer. Help me find him, damn it. Just tell me the names of your guys who might sell Rohypnol and *help me find him.*"

For a few heartbeats, he stayed eerily silent, only watching me carefully. I imagined that if an artist were to have drawn me right then, I would've had flames shooting out of all my orifices.

Eventually, he broke the silence with, "I almost forgot why we used to call you Mad dog."

"Try waking up with a bad haircut from a serial killer and tell me you wouldn't be a little pissed off."

"Oh, no, I would track the son of the bitch down and make him wish he were dead."

"That's the plan. Would be nice if I had a lead." I made a rolling motion with my hand.

Turning to my phone, he swept the screen up. "What's your password?"

I told him, ending with, "Why?"

"I'm giving you the list." As he tapped on the screen, it rang. Before I could glance and see who was calling me, he clicked the red bar. "Ox, huh? He recover alright?"

"Doesn't have the lung capacity that he used to, but he's hanging in there."

"Happy to hear it." He ignored the call and continued tapping on the screen. Then he laughed. "What did Bentley do?"

"Nothing. What do you mean?"

"You've got six unopen texts from him."

I glared. "Are you done writing the list?"

"Almost." Shooting me a smirk, he turned back to my phone. "Just like to snoop."

"Well, don't."

"Coming from the P.I.," he said under his breath. "You do any snooping on him?"

A knot formed in my stomach. For two reasons.

One: Last night, that was exactly what I'd been doing. Snooping on Bentley. The Country Killer was more than likely monitoring my internet activity, meaning he would've known I was snooping on Bentley. But I could not see Simeon as the killer. He did fit the profile in many ways, but so did almost every other CEO. Aside from that, The Country Killer likely had a stellar reputation in his community. While Simeon was well known, that was as a drug dealer. The Country Killer wouldn't have wanted that reputation.

Two: If Simeon wasn't the killer, but he knew something about Bentley's past, that would mean that Bentley was involved in a world we'd both sworn we'd escape. The girl in the photo had already led me to that conclusion, but confirmation from the area's most well-known drug lord...

"Bentley?" I asked. "Why would I snoop on Bentley?"

"You seem like the type of person who'd want to do your research on someone before getting into a relationship with them." Standing, he held out my phone. "Rumor is that's what you guys are doing. Just thought you would've found out everything he was involved in before he moved back here by now."

Had he just punched a hole through my chest? It felt like he had. "What was he involved in?"

Another half smile, this one less devious than the last. "You don't know."

"Hence why I asked."

"Ask him." Simeon waved my phone at me. "Looks like he wants to talk to you."

Grabbing it and stuffing it in my pocket, I tilted my head to the side. "How do you know then?"

He raised a shoulder. "He's the kind of person I want to keep tabs on."

What the hell did that mean? "Was he dealing?"

"Good question. Ask him." With a nod to my phone, Simeon walked to the door and held it open for me. "I don't know everyone's addresses, but none of them are far. I'm sure you can figure it out."

"Hang on. What do you know about Bentley?" Furrowing my brows, I walked closer. "What was he involved in?"

"Aren't you the P.I.?"

"Yeah, and his only record was expunged, so it's all but untraceable."

"Unfortunate." He nodded toward my car. "Now go catch your killer."

"How bad was it?" I asked. "Whatever Bentley was involved in, how bad was it?"

"Isn't that subjective when you so proudly proclaim you helped me commit murder?"

"Yes, but I'm an addict. I don't have the reputation of a proud single parent stamped on my forehead." I paused. "Wait. Did Bentley kill someone?"

"Good question," he repeated. "Go ask him."

I folded my arms against my chest. "You know, we were friends once. I would've told you if someone you trusted was a murderer."

"We partied together. We were never besties. But you know who was?" He pointed at my phone. "You and Bentley. So go talk to him."

Which was fair enough. Still left me glaring at him though. "You don't think he's The Country Killer, do you?"

I expected a half laugh. Maybe an all-knowing, serious look.

Instead, he cackled. Not a faint laugh, not a chuckle, but a cackle. "You do?"

"I didn't say that."

"But you're asking the known drug dealer and murderer?" Simeon laughed so hard that his face turned red. "Do I really need to tell you where the fault in your logic here is?"

I called for Tempest and started out the door when she was beside me. Simeon was still laughing when I made it to the driveway. "Thanks for your help. And go to hell."

"I'll save you a seat," he made out between laughs.

One more crude hand signal before I loaded into the driver's side.

Chapter 18

As I turned my car on, I read that text from Bentley.

Hey, I'm sorry, I'm not trying to blow you up. I was just hoping we could talk after I get off work today. I'll make you dinner?

As Simeon had stated, talking to Bentley seemed like a good idea. But I was now a thousand times more anxious for that conversation, because I had no idea what I had just learned.

The only thing I knew for certain was that Bentley lied. He may not have lied about everything, but he lied about why he came back here. And I just knew it had something to do with the woman in that Christmas photo.

I stared at the text for a moment, debating whether to respond, *how* to respond. Just as my fingers moved to type, *Yeah, I think we should talk too*, Ox's name lit up the screen.

Grunting, I answered it. "Yes?"

"I told you to call me every five minutes."

"I was kind of busy. I'm alive. Getting on the road to go talk to some drug dealers. Should be in the car for about fifteen minutes, and it'd be great if you didn't interrupt every song that came on the radio between now and then."

"It'd be great if there wasn't a serial killer on the loose, but there is, so suck it up."

Rolling my eyes, I shifted the car into drive. I recognized the first name on the list and knew where he lived, so I headed there first. "Can't I just call you when I get where I'm going?"

"What if he ambushes your car or some shit? No. I'll call you back in five minutes."

"Fine." Before he had the chance to respond, I ended the call.

And then, as I drove the winding back roads, my thoughts festered.

Simeon didn't seem to think that Bentley was The Country Killer. But that didn't mean he wasn't *a* killer.

BOBBY SINCLAIR HAD BEEN FIRST ON THE LIST. WHEN I SHOWED at his door, he refused to say a word to me until I paid him what my mom had owed him. I imagined I would be hearing that a lot more today.

After scrounging together my hundred and fifty bucks—at least five of which were in quarters—I showed him the police sketch, he said he didn't recognize him, then shut the door in my face.

Drew Walker was next. I didn't know him personally, but my mom had also bought from him at one point. Apparently, she'd died without being in his debt, because he looked at the sketch for a moment, said he wished he could help, but he'd never seen this man before, and offered me a pot brownie before I left. With a thanks, I declined. Come to think of it though, maybe that was why he was more sociable than the last. While Bobby dealt many drugs, Drew strictly stuck to herbs.

Next was someone I knew well. Noah Ward. He wasn't as quick to let me into his apartment as the last, but when he looked at the sketch, all the color drained from his face.

"You did," I said. "You sold to this guy."

Rubbing a hand down his beard, eyes widening, he looked past me into the apartment hallway. Behind me, a woman wrestled with a toddler and two school-aged children. When I turned back around, Noah had pulled the door the rest of the way open.

Heart skipping—partly with excitement for a lead, and partly because I was terrified of whatever I would find, given the smell wafting into the hallway—I moved inside. Walking off with my police sketch, Noah said to himself, "Shit. Shit, shit, *shit.*"

Which was what his home smelled like.

When I followed him into his living room, I kept Tempest directly at my side and didn't take the seat he offered me on the old floral sofa. Garbage was scattered all over the floor, including an open cardboard pizza box developing its own microbiome. Clothes were among the debris, with just a faint hint of body spray accompanying the scent of sweat. The incense burning on the windowsill didn't come close to disguising the stench permeating the room. Credit where it was due though, because while I smelled a million awful things, the bong on the table with smoke still inside the chamber was not one of them.

"You know him?" I asked.

"Know him, no," Noah said, still staring down at the photo in disbelief. "Sold to him? Yeah."

"Do you know his name?"

Greasy, mousy blond hair fell into his green eyes when he shook his head. "He went by Red. I thought it was funny. Like a nod to *That 70s Show?*"

Or like The *Red* Ribbon Killer. But yes, a stoner equating the name to *That 70s Show* checked out.

"What did you sell him?"

"Just weed the first couple times. You really think he's The Country Killer?"

"The waitress who saw him sitting in front of my drink makes me think so," I said. "Did he scream peace-loving hippie to you?"

"No, but..." Forehead creasing in disbelief, he shook his head again and grabbed the bong off the coffee table. "Shit, I need to get high for this."

I was sure he needed to get high for just about everything he did. "You sold him roofies?"

Lips pinched together, he held up a finger in a motion for me to wait. So I did. I waited until he exhaled, and then coughed for a solid minute and a half, before asking again, "You're the person he got the Rohypnol from?"

The whites of his eyes now red as roses, still coughing, he nodded. Once he recovered, he chugged some water. "Yeah, I sold them to him. When we first met, he said he wanted the weed to knock him out and to deal with pain."

"Should have been your first red flag. It's not hard to get a medical card and dispensary prices are just as cheap as what you charge. Not to mention better quality."

"If someone comes to you asking for your services with money in hand, do you try to send them to someone else?"

"Fair enough."

"But then he said the weed wasn't enough to knock him out, and he wanted to know if I had anything stronger. He asked for ketamine first. Said something about how it's used to treat pain?" That was true. I had read an article about that recently. Something to do with how falling into a K hole reset the pain receptors in your brain and could effectively mitigate chronic pain for months afterward. It was, however, also used as a date rape drug. "Ketamine isn't something I mess with. My customers are old heads, and K is more of a party drug. But Silas had some roofies, guess he got them on that campus he's dealing at, so I offered them to him. Took them all off my hands."

So he'd made the connection with Noah through cannabis because it was the easiest thing to get on the streets. I doubted he was using it. More than likely, he had only bought it to find a connection to what he really wanted.

Was it possible that during The Country Killer's remission, he had used ketamine or Rohypnol as a date rape drug? Maybe it was worth digging into the sex crimes reports to see who else had been drugged with either of those. It'd be a wide pool, but maybe that explained why he had used them on me, Rachel, and Josey. Since I'd injured him, and he was unable to subdue his victims physically, it was possible that substances had become a part of his signature.

How had he carried Josey this morning then? Well, part of physical therapy was muscle building. It was the same reason I exercised daily. My legs failed me regularly, but I could bust open a watermelon with my thighs. If I was in enough danger—say, on a busy walking trail with a woman I'd just knocked unconscious—adrenaline would drown out the pain long enough for me to do what needed doing. I'd pay for it later, but I *did* have the physical strength to accomplish it.

When I left, I'd call Ox and ask him to investigate any sexual assaults from the last year and a half within The Country Killer's comfort zone. He was a sadist, so any assaults with violence would narrow down our pool.

"Where did you guys meet?" I asked.

"The Pour House," he said. "I was meeting a friend there. Sold her a dime bag in the parking lot. Red saw, walked up to me, and asked if I had any more."

The Pour House. A local bar not far from Bistro Banter, the café where Bentley and I had eaten at two nights ago. "Then you sold to him? Right then and there?"

Coughing again, he nodded. "Like I said. If somebody comes to you with business, you turn them away?"

"You didn't think he was a cop?"

"Nah. I know a cop when I see one, and he wasn't."

"What makes you say that?"

"A cop doesn't walk up to you in slacks and a button-down and expect you to sell to them," he said. "Usually, they're dressed like you are right now."

Again, fair enough. Undercover cops often tried too hard to *not* look like cops. "When was this?"

"That I met him? About a year ago. I gave him a couple dime bags between then and the holidays. The roofies, I want to say that was in

March? He called me, asked if I had the shit, then met me at Silas's place to pick it up."

"Do you have his number?"

"Yeah, but dude was real paranoid," Noah said. "He used a little flip phone. Said something about how they were untraceable. I never called him either. He always called me."

Considering how vigilant The Country Killer was about covering his tracks, that came as no surprise. "Can you give me the number either way?"

"Sure." Sliding his phone from his pocket, he tapped around for a moment. Mine beeped. "You really think this is him?"

Did I know for sure? No. It was all circumstantial. Was it possible that he just so happened to be at the restaurant I had been at when I was drugged? Yes. Was it possible that he just so happened to be sitting in front of my drink? Also yes. Was it possible that he just had a hard time falling asleep and that was why he wanted the Rohypnol? Yes. Was it possible that he went by the name Red because he liked *That 70s Show*? Sure.

Were these things *probable*? Absolutely not. None of this was enough to stand in court. But I sure as hell hoped it would be enough to get a warrant for his fingerprints or DNA.

"That's where the trail is leading me," I said. "Did he ever mention what caused his chronic pain?"

"No. I tried to give him pain pills instead, but he didn't want them."

Furthering my theory that it was never about chronic pain, but all about making a connection with the drug dealer.

I prayed that he did have chronic pain, though. It was an awful thing to live with, and on an average day, I wouldn't wish it on anyone. But this son of a bitch? After what he had done to all those women, after destroying my life, there was nothing I wanted more than for him to suffer every moment of every day.

"You didn't happen to see his left upper arm at any point, did you?" I asked. "Did he have a scar there?"

Tilting his head to the side, Noah's face scrunched up in thought.

He took another hit off the bong before nodding. "He did, actually. Does that matter?"

This didn't mean Bentley was out of the woods. Especially after what Simeon had said. But it did ease my mind. "Yeah. Because I shot him there."

Squinting at me slightly, he wiped some spit from his mouth. "You wouldn't shoot me, would you?"

"Not unless you were aiming a gun at me first." Crossing my arms, I nibbled my lip. "Do you know the make and model of his car?"

"I know it was a sedan. Pretty sure it was black," he said. "Not super high-end, but not a clunker either." Pausing, Noah took yet another hit off the bong. After exhaling, then coughing for a moment, his eyes widened, and he wagged a finger. "Actually, yeah. We talked about his car once. He wouldn't do the deal in the parking lot, so he had me get in, and he drove around the block. It was an Audi. I don't know the year, but it had a Bluetooth stereo and the GPS on the dashboard, so it must've been pretty new."

That was a hell of a lot more than I had when I got here. "Black Audi, got it. Is there anything else you think might help me here? Details about him that seemed odd? Maybe anything connecting to our high school?"

"He did say that once. That he graduated from our high school. Didn't say the year, but I didn't recognize him anyway. He looked a little older than us though?" Thinking a moment longer, Noah scratched his hairline. "Oh, he was really bugged out about Silas's dog. She's just a puppy, but he was super antsy and asked if we could go to another room when she jumped on him. Is that the sort of thing you mean?"

Made sense since Bear had bitten a hole through his leg. "Yeah, that helps a lot. Did he say why he didn't like dogs?"

"Mentioned he got bitten by one when he was a kid," he said. "Actually, he had a little scar on his lip from it. He had a beard and mustache, so I couldn't really see it, but that's the sort of thing you'd want to know, right? Identifying scars? I feel like I've seen that on TV somewhere."

"That definitely helps." My heart fluttered at the thought. Good thing I kept pressing, because Noah's dumbass wouldn't have thought to tell me if I hadn't. "That everything you got? Nothing else comes to mind? Maybe he mentioned what he does for work, or where he lived?"

Frowning, Noah shook his head. "I told you. The guy was paranoid. Never even gave me his real name."

I still had far more to go on than I did an hour or so ago. "That's okay. Just call me if you think of anything else, alright?"

"Will do. And be safe out there." Stoned or not, his eyes looked concerned. "Catch this guy before he catches you."

"I sure the hell hope to."

Chapter 19

"Yes, I'm alive." Holding the phone, which I'd left in the car while I was inside, to my ear, I answered. I clicked the car door shut. "What did you give me this time? Six minutes? Seven?"

"For good behavior," Ox said. "Where you headed next?"

"Why ask? You're watching my location."

"And if it starts heading another way, I'm gonna assume someone's got a gun to your head telling you where to go."

Pinching the phone between my ear and my shoulder, I turned the car over. "Home. That's where I'm headed. I got some information. I don't know how much it'll help, but it's something."

"You want to call me back?" I knew he was referencing the burner phone, but it wasn't vital information like a name. It could wait until I made it home. "Because if you want me to meet you somewhere—"

"No, I'm only about twenty minutes from home. Just meet me there."

"Are you sure?" It was like he was waiting for me to drop the code-word. "Are you okay?"

Was I relieved to have some hope? Of course. Was I happy alto-gether? No. I couldn't get Simeon's words out of my head. "Yeah, I'm fine. Just tired. And safe. I promise."

"Alright. I'm still calling you back in five minutes."

"Of course you are," I said under my breath, pulling out of the parking space. "I'm anxiously awaiting."

Ox made a sound that almost resembled a laugh before the line went out.

Exhaling deeply, I continued out of the parking lot and onto the adjacent road. What I could really use right now was a long drive. One where the music was so loud it hurt my ears, trembled my organs, and blurred my racing thoughts to silence.

Unfortunately, even if Ox weren't watching my every move through the GPS tracker on my phone, my knee was killing me and I desperately needed to get out of the car. It was almost 3 o'clock, and I had spent the entirety of my day so far driving between the homes of drug dealers. In addition, I had almost been awake for thirty-six hours now. Everything was blurry around the edges, my stomach hurt, and I wasn't sure if I should blame the anxiety, lack of rest, or the drugs that surely hadn't left my system yet.

My top priority was finding The Country Killer. Absolutely. But all this stress, all this worry, I usually would have bounced off my best friend. Bentley would talk, or he would smile, or he would hand me a plate of food, and for a short while, my shoulders wouldn't feel so heavy. When I was listening to his voice, when I was looking into his eyes, when I was eating something he had baked love into, my thoughts were clear. My heart rate slowed, and even my pain was more tolerable.

It wasn't about romance. Sure, that may have contributed to some of it, but it was our friendship. He reminded me to take care of myself, and we laughed together, and even when we weren't talking at all, silence was never awkward.

I needed my best friend. This was the most stressed I had ever been, and I needed him, but I couldn't find the courage to dial his number. He would answer. Anytime I called him when he was at work, he answered, even if it was to say he'd call me back in five. But I wouldn't be able to look him in the eyes right now. Not until I knew the whole story of how he ended up here and what Simeon Gunn had to do with it.

If I asked him, would he look me in the eyes and lie again? There were things I had done that I wouldn't confess, even to him. Like letting Simeon kidnap a man. Of course, I felt morally justified in that. Jackson had murdered an innocent man. He could've—very well may have—gotten the death penalty either way. What did it matter to me if Simeon or someone at the corrections facility did it? Maybe it should have mattered, but I was rational enough to know that keeping my mouth shut protected me and my loved ones.

Was Bentley doing the same thing? Had he lied to me not because he wanted to, but because I would've been at risk if he hadn't? Maybe. Was it some type of *Breaking Bad* situation? Was that what he was involved in with that girl?

Ugh. The thought of him being with that girl made my stomach hurt so much worse. Bentley selling or making drugs bothered me less than the thought of him in a relationship with that girl. While I always had sympathy for addicts, for people who struggled financially and did whatever was needed to make ends meet, there was no way in hell I could sympathize with a grown man chasing a little girl. And that's what she was. Even if the girl in that photo was legally an adult, she was too young for someone our age.

Would Bentley even do that? I couldn't see it, but why else would she have been present for Christmas? Who was she? What did it have to do with Simeon Gunn? Simeon's involvement at all was enough to make me nauseous, but—

My phone rang again. According to the clock on the dashboard, it had only been two minutes. Annoyed, I grabbed it from the center console, ready to tear Ox a new one.

But *Private Number* slid across the screen.

Stomach aching, Gayton's words this morning pulsed through my mind. She'd said he'd make contact soon. As she'd instructed, I dialed her number on the burner with shaking fingers. While it rang, I stared at that *Private Number* and swallowed the bile that stung up my throat.

I had to answer, especially if he had Josey. But this was not the sort of conversation to have while driving.

Pulling off to the shoulder, I fumbled with my cell phone as it rang again, and again, while I searched for my recorder in the center console. Typically, the recording app on my phone was more than enough for my job, but in case my phone died on me at some point, or in case of situations like this, I always made sure to have an old-school recorder in my car.

Holding my foot on the brake, ready to get back on the road in case he showed up, I clicked the red button on the recorder, swallowed hard, and slid the green bar to answer the call. "Hello?"

"Mad dog. That's what you go by, isn't it?"

I'd never heard him speak, but somehow I knew. That voice did not belong to Bentley, it didn't belong to anyone I knew, nor was it the slightest bit familiar, but there was a certain edge to it that made my limbs lock up involuntarily. His tone was casual, even friendly. But it was the same sort of voice you would hear from the "nice guy" at a club. The nice guy who gave you no logical reason to fear him, but something inside you just screamed, *Run.*

Like there was some biological imperative to know that no matter how charming that voice sounded, no matter how good of a job he did at faking the nice guy routine, my body wouldn't let me. It was like some type of ancestral memory. Like thousands of women throughout history had been fooled by men like this before, and they were all screaming from the clouds, *Run.*

I couldn't run. I had to pretend like I didn't want to. There was an innocent woman in his custody, and she needed me.

God, I prayed she still needed me.

"Red. That's what you go by, right?" I did my best to sound as confident as he did. "Too bad though. I prefer Country Killer. It sounds stupid, and that's the reputation you deserve."

He chuckled, and that sound should've been endearing. Maybe even sexy. Like his voice, it was deep. Raspy. The kind of voice that would make a woman swoon if he had the right accent.

Instead, that sound rushed adrenaline to my limbs and again whispered, *Run.*

"And here I thought you might be nice," he said. "Josey's life depends on you being nice."

A stab ached through my chest. It took everything I had to keep my voice steady. "Like Amber? Did she depend on me being nice to you too?"

"Oh, no. She was done for months ago. As soon as I decided, there was nothing you could have done."

"You're making yourself look so much better."

"I know exactly how I look, Mad dog." The rest of his tone was playful, teasing, but he spat those words, like my nickname tasted like vinegar on his tongue. "Know exactly how you look too. Gotta say, I prefer the blouse. The homeless aesthetic seems to be your preference, but maybe you would've gotten farther in life if you cared a little bit more about your appearance."

Hated that I knew this routine. Just like a "nice guy" to throw out a backhanded compliment in such a poorly attempted, seductive tone.

"You realize women don't dress ourselves each morning thinking about some chauvinistic pig's opinion of it, right?" As stupid as it sounded coming out of my mouth, this was what they'd told me to do. Stand my ground. Be a bitch. "But I guess you wouldn't know that. The only women you talk to are defenseless old ladies. That is, before you kill them." I hated saying that. Hated, hated, *hated* saying that. It was a smack to his ego though, and that was what I was supposed to do. Even if it meant insulting the dead. "Or, maybe you prefer them once they've gone cold. You strike me as that kinda guy."

Another chuckle, but this one less of a taunt and more of an assertion. Like just the sound told me that he was broadening his shoulders and lifting his chin. "Or maybe I prefer them on leashes. Where a bitch belongs."

Metal rattled on the other end of the speaker and, muffled by a gag, a woman squealed.

Bile rose up my esophagus. I swallowed it back down.

"Speaking of bitches, how's Bear? That's his name, right?" His laugh teetered on a cackle. "My apologies. Was. That *was* his name. Have you visited him recently?"

That meant something. It had to. The first half could have been him taunting me, trying to make me afraid or angry, but he wouldn't have asked that unless he had a reason.

No matter how much it made me want to reach through the phone and strangle him.

"That's gendered language, and you're using it incorrectly," I said. "Bear was male. He wasn't a bitch. But hey, coming from the piece of shit who can only stand up to a woman when he sneaks up on her in the middle of the night, you know a thing or two about bitches, don't you, Red?"

"I know a thing or two about yours. What's her name? Temperance? Tempest? That's it. Tempest." The clink of metal sounded again, followed by a muffled sob. "She really likes her bed. It's funny, because I thought you weren't going to give her one. You kept saying so. That she wouldn't stop resource guarding if she had things to guard. And then it occurred to me. You didn't take away her belongings. You just gave her a new one. Yourself. Just like Bear did, she'll die to protect you."

As though I didn't hear her panting in the backseat, I whipped my head around to look at her. She was fine. Sitting in the middle seat without a care in the world, gazing out the windows.

Quickly, I put the phone on mute and told Tempest, "Floor."

She dropped between the seats in a heartbeat.

To my knowledge, he wasn't a sniper, but I wasn't taking any risks.

Rationally, I knew that wasn't his point. He didn't want to kill her. Not right now. He wanted me to be afraid that he had not only been watching me through my cameras but listening in on my conversations.

"That would be too bad, wouldn't it?" he asked. "I would hate to do that to her."

"You'll never get within a hundred feet of her," I said, doing my best to keep my tone flat and even. "What's your point here? Are you just trying to scare me? Torture me? Because it isn't working." It was one-hundred percent working. "You want to make a deal? Stay on the line. I'll conference in the FBI."

"Do I want to make a deal? Yes. With them?" He chuckled one more time, softer than any of the others had been. The woman's sobs joined the sound. "You're who I'd like to make a deal with, Mad dog."

"Too bad. Thanks to you, I'm no longer a cop. Don't worry though. Detective Taylor should call me any second. You can talk with him yourself."

"If you answer a call from him right now, Josey dies." Still, his voice had the playful edge to it. "You don't want her blood on your hands, do you? Amber's death, that's already on you."

A lump the size of a truck formed in my throat. There was no swallowing it down. The most I could do was snap, "Just tell me what you want."

"You. I thought that was obvious," he said. "Leave the dog, and your phone, in your vehicle. Walk to Holly Park. You're not far. Go into the woods, wait for the signal, and then I will direct you from there."

"It's not gonna happen," I said. "But if you let Josey go—"

"I'm not negotiating with you, Maddie. Either you do what I have just told you to do, or Josey dies. You don't want that, do you?"

I had to keep the phone on speakerphone and away from my face so that he wouldn't hear the rapid pace my breathing picked up to. They said to keep him on the phone if he called, and I didn't know how much longer I could keep it together, because I knew what was about to happen. I knew, and I didn't want to face it.

"Tell her," he said. The woman's sobs were louder now, no longer muffled, as though he had removed a gag from her mouth. "Tell her you need her help, Josey."

"Please," Josey sobbed. "Please don't let me die."

I couldn't form words.

They lodged somewhere deep in my throat. The only thing that was gonna slither its way out was a scream.

"Tell her what we were just watching, Josey," he said.

"Th-the news. The news last year. You're a hero." The most wretched, heartbreaking weep billowed from the speaker. "That's what they said. They called you a hero. You saved that girl. Rachel? You saved her, so you'll save me, right? Please. Please just do what he says. Please save me too."

I opened my mouth to speak, but nothing came out. Tears stung across my eyes and burned aching trails down my cheeks.

"Maddie? That's your name, right?" she sobbed. "You're coming, right, Maddie?"

I wanted so badly to. I wanted to save her. But Gayton's voice played over in my head again, reminding me that if he got ahold of me, he would kill me. Killing me would only add to his ego trip. He would kill again, and again, and again. He would continue to get away with it, just like he had a year and a half ago.

Since I had become his enemy, I had become his weakness. The only chance we had at stopping him, and stopping him for good, was me.

Amazed that my voice didn't quiver, I said, "Is there anything you want me to tell your husband?"

She sobbed again. That awful, almost indescribable sob. It was unlike any other sound I ever heard in my life. Pained, grief-stricken, terrified, and something so awful that I didn't know if there were words to assign to it. Or maybe we just used words like pain and grief and terror too often. Maybe moments like this were exactly what they were meant to describe. "I love him. Tell him I love—"

A scream.

A scream so bone curdling that I wasn't sure I would ever be able to forget it. The moment I heard it, I knew that for the rest of my life, I would never stop hearing it. From here on, Josey Hall would forever hold a place in my heart. And so would her scream.

It would live and fester within the darkest part of myself. It would reverberate through my mind every time I considered picking up a little orange bottle. It would haunt every peaceful dream. It would ache deep inside my chest until the day I died.

Josey and her scream.

"This is your fault, Maddie!" He yelled over her scream. "You did this! You let her die! Don't forget that, Maddie!"

It was. I did. And I would never be able to.

Muting the phone, I cupped a hand over my mouth and listened. I listened to her beg, I listened to her sob, and I listened to her scream. All I wanted was to chuck that phone out the window and drive a million miles away. Or climb through its screen and stop him. Kill him. Make sure no one else could ever feel this way at his hands again.

But if I hung up, he would think he'd won. He would think he had broken me.

He had to think that I was an evil bitch who could not be broken.

"I'll tell him, Josey," I managed to get out. "I'll make sure he knows you loved him."

I didn't know that scream could become any more awful, but it did. I didn't know what he did to her, I didn't want to, but my false strength was like his ammunition.

The most awful sloshing sound bounced from the speakers so many times that I lost count. I didn't know what that sound was, and I could've gone my whole life without knowing.

There was a *thump*, and another, and a *thwack*. There were so many, and I didn't want to know what they meant. Was he beating her? Stabbing her? Torturing her?

All three, I had to imagine.

I hated the relief I felt when I no longer heard Josey's scream.

Winded, panting, he said, "It's your fault."

The line went dead.

Chapter 20

Ox had called. I didn't answer. I *couldn't* answer.

I sat there in my car on the side of the road, and I sobbed. I sobbed until I was sure I was going to faint, but I didn't. It would've been nice if I had. It would've been nice to get a break for a moment, for a few minutes. But I supposed my instinct was louder than my desire. The instinct that said, *He's been watching you. He knows where you are at this very moment. If you faint, Josey's death was for nothing. Run.*

I couldn't run, but I could drive.

I had never slammed onto the gas so quickly. I tore off onto the winding back road with a plume of dust in my wake. When Ox called again and again, I attempted to grab my phone off the passenger seat, but it fell out of my sweaty, shaking fingers.

I couldn't catch my breath. It was like a vacuum had just been shoved down my throat. I rolled down the windows to let in the fresh, humid summer air, but I still couldn't breathe. My phone dinged with a text message, but I couldn't breathe. All I could think about was trying to breathe.

When a quiet cry tore through my lips, it finally felt like I could breathe. That crushing sensation sitting on my chest wasn't gone, but it was lighter. As though instead of the world sitting on my sternum, it was down to a pickup truck.

I didn't cry often, but how could I retain my composure after that? I knew that wasn't fair. Who was I to cry? Josey was the one who'd died. I was alive. I was breathing in the warm, humid air, and Josey was dead. I didn't even know Josey.

Who did I think I was to cry? Josey was the one who deserved tears. Josey was the one who deserved...

Josey deserved none of this. She'd been an innocent woman on her morning walk, and she'd just so happened to look like me. For that, she was dead. What twisted, evil world did we live in that Josey could die for *looking* like me, and I got to drive away and breathe the humid summer air?

If you faint, Josey's death was for nothing, rang through my thoughts once more.

That was just it. Josey's death *was* for nothing.

She was dead, and no good had come from it. No good *could* come from it.

That was the thing that I could never make sense of when The Country Killer began. Murder and killing may have fit in the same Venn diagram, but often, I could understand killing. Killing happened in the heat of the moment between spouses when one found out the other was unfaithful. Killing happened when a verbal altercation turned physical, and someone saw red as they fought for their lives. Killing happened over drugs and money, two of the most vicious substances known to humanity. Killing happened far too frequently, and never beautifully, but there was normally a reason. Stupid as that reason may have been, there *was* a reason.

But there was no reason for a murder like this. There was no reason to kidnap that woman on her walk and make me listen to her die. There was no reason to break into Rachel's house that night, to kill Bear, to shoot me. There was no reason for Audrey, or Amber, or any other murder this man had committed.

There was no reason.

Hunting Grounds

Flashing red and blue lights shined straight ahead. I didn't realize they were Ox's until he was swerving past me at seventy miles an hour in the twenty-five zone.

I again considered reaching for my phone, but my hands were trembling so much on the wheel that I wasn't sure if I'd make the stretch to the floorboard of the passenger seat. In my rearview, those flashing red and blue lights shined. If I hadn't seen Ox in the driver's seat, I would've pulled over, but he could wait. I was already turning into the trailer park. When I got to my driveway, I would stop, and I would tell him why I hadn't answered the phone. I would try to at least, if I could stop hyperventilating. That's what the tears had turned into at some point in the last mile. Hyperventilating.

Ox was so close to my bumper, I was surprised he hadn't rear-ended me. Actually, he very well may have. I wouldn't have noticed.

When I made it to my driveway, he didn't pull in beside me. He blocked me in from behind. I wanted to be angry about that. He thought that his controlling tendencies were so endearing, but it only infuriated me. Except, they didn't. Not this time. Because this time, all I could think about was Josey.

In my peripheral, I saw him getting out of the driver's side. I couldn't get out. Not yet. I needed to breathe first. I needed to pick up my phone, and reach into the backseat to pet Tempest, to make sure she was okay after the chaos of my anxiety-riddled drive here.

As I grabbed my phone, something cool touched the back of my arm. I jolted, only to realize that it was Tempest's nose. Just beginning to regain a somewhat normal breathing rhythm, I reached back to pet her as I swiped open my phone.

I shouldn't have swiped open my phone.

In my texts, from a sender whose information was undisclosed, a series of numbers and dashes symbols, was a photo. A photo I should have never seen. A photo *no one* should've ever seen.

Josey's body. Josey's body, adorned in a flower printed nightgown dampened with splotches of crimson. She lay lifeless on a small bed. That was all that was visible. The bed, and Josey's body. A slice of maroon lined her throat, dripping streams of red onto the brilliant white linen. Her hands were bound in cuffs lined in red ribbon.

Aside from a busted lip, her face was recognizable. Beautiful even. She wore no makeup, but she looked at peace. As though death had been kinder than the day she'd had. Like it was relief.

Her body? Describing it as overkill didn't do the damage justice.

Ox pounded on the window, screaming something I didn't hear over my thumping heart. I jammed the car door open. Probably should've cared that I hit Ox with it, but I had to get it out of my hand. I couldn't keep holding this phone with this picture of Josey.

I jammed it toward him, called for Tempest, and bolted to the porch. The bile rising up my esophagus forced me to stop at the trashcan on the corner. Like I had so many times in the last thirty-six hours, I hurled until there was nothing left inside me.

Tempest brushed my calf, then tucked her head against my hip. As if to say, *It's okay, Mom. I'm right here. I know you're not okay, but I'm here.*

It was only then, reaching down to run my fingers through her fur, that I could hear Ox over the slamming of my heart. I heard his voice, at least, not what he was saying. Not until he was beside me with a hand on my back.

"You need to sit down."

That much, I couldn't argue with.

Chapter 21

ONCE I STOPPED HYPERVENTILATING, THEN PUKING FROM THE bottle of water Ox insisted I drink, I told him what'd happened. I showed him the recording and had to walk away while he listened to it. When he had, he stowed it to his pocket, then attempted to do the same with my phone. I would've let him take it, but a text from Bentley flashed across the screen just as he reached for it.

It said, *I just saw you pull up. What happened? Are you hurt?*

I couldn't respond, but I also couldn't be left without a way to contact him. I needed to understand what Simeon meant earlier. Why that was the first thought that came to my mind, was beyond me. My head was a thousand places, and I couldn't get it on straight.

"It's evidence, Maddie," Ox said. "The FBI are gonna need it—"

"Then they can have it when they get here." Lifting either hand to my head, I threaded my fingers through my hair and grabbed two fist-fuls at the back. "I called them. When he called, I called them. Did they tell you?"

Frowning, Ox gave a nod. "That's why I was flying to follow you."

I nodded too. "Good. That's good. That means that they were able to trace the call, right? Or probably not. Considering everything else he's done, I'm sure making a phone call untraceable was easy enough.

But we have something now. Right? We have more to go on than we did. M-my connection. He met him. He thinks. It lines up. Maybe. It's all circumstantial, but—"

Ox reached out and grabbed my hands on the sides of my head. He kept his shoulders square, his chin up, but his hands were as soft as the warm breeze. While his face remained mostly blank, emotionless, his tone was synonymous with a lullaby. Soothing and kind. "Before we talk anymore about the case, you need to go calm down. Sit on the couch, and listen to some music, or watch some TV, or eat something, or meditate, or whatever it takes for you to calm down. Gayton, Phillips, and Martin are on their way here. We can talk about everything once they are. I'll fill them in on the phone call. And then we can all talk about what you learned. Okay?"

None of what he just said was unreasonable, nor particularly endearing. It was logical. My state was too panicked. I would forget details, I would leave out important bits of information. This was what we were taught to do in law enforcement. Whether a domestic dispute or a traffic violation gone wrong, the first way to get anything concrete out of the witness was to make sure they were calmed down first.

But it felt like compassion coming from him, the guy who had no concept of emotional intelligence.

Carefully pushing his hands away, I nodded once more. "I need to brush my teeth and get the taste of puke out of my mouth."

"Alright then. We'll start there." He called for Tempest, and she joined me at my side. Then he took my elbow like it was a handle and led me up the stairs. There went that edge of compassion. "Do you need anything else?"

"You to stop manhandling me," I muttered, shaking my elbow from his grasp. "I can walk to my bathroom by myself."

"I'm walking with you." The pathways around my home were small. Maneuvering them with the giant named Ox at my side wasn't easy. That's where he stayed, though. Practically glued to my hip. "You've been hyperventilating for the last twenty minutes. I'm not letting you fall."

I didn't have it in me to argue. The most I managed was an annoyed wave of my hand in his direction until we were in the hallway beside my bathroom. "You gonna wipe my ass for me too?"

"I would offer, but I doubt you'd take me up on it." He likely intended it as a joke, but he didn't laugh or smile. "If you're not out of there in fifteen minutes, I'm coming in."

"Of course you are," I said under my breath.

Tempest barreled past me into the bathroom. She always did that. Everywhere I went, she came too. Probably because the damn Country Killer was right, and I was now the resource she guarded with her life.

But I didn't have the energy to worry about that at the moment.

Instead, I shut the bathroom door, collapsed on the toilet, and dropped my head to my hands.

My heart was still racing. It seemed to beat harder behind my ribs when there was no one around. I knew I was a mess in Ox's presence, but I was even more of a mess now.

At some point, listening to that pounding in my chest, certain that I was going to have a heart attack, I started hyperventilating again. Grabbing the support bar on the tub to keep me upright, I hurriedly flicked on the hot water to drown out the sound. The last thing I needed was Ox coming in here and telling me to calm down while my pants were around my ankles.

It wasn't a pretty image. None of this was even close to the strong, *screw everyone* persona that I had crafted for so long. Hyperventilating on the toilet, only to morph into sobbing on the toilet, with my dog's head in my lap, sleep deprived, still under the influence of the drugs that had been forced into my body two nights prior, was far from how I wanted anyone to see me.

I looked pathetic. I felt pathetic. Especially because it was Ox who saw me first in my panic-ridden stupor.

Why the hell did that matter right now? While my image didn't, my mental state did. I needed to get it the hell together. I needed to do something with all this pain, all this fear, all this worry, and all this guilt. All this damn guilt.

Breathing slowly, I struggled onto my feet only to be greeted with shooting pain up my thigh. In the mirror, I watched as my face screwed up in pain, and then in fury. My teeth gritted and my eyes narrowed. That damn chopped off piece of hair dangled in my face.

And then I remembered how I crafted that strong, *screw everyone* persona. When I was hurt, I spun that pain around into anger. That was how I'd survived. In my childhood, in my failed relationship with Ox. When I'd gotten this bum knee.

That was how I would survive this.

Staring at that chopped off piece of hair in the mirror, dangling just a few inches below my collarbone, I wrenched open the drawer on the vanity. I yanked out my scissors, ran my fingers through my hair, and started chopping.

Why? Because I would've preferred calling Simeon for a little orange bottle. Because I would've preferred getting in my car and driving to the liquor store. Because cutting my hair wasn't going to find the killer, but it was better than the other two options. And it was better that my whole head looked like shit than staring at that chunk that he had taken away from me.

I would have to stare at the scar on my knee every time I was in shorts or a bathing suit. Hell, even when I needed to take a piss. But I refused to continue to look at the hair he touched, the hair he had taken away from me, the hair that barely fit into my ponytail, when I knew it would grow back. I had considered chopping off my leg several times so that I didn't have to deal with the pain he'd left, only to decide that that probably wasn't the best idea. Unfortunately, it would not grow back. But my hair would, and until it did, it would at least be even.

Just as I finished—looking not at all like any woman who'd had a meltdown in the bathroom mirror and chopped all her hair off in the movies, well aware that the back was not at all even with the front—I dropped my scissors into the sink and propped my hands on my hips. It did not look good. But this haircut did, in fact, say *screw everyone*. Because no one would want to go out in public with me like this. And maybe it looked strong too. No pathetic person had the balls to walk around with this head of hair.

Persona restored, or falsely restored, I wiped away the tears and sweat. Sweat, courtesy of the shower that was still steaming away.

I couldn't tell you what happy chemicals released in the brain when you cut your hair in the bathroom mirror, but I could announce with pride that it made me feel a little bit better.

At my feet, Tempest howled, "*A-woo-woo-woo!*"

A few golden locks laid on her back. Laughing, I bent down to brush them away. "Do you like it? You think it looks better?"

She leaned in and licked my cheeks.

Laughing again, I massaged her scruff and rested my head against hers. "That's my good girl."

She licked and licked.

My phone rang.

Heart dropping to my gut, I pulled it out of my pocket, expecting *Private Number* to slide across the screen. But it didn't. I didn't know the number, but now my heart was hammering again.

614 area code.

Columbus, Ohio.

Slowly lowering myself to the bathroom floor, I answered the call. "Hello?"

"Hey there, this is Officer Anthony Clark. Is this Maddie Castle? Did you call me about Bentley Roycroft?"

Chapter 22

"Yes," I sputtered, bringing myself to my feet. "Yes, this is Maddie Castle. How are you?"

"I'm not doing too bad. What about yourself?" Judging by his voice, he was an older gentleman. Likely nearing retirement age. In my experience, the middle-aged and older cops were the best cops. The least likely to be roped into little schemes and coverups for people they cared about. The job could make you jaded, and if they had made it this long without becoming so, it was usually because they wanted to do good in the world.

"Oh, you know." I gazed down at my hair on the bathroom floor. "Living the dream."

He chuckled, a deep belly chuckle that I found comforting. "Aren't we all. Any who, you called about Bentley?"

"I did, yeah." Swallowing, I raked a hand through my hair. "I was just hoping you could tell me about what happened that night? The night that he was arrested?"

"You're a cop, your message said?"

"I was. I'm a private investigator now."

Officer Clark made a noise in his throat. "Somebody's paying you to investigate Bentley?" He almost sounded offended.

"No, nothing like that." Although, I did debate lying. Maybe if he knew that I found a connection between him and The Country Killer, he'd be quicker to help me. Or maybe he would grow even more defensive. As established, private investigator wasn't a title many officers liked hearing. What every middle-aged or older gentleman did like hearing was a sweet young girl concerned for her safety. "He's my neighbor. Also a friend of mine growing up. But I found out about this arrest, and I'm just worried he's not who I thought he was. I just want to know the story so I know whether I can trust him."

"Aw, hell," he spoke under his breath, and I could practically hear him frowning. "How'd you find out about it? You know how these things work, Ms. Castle. The arrest was expunged. It's not on his record. I really shouldn't be talking about this with you."

"I know, sir." Whether I was proud of being a master manipulator or not, I was one. I didn't make my voice sound innocent per se, but I did make sure it was soft. Concerned. And as angry as I was about everything else going on in my life, I genuinely was concerned. I didn't have to fake it. "It's just, Bentley made it out like he's nothing but a family man. And we're sort of becoming more than friends. That arrest says it was a domestic dispute, and we both grew up in not-so-great situations, and I don't want to be the statistic who ends up in another."

A breathy sigh echoed through the speaker. "I really don't think you will. And I really don't want to talk about Bentley in any sort a way, Ms. Castle. He's a good kid."

"I understand." Still, I kept my voice soft. Maybe even a bit sad. Again, that wasn't faking. I was heartbroken over the thoughts that had been running around in my head. I didn't *want* to think this way. But I needed a reason not to. "You can't tell me anything at all? Even who the fight was with?"

"It wasn't much of a fight if I'm being honest," he, again, said under his breath. "Have you talked to Bentley about any of this?"

"No, sir." A bit of a southern accent tinged his voice, and I had the feeling that the *No, sir,* would pull on his heartstrings. The southern bells had a thing for formalities. "Like I said, our family lives growing up weren't very good. I don't like to poke bears, if you know what I mean."

"The only type of bear I would describe Bentley as is a teddy bear," he said. "But I'll tell you what. What happened with Ms. Miller that night had nothing to do with Bentley. Not really, anyway. I took him in, yeah, and I agreed to drop the charges by morning after I heard from him and Ms. Miller. But no, ma'am, she was not hurt that night. The son of a bitch deserved what Bentley did to him. Once I talked to his little girl, I had no doubt. His life did not deserve to be ruined over it."

"Ms. Miller?" That sounded familiar. I'd heard Miller somewhere. Obviously, it was a common enough last name, but something to do with Grace. Maybe on one of her social medias? "Do you know what her first name was?"

Another deep breath. "I've already said more than I'm comfortable with, ma'am. Now if you want to talk to Bentley, and then call me once you hear from him, to corroborate his story, I will. And if he gives me permission, I'll tell you everything. I'm sure if you ask, though, he'll tell you all about it."

Pulling the phone from my face, I shut my eyes and let out a deep breath of my own. Apparently, master manipulator or not, Clark had his loyalties and his duty in check. Like I had already thought. Older cops were cops because they believed in the law.

But I had something I hadn't before this phone call. The name Miller.

"I understand, sir." Turning around, I got a glimpse of myself in the mirror. I'd almost forgotten that I cut my hair. Without looking at it so closely, maybe it wasn't too bad. "Thanks for calling me back."

"No problem, kid. You have a nice evening."

After repeating the same, I ended the call and went to Instagram. I had scanned through all of Grace's followers both last night and several months ago when I'd set up my account. That must've been where I'd seen the name Miller.

And sure enough, after about two minutes of searching, I found it. Also found out why I hadn't thought to do any digging on this account.

User tag: Daisy.Miller, followed by a thousand emojis.

The profile picture was a Daisy. I had assumed the account belonged to another preteen girl. Most teenagers or young adults didn't put pictures of flowers as their profile pictures.

Her account was private, so I couldn't see past her bio. Her bio, however, contained a link to an adult website, which only made my stomach hurt worse. Not because I had any moral issue with that industry, but because if Bentley had been taking advantage of a young girl who got into that business when she was barely legal, I may have had to move just so I never had to see him again.

There were no other social medias linked in her bio, but I had a name now. Daisy Miller. With my laptop, I could run a background search. Considering everything else that'd happened today, probably not what I wanted Ox to see over my shoulder.

For now, Google it was.

Shutting out the app, I opened my browser and typed—

"Maddie." Ox rapped on the door. "You didn't fall in, did you?"

Jumping, I nearly dropped my phone. "No, Ox. I didn't fall in. What do you want?"

"They're here. Gayton, Martin, and Phillips. We're gonna need that phone. And to know everything you know."

With an annoyed grunt, I backspaced everything I was typing. I didn't want Ox to see the name before I did my research. Also went into my call log and deleted the record of my call with Officer Clark. Just in case. Just until I knew more.

With that settled, I slipped it into my hoodie pocket. "I'm coming."

When I swung open the door, Ox arched a brow at me. "Nice."

I couldn't tell if that was a compliment or an insult. "It looks better than it did."

"It does." Compliment then, I supposed. "You had your hair like that when we met. Looks good on you."

Damn it. Maybe I would've preferred the insult. "Thanks."

"It's really uneven, though. When this blows over, go to a professional."

Wagging a finger, I continued ahead, not so much as looking over my shoulder. "I knew the insult was coming."

Chapter 23

Y<small>ET AGAIN,</small> I <small>LEFT THE ROOM WHILE THEY LISTENED TO THE</small> recording. Never again did I want to hear that phone call. I wished I hadn't heard it at all.

Ox told me when they were done, and I came back in. Sitting beside Gayton at my kitchen table, I scanned the three of them. "You're here. So I'm assuming your techs weren't able to trace the call."

"Unfortunately," Phillips said.

"It bounced off every tower within a hundred miles," Martin said. "We expected that, but it would've been nice if he slipped."

"Hasn't yet," Ox said.

"He did once," Gayton said. "The first fire." The night Bentley was in town. "He *will* slip again. He's smart, and he's experienced now, but he has a weakness."

"Her name is Maddie Castle," I said. "But I don't know what you expect me to do with that."

"Exactly what you did today," Phillips said. "I know how much that must've hurt, but you did exactly what you had to do. Thank you."

I didn't intend to glare, but I did. This went beyond *hurt*. He had no idea how much pain that woman died in for simply looking like me, for living in my area.

Or maybe he did. Maybe all three agents had been to blame for innocent people's deaths. Whether by proxy, or because of situations like today, maybe they all knew exactly how what I had just experienced felt. Maybe he downplayed it to keep his own emotions in check.

But to thank me for it? To thank me for letting a woman die was awful in a way I couldn't put words to. I didn't want them to apologize because I hadn't known Josey. I wasn't grieving her, I didn't deserve apologies that weren't mine.

Thanking me, however, was like saying congratulations. Like a good old pat on the back. Like saying, *Good job, sport.*

Sickening. Congratulating me for what I had just done was sickening.

"Anyway." Ox nodded my way, likely picking up on my animosity. "Maddie got some intel from her connection."

"Great." Phillips flipped open his notebook and clicked his pen. "What's his name and address?"

I snorted. "Not happening."

Ox gave me a look. Brows furrowed, jaw set. If we had ever had kids, it was the same look I imagine he would've given a toddler who'd scribbled on his face while he took a nap.

But I was not a toddler, and FBI or not, I wasn't giving away my contact.

"I'm sorry?" Phillips asked.

"If I send the FBI to this person's house, I'm putting my life at risk," I said. "Aside from that, these people trust me. I have a career that isn't as cushy as yours. All it takes is one drug dealer to drop my name to their circle, and I lose all my connections. You're not gonna get any more out of this guy than I did. You're not gonna get a damn thing out of him. I did because I know him, and because I promised his name wouldn't end up in any records. This information includes him admitting to dealing illegal substances. Whether you guys would charge him isn't the point. The point is you have the information. It doesn't matter where it came from."

Gayton frowned at me. Martin arched a brow and raised a shoulder, as if she understood my perspective.

Phillips narrowed his eyes. "We understand you've been through a lot today, but in order to get rid of him, we need to—"

"This has nothing to do with what I've been through today. I would've been just as bothered by you insisting that I give you my connections last week. But don't you dare try and spin this."

"I'm sorry?" he repeated.

"You just said 'in order to get rid of him.' Like I don't want to get rid of him. Like I don't want to catch this guy. I just listened to him torture and murder an innocent woman because all of you told me that's what I needed to do," I said. The rest of the room stayed silent. "More than any of you, I want to see this bastard with a bullet in his head. I lost my entire life because of this man, so you'll never understand how *badly* I want to get rid of him. But you want my information at your full disposal, so you're trying to pull on my heartstrings to make me give it to you. I was a cop too. I know that trick, and it's really damn low.

"My contacts' information isn't necessary. Catching him isn't worth me getting killed by the local mafia. But let me guess. Ox told you who my contacts were, and the FBI has already been looking into them, and you figure that if you bring them in for questioning, you might be able to cut a deal with them. Just to get a confession, catch them on dealing, you might find a way to charge them with this. Even though we both know they aren't the killer. But hey, anything to look good to the guys upstairs, right?"

It was almost undetectable, but Phillips's teeth tightened to a line.

"You're here for a murderer. You want to bust these guys for drugs? Do it on your own time. Build your own case. But you're not gonna build your career off of my dead body." Okay, maybe they were right. What I had been through today did play a part in why I spoke to FBI agents the way I just had. But the fact remained. "So either take the information I *am* willing to give, or I'll dig into the lead myself. I mean, why shouldn't I? I've done more damage to this guy than anybody else. Maybe I'm our best shot."

"That's alright, Castle," Martin said, raising her hands in a defense gesture, likely to get me to calm down. "Just tell us what you know."

Martin and Gayton, I liked them better than Phillips.

I didn't leave out a single detail Noah had given me. At the end of it, Ox said, "What do you know about this bar? How do you think they'd feel about us walking in there?"

"It's not a sketchy place," I said. "I go there just to eat sometimes. The owner, Carrie, even before I was the Maddie Castle who put a bullet in The Country Killer, she gave me a discount, or my food for free. She loves cops. Loves the Army. Has an American flag behind the bar, her husband's folded up flag. Her son is still a marine. She's gonna tell you anything you need to know."

"Looks like they're open till one AM," Martin said, tilting her phone for Gayton and Phillips to see. "We should go now before the evening crowd comes in."

"We should." Gayton stood and grabbed her jacket off the back of the chair. "How far is this place?"

"Fifteen minutes, traffic depending," I said, standing as well. My jacket was behind Ox, so I gestured that way. "Can you pass me that?"

"You won't need it." Phillips gave me a smug smile. "You had such a long day. Get some rest."

Mouth falling open, I shook my head. "You wouldn't even have this information if not for me."

"And we're very grateful for it," Phillips said. "But we can handle this. You just try and relax."

With a huff, I looked at Ox. He was the detective on this case, so he got to make the call.

And much to my disappointment, he frowned at me. "It has been a long day, Mads. What did you get last night? Two hours of sleep?"

None. "I'm fine. And it stopped being your job to worry about my mental state a long time ago. Just let me come. I just told you, I know the owner of the bar. She—"

"She loves cops," Ox said. "I'm not going to keep anything from you. If I learn something, I'll tell you. But after everything today, you need to get some rest."

"I don't need rest. I need to do whatever I can to help you find—"

"You aren't going to do us any good if you mouth off to every person we come across," Ox said. "That isn't me calling you dramatic. You're not. But you just cut your hair in the bathroom mirror, have such dark circles under your eyes that it looks like somebody gave you two shiners, and the last time you ate was at—What? Four AM? I'm not doing this to be a dick. I'm doing this because you're no good to me when you're like this."

So close.

Ox was so close to sounding like he had a smidgen of compassion in there. Then he hit me with that last sentence. Apparently, I only existed to Ox as an asset.

Reaching past him to grab my jacket, I snapped for him to do something inappropriate to himself, shot Phillips a glare that must've looked deadly above my dark circles, and stomped to my bedroom with Tempest.

But I needed to do more research on Daisy Miller anyway.

Chapter 24

First, I did that background check. Daisy Miller, born May 1, 2002, in Columbus, Ohio. So at the time of that Christmas picture, I was correct. She was in her late teens.

Her record came as no surprise. While Daisy had never been arrested for violent crimes, she had a laundry list of arrests for possession of illegal substances. Two for marijuana, one for cocaine, and four for methamphetamines. Alongside those, in June 2020, she'd been arrested for solicitation. She'd been arrested again for solicitation in November 2020. By the end of 2021, she'd been arrested six times for prostitution.

Yet all I could think was, *Poor kid.*

I wanted to know more for certain, considered taking a drive to Ohio just to ask around, but if I had to guess, she was a kid from a rough place. Got hooked on drugs when she was young to deal with the pain of whatever her life had been. With no money, no way to buy the drugs her body now depended on, she'd turned to the one thing she knew could make money. Her body.

I knew the type. A few girls who had grown up in my trailer park had the same stories. *I* could have had the same story. Honestly, I couldn't tell you why I hadn't. Maybe it was because I'd hated my mom so badly, and just to spite her, I'd sworn to not be like her. I knew a thing or two about sex work because when my mom hadn't had money for drugs, she'd resorted to what Daisy had.

Guess I had to give Mom credit on that front. It was one thing she'd drilled into my head. *Never sell yourself to a man. 'Cause the things he'll do to you before that timer goes off, while he owns you, you'll never look at men the same again.*

Maybe not peak parenting, but solid advice either way.

But when it was all you knew, it was what you did. It was a cycle. A cycle my mom had lived through, and a cycle that I had chosen to end. I had to assume that Daisy had been born into the same one. Unfortunately, she had yet to escape it.

Once I had a record in hand, I went to social media. Not the adult website, but the ones everyone used.

Except for Daisy. She had a Facebook account, but only one profile picture. It was posted in 2020. She hadn't made a status update since. Or maybe her account was private. I didn't know, and I wasn't sure that it mattered, anyway.

I considered sending her a message. But what the hell would I say?

Hey there, sorry to bother you. Do you know Bentley Roycroft? Well, Officer Anthony Clark claims you do. I was just hoping you could tell me about whatever happened the night that he was arrested. Apparently you were there. Oh, and by the way, I'm an ex-cop. And a private investigator.

I had a stamp on my forehead that said, *Criminals, stay away.*

Back to Google I went. Maybe if I could find her address, if she *had* an address, I could drive out there. Not today. As much as it burned me, Ox was right. I did need to sleep. But meeting me in person would send a clearer message.

Hey, fellow trailer trash over here. See this bleach-stained hoodie covered in dog hair? I can't remember the last time I washed it. I may be an ex-cop, but I'm also an addict. We're not so different. Swear I'm not trying to get you put away. I just want to know if the cop in your town is lying to me to protect Bentley.

The moment I googled her name, however, stomach acid burned its way up my esophagus.

Daisy Miller, Missing.

Breaths hard and uneven, my shaking fingers scrolled across the screen. The photo they used was her mug shot. They used her *mug shot* for her missing persons file. I could rant and rave about how cruel that was, how much it limited her chances of being found, how people would glance at that picture and not care that she was gone, but I was more concerned with the paragraph beneath.

Daisy Miller was last seen at Club Xstasy on September 3, 2021. She was reported missing by her coworker. Call 614-555-5555 if you have any information about her disappearance.

And that was it.

They didn't mention family or friends who missed her. They didn't even attempt to make her look like the type of person they wanted to find. That shouldn't have come as a surprise. Girls like her, guys like her, trailer park trash, inner-city kids, addicts, sex workers—authorities didn't want to waste resources on us.

Me, if I went missing, they would search for me because I was a hero now. Because I had shot The Country Killer. But ten years ago? If I had gone missing? Well, they might have used my mug shot too.

Tempest jumped up beside me, climbing over me to lick my face. She must've sensed my anxiety, and I usually found that endearing. The most I could manage for her at the moment was a quick pet on the neck.

I went back to the Google search results. Two pages down, that name popped up again. Club Xstasy.

The coworker who'd reported Daisy missing, Katie White, had done a video interview with a blogger. One of those amateur journalists who reported on the city from the comfort of his couch. I wished I could thank him for that, because at least someone was shining a light on the people who needed it. The local news station certainly hadn't reported on Daisy.

Of course, I clicked on it.

"So how long have you known Daisy?" the interviewer asked. He was a short guy, likely not much older than Daisy herself, with thick black glasses, a short brown beard, and a plump figure. "Were you guys friends before she started working at Club Xstasy?"

"We were, yeah," Katie said, running a hand through her curly blond hair. "She babysat for me a few times when she was a minor, and then she asked if I could get her a job."

Nodding, the interviewer jotted in his notepad. I appreciated his relaxed expression. He didn't rebut with a, "And you thought it was appropriate for an eighteen-year-old to work at a strip club?" He wasn't trying to paint her as a villain. He just wanted the story out there.

"And she didn't have any problems with anyone, did she?"

Shaking her head, tears formed in Katie's eyes. "Not really, no. Everybody loves Daisy. She got in trouble sometimes, but she was a good kid. Sweeter than pie."

"When I talked to the local police, they made it sound like they suspected Daisy had overdosed when no one was around to see it. It's my understanding that she didn't always have a home."

The tears in Katie's eyes flooded the whole way across them. "You know how hard it is to overdose on meth? Because it's not easy. It can happen, yeah, but Daisy wasn't a junkie. Pain pills, dope, those are easy to kill yourself on. It ain't like that with meth."

Agreed with every word of that. Although I never did heroin, I knew that prescription opiates were no different in the brain or the body. Alongside that, I knew plenty of people who had killed themselves on dope. Combining all the overdoses I'd witnessed as a cop, along with all the funerals I had attended for people I'd gone to school with, I knew of at least five dozen opiate related overdoses.

To this day, I knew of two people who'd killed themselves on meth. One was a call I had been on as a cop. The guy was tweaking, he accidentally shot himself, and called 911 before he bled out. So, not an overdose. But never got the whole story on it because he'd been dead on arrival.

The second was a woman who'd had a heart attack.

"What do you think happened to Daisy, Miss White?"

"I think someone killed her and got rid of her body." Struggling to retain her composure, Katie's face screwed up in grief. "Even if she had overdosed, they would've found a body. I've been everywhere she usually goes. I checked all the motels, in the woods where she camps sometimes, and the bridge that she slept under, and everywhere else. Maybe it was her own stupid fault, but I'm telling you, somebody messed with her body then."

"And why do you think the police aren't doing anything about it?"

Katie snorted a laugh. "Because they're protecting him."

"Who's that?" The interviewer leaned in, eyes creasing in focus. "Who do you think did this, Katie?"

"I don't know his name. Daisy never talked about him much. One of her Johns, I think." Sniffling, she wiped her nose with a tissue. "All I know is that he's a paramedic, and he's friends with the cops."

There was no stopping it. The vomit burned up my throat, and I leaped from the bed to get to the trashcan in the corner.

Chapter 25

How the hell did I still have anything inside me to throw up? I had no unearthly idea. Also had no idea why this was becoming my new anxious reaction. Anger was better than this. Sure, maybe when I got angry and tossed my phone, I had to get a new one, but that was better than vomiting every time I gathered uncomfortable information.

I needed to eat something. Or drink something. When was the last time I drank any water? But before I did any of that, Bentley and I needed to have words.

After I composed myself, I found my phone from my pile of junk on the bed, swept it open, and typed.

Yeah, I'm okay. You want to come over and talk?

Before I even shut the screen, he texted back, *Of course. I'll be right over.*

Acting fast, I ushered Tempest into her crate and locked her in. My heart pounded against my ribs so hard that it hurt as I walked around the bed to my nightstand. Yanking the drawer open with shaking fingers, I grabbed a handful of ammunition. Shaking a moment ago or not, they were steady as stone as I loaded the bullets. My revolver opposed to my semi-automatic. It was quicker and simpler to operate if

I needed it. Also had less chance of misfiring. From the same drawer, I dug out my old phone and clicked record in the voice notes application.

Holding the wall for stability, I kept my fingers around the grip. As soon as he walked inside, it would be on the trigger. I had no plans on releasing it until he told me exactly what I wanted to know.

The awful thing was that I was fairly certain I knew. It was exactly as I feared it was. Bentley Roycroft was not the boy I remembered.

IMPRESSED WITH MYSELF FOR HOW QUICKLY I MADE IT TO THE living room, I peeked out the curtains just in time to see Bentley cutting through my grass. When he knocked on the door, Tempest howled in the back room. I yelled the command for quiet as I limped to the door.

Was the gun taking it a step too far? I didn't think it was. The truth of the matter was simple. If Bentley had killed Daisy, he would kill me for questioning his involvement. He was over six feet, his arms were almost twice as big as mine, while I was only a few inches over five feet, relatively small in stature, and lived with a jacked up knee.

It would be effortless for someone Bentley's size to take me down. That was just the fact. I could have screamed that I was a badass until I passed out, but I wasn't stupid. I was a private investigator living with a lifelong injury and chronic pain. I was no hero. No superstrength. No x-ray vision. No ability to fly if this went badly.

But I had a gun. If I had to, I would use it.

Swinging the door open, those warm brown eyes and that sweet boyish smile I had once found so welcoming now made me nauseous. "Oh, hey. I like it." He gestured to my head. "Short hair's pretty on you."

Stealth was key.

"Thanks. Just got tired of looking at it." Forcing a smile, I tugged the door the rest of the way open for him. "You're letting all the cool air out."

"Sorry." His smile got a bit bigger as he brushed past me. "Seemed sorta insensitive to just barge in."

"Yeah, well." Pushing the door shut with my hip, I spun the lock. "With everything considered, I'm gonna be changing the location of that damn spare key."

"Told you you should have done that a long time ago." Squinting, he glanced down the hall. There was my opportunity. "Where's Tempest—"

Gun in hand, I shoved him into the wall beside the couch and jammed it into his chin. Barely registering what was happening, his eyes flicked between me and the butt of my gun. "What the hell, Maddie? What are you—"

"What happened with you and Daisy Miller?" I snapped. "How was she connected to your arrest in 2020, and where the hell is she now, Bentley? Who put the bullet in your arm? And why the hell haven't you mentioned any of it to me?"

Slowly, all the warmth drained from his cheeks. Eerie silence stretched on for far too long.

"I'm begging you to give me a reason not to put this bullet in your head," I said behind gritted teeth. "What did you do to her? Why does Simeon Gunn know? Who are you, Bentley? Because you're clearly not the sweet single dad you wanted me to believe you are."

Swallowing, he shook his head slightly. "I never hurt Daisy. And I... That scar's a long story, but I-I'm me, Maddie. I'm the same person I've always been—"

"Don't bullshit me right now. I'm running on caffeine, adrenaline, and no damn sleep. So don't think for a second that you can sweet talk me into shutting my mouth. Tell me the truth, Bentley Roycroft."

I sounded far too much like his mother with that last sentence. It did the job though, because he shut his eyes, lifted his hands at his sides, and breathed out slowly.

"Do you think I'm bluffing? Because I promise—"

"No. No, I just... I don't know what you found, but I can imagine how bad it looks." Keeping his hands up, he slowly opened his eyes.

There were tears in them. Not tears of fear, but grief. He didn't let them escape as he nodded to his pocket. "Go into my phone and open my photo albums. This will make a lot more sense."

"How about"—I pushed the gun so far into his chin that he was practically looking at the ceiling—"neither of us move until you answer my damn questions?"

"Now I remember why we called you Mad dog," he muttered, as though I didn't hear it when we were standing chest to chest.

"You really shouldn't patronize the person who has a gun to your head." I pressed my thumb on the hammer and watched him shudder. "How many times do I need to repeat myself?"

"I'm sorry," he said quickly with wide eyes, followed by some choice words. "I didn't hurt Daisy. I *would never* hurt Daisy. I love that little girl—"

"*That little girl?* What—Were you paying her when she was a minor too?" I snapped. "I really thought you were different, but you're just like every other piece of shit from this place, aren't you?"

A second ago, he looked anxious. Now, he may as well have had a giant cartoon question mark over his head. "Wait, who do you think Daisy was to me?" Pausing, disgust scrunched up his nose and curled his lip. "You think I hired her for sex?"

Well, I had. 'Til he looked at me like that.

"All that research you did, and you never once thought to figure out what my wife's maiden name was?" His tone grew more defensive with each word. "Isabella Miller. Daisy Miller was Bella Miller's baby sister. Grace's aunt. Yes, she was a sex worker, but that's not how I knew her. She was family. *I did not hurt her.* All I ever wanted was to help her, and once she disappeared, I had nothing left in Ohio."

Oh. Shit.

"*That* was why I came back here. Because Bella was gone, and Daisy was gone, and I got wrapped up in some shit I'm not proud of *trying* to help her, and I wanted to get away with my daughter before she ended up like her aunt." Stiff jaw releasing ever so slightly, Bentley shook his head. "Do you really want to know what happened? Or are you just looking for a reason to hate me like you do to everyone else in your life, Maddie? Because if you want to see every bit of my dirty laundry, I'll hang it all up in the front yard for you. But if you want to hate me, I don't think this story is gonna give you that. I'm not proud of it, and no, I'm not just a single dad. But I'm not whatever your paranoid, screwed up head has spun me into."

Chapter 26

Alright. Maybe I took things a bit too far.

In my defense, I was sleep deprived, hungry, and still under an influence. Also, Ox had told me not to mention anything to Bentley. I should've trusted my instincts and asked him directly. But I did give Bentley the opportunity to bring me up to speed. He chose not to.

Supposed it was time to hear him out.

Slowly lowering the gun, aiming the barrel at the floor, I took a step back. "Are you just going to tell me, 'I don't know?'"

Bentley frowned, but there was still annoyance in his eyes. "Maybe if you would've asked me a direct question instead of, 'why did you come back here?' I would've had a better answer for you."

"Maybe you shouldn't have tried to make me think you walked out of a damn Hallmark movie if you've got this many skeletons in your closet."

Rubbing the bridge of his nose, he ran his tongue along his teeth. "Look, do you want to know the story? Or do you want to be mad at me?"

Propping a hand on my hip, I said, "Both." An unwilling smile twitched at the corners of his lips. I nodded to the couch. "But let's start with the former."

Walking past me, Bentley pointed to his usual seat on the sofa. "It's not rigged with a bomb or anything?"

I glared.

"Well, you just held a gun to my head. Pretty sure it's still cocked." He held up his hands in surrender as he sat. "Forgive my paranoia. I guess we both have it."

"Do you want me to be mad at you?" Gun still in hand, I walked around the coffee table and sat on the opposite end of the couch. I did need to decock it, but that wasn't the sorta thing I wanted to do inside the house. Plus, wasn't a hundred percent sure I wouldn't need it yet. Keeping it aimed at the floor for now seemed best. "Or do you want to tell the story?"

"Touché," he said under his breath. Resting his elbows on his knees, Bentley held his hands together and avoided my gaze. "Where do you want me to start?"

"The beginning. I guess when you met her."

"She was a kid. Six or seven, I think." Raising a shoulder slightly, he gave me that offended look again. As if to say, 'How dare you accuse me of being attracted to her?' "She was my girlfriend's baby sister, and then my wife's baby sister. She was almost like my kid."

Well, if that was true, I couldn't blame him for getting defensive. That did sound a lot more like the Bentley I knew than the version I'd conjured up. "How so?"

Another breathy exhale, finally meeting my gaze. "Bella grew up like we did. Her mom was a lot like yours. When she graduated high school, she moved to her college campus, but every day, she went home to take care of Daisy. Made sure she got a bath before bed, ate dinner, laid out her school clothes. When we got more serious, when she realized she was pregnant with Grace, I went with her. On the weekends, we took Daisy to the park, the movies, fairs. Bella pretty much raised Daisy, and then I was with Bella, and then we had Grace, and then I was pretty much raising Daisy with Bella."

I wish I had someone to corroborate his story, but I imagined the photos on his phone that he told me to look at would be proof enough. "How old was Daisy when Bella passed?"

Biting his lip, his eyes creased in thought. "Thirteen? Fourteen? I don't know, somewhere around there. Bella tried to get guardianship of her a thousand times, but they wouldn't do it. 'Course Eve would've lost her housing, welfare checks, food stamps, and the tax benefits if she willingly signed custody to Bella. And Eve was there. Out of her mind on meth or not, she was there. And you know how it goes. They want to keep the kid with the mom.

"By the time Bella died, Daisy was smoking meth with Eve. Her mom was the first person who gave it to her." Gritting his teeth, he shut his eyes and shook his head again. "No matter how many times we went to court, no matter how many times we tried to get Daisy into rehab, no matter how many times we called CPS on Eve, they wouldn't give Bella custody. She was too young, and then we didn't make enough money, and we didn't have enough room in our house, and a thousand other bullshit reasons."

That sounded about right. In the US, if they could keep a child with the mother, no matter how awful the mother was, they did. The exception was when a father was involved enough and wanted custody of the child.

Sometimes, it was better that way. Children were better off with their shitty biological parents than shitty foster parents. My maternal and paternal grandparents were gone before I was born, and neither my mom nor my dad had siblings. No one had fought for me. So I'd stayed with Mom, because even though she'd been an awful parent, I'd at least known what to expect from her. I wouldn't have known what to expect from the foster homes.

It wouldn't have been up to me either way, however. Children didn't have a choice in custody battles. If the parent could prove they were fit, if they could pass a drug test and get the house clean when CPS came to visit, the parent kept the kid.

"So Bella was still alive when Daisy started using."

Giving a nod, Bentley raked a hand through his hair. "When she didn't have money, she came to us. When she got into a fight with Eve, she came to us. When she didn't have food, she came to us. When she was having trouble in school and Eve wouldn't answer the phone for the teachers, they called us." Pausing, he gazed at the floor for a minute. "We were kids. I get why they wouldn't give her over to us, but she would've been better off if they had."

More than likely, yes. She would've been.

"But a month after Bella died, Eve died. Mixed stims and dope. Her DOC was meth, but she was a poly addict. She'd take anything she got her hands on. Warned her not to mix uppers and downers, but telling an addict how to do drugs is like bashing your head against a wall." DOC stood for drug of choice, stims meant stimulants, and dope was the slang term for heroin.

"Daisy found her when she came home from school. On one of the few days she went." That part, he mumbled, like any disappointed parent would. "Daisy had been at my house a lot after Bella died. She was trying to get clean. Couldn't exactly do that around someone who was smoking in the kitchen." Biting his lip, he still stared at the ground with his elbows on his knees. Like just talking about this ripped him apart. "Kept me busy too. Distracted. I just kept thinking, 'I gotta keep her clean. I gotta help her get her life on track.' Those were some of Bella's last words to me, you know." His voice cracked a bit there, and it took him a moment to continue.

"Bella was supposed to be home the day she died. She told me to take the truck to work. We had another clunker I was working on, and when we both had somewhere to go, I drove the piece of shit because I didn't want her and Grace in it. Grace was at school, I dropped her off that morning, and I was gonna pick her up on my way home, but she started running a fever, so they called, and Bella went to pick her up, and the brakes gave out on her way." Pausing again, he looked up. "Never tell Grace that, okay?"

There was no need to ask me that. I wouldn't dream of telling Grace anything that'd hurt her.

"Anyway." Focusing again, his eyes went back to the floor, as if trying to remember where he was going with that. "She'd already lost a lot of blood by the time we got there. She knew. I knew. She kept telling me she loved me, and to tell Grace she loved her, and she was begging me not to give up on Daisy. She kept saying, 'She doesn't have anyone now. She doesn't have anyone now.' I told her I'd make sure she was okay.

"That was why I let a teenage girl come over to my house when no one else was around, Maddie. Because she was family. It was never anything weird, and it really pisses me off that you thought that's who I am."

Now it was me biting my lip and gazing at the floor with the still-cocked gun tucked in my hand.

It wasn't that I had believed wholeheartedly that he'd been sleeping with Daisy, nor that he had killed her prior to this conversation. I just hadn't known *what* to think. All I believed, beyond any doubt, was that he wasn't who I'd thought he was.

"I'm sorry for thinking the worst," I said. "But you lied to me yesterday, Bentley. So yeah, I started digging, and it didn't look good."

"Because it isn't. It's a shit storm. But not because I'm a piece of shit who takes advantage of young girls."

The real problem here was Bentley's inability to see someone suffer without trying to help them. I looked back up to his face. "Is that where the story ends?"

"It's barely the beginning."

Chapter 27

"I TRIED TO GET HER AS A FOSTER KID, BUT PARAMEDICS DON'T make great money, and CPS probably thought the same thing you did. I even got a lawyer. I used up way too much of Bella's life insurance on a damn good one, and they still denied me a thousand times over. It didn't help that she kept running from foster homes to my house. I convinced her to go back the first few times, but then I was the one who dropped her off, and I showed up on the court records, and it looked bad. It *was* bad." Hanging his head, he massaged his temples.

God, this was awful. There was a lot of awful in this room over the years. My mom had overdosed once in the exact spot where Bentley sat. The couch was new, suede opposed to Mom's cigarette hole riddled, floral printed, thrift store sofa, but it was positioned the exact same way. I had given her CPR until the cops came, barely keeping her alive. That had been a horrible moment of my life, but seeing Bentley like this was so much worse. Especially knowing that I was the one who forced him to discuss such a heartbreaking experience.

"By the time she was sixteen, it was hell. She was *in* hell. Those foster homes, the way she got treated, the other foster kids, specifically the boys—" He cut himself off with a sharp breath. "A lot of terrible things happened to her. So when she showed at my door, or in my kitchen, or in the guestroom, or in the backyard, I stopped taking her back there.

"When her caseworker would call, I'd lie and say I didn't know where she was. And when they came to look for her, knowing that my house was probably where she ran to, we had a whole routine down. She would go out the back door, squeeze herself into the gap between my house and the neighbor's house, then sneak into the neighbor's through her basement window. She's a nice old lady. She was there the night that I was arrested, by the way." He shot me a look. "I can call her if you need an alibi."

Nothing about his demeanor suggested he was lying to me. I could track down the neighbor myself, if doubts came to fruition at some point, but for the moment, I was content to listen.

"That's okay," I said. "Was Daisy using at this time?"

"Aside from that month after Bella died, I don't know if Daisy was ever *not* using," he said. "Around the time she was sixteen, almost seventeen, still a runaway foster kid, she got into some really bad shit. Which is how I ended up with this." Lifting the arm of his shirt, he exposed the scar on his bicep. "But maybe that's not the right way to phrase it." With an audible breath, his eyes turned to the ceiling. "She would steal things. Not from people, but from stores and shit. Then she would sell it, and I know it sounds bad, but I preferred that. Because then she started dating this kid. Or, *not* kid. He was twenty-six, I think? The guy was not much younger than I was, dating a teenager, and he sold meth. Sold *her* meth. He was on it too. But that's not the point.

"Point is, he was a dealer, and she stopped stealing and started selling with him. His whole family made it and supplied to dealers all throughout the state. Later realized they were supplying Simeon. Which is part of why Simeon has been keeping tabs on me." Pausing again, like he lost where he was going with this, he stood and paced.

When he was in trouble, when he was anxious, that was always what Bentley did. He paced. Otherwise meaning we were getting to the bad part of the story.

It was all convoluted and messy, but I understood. When I tried to tell my life story, when I'd tried to tell Ox about specific events from the chaos that I had grown up in, I would get lost and go on side tangents. Nothing was neat and tidy in the world of drugs and poverty. It didn't make for a great story, because stories were logical. But when people were fighting for survival, or for drugs—which was the same to an addict—things got messy.

"Me and Daisy got into it about it. I told her that if she didn't stop seeing him and selling, I would call CPS. She'd storm off, and he'd drive by and pick her up. Then she would call me later and say she was sorry, but she just loved him, and she couldn't go back there. Then I would feel guilty, and we would make up.

"Then she'd show up with a black eye, and I'd ask where she got it, and she wouldn't tell me. But I knew it was him. I'd say something to him when he came to pick her up, and he'd get smart with me, and then he'd storm off with her in his car, and then I wouldn't see Daisy again for a month or two.

"Six months after they started dating, I got a call from a number I didn't recognize. It was Daisy at a new foster home, after she got arrested for prostitution. Mind you, Grace and I hadn't seen Daisy in, like, two months at this point. So I was thinking she started selling herself to pay for the drugs. But she asked if she could come over, and I said yes, of course, but she wasn't right when she got there. Even with the drugs, and the shitty mom, and Bella's death, she was an upbeat person. Bubbly, funny. A lot like Grace. But she wasn't that day. She said she was sober, and she wanted to stay that way. And that part, I wanted to be happy about, but she just seemed... broken."

Frowning, a lump formed in my throat. "Was the boyfriend pimping her out?"

"To hear her tell it, no." He returned to his seat on the couch and rubbed a hand through his beard. "But that's what it looked like to me. That's when I started thinking about coming home. Coming back here, I mean. With Daisy. I didn't know how to do it, and I knew I'd be breaking a thousand laws, but I wanted to get her out of there so bad.

"I started planning it while she and Grace were sleeping that night.

I could sell the house me and Grace were in, use the ten grand profit plus what I had left of Bella's life insurance to get us a little house, or a trailer, and Daisy could get a fresh start. *I* could get a fresh start with my kids. Daisy would need a fake ID since she was a runaway foster kid, so I got in touch with Simeon about that. He was willing to help, but Daisy panicked when I suggested it the next day.

"She said he'd find her, they'd all find her. I told her I'd handle the little shit if he followed us. She wasn't the center of their operation or anything. Sure, she sold drugs for them, but she was just another one of their worker bees. They didn't care enough about her to hunt her down. Which is when she broke down. Apparently she owed Kevin and his family somewhere around eighty-thousand dollars' worth of meth."

My jaw dropped. "That was why she started selling herself."

Expelling a long, shaking breath, he nodded. "Because if she didn't, they would kill her. But she was only seventeen, and she had no way to come up with the money. If she didn't get it to them though, they were either going to kill her, or make her 'work'"—he held up air quotes—"for them until she paid it off. Plus interest."

I was certain I saw where this was going. "So you agreed to sell for them."

His brows furrowed and eyes squinted at me. "You really think that I'd deal meth? Who the hell would I sell it to?"

Touché. "What did you do then?"

"I had sixty grand left from Bella's life insurance. I gave them that and agreed to work off Daisy's debt. They were tweakers, Maddie. They hurt themselves, and each other, *all* the damn time. I'm a para-medic. So when one of them shot another, I stitched them up. Just like I stitch your ass up." His brows were still furrowed, but he gave a half smile. "Did you think I was gonna let them pimp me out?"

"Hey, lots of folks would pay a pretty penny for your company." I returned the smile, and he chuckled. It was the nicest sound during such a grim conversation. "So you paid off the twenty-thousand dollar debt stitching up meth addicts?"

"And dollar store chemists, and their dealers, and anybody else they brought to my house," he said, the joyous tone in the air dissipating again. "The condition was that they never messed with Daisy again. Didn't deal to her, Kevin didn't come near her, and they made sure anybody on the streets, their guys or not, stayed away from her. They agreed. Within six months, by the time Daisy was eighteen, the twenty grand was paid off."

"So the arrest, that was before the deal?"

Frowning, Bentley shook his head. "As soon as the debt was paid off, they started fronting shit tons to Daisy again. Daisy was dating Kevin again. But she was an adult now. She was officially out of the system, and at least I knew she could come to me without having to run from CPS."

"The fight had nothing to do with you then," I said. "That's what you're saying?"

"Oh, no. It had everything to do with me." Sitting back on the sofa, he rubbed a hand down his jaw. "I was working late one night. Tried to get day shifts, but it wasn't always up to me. And my savings was pretty much shot, so I took any overtime I could get. I think I was on eighteen hours so far that day.

"Grace was at my neighbor's. She watched her when I worked. Sometimes Daisy watched her, but I didn't like doing that for obvious reasons. She never got violent when she was high, so if I had to run out while Grace was asleep, and Daisy was sleeping a few rooms over, that was one thing. But if I was working a double shift, my neighbor was a huge help.

"That day, I was on my way home, exhausted, and I got a call from Grace. She was crying, and she said that Kevin was there. She was next door, but Kevin and Daisy were in the yard. I guess they were fighting, God knows what about, and he was hitting her. I was close to the house, and I stayed on the phone with Grace while I was driving, but I could hear them through the speaker.

"My neighbor was on the phone with the cops, but they were both so high that it didn't seem to matter. And Daisy was like my kid, you know?" I could see the pain in his eyes when they met mine. "I got out of the car. Me and Grace were still on the phone, so I told her to go in the house. I went in through the back gate. His back was to me, but I saw Daisy. Her nose was bleeding, she had a cut on her forehead, and she was crying. Then she looked at me, and her eyes got wide, and I remember nothing after that. I saw red."

That sounded a lot more like the Bentley I knew. And couldn't say I blamed him. I would've done the same thing.

"So it wasn't about Daisy. You were arrested for hurting Kevin."

"I didn't just hurt him." Scratching his forehead, he pressed his lips together. "I almost killed him."

"And he didn't file charges?" I asked. Of course, that was common enough for addicts and drug dealers. But I couldn't see the case getting thrown out if the damage was that bad.

"One of his friends was with him. Between Daisy, my neighbor, and her husband, they got me off him. His friend dragged him out of my yard when the sirens got close. Literally just as their car pulled out, the cops pulled in. They saw Daisy all beat up, they saw my bloody hands, and they arrested me. I don't even remember everything I said to Clark in the car. I think I cried. About Daisy. About Grace. About Bella, how I'd failed her. I realized once I was in cuffs that Grace was at the window. She saw it.

"He just told me to get some sleep. The next day, he drove me home. Grace stayed home from school, and Daisy was there. They were both really upset, worried about me. We ate. Daisy promised me that she was never going to talk to him again. Grace mentioned leaving Ohio and going to stay with Grandma. And that's when I decided I was gonna move back here. But not before Kevin's brother jumped me when I was walking to my car the next day and said that I owed them again." He gestured to his scar. "That's another long story though."

Oh, if he thought he was done, he was so incredibly wrong. "I've got all day. But, does that mean that you're still in debt to them?"

Pressing his lips to a thin line, Bentley scratched his head. "See, it's a long story."

Chapter 28

The scent of cigarettes merged with booze, cheap cologne, and French fries as Ox stepped through the threshold with the others at his tail. Blue lights shined below the bar, green ones illuminated the *Pour House* sign that glowed behind the bartender's head. Old soft rock bounced from the speakers, likely originating from the jukebox in the corner.

Ox hated these places. Bars. Clubs. He had tried to go to a few after realizing there was no chance he would ever get Maddie back, and he hadn't seen the allure. Why was this the only place where adults could meet one another? Why was there nothing better to do than to go to a bar? It was like everyone had decided that people couldn't enjoy one another's company unless they were under the influence. Not to mention that even one drink at these places could put you over the legal driving limit. So how was everyone here supposed to get home?

Farmer's markets, he liked. Unfortunately, the only people Ox met at those were retirement aged. Not exactly who he was looking for in a partner.

Walking through the park, Ox enjoyed as well. But a thirty-something-year-old man walking through a park by himself without so much as a dog at his side wasn't a great image. He got some very dirty looks from mothers with their strollers. So he hadn't done that again either.

"Should've asked Maddie if the food's any good," Martin said, looking around. "There aren't many options out here."

"You can't screw up fries." Phillips brushed past Ox to the bar.

Ox shot him a look. Phillips didn't notice.

Ox did not like being brushed past. Specifically, he didn't like that Phillips had been the one to brush past him. Had it been Martin or Gayton, Ox would've thought nothing about it. But he didn't appreciate Phillips. Not after the way he'd spoken to Maddie.

It was no secret that Ox had a hard time understanding human emotion. Phillips, however, knew how Maddie felt and attempted to manipulate her. Why? Why try to hurt her after everything that she had been through in the last forty-eight hours? Why make it worse?

Ox understood wanting a new or better position. Who didn't want a promotion? If Ox had a shot at a job with the DEA, as he'd overheard Phillips and Gayton discussing, he would take it. But not at the expense of one of his CIs.

That was the thing. Ox was an ass. Everyone knew it, and that was fine. What they could not say was that he was cruel. Selfish wasn't even a fair descriptor. He was logical, so logical that he hurt those around him inadvertently, but he couldn't fathom someone entering this field purely for the sake of business.

That was what Phillips had done. When he'd drilled Maddie about giving over the name of her informant, it was because he wanted a bargaining chip to use in a business move.

That wasn't how Ox thought of his job. Law enforcement was not about making money, or an ego boost, or a badass title. It was about helping people who were hurt. Stopping people from *getting* hurt. Removing dangerous people from society so that the innocent ones could go on living freely.

Maddie was one of those hurt people. She always had been, in some regard, but now she hurt in a way she had never hurt before. And today, all Phillips had done was try to hurt her more. From his condescending rhetoric to his attitude when Maddie said she wanted to come. Ox agreed it was best for her to stay home, but that was for her well-being. Phillips had done it just to hurt her, and Ox couldn't wrap his mind around that.

Approaching the bar behind Phillips, Gayton on his left and Martin on his right, Ox cut in just as Phillips opened his mouth to speak. "Carrie Harris?" Ox held a hand over the bar.

Squinting, Carrie stretched a hand over the bar as well. "And you are?"

"Detective Lenox Taylor from the Pittsburgh P.D., and Agents Gayton, Martin, and Phillips with the FBI." Holding up his badge, Ox worked with all his might to muster up a kind smile. Judging by the face Carrie made, it looked as pained as always. This was why he'd loved working with Maddie. Her friendly smiles actually looked friendly. "Maddie Castle told me you own this place?"

"You know Maddie?" Just the mention of her softened the tension in Carrie's posture. "How 'bout that. What can I help you with, Detective?"

"I'm sure you've heard about the murders." After returning his badge to his pocket, he leaned over the counter. "We're investigating them. Maddie thought you might be able to help."

Tucking her dishtowel into her waistband, Carrie's eyes twinkled. She was an older woman, pushing seventy, with wispy gray hair tucked into a long ponytail, just a hint of mascara over her blue eyes, and warm, sandy skin. Her expression was welcoming, even a bit excited.

"What can I do?" Pausing, Carrie scanned the bar behind Ox. "Where's Maddie? She alright?"

"She's at home." Phillips leaned over the bar as well. He gave a friendly smile. It looked genuine. Damn him. "She's been unofficially assisting in our investigation, but it's taking its toll."

Ox fought with all his might not to glare. While that was true, these were Maddie's people. This was Maddie's town. A town where she did business, a town where people trusted her to investigate what the police didn't, and Phillips had to make jabs that depicted her as weak? Incompetent?

Ox didn't like Phillips. Not one bit.

"Sure." Carrie's eyes grew sympathetic once more. "With what he did and all, I'm sure she's really struggling."

"Well, you know Maddie." Ox tried again to give that friendly smile. "She can handle it. Just a little sleep deprived."

"Ain't that the truth. Not much the girl can't handle." She returned the smile, assuring Ox that his had done its job. Gradually, Carrie's brows furrowed. "But how can I help?"

"Hopefully with identifying this man." Martin extended the police sketch across the bar. "We have reason to believe he's connected to the murders. Does he look familiar to you?"

Lifting her glasses from the chain around her neck to the bridge of her nose, Carrie harrumphed. "You think Red's The Country Killer?"

So she didn't know his real name.

"We don't know." Gayton rested her arms on the counter and leaned in as well. "But we would like to speak to him if you can help us track him down."

"Wouldn't surprise me if he were. But I'm sorry, ma'am, I can't help you there." Carrie frowned. "He always paid in cash. Wasn't the personal anecdote type either."

"What do you mean?" Ox asked.

"Bartenders are free therapists." Leaning against the counter behind her, Carrie crossed her ankles. "Most folks sit down, get their drink of choice, then rant and rave to me about their lives. They talk about their kids, their parents, work, their wives. You know. Any and everything. But not Red. Most Red ever talked to me about was the weather. He talked to every woman who walked in here, though. Not about anything important. Mostly bragging about his car, all his money. You know men like that. The ones who just want everyone to know how great they are."

Textbook narcissist. But why not talk that way to Carrie? She was at least twice his age, sure, but the killer's ideal victim when he began were women in the same demographic. Carrie was no worse on the eyes than any of his other older victims. Their body types were similar as well. Short and petite.

So why hadn't he made conversation with her like he had with other patrons? Not unless this establishment had been his hunting ground as well. If it were, he wouldn't have wanted the owner to have any specific information on him when the police came to ask questions.

"You have spoken to him, though?" Phillips asked. "Is he a regular?"

"For a while, he was." She raised a shoulder. "Now, he's not allowed on my property. Last I saw him, I was aiming my shotgun at his head."

That escalated quickly.

"What happened?" Phillips asked.

"I was up here doing my usual. Red walks in and sits at that stool." She nodded to the one at the end. "Asked him what he was drinking. Rum and coke, like always. I get it to him and go on about my business. Don't think much of it.

"The night goes on, and he starts chattin' up a lady. They head over to that booth over there. She was eating it up, all that bragging of his. Girls like her do." Another frown, followed by a headshake. "He said he had money, and she saw someone who'd give her what she needed to get high. Sad thing.

"But anyhow, the girl only had a few glasses of wine. Two, to be exact. And outta nowhere, she starts falling over herself. Now, I know who this girl is. Word travels in a small town, you know? The thing was, she didn't get up from that booth once. I know addicts. I've seen the girl's forearms." Carrie tapped the vein in the crease of her elbow. "Even if she popped a pill or two in that time, she wouldn't have been that out of it. Not if she was a habitual heroin addict, you know?"

"Sure," Ox murmured.

"Then Red gets up. And he's putting an arm around her shoulder like he's gonna carry her out of here. I said hell no and walked my ass over there. Told him I'd call her a cab or her friend. He says he'll drive her home. Then he starts acting all big with me. Puffing up his chest and standing all big and tall.

"I ain't a big woman, so I let him go at first. He gets her out of the booth while I'm walking around the bar. Grab my gun from down here" —she nodded below—"walk on over, hold it to the back of his head, and I tell him to let her go. He spouts off something about suing me, calling the cops, all kinds of nonsense. I tell him to go ahead, and then I'll tell them to search him for whatever he put in that girl's drink.

"By then, a few other guys are crowding around. Big guys. My biker boys." Carrie chuckled. "Red gets a little antsy, sets the girl down, and I tell him his fancy shoes better never get within a foot of my business again. All these guys around, he shuts up and walks away. Then he gets to the door and calls me a stupid bitch." Another chuckle. "And, well, some of my friends followed him to the parking lot. I couldn't tell you what happened out there. I was helping the girl who couldn't keep her eyes open. But they came back in with a little baggie of white pills. I gave 'em to the nurses when I dropped her off at the hospital."

"Rohypnol?" Ox asked.

"Yes, sir. That's what the doctors said," Carrie said. "Haven't seen Red since that day."

"And when was that?" Gayton asked.

Flapping her lips together in a trill, Carrie cocked her head to the side in thought. "Six months ago, I think? Something like that."

"You don't happen to know the name of this woman, do you?" Ox asked.

"I don't know her personally, no," Carrie said. "But the girl who's come in here with her before, I do. You give me a few minutes. I'll try and find her information for you."

Chapter 29

"It's a long story?" I blinked hard at him. "It seems pretty simple. Either you're in debt to them or you're not."

"Aside from paying off Daisy's debt, I didn't owe them anything. I'm not proud of it, but he deserved what he got."

"I think he deserved a bullet, so you don't need to defend yourself." Well, I hoped not. Still wasn't sure that I believed every word, but I certainly wanted to. "But if some drug dealers are after you, I feel like that's something I should know. Since you're—oh, I don't know—sitting on my couch."

"That gun's already cocked if they come barging in."

I narrowed my eyes.

He smirked.

"When did you get funny? That's my thing." Gesturing to the gun, I made a rolling motion with my hand. "In case you forgot, I am still holding said gun, so now would be a good time to answer my damn questions, Bentley."

If this man sighed one more time, I was sure he'd faint. Much to my surprise, he did sigh again, but he did not faint. "Dale says I'm not. Kevin says I am. Dale is Kevin's dad, the leader of whatever you wanna call them. Hillbilly mafia? Gang? I don't know. But Kevin just hates me because I beat his ass. Nobody takes him seriously anyway, not even the other dealers. Ask Simeon. I'm sure he'll tell you all about him."

"So you have spoken to Simeon."

"He's called me a couple times." Glancing at me out of the corner of his eye, Bentley picked at the cuticle on his thumb with his pointer finger. "Offered me cash to help him out when he or one of his guys get hurt."

"And you have."

"I didn't say that."

"You said it without saying it."

"How?" He swiveled to face me better. "How do you know? You always know, and I don't understand how you always know."

My turn to smirk. "How do I know when you're lying?"

"I didn't lie."

Fine, he got nervous. It wasn't technically a lie. But it was an attempt at an omission.

I didn't know if he did it every time he lied, but I knew when he was avoiding direct eye contact and picking at the cuticle on his thumb, he was at least hiding something. He thought it was the eyes that gave him away. Nope. The cuticle.

"Does Simeon have you on his books?" I asked.

Bentley frowned. "No. Of course not. When would I have time to stitch people up for Simeon? I'm always with you, Grace, or at work."

"But you *have* stitched people up for him."

His frown deepened. Eventually, he nodded. "Twice. That's my savings. I lied to you about Bella's life insurance money. After all that shit with Daisy and Kevin, it was gone. But that's the only thing I lied to you about. I swear, Maddie. That is the *only* thing I have lied about."

No cuticle picking. I nodded and asked, "Why were you here that night?"

Bentley's shoulders slumped. "You really think I'm the killer? You're the lunatic with a gun."

"If you would've just told me the truth yesterday, we wouldn't be here. But you lied, at least by omission, and you weren't gonna tell me the truth until I did something drastic." Keeping the gun aimed at the floor, I leaned back into my corner of the sofa. "I don't think you're the killer. You couldn't be because Ox told Derek to watch you, and you were in your house all night while the bastard killed again."

Still, he frowned. "You really think that's the type of person I am?"

"You had a whole secret life of crime you never told me about."

"Providing emergency medical attention is not at all equivalent to raping and murdering almost a dozen women, Maddie."

"I didn't say it was. I said you lied to me, and if I wanted to find out the truth, I was gonna have to find it on my own. Or find enough of it to have a good reason to hold a gun to your head." Again, I lifted it but kept the barrel aimed at the floor. "And by the way, you're now dancing circles around the question I asked you. So what were you doing that night, Bentley?"

Looking a bit like Tempest when I scolded her for guarding when I first got her, Bentley hung his head. "Taking a bullet out of Noah Ward's foot the first time."

"Noah got shot in the foot?"

"Noah's an idiot who shot *himself* in the foot." Waving at my gun, Bentley said, "Speaking of which, can you decock that?"

"Are you crazy? I can't do that in the house."

"But you had no problem cocking it against my chin," he said under his breath. Apparently, I was never going to live this down. "The second time, I was stitching up one of Simeon's guys. Cut his leg open running from a few cops. I was trying to save up enough money to get out of Ohio with Grace and Daisy. That's it. That's what I didn't want to tell you. Do you still think I'm a rapist? Or a murderer?"

I thought that I still didn't know what happened to Daisy. "I never *thought* you were a rapist or murderer. But you didn't give me any reason to believe you weren't."

"Every day that we've spent together for the last six months wasn't reason enough, Maddie?" His furrowed brows and annoyed tone were understandable. "I get being mad at me. I even get why you think that something might've happened between me and Daisy. It didn't, and that's disgusting, but I get why your head went there. Accusing me of *this* though? That's how little you think of me?"

"No. I don't think little of you at all. Just like I wouldn't have thought little of you if you'd told me this story a month ago, or two months ago, or the day you showed up here. Which is the problem, Bentley. I had you on a pedestal, and I was blind to the red flags. The fact that you never had a real reason for coming home. That you claim to have this money in savings, and you're living in a double-wide trailer in this piece of shit park you swore to hell and back that you'd never come back to. You *wanted* me to be blind to the red flags. And that wasn't fair. You shouldn't have lied to me when I asked you. I told you why I'm back here, I hung out all my dirty laundry for you, and you hid yours. You know I don't trust anyone, but I trusted you, and you didn't trust me enough to tell me the truth until I held the gun to your head."

I did not know how the man hadn't fainted yet, because he sighed again. This one was more of a grumpy harrumph, paired with a frown. His forehead was scrunched up just like Grace's had been last week when he told her that she could not get the four-hundred dollar dress for her end-of-the-year middle school dance.

Otherwise telling me he wasn't all that mad about the gun to his head. He was mad that I didn't trust him, and that I was *right* to not trust him.

"I should've told you," he said after a moment. "But I know how you are. I know you want proof, and I just don't have it. I wish I had recordings of the past decade. Maybe I can find some court dockets? I guess I could call my lawyer? She's not gonna be able to confirm that I never slept with Daisy though." He visibly cringed when he said that last sentence. "I didn't kill Daisy, but I can't prove that I didn't. One day, Daisy, Grace, and I were shopping for groceries and making s'mores in the fireplace, and the next, she was just gone. No idea where, no idea why. All I've got is the alibi of having worked an overnight when she vanished. I don't know why you think I could cover up a murder.

"Because, sure. I'll stitch up some addicts, and drug dealers, and meth cookers, but that is a different level of illegal. Providing medical attention is helping people. Were they all people who deserved help? I don't know. Maybe the world would be a better place without some of the people that I saved, but judging whether someone deserves to live or die is not my job. Helping someone who's hurt is my job. And they paid better than the city does. So yeah, I stitched people up, but I never killed anyone. Especially not Daisy. I would've died for that kid, and I would've killed to protect her, but if I hurt her, I *would not* live with myself. It'd be like killing Grace, Maddie. Never, not in a million years, could I harm a hair on either of those girls' heads. But I can't prove that to you. Even though we both know it's much more likely that you would commit murder than me, I can't prove that I haven't."

Probably. I'd always been the more aggressive one of the two of us.

"I don't believe that."

Jaw falling open, Bentley scoffed. "What do you want me to do? How am I supposed to prove to you that I didn't hurt Dai—"

"I don't think you did." Did I believe the entire story beyond a certain doubt? Absolutely not. I believed *no one* beyond a certain doubt. I did believe their relationship was platonic and that he went too far attempting to help her, but I didn't think he'd hurt her. "But I don't think that's why you omitted it yesterday."

"Yeah?" Crossing his arms, he leaned back on the opposite side of the sofa. "Enlighten me. Why didn't I tell you?"

"Because you wanted to be on that pedestal," I said. "Because Ox was on your ass. Because you liked me thinking of you as the perfect, small-town single dad. You wanted me to like you more than I like the overbearing detective." And I did, but that wasn't the point here.

All the snarky, nearly playful energy in the air disintegrated with every word. In movies, there was always that line about how *the world stopped spinning*. It was usually in a good way. Like when star-crossed lovers saw one another for the first time, or the moment the love interests finally kissed in a rom-com.

This was one of those moments, but not the good kind. The look on his face was not the kind anyone made for one of those love-struck *the world stopped spinning* moments. It was more like a *world stopped spinning* moment from a post-apocalyptic.

Bentley's always-warm brown eyes were now vulnerable. Afraid. Not so shaken that he had to run, but afraid that I hated him. Afraid that whatever we had a few days prior was gone. Whether it was friendship or more didn't matter.

Bentley thought that I was ready to cut him off like I cut off everyone else who hurt me. He was worried that I had just decided I was done with him like I had been done with my mom, like I had been done with Harper, and like I had been done with Ox.

I wasn't.

"That was it, right?" I asked. "You wanted me to see you as my knight in shining armor?"

I expected him to look away. That was usually what he did when he felt uncomfortable. But this wasn't discomfort. It was fear.

Swallowing, he shook his head. "You've never needed anyone to save you."

"Then why didn't you tell me?"

For a few more seconds, he was quiet. He just stared at me. Stared at me with an expression I could only describe as desperation. His eyes were still so soft, scared, but his forehead creased the way anyone's would when they were going to cry. He didn't. No tears escaped him.

"I wanted you to see me for the person I'm trying to be," he said. "I didn't want you to look at me and see another screwed up piece of shit from this hell hole who's gonna let their kids turn out the same way they did. I tried really hard to break the cycle, but then Bella died, and Daisy was alive, but she was dying too, and I didn't know how to turn it off. I didn't know how to stop taking care of her, and enabling her, trying to give her what *we* needed when we were kids. I just fell deeper and deeper into a life I never wanted. Now she's gone, and I don't know if she would've been better off if I'd left when Bella died. I don't know if I didn't fight hard enough for her, or if I should've called the cops every time I knew she was getting high, or if I messed up Grace like our parents messed us up, or if I'm even a half-decent person, but I want to be. I'm trying so goddamned hard to be.

"It was never about wanting you to think I was perfect. I just wanted out. I wanted a fresh start. I wanted that life with the little picket fence that we used to dream about. I wanted you to know that you and I want the same things. I didn't want you to know how shitty of a dad I've been. I didn't want you to think that I think the things I've done are okay because I know they weren't. If I'd told you everything, you'd think I was just like every other kid who grew into a watered-down version of their shitty parent. I didn't keep this from you because I'm some psychopathic narcissist who wants you to think he's perfect. I kept it from you because—"

He stopped. Just stopped. His mouth was still open, like the reason was trapped inside him. Like those words were as heavy in his esophagus as the entire planet, and there was no way they could fit up that narrow tunnel and leave his body. Like they were too big, and he was too small.

He always thought he was too small.

I hated that he saw himself this way. I hated that I brought it all to the surface the way I had. I hated that I'd forced him to open up to me.

But maybe he needed that. Maybe he needed someone to coax it out of him so he would realize those thoughts weren't too big, and he wasn't too small.

"Why, Bentley?" In black and white, those words seemed harsh. But they rolled off my tongue softer than silk. "Why did you keep it from me?"

His eyes flicked between mine like he was waiting for me to say that I agreed. That I suddenly thought he was an awful person or a terrible father. That I wanted nothing to do with him.

I didn't. I couldn't.

Wetting his lips, he swallowed hard again. "Because I want you." More fear shined in his eyes than ever before. When my expression didn't give him a reason to stop, it dwindled. "I've wanted you since we were pre-schoolers. But you didn't want me. Not until you saw me as someone better than the lives we were born into. I didn't know how to tell you I'm just as bad as everything we ran from.

"Or I thought you did, anyway. I thought maybe you wanted me too. Maybe I made that up. Maybe admitting this is as stupid as it was of me to kiss you when we were kids. I'm sorry I didn't tell you every-thing. I'm sorry I'm not who you thought I was, and I'm sorry I made everything you're going through so much worse by dumping all this on you. I'm so sorry, Maddie. But that was why I didn't tell you. Because I want to be who you thought I was. I want to be someone you want."

Chapter 30

Ox and the others accepted a few drinks and French fries to keep them satisfied while they waited to hear back from Carrie's friend. Just when Carrie came out with the food, her phone rang. They'd made it through all of two bites before Carrie told him that she had the address of Abigail Reynolds, the woman "Red" had drugged.

Following that night, she'd checked herself into rehab. After a ninety day stay, she'd checked herself into a halfway house. She had only just gotten her own apartment a month ago, just outside of Oil City in Franklin County. Two and half hours from the bar in Somerset.

Carrie's friend got them Abigail's number. She didn't answer when they called. Carrie's friend found that odd. Abigail always answered her. Which left Ox concerned.

A two-and-a-half hour drive, five hour round-trip, wasn't ideal when it was already nearing 4 o'clock. While The Country Killer attacked at night in this area, Ox doubted staying close would make a difference. He never knew what The Country Killer was doing until he was done. Considering what had happened on the phone today, he didn't want to leave Maddie here alone.

Gayton said she would stay back so she could be first on the scene if something did arise before Ox returned. Before deciding if that was something he wanted to do, Ox sent Maddie a text.

Hey. We might have a witness. She's all the way up in Oil City though. You don't mind if I head that way with Martin and Phillips while Gayton stays in town, do you?

It was only heartbeats before she responded. *Nope.*

Just one word, a typically friendly word, and Ox heard it like the crack of a whip. With an eye roll, he texted back, *Eat something. You're being a bitch again.*

Maddie then responded with some less than kind emojis.

No matter how rude it was, it still made Ox's chest warm. On the drive to Oil City, he thought about her. Maddie, and all the things she'd said over the years. What their relationship would come to. How even when Maddie was angry, even when she cussed him out, even when he taunted her, and she teased him, they still had something that few people would ever experience in their life. A connection like no other.

They weren't meant to be a couple. Ox knew that now. Maddie would never forgive the things Ox had done, and that was best. They were better this way. Friends who occasionally worked a case together. Friends who had seen every inch of one another, in both the literal and metaphorical sense. Friends from practically different universes who'd met and merged over one common denominator.

They both wanted to help people.

From that one thing in common, a thousand other small similarities stacked together to build the blocks of their relationship. Not only did they like helping people, but they liked solving puzzles. They used to do that for fun, in fact. Make puzzles, glue them in place, then hang them on the walls like trophies. When Ox was first promoted to detective, Maddie had gotten them their first puzzle. As he worked the case, anytime he racked his brain for too long and was out of good ideas, he and Maddie would click the pieces of the puzzle together. That was when he got to pick Maddie's brain. Over that puzzle, discussing the case together, was how he solved it.

That was what they were good at. Solving puzzles. It was formulaic, of course, and that was what they loved about it. Ox always loved logic and reason, while Maddie loved to turn chaos into something sensible. That was why they'd bonded. That was why they'd fallen in love.

In the last few months, Ox had accepted that. It was okay. They weren't a couple, and they didn't have to be. As long as he got to spend the rest of his life solving puzzles with Maddie Castle, Ox was happy.

Abigail's apartment complex was a decent enough place, but nothing extravagant. It may not have been in the best part of town, but the five-story, red brick building was inviting. Little white shutters framed each window, many of the Juliet balconies and fire escapes decorated with pretty spring blooms. Even the stairway to Abigail's home on the fourth floor was nice. Roomy metal steps that rounded all the way to the fifth floor. Ox had always liked rounded staircases. They felt Victorian, classic. He'd wanted to put one in the house he and Maddie had once dreamed of building, but she'd reminded him that rounded staircases were quite small, and Ox was not.

Nonetheless, Ox was not surprised when he and the others showed Abigail their badges through the peephole, and Abigail held open her door with wide eyes and trembling fingers. "I-I don't think I have any warrants, do I? I go to all my hearings. I haven't done anything. I swear, I—"

"We know," Phillips said, extending his hand and giving a warm smile. "You aren't in trouble. We're just hoping you might be willing to help us with an investigation."

To the average person, that would be a relieving statement. To an addict? That sounded a lot like a threat to blackmail her into snitching on someone. The color draining from her rosy cheeks proved it.

"The Country Killer," Ox said. "We think you may have had contact with him a few months ago."

Blinking hard, Abigail's face screwed up in confusion. "What? How? I thought you guys didn't know who he was."

"We don't for certain." Ox held out the police sketch. "But we believe he goes by the name Red. This is the man who drugged you at The Pour House, isn't he?"

Ox hadn't realized that Abigail's face could get any paler, but it did. After cupping her hand over her mouth, breathing through the realization that she could have become one of his victims, she invited Ox and the others inside.

Again, a nice place. The furniture was old, a nicked up wooden coffee table, a few mismatched end tables, and an old box TV in the corner, but it was clean. Abigail's beige carpets were so well-maintained that he could still see the sweeper marks. He liked to respect people's homes, even considered taking off his shoes, but decided it was best to be ready to go in case he had to rush back to Maddie.

Martin and Phillips sat on the sofa, Abigail took the pink corduroy recliner, and Ox stood. Ox preferred to stand anyway. Abigail was still gaping at the police sketch when Ox said, "Is that surprising? Do you believe he could've been the killer?"

Swallowing, she laid the sketch on the table. "No. It's not surprising. But I don't remember that much about him. We only met that one night, and mine ended in the hospital."

"You don't remember anything at all?" Martin's eyes were sympathetic. "Those drugs do have that effect, but if there is anything that stands out about him, it might help us figure out who he is."

"I don't know," Abigail whispered, still staring at the sketch. "He was a big shot? Talked a lot about how much money he made. He was really into me. I thought he was, anyway. Maybe he was just really into the idea of killing me."

Ox snorted. Abigail gave a half smile, like a nod to someone else with her style of dark humor.

"Did he mention what he does for a living?" Ox asked.

Biting her lip, Abigail shook her head. "Maybe? I really don't remember much."

"We understand," Phillips said. "But even a rough idea could help."

Focusing, Abigail shook her head. "I thought he said it had something to do with technology. Maybe? It was so long ago, and I was really messed up."

"What is the first thing that you do remember about him?" Ox asked.

"Oh, geez." Scanning the carpet, Abigail slid her hand up and down her arm, as if to self-soothe.

That simple gesture was common enough, but it reminded Ox all too much of Maddie. Until the last few days, Ox had never seen Maddie need to soothe herself. Usually, her emotions manifested in anger. But several times since this all began, Ox had noticed Maddie rubbing her hands up and down her arms.

It wasn't surprising that Abigail looked like Maddie. Clearly, Maddie had become Red's type. But the longer he looked at Abigail, the more similarities he saw. Physically, of course. They both had small noses, thick lips in an eerily familiar shape, and similar statures. That little gesture, in tandem with the dark joke Abigail had just told, however, raised Ox's suspicions.

He had no doubt that Red had been watching Maddie. He would've gathered enough from watching Maddie through her cameras. But Abigail even had a similar life experience to Maddie. Both addicts. Both from rough walks of life. Both enjoyed drinks at the same bar.

Obviously, Red's interest in Abigail stemmed from his obsession with Maddie. But was it possible that Maddie had met him? It wasn't uncommon for stalkers to get close to their victims. That was why Ox's mind had initially gone to Bentley. But what if he'd been involved in her life in some other way? What if they had a mutual friend? What if it was more than just a drug dealer they had both known?

"He made a comment about the dog hair on my pants," Abigail said. "Right after we started talking, I mean. I had just been at my friends', and they have huskies. My pants were black. I don't know. It didn't seem like a big deal to me, but is that the type of thing you're talking about?"

"That's exactly the kind of thing we're talking about," Ox said. "Another witness mentioned his dislike for dogs. Was there anything else like that? Things that seem silly, or maybe even stupid, that just sort of stuck out to you?"

Running her fingers through her hair, much like Maddie often did, Abigail shrugged. "He asked me if I like hunting? Then rambled on for a while about different guns? I told him I did, just because that's what you do when you meet a nice guy. Try and make it sound like you like the things they like."

"Did he mention where he hunts?" Martin asked.

"I don't think so. But it really is choppy," Abigail said. "Do you have any specific questions?"

"Did you realize he drugged you?" Martin asked.

"I remember when my legs started to feel heavy," she said. "It made me think something wasn't right, but that's around the time that I stopped remembering anything."

Ox understood where Abigail was coming from. She remembered very little from the night already, and they were asking her incredibly vague questions. There were two exact ones he could ask, however. "Did he mention where he lived?"

Gasping softly, Abigail's eyes sparkled. Like something just clicked. "Not an address, but he said it was close. That's why he wanted to know if I liked hunting. Because if I did, I was used to walking in the woods in the dark." With excitement, Abigail wagged a finger. Almost like she was pointing at the light bulb over her head. "He said that he drove his quad there that night. He didn't want to risk getting a DUI. I think he said that it would take us about half an hour to get to his house on the quad? Or maybe less? Maybe more? Does that help?"

"It very well might," Ox said, but he doubted it.

Quads could drive as fast as ninety miles per hour. Granted, if Red had planned on riding through the woods to his home, Ox doubted that he would go above thirty. Even so, if he lived thirty minutes away, and he were driving thirty miles an hour on his quad, that would equate to a rough fifteen mile diameter. Which was the same diameter they'd already expected Red to live in.

But maybe one of those quad trails bordered a high-end neighborhood. That might tell them something.

"Do you remember his face well enough to pick him out of a lineup if we find him?" Phillips asked.

To that, Abigail nodded.

Ox looked from Phillips to Martin, speaking without words. As if to say, "Is there anything we missed?"

None of them spoke.

"I'm happy to hear that." Ox extended a card to Abigail. "Thank you for your help. If you think of anything else, give me a call."

After a few more formal farewells, just when they made it to the door, Abigail said, "I remember one more thing."

Ox looked at her over his shoulder.

"Moirah? Or Mayrah?" Laughing halfheartedly, uncomfortably, Abigail shrugged again. "I don't remember what it means. I just vaguely remember it from that night. Does that mean anything to you?"

Ox did a mental memory search, but nothing surfaced. "I'll keep my eye open for it."

Chapter 31

"THAT'S NOT TRUE," WERE THE FIRST WORDS THAT FELL OUT OF my mouth.

Bentley was wrong. He was wrong in the same way when he'd kept everything from me. If he hadn't always been so damn self-deprecating, and if I hadn't always been so damn determined to ruin every good thing that happened to me, maybe we would have been past this point much earlier on. Maybe he would have felt ready to tell me everything without me holding him at gunpoint. But that's not how it turned out, and it wouldn't get better unless we addressed it.

For a few seconds, Bentley stared at me in disbelief. Probably waiting for me to explain.

I didn't. Why? We'd need to resurrect Freud to answer that question.

"What's not true?"

"You're not as bad as everything we ran from," I said. "You're not even close to as bad as everything we ran from."

Again, his forehead wrinkled the way someone's did when they were about to cry. He didn't. It didn't make me feel better, and it still felt like that wasn't the answer he was hoping for.

"You enabled Daisy." Sitting forward, infuriated with myself for still holding a loaded gun at a moment like this, I did my best to keep my voice soft. "When she was alive, I enabled my mom. That doesn't make us bad people."

His eyes crinkled at the edges, confused that this was where I was leading the conversation. It also confused me that this was where I was leading the conversation.

Feeling my cheeks warm, I shook my head. "Enabling someone isn't good. Obviously, but you don't enable someone because you hate them. You don't enable people because you're cruel. You enable people because you love them. Because you love them too much. And you do that so much that you lose yourself in the process. You end up leading an entirely different life than the one you want. And *that's* bad, but it's bad for you. It erodes your sense of self, and it drains you, and it hurts. But it doesn't make *you* bad. A bad person wouldn't question whether enabling a teenager they'd practically raised was a bad decision. A bad person would feel no guilt now that she's missing. A bad person wouldn't care, and you do."

Again, he just stared at me. Still as confused as he was a moment prior.

But I still had to answer the question he was really asking. The question I had intended to answer in the first place.

The words wouldn't come out. I guessed Bentley wasn't the only one who saw himself as too small.

"That's it?" Staring at me, he looked confused and on the verge of tears at the same time. "After everything I just said, that's it?"

I tried to open my mouth, but I couldn't even do that.

Not because I didn't want to. I did. I'd wanted this conversation for weeks, maybe months. Hell, maybe a decade and a half.

Why couldn't I speak? Why couldn't I have the courage that he just had?

Pressing his lips to a line, Bentley gave a slow nod. "Alright then. Guess I'm going to go home. I'd appreciate if you didn't shoot me on my way out."

Typically, I would think that was a joke. But his expression made it very clear that he was not in a joking mood. Not since I'd coerced him into telling me how he felt, only to stay silent once he had.

This wasn't how I wanted it to go. I didn't know how I wanted it to go, but it wasn't this. This was bad. This was stupid. *I* was stupid. Why was I so stupid? Why was he already at the door, not sparing me so much as a glance, and I still sat on the couch holding a loaded, cocked gun that I had just held to his head?

How could he say that *he* was the bad one here when my dysfunctional ass thought that this was a good idea? How could he think I'd hate him for knowing that he took care of his dead wife's baby sister when she'd spiraled into full-blown addiction? How could he think I wouldn't understand? How could he hate himself when he was so good, and I was the one who was so screwed up?

I was the addict. I was the one who'd lost her career because she hadn't done her job well enough. I was the one who *had* escaped the cycle, only to fall right back into it. I was the one who had an innocent woman's blood on her hands today.

And that was why I watched him walk out the door.

Because he was good, and I wasn't.

As my fingers trembled around the gun in my hand, as a lump formed in my throat, it clicked. Suddenly, I understood why I had done all of this. I told myself it was because I was afraid.

That was a lie. No part of me believed Bentley would ever hurt me. But I pretended I did. Just to do what I had always done. To repeat what I had when we were preteens in that field in the center of the trailer park under the stars.

It was easier to be the screw-up. Even when I knew exactly what I wanted, even when I knew how to get it, I screwed it up on purpose. A habit I had broken when I'd left this trailer park at eighteen, and one I'd fallen right back into when I lost my knee.

When I was more ashamed than I had ever been, I'd pushed Ox away. So far that he'd leaped into my best friend's arms. I wasn't to blame for his actions, but I was to blame for the pattern. It wasn't until this very moment that I saw it. It was in front of me now, and I had to face it.

Literally the day that I'd learned of Ox's affair, I drank a fifth and took I couldn't even count how many pain pills. I hadn't intended to kill myself, but I had intended to ruin my life. And I did. No more pain pills after that, and no more chances at returning to life as a cop.

The following day, when Alex had offered me a way to get back on my feet, I turned her down. I asked for her help packing my things and moving me into this trailer park instead.

In the days, weeks that followed, then months, and the year, I'd become my mother. I'd sat in her living room, maybe on a new couch, but positioned just as hers had been, staring at the same four walls, and popped pill after pill.

Today. The man I cared for most in the world, the man I had been falling in love with since childhood, told me he felt the same way that I did. Even after I had just held a gun to his head.

Then I watched him walk away.

Why did I do that if not to torture myself?

This was how I punished myself. Mom wasn't around to beat my ass anymore, so I beat my own.

That son of a bitch did this to me. I had escaped the cycle, and all it'd taken was one severe trauma to throw me right back into the eye of the thing. The Country Killer, or The Red Ribbon Killer, or Red, whatever the hell his name was, had taken the life that I was prouder of than anything. And I'd let him. I'd let him ruin everything I loved about myself all the way down to how I felt when I looked in the mirror. He crawled inside my head and made me hate myself again.

Bentley had helped me get out. When he'd showed up next door, helped me get sober, made me dinner each night. He'd extended the life rope down to the center of my hurricane of a life. Then that evil bastard returned, and I'd started spiraling right back into its vortex. His voice, screaming that it was my fault when he killed Josey, hadn't left since. I'd let it paralyze me to this damn couch.

The only way to get out of the eye of that hurricane was to get up. I had to get off the couch.

Silent tears trickling from the corners of my eyes, I grabbed the sofa's arm and relied on it for strength as I stood. Knee aching with every step, nearly giving out on me a few times, I wobbled to the door. By the time I swung it open, Bentley was already rounding the bend to his trailer.

Scanning the grass to my right, making sure Duke wasn't outside in Greg's backyard, I wedged my thumb in front of the hammer. The moment would've been far more intense had I just shot the gun, but I'd already aimed it at Bentley's head today. Firing a shot anywhere near him was a sure way to keep myself stuck in the eye of the damn hurricane.

Carefully setting it on the ground once it was de-cocked, I yelled, "I did!"

Bentley stopped. When he turned around, he was as confused as he had been on my couch. "What?"

"I did want you. When we were kids. I did want you. But I also wanted what was best for you. You didn't just want out of this park. You wanted out of the state. You wanted to go as far as you could, and I didn't, but I knew you would've stayed. If I had asked you just once to stay, you would have, and I couldn't do that to you. I didn't want to ruin your life the way I wanted to ruin my own. I wanted you to get what you wanted, what you needed. So I let you go." I took a shaky breath. "But I wanted you to stay."

Chapter 32

BENTLEY ONLY STARED AT ME. HIS BROWS WERE STILL FURROWED, but his jaw was softer now. His eyes seemed to plead, *Give me more than that. Tell me what I need to hear. Don't just say you care about me. Tell me how you care about me. Tell me I'm not the only one who feels this way.*

It was my turn to pour my heart into this. I started limping across my porch, having to rest after each step. "When you kissed me, I told you we were better as friends. That wasn't because I didn't want you. I just didn't want to *lose* you. You were the best friend I ever had. I didn't want to ruin it. Relationships ruin friendships, and I needed a friend. I needed you. And I wanted you. I still want you. I've *always* wanted you."

As I spoke, he listened to each word. His scrunched up forehead gradually softened. Initially, only the confusion vanished. He still looked upset, angry. Until that last sentence.

He ran to me.

I was on the third to last of the steps, attempting to make it to the bottom, but he was already in front of me with his hands on my cheeks and his lips against mine.

The world didn't stop spinning like it did in the movies. It spun faster and faster, like I was a little girl on the merry-go-round howling with laughter as those butterflies took hold of my torso. They weren't just flapping their wings. They were on fire, warming every inch of me as Bentley circled his arms around my waist, hoisted me off the porch, and spun me around.

First kisses were awkward, but this wasn't. Then again, it wasn't our first kiss. That one hadn't felt awkward either, though. It'd felt scary. Like he had been a teddy bear whose hems were fraying, and if I squeezed him too tightly, I would lose him forever.

What came next, I wasn't sure, but I knew we had lost each other once. Neither of us would ever forgive ourselves for that. I would never let that happen again, not over something as silly as fear. Especially not because a serial killer had gotten in my head and launched me onto this path of destruction.

"Well, it's about damn time!" Greg called.

"I was just about ready to say the same," Derek said from the opposite direction.

Ah, yes. What a perfect way to end an even more perfect moment.

Although, that was horseshit. Nothing about this was perfect.

I hadn't slept in almost two days, couldn't remember the last time I brushed my teeth, likely reeked of vomit, and the corners of my eyes were chafed from all the crying. Bentley had just gotten off work, only for me to bombard him with the most personal questions imaginable. And threaten his life.

This was not even *close* to perfect.

But the smile across his lips as he pulled away was. The comfort intertwined with passion in his eyes was even better. "Guess there's no keeping this quiet."

Normally, I'd be pissed anyone had picked me up at all, let alone that they were suspending me in the air for this long. I felt like that joyous little girl on the merry-go-round instead. "Did you want to?"

"Did *you* want to?"

Smiling, I shook my head.

I didn't realize his could get any bigger. Yet it did. He came in for another kiss, this one slower and softer than the last. It only lasted a heartbeat before Bentley's phone rang, and he grumbled with annoyance.

It was Grace's ringtone. She had a special one, so he knew she was calling when he was at work.

"You can set me down," I said. "I'll still be here."

Letting out a half laugh, he shook his head. "She can wait a minute."

"There's a serial killer on the loose, Bentley."

"Which is why she's calling me." Effortlessly, not so much as trembling, he returned me to flat feet. "I've been walking down to the bus stop to pick her up since everything started. I don't want her going anywhere alone. She calls me when she's leaving the school."

"Or she's calling you because she missed her bus." Smiling still, I took a step back. "Go ahead. Answer it."

With a heavy sigh, still smiling, he did. "You on your way home, kid?" Some chatter sounded on the other end. "Alright. I'll start walking." Some more chatter. "Yeah, I'm standing outside with Maddie. Why?" More chatter, followed by an eye roll. "I'll ask her."

"Ask me what?"

"If you and Tempest will walk down to the bus stop with me, then come over for dinner," he said, holding a hand over the speaker. He said in a quieter tone, "You don't have to."

After all this? No way I was walking back into my trailer alone. "As long as you double the recipe. I missed dinner yesterday, and I'm starving."

Bentley's smile widened. "Yeah, she's coming. Now let me get off the phone so that we can meet you down there."

* * *

AFTER CAREFULLY RETURNING MY GUN TO ITS SPOT BENEATH THE bed, I freed Tempest from her crate. She was more energetic than usual when Bentley greeted her, probably because we'd yelled and she could sense the tension. The two of them had to rush through their greetings so we could get to the bottom of the hill. Normally neither of us would have minded, but we didn't want to take any chances of Grace walking alone right now.

The moment I stepped out of the house with Tempest on her leash, Derek leaned against his cruiser and hooked his thumbs around his bulletproof vest. "Where we going?"

"We"—I gestured between myself and Bentley—"are walking to the bus stop to pick up Grace. Don't worry. Doubt we're going to cross The Country Killer's path."

"Well, tough." Derek stretched his arms overhead. "The FBI told me not to let you leave alone. So I'll be chaperoning."

"Yay," Bentley said under his breath.

There was no point in arguing. Derek wouldn't give here. I didn't blame him. If I were in his shoes, I wouldn't either. But a little privacy would've been nice, because I didn't know what Bentley wanted to tell Grace.

He kept his distance though. As we trekked down the hill, staying on the road despite our usual course through the woods to the entrance of the trailer park, Derek stayed at least fifteen feet back. I half expected him to be taking photos behind us.

The first five minutes were quiet. Couldn't say if it was the exhaustion, all the happy chemicals firing in my brain, the hunger, or that it had just been a long time, but I didn't know how to get the conversation going. I kept glancing at his hand. A silly thing, but there it was. Dangling at his side. Not holding mine. Should I have been the one to reach for it? Would Bentley feel emasculated if I had? Was Bentley even capable of feeling emasculated? The man was tuned in on his emotions and wasn't afraid to say so.

"You okay?"

I looked up at him. "Huh?"

He laughed. "Are you okay?"

Smiling, I nodded back.

"You're awfully quiet. It's rare for you to be quiet."

"Was that an insult?"

"It was a compliment." That smile. He just would not stop smiling. "You sure you're okay?"

"Did I taste like throw up?"

His face scrunched up. "What?"

"I've puked a lot in the last couple days, and we ran out of the house at three in the morning to go to the scene, and I don't think I brushed my teeth, and then I puked again right before you came over, and I'm wondering if I tasted like throw up."

Laughing, Bentley nodded to the bottom of the hill. "Should we talk about what all this means before I tell Grace?"

"Why do you do that?" I said, glaring at him. "Why do you avoid my questions?"

"Because you did taste a little like throw up, but I didn't want to make you feel insecure about it. It was a great kiss. No regrets."

Tempy smiled up at me, as if to say, *I don't care that you smell like throw up either, Mom.*

Jaw falling open, I smacked him in the arm. "You could've lied. You didn't have to tell me the truth."

"Last time I lied, you held a gun to my head. Forgive me for not wanting to do it again."

"Okay, we're not gonna tell Grace about that," I said. "Right?"

Again, he laughed.

"No, seriously. I don't want her to know I did that, Bentley."

With a teasing smile, he shrugged. "Then maybe you shouldn't have done it."

"Well, you should've known better than to lie to me."

"And yet, you *want* me to lie. You tasted like cake. Oh, and you smell like roses." He smirked. "Happy?"

Pulling my hoodie up to the side, I sniffed my armpit. "I stink?"

"You smell like roses."

I smacked his arm again, which only made him laugh. "It's not funny. What do I smell like?"

"Throw up. And weed." Leaning closer, he sniffed me a few times. "Why *do* you smell like weed?"

"Because I questioned Noah Ward earlier and he can't go five minutes without taking a bong rip. Now why do you smell like..." Searching for a comeback, failing to find a good one, which he laughed at yet again, I thrusted a fist down at my side. "It's been a long ass week. Forgive me if I don't have the energy for banter. But you're mean. Even if I came up with a good one, you would just mock me."

Bentley's hand brushed against mine, and he caught it. Smile softening, he laced our fingers together, bringing a layer of warmth to my hand that traveled up my arm and over my entire body. "I'll stop mocking you. After this." He pointed to my cheeks. "Are you blushing? Or are you coming down with something?"

Yanking my hand from his grasp, I shoved him this time. "I hate you."

He just laughed, found my hand again, and lifted my knuckles to his lips. With a smile, he said, "You're pretty when you blush."

Which only made me blush more.

Chapter 33

Tempest and I stayed a few dozen yards behind while Bentley walked closer to the bus stop. Tempy had gotten a lot better about her excitement around people, but she was still tense from earlier. It was best that she stayed far from rambunctious children.

"Did you aim that gun at him?" Derek's voice made me jump. He'd stayed a few steps behind us as we walked. "Or do you just regularly hold a cocked gun when a friend comes over?"

The biggest wave of shame washed over me. It was bad. I shouldn't have done it. I knew very well that you were to never point a gun at something—someone—unless you had a reason. Unless you planned to shoot.

I shouldn't have had access to a gun today. For protection, I needed it, but gun safety required a level mind. I didn't have that today.

I was already ashamed of what I had done, but Derek knowing made it worse. Derek hadn't been my father, but he was the closest I had to one growing up. The only male figure I knew with redeeming qualities. And he cared about me. I wanted to make him proud.

What I had just done would make no one proud.

"You saw that, huh?" I asked.

"Sure did."

Now was the time to come up with an excuse. To explain it away. But there was no good excuse.

"You saw the video, didn't you?" Derek kept his gaze ahead on Bentley as he waved at the bus to embarrass Grace for the remainder of her ride. "That little punk of a reporter with a blog?"

"You know about that?" Cocking my head to the side, my heart slowed. "You knew about Daisy?"

"I know everything." A playful smile. He used to say that anytime he caught me and my friends getting into trouble. "When she was still underage, he called me and asked what might happen if he took a minor in foster care across state lines. I told him. He would go to jail. Then not long after, he came out this way to help Phoebe with that tube baby." That was a unique way to describe artificial insemination. "We met up and got some drinks. I gave him legal advice where I could, but mostly, I gave him dad advice. Told him that if he wanted to help her, the most he could do until she was eighteen was let her crash on his couch. Maybe that was bad advice. But I don't think he'd forgive himself if he hadn't, considering everything that happened."

Frowning, that ache of shame in my chest got deeper. "Did you ever meet her?"

"Yeah, a couple times." Derek's smile was sad. "She had a drug problem, but she was a good kid."

"Most people with drug problems are good," I said under my breath.

"Most." Derek nodded, still looking at Bentley. "He sent me that interview. Then he called me, bawling his eyes out. Said he didn't know what to do. A rumor had gotten out in his P.D. that it had something to do with him, and *that* was why he was moving, so I went over and helped them finish packing. You should've seen that boy, Maddie." Kind brown eyes growing even softer, a frown weighted the edges of his lips. "You ever have to tell a parent their kid's dead? That look on their face? How hard it is for them to even speak?"

A chill crept up my spine at the many memories. I'd had experience with that. Every city cop did. Far too often, I had been the first to arrive at an overdose, so I administered the naloxone and started CPR, all too late. Then, as the paramedics loaded them onto a stretcher, I had to be the one to tell their loved ones.

It was always hardest with the parents. When it was someone's sibling or partner who had died, it was terrible enough. Death was cruel. Grief was the hardest battle people had to fight in their lives. But telling a parent that their child was gone forever was like punishment for a crime on its own. The scream of the first mother I'd had to inform haunted my dreams to this day. Much like Josey's.

All I could manage was a nod.

"That's how he looked. Like his whole world had just been yanked out from under him." Frowning, Derek shook his head. "I don't know what happened to her. I looked into it, and I don't think the cops did anything wrong. It was one of those cases where there just wasn't any evidence to follow. But I can tell you for damn sure that he had nothing to do with it. Look at him. Just look at the way his face lights up when he sees his little girl." As Grace stepped off the bus, glaring at him, Bentley scooped her up and spun her in a circle. "He looked at Daisy the same way. It's a lot different than how he looks at you, if you hadn't noticed."

The longer I looked at them, watching Grace try to disguise her embarrassed smile, seeing the light that shined in Bentley's eyes, I felt so much worse for what I had done today. All the paranoid theories that had run circles around my mind since my hair went missing were beyond unfair. Bentley was right. How the hell could I believe that he was the man I had made him out to be?

"He moved in here a few months after that interview. Then he started spending time with you again. He started looking happy again. Not that fake happy he puts on for Grace, but *really* happy." Derek nudged his elbow into mine. "So I'm sure it hurt when you did that."

"Thanks," I muttered. Just what I wanted to hear.

"I bet he was glad to get it off his chest. Just like you were glad to get it off yours when you admitted you had a problem." Was that supposed to make me feel better? It didn't. "Come on, kid. You've known him all your life. You know that if there's a chance something'll hurt, he avoids it." That was true. Much like the bike thing when we were preteens. Bentley had borrowed mine, his dad broke it, and he avoided me for a week. Even though it hadn't been his fault. "Maybe he needed you to hold that gun to his head to get him to open up."

I arched a brow at him. "You think it was totally cool that I held a gun to his head?"

"Wasn't that a double-action revolver? You wouldn't have accidentally pulled the trigger. He was fine."

I laughed. I had thought about that when I grabbed the revolver instead of the automatic. The trigger pull on a modern revolver was practically an internal safety. It was so hard to pull one that I only kept the revolver because I liked the way it looked. The pistol was the one I relied on for protection.

"But hey, I already told you. I ain't all that good at giving advice." Derek smiled. "I'm glad you two worked through it though. Only took you your entire life."

Narrowing my eyes, I gave him a half smile. "Thanks."

He roughed up my hair. If it were anyone else, I would've smacked them. But never in a million years would I disrespect Derek like that.

"Maddie!" Grace yelled, running in my direction. "Are you okay? You didn't call me back last night!" Already before me, she tossed her arms around my waist and hugged me tight. "I was worried about you."

"Yeah, I'm okay." Hugging her back, I was half-tempted to jump around and tell her. She had been hounding me for months about finally moving past the friend stage with her dad. As odd as it sounded, this preteen was one of the best friends I had. I wanted to share this exciting new thing with her. But Bentley wanted to talk to her first. So instead, I said, "Do you like my hair?"

Pulling away, her jaw dropped. "You want me to be honest?"

"Don't be mean," Bentley called, lugging her million bags as if he were her mule. "I think it looks pretty."

In a not so discrete whisper, Grace cupped a hand around her mouth. "He always thinks you look pretty." When I chuckled, she continued, "But he's wrong. It's bad, and you need to go to a pro."

Such a sweet kid. Rude, but a sweet kid.

Chapter 34

"Maddie," Grace said, scooping some lasagna onto her plate, "you're probably gonna be busy tomorrow, huh?"

"I don't have any open cases right now." Topping off my cup with some water, I leaned against the kitchen counter. "Why?"

"Because I was talking about you at school today." She gave a bashful smile. "Apparently you're a hero. Everyone wants your autograph. My teacher said you could come in and sign some yearbooks if you wanted to."

Good thing I hadn't sipped my water yet because I may have choked on it.

Since walking back from the bus stop, I'd almost forgotten about everything. The excitement over the smirks Bentley gave me while he cooked allowed me to zone out for a while. It wasn't some monumental picket fence fantasy of the two of us living in suburban, domestic harmony. Just a little hope during a really shitty time.

The distraction was nice, and now it was over. It was especially hard to hear myself referred to as a so-called hero when a woman died after having begged me to be hers today.

Had that really only happened today?

"Oh," I murmured. "I don't know, kid. I've been helping Ox and the FBI agents whenever something comes up. They might need me."

"Aw, come on." Grace's eyes still smiled as she puckered her lower lip. "Just for, like, ten minutes. You don't have to stay long or give a speech or anything. People just want to meet you. And you'd give me some bonus points with my teacher for next year. He's an ass face, but he was supervising lunch today, and he heard me talking about you, and he said he'd love to meet you. Oh, and Harry." She laughed. "The security guard. He said you'd remember him. Apparently he hasn't seen you since you were a kid, but he credits himself for how far you've made it in your career."

"Harry's still alive?" I asked. "He was ancient when we were your age."

"That's mean." Bentley passed Grace a napkin over the table. "And I don't know why you think that you can talk like an adult when Maddie is here, but the rules are still the same. No cussing 'til you're old enough to drive."

Waving him off with one hand, she wiped the spaghetti sauce from her cheek. "Please, Maddie? For first period, that's all we're doing. Just signing yearbooks. All you have to do is make an appearance. Say hi to Harry, sign a couple pieces of paper, then leave."

Accepting praise for my failure that night made no sense in my mind. The thought of it made me sick. But I loved Grace. All things considered, now was the time for me to make a good impression.

So I opened my mouth to say I'd stop for a few minutes, but Bentley shook his head. "No, she's not gonna do that."

"Since when do you tell Maddie what to do?"

"Since she looks like she's at death's door." He paused to chew his lasagna. "She's going through a lot right now. Two more women are dead, Grace. This is not your opportunity to ride Maddie's trauma to popularity. I raised you better than that."

Slowly, Grace's eyes softened. Her mouth opened and shut a few times, as if she wasn't sure what to say. "Shit. I'm sorry. I didn't mean to —I'm sorry. I don't know what I was thinking."

And that wasn't what I wanted. She was just a kid. She wasn't intending to exploit me for what happened that night. The prospect of more people liking her fell into her lap, and she thought it was cool.

So I smiled and shook my head. "It's okay. You don't need to apologize. Not to me, at least. Your dad just told you not to cuss and you said 'shit.'"

Cheeks turning red, she gave Bentley an awkward smile. "Sorry."

"Mhm." Although he glared, it was a playful glare.

I chimed in. "Subject change. Tomorrow's your last day, right?"

"Yeah," she said. "We're just doing games and stuff. My friend Olivia was complaining about why we even have a last day of school even though we don't do anything, but I think it's cool. If the weather's nice, we're gonna play a bunch of games outside. Then we get pizza for lunch. My old school didn't do that."

"It was always my favorite day of the school year," Bentley said. "The last day, and the day right before Christmas break."

"I don't know. Today was cool too. We finished our tests yesterday, so we just got to sit on our phones and talk a lot." Grace turned my way. "Did you find out anything important today? About the killer, I mean. Do the cops have any leads?"

Now it was me opening my mouth only for breath to come out. There was no way I could tell her what happened today. I hadn't even told Bentley. So I just shook my head.

"I thought you said you were *soo* busy." Another playful smile. "What did you do today, then?"

Again. I was at a loss. Where to begin? The part where I'd driven around to a bunch of drug dealers' houses? How about when I listened to an innocent woman beg me to save her, only to hear every stab The Country Killer slashed through her body when I didn't? Maybe when I'd snapped at an FBI agent and likely ruined any chance I had at ever getting a job there? Or how about the part where I'd threatened to kill this little girl's father?

"I told her about Daisy," Bentley said, casually taking another bite of lasagna, then sparing me a glance, as if to say, *Looked like a cat had your tongue.* "That's what she was busy with today."

I wasn't sure if that was a better alternative topic, but he left out the gun to his head part, so at least there was that.

Grace's eyes got big. "Did she call?"

With a frown, Bentley shook his head. "Sorry, kid. She didn't."

Grace's shoulders slumped. "Figured, I guess. But why were you guys talking about her? Did something come up in the investigation?"

Still frowning, Bentley shook his head again. "I wish. But no, the cops were just looking into everybody close to Maddie since the killer's been stalking her. They found that record from my arrest."

Grace's face screwed up in a combination of confusion and rage. "And what do they think? That because you beat up some woman-beater and drug dealer that you're a serial killer? How does that make sense? And that was private property. Maddie says that on private property, you have the right to—"

"They were just checking on everybody who's close to her." Laughing, he held up a hand for her to stop. "All her friends and neighbors. Then Maddie had questions, so I told her. That's all. Nobody thinks I'm the killer." Turning my way, he gave a half smile. "Right, Maddie?"

I resisted the urge to narrow my eyes. But I saw why he brought it up like this. Discussing this when she had only just gotten home, and he hadn't been on his phone long enough to text her, was his way of proving that he was telling the truth about his relationship with Daisy. Closest thing to proof he could give me, anyway. "Right."

"Good," Grace grumbled, stabbing her last bite of lasagna. "Because that doesn't even make any sense. The killer likes women. All you did was punch a bad dude. Probably more than you needed to, but still."

Her annoyance at the prospect was, in fact, the proof I needed. I had already believed him, but if I knew one thing with absolute certainty, it was that Bentley wouldn't manipulate his kid into telling me an elaborate lie. Doubted he could convince Grace to cover up all the conspiracies I had concocted, anyway. The kid may have killed him herself if she thought he was responsible for any of it.

"I think you're rubbing off on her," Bentley said.

"Looks like it," I said.

"I never talked to you about Daisy either, have I?" Grace asked me.

Ironic that she mentioned it, because I was going to ask why she hadn't. Not because she owed me every inch of her life story. Purely because of her reaction when Bentley mentioned her. Did she still think she was alive? "No, I don't think you did."

"It's kinda hard to talk about," she said after a moment. "I don't really remember my mom that much, but Daisy was my best friend. It's different, ya know?"

Talking about my mom wasn't all that hard. The same went for my dad, if he was dead. But talking about Bear? The moment he popped into my head, I had to reach down and pet Tempest below me just to soothe the ache in my stomach. "Yeah, I get it. That's gotta be hard. I'm really sorry."

Grace shrugged again, sliding her fork through the smeared sauce on her plate. "It's okay. I know it's stupid, but I just hope that she decided she was sick of us." The sound she let out was barely enough to call a laugh. "Sometimes she would do that. Just disappear for a few months. But I know what she was doing, and... I don't know."

I knew she hoped Daisy wasn't dead, but she suspected it.

I did too when I found that missing person file. Daisy fit a type, the kind who vanished forever. Maybe I could look into it, though. Once everything settled down, once we either caught the killer or he went back into hiding, I could request the case file. Ox might be able to pull some strings.

"You would've liked her." Grace's smile was still sad, but it was a bit more genuine. "She would have liked you too. Maybe you guys would have been friends."

If I'd still had any doubts, they were gone now. Looking into that little girl's eyes was every bit of proof I needed. Biologically, Daisy may have been her aunt, but in Grace's mind, she was her sister. It was the same expression every sibling made when I told them their counterpart was dead. Unimaginable grief. I had already told myself that I believed Bentley, but that look Grace gave me was all the proof I could've ever needed.

"Maybe." I forced the same sad smile. "If she was your friend, anyway. Any friend of yours is a friend of mine."

Another faint laugh, followed by her eyes dropping to the tabletop. The air was suddenly thick, and I felt awful. This kid was supposed to be celebrating her last few days of school, only for her worst experiences to be dredged up over dinner.

"I'm in the mood for cookies." Grace stood, pasting on a fake smile. "Anybody else?"

"I never turn down cookies." I gave her a smile in return. "Scratch? Or the old-fashioned in a tub?"

Grace's laugh was more genuine than her smile had been. "I think I used up the last of the flour last night."

"Are there any left?" I asked.

"There are not." With flushed cheeks, Bentley scratched his head. "I'm a stress eater. Don't judge me."

"Lucky for you, I always keep a stash of cookie dough in the freezer." Patting my hip for Tempy to join me, I nodded toward my house. "Wanna go make some at my place?"

Chapter 35

THE HUMID SUMMER WIND DRIFTED OVER OX'S SKIN AS HE climbed the stairs to Maddie's trailer. Light still shined inside, but that suggested little. For many, that would mean they were awake. Not Maddie. He and Maddie used to argue about the fact that she would stay up later than him and leave the lights on all night when she fell asleep. She used to say, "I just have to finish this episode." Then he would get up to use the restroom at 3 AM, the bed would be cold and untouched beside him, and Maddie would be passed out on the couch with the sofa pillow under her head.

Deep down, he found it endearing. She looked cute bundled up in that tiny throw blanket. Small. Vulnerable. It was a rare occurrence for Ox to witness Maddie like that, even back then, but he treasured the glimpses he got.

This time was different. She still looked that way when he opened the door, small and vulnerable with a tiny throw blanket, but it wasn't a sofa pillow under her head. It was Bentley's thigh. His fingers were in her hair, gingerly stroking it away from her face.

On the floor at his feet, Grace lay with a throw blanket as well. Her pillow, Tempest, opened her eyes and yawned at the sight of Ox. She wagged her tail a bit, then glanced at Grace. Almost as if she was saying, *I'd come say hi, but look how cute she is.*

Ox had thought that a moment like this would make him feel nauseous. Maybe even that it would hurt. But it didn't. In a way, he would treasure this glimpse just as he had treasured all those other vulnerable moments.

For a moment, it was like he was living in the dream that had always floated through Maddie's psyche. A kind, soft partner who merged with her headstrong nature. A kids' movie playing on the TV while she cuddled up beside him. A big, fluffy dog used as a pillow for the child. The traditional family that Maddie always wanted, and Ox had never been willing to give her.

"I didn't want to leave her home alone, you know?" Bentley said. "I didn't want to wake her up either. I don't know when the last time she slept was, but she didn't look good. Then Grace passed out, so we just stayed."

Giving a tightlipped smile, the closest Ox could get to a genuine one, he said, "Sure. You know what time she fell asleep?"

Carefully lifting Maddie's head off his lap and onto the sofa, tiptoeing around the child on the floor, Bentley struggled to his feet. Stifling a yawn, he stretched his arms overhead. "Around eight? Maybe nine?"

Ox glanced at the clock reading 2:46 AM and gave a nod. Somewhere between five and seven hours then. Almost enough to count as a full night's rest. "That's good. She needed it."

With a dry smile, Bentley dipped his head. "Probably best we head out. Grace's got school in the morning."

Ox returned the curt nod. Seemed to be the best communication skill these two had available. But he wanted to say more. Ox was no good at talking. Never, not about anything aside from cases. But he wanted to say it because he knew if he didn't, if he didn't build some type of rapport, he could lose her indefinitely.

As Bentley bent over to pick up his daughter, Ox blurted, "Don't ruin it."

Puzzled, Bentley straightened. "Huh?"

"With her." Ox glanced at Maddie. "She's in love with you. Even if she doesn't say it, she's in love with you. And you're in love with her. So don't ruin it." Bentley made a face at that, like he was trying to decipher if Ox was threatening him. He wasn't. "I'm not saying you will. People screw up, though. We make mistakes that change the course of our lives. Sometimes for better, sometimes for worse, and sometimes you can't tell which until years later. I did that. I hurt her, and it rewrote the life we had planned.

"And that's what Maddie does. The moment she decides loving you hurts more than leaving you, she leaves. That's what I loved about her. She stands up for herself. She doesn't forgive easily. That's how she protects herself. So don't ruin it, because I think you're what she's always wanted. And if you hurt her too, I don't know what it'll do to her."

For a few too many cricket chirps outside the window, Bentley and Ox only stared at one another. It wasn't an intense moment of masculine posturing. It was one of understanding. Maybe even bonding. Ox wasn't sure. Like he struggled with relationships, he also struggled with friendships. He'd had a few over the years, but they'd hated the same things about Ox that Maddie had. He was just no good at understanding how people felt and how to tiptoe around their emotions.

Eventually, Bentley broke the silence with, "Loved?"

"What?"

"You said that was something you loved about her. Does that mean you don't love her anymore?"

Love. Loved. Those words rolled so effortlessly, so softly, off Bentley's tongue. Ox envied that. How casual love was for him. For Ox, when he loved, it was all-consuming. Distracting. Painful, at times. The people he loved became so deeply embedded in him that without it, he felt like a car running with low motor oil. Nothing moved quite right once it was gone. For that reason, he was very careful with who he gave it to and who he took it from.

The gears had shifted more fluidly in recent months. Since his and

Maddie's relationship had mended. Since they could be friends. It was that connection, regardless of whether it was romantic, that he had been missing. Aside from his mother, Maddie was the only person he had that deep love for. Now that they were on better terms, he was functioning smoothly again.

"There isn't anything left for us." Ox kept his gaze on Bentley's, but he looked at Maddie out of the corner of his eye. Saying this hurt, but not like it had when she was out of his life completely. "She made up her mind. I don't think I'll ever stop loving her, but it's different now. It isn't the same type of love. It's familiar. It's safe. I don't want to never see her again, but I'm not in love with her anymore."

Again, they only stared at one another for a while. Bentley's eyes were soft again, like they'd been when he was stroking Maddie's hair. Like he was understanding. Or at least, Ox hoped he was.

This wasn't a threat. It wasn't Ox waving a red flag in front of a bull. It was a man assuring another man that he was done. Ox would not try to take Maddie out from under Bentley. He had loved her, enough to let her go. He loved her enough to let her have the love she had always wanted. Even if it wasn't from him.

It was also a proposition. It may not have sounded like one, but it was. It was Ox saying, *Please don't take her away from me.*

For Ox, it was enough to plead with a straight face and a flat tone.

"I'm sure she doesn't want to go the rest of her life without seeing you either," Bentley said eventually.

Ox's chest felt lighter. Was this bonding? It felt like bonding.

Ox knew that was the defining difference between Bentley and himself. That was why he was better for her. Maddie's and Ox's personality types were too similar. She was better with the emotions than he was, but they were both headstrong. Maddie needed someone sweeter, like how lemons tasted better with sugar than more lemons.

"I won't ruin it, man," Bentley said. "I won't hurt her."

Maybe it *was* bonding. The 'man' at the end of the sentence suggested as much. Ox had never been one for terms of endearment, but he knew people used them as just that. Endearment. Maybe the two of them could be more than civil. Maybe they could be something akin to friends. "Good. She deserves that."

Bentley's smile was still forced, but his posture was softer than it had been when he first stood. He nodded to Maddie. "You want me to take her to her room?"

"I'll wake her up after I get a shower. She's gonna want to know what I learned today."

"And I'm sure she'll be pissed if you make her wait till morning." Another smile, this one a bit more genuine. Like this was something they could bond over. Their mutual understanding of the creature they called Maddie.

Ox was able to give a smile as well, hoping this one didn't look as constipated as the ones he was known for.

"Really should get her to bed, though," Bentley said with a gesture to Grace. "Have a good night, man."

"You too."

Chapter 36

Cool water dripped onto my forehead as a hand shook my shoulder.

I grasped for my slumber, only to find Ox's eyes on mine.

Wasn't sure what I expected to see, but the last time I'd woken up I'd found out a serial killer had been in my house. My reaction was valid.

Per usual, his face was flat. As my shock dwindled, he held out a steaming mug. "I sent your boyfriend home."

Out of habit, I almost said he wasn't my boyfriend. But maybe he was now? We hadn't gotten to have that conversation. The three of us had made cookies together, turned on a movie, and I was out cold before the opening credits ended.

Sitting up, I accepted the tea and took a sip. Chamomile with honey. I was never much of a tea drinker, but Ox's mom had made me some the first time I'd met her. I liked it. Ox bought a bunch, then made me tea anytime I was stressed, or when he was going to tell me something that would stress me out even more.

"I like him for you." Ox sat on the cushion beside mine. "I'm sorry I made you paranoid about him."

Still half asleep, I rubbed my eyes. "I'm sorry, am I dreaming? You literally just accused him of murder."

"I was suspicious of him altogether. But I did speak with that arresting officer today, and I think that my opinions might've been rooted in some jealousy. He's likable. I'm not, and that pisses me off." He sipped his own tea. "Bentley seems like a good guy. And Alex likes him. Alex doesn't like most people. Tempest likes him, and I trust her opinion too. And yours, I guess."

Was that a joke? It may have been intended as one, but there was only the faintest rise at the corner of his lips to suggest so.

"Thanks?"

"Plus, he couldn't have been the killer. He didn't leave the house last night." Ah, yes. Should have known that it had less to do with judging character and more to do with hard facts. "I'm guessing you talked to him about the arrest."

I frowned. "I wasn't going to, but I heard back from the arresting officer too, and I started doing research. I just had to know his side of the story." I shifted in my seat to sit up straighter. "That reminds me, actually. Would you be able to get me some files about a missing person?" I briefly explained the situation with Daisy, leaving out the illegal acts Bentley had committed. "It's harder to access information like that than it used to be."

"You don't think he's connected to it, do you?"

"I don't. She was like his kid." Raising a shoulder, I gulped up the last bit of my tea. "I know you don't like gut feelings, but I just can't see it."

"I don't think he's involved with it either. But situations like that, we know how they go most of the time. I can't even count how many missing persons we have in the city. Most of them are like her. You know there isn't usually much we can do."

I would say that sounded like compassion for Bentley, but it wasn't. He didn't agree with me over a gut feeling. He agreed with me over statistical evidence he'd seen time and again. Which was fair enough. "I know. They asked me if I could look into it, so I just want to help."

"When this calms down, I'll get you what I can." Putting his empty mug on the coffee table, Ox dug around in the pocket of his sweatpants. "So, you know how Red said something on that call about Bear's grave?" I nodded in answer. He swiped around on his phone, then turned it toward me. "I went by my place to grab a few things. On the drive back, I found this."

An image of the tree beside Bear's grave lit up the screen. Mounted just above the lowest branch was a camera. It was aimed at the backside of Ox's condo. "We already assumed he's been watching you too."

"Probably trying to get in my head." Ox shuttered the screen and stowed it back into his pocket. "Gayton and Martin stayed back to get info from it to send their tech analyst."

"Did it work?"

"Did what work?"

Softening my voice, I did the same with my eyes. "Did he get in your head?"

"Because he had a camera aimed at my house?" Ox snorted a laugh. "No. The fact that he's killing women who look like you, that's what's done the trick."

That was more heartwarming than he realized. "You don't think he did anything to Bear's grave, do you?"

He was quiet for a few heartbeats. "I don't spend that much time in the yard, but I would've noticed if he'd dug it up or anything. And that would seem out of character for him, wouldn't it? He doesn't seem all that interested in the bodies."

"Eh, debatable." I cracked my neck from one side to the other. "He does stage them. But you're probably right."

That seemed to soothe Ox's tense posture. "Anyway. You're not too tired, are you? Want me to bring you up to speed?"

Crossing my legs into a lotus position, I propped my elbows on my knees. "Throw it at me."

* * *

So, HE DID. HE TOLD ME EVERYTHING HE HAD GATHERED TODAY, ending with, "I really think he's met you at some point. He isn't just picking women who look like you. He's also picking women who act like you. And yeah, I guess he could've gathered that from stalking you. But it just seems deeper. The little mannerisms, the common life events, the way you look. I don't know."

"I guess it's possible. But it's not like I meet tons of new people regularly. I meet people through work, but it's not like I'm in customer service."

"When it all first happened, or when you moved in here, you didn't meet anyone who made you feel off?" I couldn't tell if Ox was concerned, or if this was the face he gave people he was questioning. "Maybe at that bar? Did you meet him there?"

"The only person I talked to at the bar was Carrie. I'm not exactly the social type. You know that."

"Maybe he was just following you then," Ox murmured. "I just can't see someone with his level of compulsions stalking his victim for this long without ever having interacted with you. He couldn't sit and watch you from anywhere outside. You're surrounded by other trailers. None of the neighbors fit his description."

"None of my neighbors fit the profile either," I said. "They're all people who have been here my entire life. It's not like they're rich people who moved into the trailer park to get closer to me."

"Not like you were in the best state of mind to be paying attention to people who were around you when you first moved in here either," Ox said.

While that could have been interpreted as a jab, it was the truth. I'd been high all the time. I'd kept my gun on me. Looked over my shoulder in parking lots. Paid attention to anyone paying too much attention to me, or other women who were out on their own, just as most women moving through the world did. But if the same guy had been at the bar I'd gone to on Monday, and then the restaurant on Friday, I wasn't sure that I would've noticed.

"What about the name Moirah?" Ox asked. "Does that ring any bells?"

I chewed my bottom lip as I thought for a moment. "Not that I can think of. None of the victims were named Moirah, were they?"

Shaking his head, Ox's gaze focused on the tabletop. "No. I even checked all their immediate families. There was a Marissa, but no Moirah. Maybe that's not the right word though. Abigail said that it sounded like Moirah or Mayrah? She didn't even know what it meant. Just a word that sticks out in her mind from that night."

That made sense. When under the influence, there was no way to ascertain what did and didn't stick, nor why it stuck. It could have been as simple as a phrase somebody else had said. She may have read it on a sign somewhere. Hell, it could've been the company logo on someone's shirt.

It could've been a company logo.

"Could mean nothing, but—"

"Hang on." Scanning the couch around me for my phone, I found it under the throw pillow. Onto Google I went, and I typed. "Start saying words that sound like that. Just give me different combinations with those same sounds."

"What are you doing?"

Into the search engine, I typed, *Moirah Technology.* "It's a long shot, but we'll see. Just give me words."

"Uh, Mara?"

No cigar. But I kept trying with a thousand combinations.

Moirah Technologies. Madara Technologies. Marmara Technologies

When none of those brought me anything valuable, I searched for words that rhymed with Moirah. Kara. Lara. Chiara. Cantara. Delara. Again, came back with nothing.

"Maybe we're looking at this wrong," Ox said. "What if she didn't hear it? What if she saw it? What if that's why she doesn't know how to pronounce it?"

Snapping in his direction, I wagged my pointer finger. "I like the way you think."

With a pen and paper from the table, each of us spelled out the word Moirah and Mayrah. We figured two sets of handwriting might make for a better comparison. Below the words, we wrote out letters that were similar. This trick had worked for me before.

Letters that looked similar to M in certain styles, at least in the mind of someone who was stoned out of her mind, were capital N, V, lowercase R, and an upside down W. By the time we'd gone through both sets of word, our key looked something like:

MOIRAH

M—N, V, r, upside down W

O—e, a, c, C.

I—l, j

R—v, n, P.I.

A—o, e, c, C

Y—L, K, k, t

Then we started stacking them together into syllables that resembled words.

Melnach. Melrach. A thousand others, until they all looked like a foreign language spread out across the page.

Then Ox said, "Weirah. Almost sounds like a name, doesn't it?"

My brain tinged.

"O'Merah?" I murmured, thinking hard for the vague memory.

"What?" Ox asked.

Waving him off, I resumed typing. Switching things up this time, knowing that search engines worked in a variety of ways, I started with *Somerset County PA Technology* and followed with, *O'M—*

And there it was. Suggested search number one.

Taking in a quiet gasp, I turned my phone toward Ox, reiterating the words aloud. "O'Meinah Cyber Security."

His eyes widened. "You know them?"

"One of my first cases as a P.I. An employee there, Kathy something, hired me to look into her daughter's boyfriend. It was a simple case, just gathered enough information to prove the kid was a punk. When I asked where she'd heard of me, she said in the paper. The local one wrote an article on me when I tried to buy ad space. But in business, we have something called the seven touches rule. You don't purchase something until you've seen it talked about or advertised seven times. What if one of her coworkers mentioned me each time she talked about her daughter's punk boyfriend? What if he left my business card laying around somewhere for her eyes to graze over?"

"Did you meet her there? At her work?"

I shook my head. "Not inside her building, but several times in the same parking lot at a food truck. Easily could've watched us through the windows."

Joy shining in his eyes, Ox dialed Gayton's number. "A link's a link. Let's see if the judge'll give us a warrant."

A lead? A *real* lead after almost two years with absolutely nothing? I'd never been so excited in my life.

Chapter 37

GETTING A WARRANT WAS HARDER THAN EXPECTED. THERE WAS reasonable suspicion, but suspicion was circumstantial. Abigail's testimony was enough for us to look in O'Meinah's direction, but for a warrant, we needed evidence that was credible, reliable, and had a probability of proving a crime. A drugged woman's testimony of the vague memory of a word was not exactly credible or reliable. Especially considering she was an addict.

Overnight warrants were especially hard to get. No judge enjoyed being awoken at 4 AM. Especially not for a case like this, where there just wasn't much. Signing a warrant for the business's records didn't guarantee that it would save any lives. Which certainly didn't help.

While Ox argued with the judge, I got to work. O'Meinah Cyber Security. Who owned it? Luckily, not a hedge fund manager or corporate CEO. It was a small business, run by an everyday Joe. Literally. Joe O'Meinah. Joe, who had an American flag in his banner on social media. The kind of guy who liked cops, from what I could tell.

With a bit more digging, I found his home address. It was pushing 4:30 then, and he lived about thirty minutes from me. Having accepted his defeat, knowing that I was always the smooth talker in our partnership, Ox got off the phone with the judge, and we drove.

Only took us about twenty minutes to get there with Ox's driving. Surprisingly, without killing us both.

It was a nice house in one of those neighborhoods that wasn't too far from civilization, but also wasn't a mass commercial development. It was a luxury home, if that was what they called them.

Either way, I practiced batting my eyelashes a few times before approaching the door. It took somewhere near ten minutes for Joe to answer, stomping all the way. It looked like he was about to say something to the effect of, "This is private property," before Ox waved his badge.

The tone changed rapidly. Still in his bathrobe, tugging it shut, Joe said, "Oh, I didn't realize. Is there something I can help you with?"

"We think so." Reaching into my bag for the police sketch, I gave him a smile. "We're investigating The Country Killer. We have reason to believe that this man might be involved somehow. You don't happen to recognize him, do you?"

Rather than looking at the image, Joe squinted at me for a few heartbeats. "Wait, you're that cop who got injured shooting him, aren't you?"

"Yes, sir. I am. Which is why I'm knocking on your door before the sun's up. There's nothing I want more than to catch this guy."

"Sure, sure. Thank you for your service," he murmured, finally turning his attention to the paper in my hand. "This sketch, does it look like anyone I know?"

"We're thinking he may be one of your employees," Ox said. "We're not certain, but there is a connection."

Cocking his head to the side, Joe nodded. "Maybe. Maybe, yeah. Kinda looks like Eric Oakley, but with a beard. But he's not one of my employees. Not anymore."

A name? Did we really, *finally*, have a name?

"Was he fired?" Ox asked.

"No, he never gave me any problems, really," Joe said. "He was my lead programmer for years. I didn't see him much. Back before the pandemic and all, when we were all still in the office, that's where he

231

was all the time. In his office. Even ate his lunch is in there. He was friendly when he came out for coffee and to use the restroom, fun once you got talking to him. Just always kind of a lone wolf."

Friendly when he had to be, but a recluse as much as possible. Fit the profile. "When was the last time you spoke to him?"

"Whew, let me think. We switched him to work from home in 2020, and I didn't see him for—well, geez—a year and a half? Last time we spoke was when he gave his two weeks. I think his folks weren't doing great. But you know what, my wife never liked him. At work parties and whatnot, she said that she didn't like how he looked at her and my daughters. They're off to school now, but anyhow." Joe yawned. "You really think he's the killer?"

"We've just found some connections," Ox said. "We're not making any accusations. We'd appreciate if you kept this between us until we know more."

"Sure," Joe murmured, bulky shoulders slumping with something between shock and disbelief. "Wait, you don't think he used my technology to learn about these women, do you?"

"No, we don't," I answered before Ox could. "None of his victims had security systems."

Almost like he intentionally avoided them. Which was logical. Had he used his knowledge of computers to spy on or break into those women's homes, it would've been far easier for us to tie his career to his identity.

Before this recent spree, he was smart enough to conduct his violence below the radar. Because those had been senseless killings. Murder purely for the sake of murder. Now, it was emotionally motivated. Revenge against me.

Really, none of this mattered anymore. I could debate and dissect the psychology of a serial killer until my brain was in knots. I didn't need to care about his thought pattern at the moment.

"You know where he lives?" Ox asked.

"I can run into my home office and dig through my records for you real quick." Joe nodded inside. "I can put a pot of coffee on if you'd like."

Passing him a business card, I gave a smile. "That's alright. If you think of anything else, give us a call."

"Sure thing. You take care."

Turning away, ready to return to Tempest in the car and start up my search engine, Ox said, "This is the most we've ever had."

I couldn't pull down my smile. Not only was it exciting to solve the case, but because we could finally end this. My home, my town and neighboring ones—we could feel safe here again. We could find justice for all the innocent women he'd killed. I wished it had happened sooner enough for Josey, for Amber, and for all the others, but at least we could stop anyone else from joining the list.

"I think this is it," I said. "This was the missing piece. I've got a feeling, Ox. You know my gut. It's usually not wrong."

It was hard to believe, but his smile was as big as mine. "It's usually not."

"Detective. Ms. Castle," Joe called from the porch. When we turned to face him, his eyes were wide. "Anytime I hire somebody, I fingerprint them for the background checks. I hold on to those records too, in paper. Could that help you in any way?"

Heart fluttering, a laugh escaped me. "You still have his?"

"Under lock and key in the safe." He pointed off into the distance. "Not here though. At the company, I mean."

"Do you have time to take us there now?" Ox asked.

"If you need me to," Joe said.

"Yes, sir. We need you to." The adrenaline coursing through me numbed any of those early morning pains in my knee as I jogged to Ox's car. "The sooner the better."

Joe said something else, but it was indistinguishable. I was already climbing into the passenger seat, and Ox was already turning the engine over. Still in his bathrobe and slippers, Joe jogged from the house as well.

"If they match the fingerprint from Rachel's attack," Ox said, smile stretching wider, "we've got him."

Laughing, I nodded. "We've got him. I know we do."

I wasn't sure if the two of us had ever smiled at one another with such joy. I almost wanted to reach over and hug him, maybe kiss him, just to celebrate. It was surreal. If this was right, if Eric Oakley was the killer, the worst part of mine, Ox's, Rachel's, and everyone else who he'd harmed was finally coming to a resolution.

Then my phone rang.

Simeon Gunn lit up the screen.

Chapter 38

"This is on you, Maddie," Simeon snapped, just after I said hello. "I blame you for this one hundred percent. If you hadn't come around asking questions, putting your nose in—"

"What's on me?" It shocked me that my voice didn't come out confrontational. Usually, it would. I never appreciated when anybody used the tone Simeon was using. But if my questioning him or his guys had resulted in someone getting hurt... That *was* on me. "What happened?"

"Noah's in the hospital." As hard as it may have been to believe about a drug dealer, there wasn't only anger in Simeon's voice, but fear. Worry for his friend. "Somebody broke into his house at, like, three AM and shot him, dude. Who the hell do you think that was?"

"Oh my God," was all I could manage.

"You know Noah. He's one of the coolest guys I've employed." Simeon's voice wasn't quite a yell, but it was raised enough. "Nobody has any beef with him. Everybody who buys off Noah loves Noah. And his stash was still there. So this wasn't a robbery. Noah is pretty sure he saw him too. It was that son of a bitch serial killer, and I swear to God, if I get my hands on him—"

"Noah saw him?" The heavy, tight feeling in my chest lightened. "He's okay?"

"Is lying in a hospital bed okay, Maddie?"

Of course not but injured was better than dead. I knew that plenty. "Is he alive?"

"He wouldn't have been," Simeon said, deep breath escaping him. "If he would've been asleep, he would be dead. But I guess he was in the bathroom when the guy came in. He came running out with a baseball bat, the guy fired, but Noah got a hit in. He hit him hard enough to make him drop his gun. And don't ask about the serial number because I already checked. It's filed off. The guy ran, but that's not the point. The point is that you questioned him about this shit, and then the guy tried to murder him, Maddie."

I didn't mean to, but I responded in the same tone. "And what the hell do you think I can do about that, Simeon? I'm sorry that happened to Noah, but I didn't do this. Drug dealers mess with shady people. Getting shot is a possible job hazard. Unlike the innocent women whose homes he's been breaking into and torturing and raping and killing just for the hell of it. Unlike you, I'm actually trying to stop the bastard. So, what? Am I on your hit list now? Are we sworn enemies?"

Through the speaker, I heard him growl his annoyance. "Tell me you're close to finding him. Tell me right now, or I'll find a way to learn everything you know and take care of him myself."

"We're close to finding him," I said.

"If you don't find him within a week, you better tell me everything you know."

There was no reason to threaten me. I would tell him everything I knew regardless. No one would want to be on the bad side of someone like Simeon Gunn. Including The Country Killer.

Clearly, he wasn't afraid of innocent old ladies in their homes, or young women who lived alone, or teenage girls still living with their parents, home alone for the weekend. Maybe he would be afraid of the most powerful man on this side of the state. That was usually how it worked for men like him. Women? No match. Big, scary men? I had no doubt he'd go back into hiding.

"Deal," I said. I expected him to hang up, but he stayed on the phone a few heartbeats longer. Like a silent way of apologizing for his attitude.

When the silence continued, only the sound of Ox talking in the driver's seat to Gayton filling the space, I asked, "Where'd Noah get hit?"

"His thigh," Simeon said. "I guess it was really close to hitting his femoral artery."

"It didn't though?"

"It didn't." Another deep breath. "They think he's gonna make a full recovery. But that doesn't mean that this was okay."

"Of course not." Still, my voice was soft. "I really am sorry. I wouldn't have gotten him involved if I knew it would come to this."

"Doubt he'll hold it against you," Simeon grumbled. "Did it help at least? Whatever intel he gave you?"

"It did. We're pretty sure we know who he is now," I said. "It's just a matter of proving it and getting a warrant for his arrest. I would tell you who we think he is, but I don't think you want to be there when it goes down."

Another growling noise in his throat. "Probably not. But that'll make Noah smile. Getting to be the hero."

"It's not all it's cracked up to be."

"Eh. The kid could use the ego boost."

I chuckled. Simeon did too. When silence returned, I said, "But we're good?"

"We're good. But if you have a chance to kill him instead of put him in cuffs, please do."

"Trust me, I'm praying he gives me a reason."

One more chuckle. "Let me know if it goes south. I'm gonna get back to Noah. Don't let him take out your other knee too."

With an eye roll, I said something universally unappreciated before ending the call.

Simultaneously, Ox ended his. "Who got shot?"

"My informant. He's okay though. But now our guy has a baseball bat wound somewhere on his head."

Ox's face screwed up in confusion. "What?"

"He tried to kill Noah last night. Probably because he identified him, and he somehow knew we were getting close. Maybe he tapped into the phones Gayton gave us? Maybe he knew we found Joe O'Meinah?"

"You got Carrie's number?"

I was already dialing. "Probably not a bad idea to send someone over to her."

Eyes flicking between the road and his phone, Ox clicked away. "They got me some info on him while we were on the phone. You're never going to guess what Eric Oakley does for a living now."

"Hello?" Carrie answered.

Holding up a pointer finger in Ox's direction, I said, "Thank God. This is Maddie Castle. I was just checking to make sure you're alive."

Laughing, Carrie said, "Why the hell wouldn't I be?"

I briefly explained, shaking my head with worry. "You got your gun on you, right? Just in case?"

"Always do," Carrie said. "But I'll lock myself in the back room for now just to be safe. You tell the cops that I won't open the door until they do their little *whoop-whoop*."

It was nice to smile. "I'll pass it along. You just stay safe."

"You too, kid."

By the time I had the phone back in my lap, we were pulling into the shopping center parking lot where O'Meinah Cyber Security was located. Ox was still on the phone, with Derek. Unbuckling his seatbelt, he motioned that he was going inside.

"Go ahead," I said in a hushed tone. "I'll do some digging."

Once he was out of the car, he clicked the lock twice to activate the alarm. And I started searching.

Who was Eric Oakley?

From what I could tell, exactly what the profile said he would be.

White male. Attractive. Intelligent. So intelligent they had believed he didn't work in the service field, and they had been correct.

Regardless, he'd graduated top of his class from Carnegie Mellon University, the fourth top college in the country for computer engineering. He was older than me, but not by much. Late thirties to early forties, judging by his profile pictures on social media. Which there were a lot of. Most men in his age range—most men, period—had no more than twenty selfies on their social medias from the last decade. Eric Oakley had a hundred and fifty. Not surprising for a narcissist.

In some holiday pictures, his mother Kendra Oakley had tagged him. Like I had scrutinized that image of Grace, Bentley, and Daisy for hours, I studied this one the same way. Most family holiday photos featured a dozen or so people. Not this one. Only Eric, Kendra, and Robert, who I assumed was his father. Robert didn't smile for the photo. Looked like he was only allowing it to be taken because he had to. Also an attractive man, but very astute. Even at Christmas dinner, he was in a suit. It wasn't much different for Kendra. A pretty woman, with gray hair, wearing a gown that would've fit in at a gala.

The odd thing was, looking at Eric and Kendra side-by-side, one might assume that they were the couple. After all, they were both smiling ear to ear. Rather than resting a hand on her husband's chest, Kendra rested her manicured fingers on Eric's. An arm around the waist wasn't all that peculiar, but Eric's hand looped around his mother and clutched her hip.

I didn't know if there was a story there, or what the story was, and I wasn't sure that I cared. Even if his mother had sexually abused him, he'd still made the choice to rape and murder innocent women. Contrary to the popular phrase, hurt people did not always hurt people.

What did pique my interest, however, were her other photos. Photos of her as a young woman.

Dark hair. Light skin. Petite.

Until his infatuation with me, Eric's type.

The deeper I dove into Kendra's profile, the more I found. Her account was set to public. A rare occurrence, one most people didn't dream of, but it made me wonder if Eric's narcissism was inherited. So did her frequent posts. Many of which mentioned her son.

I had a wonderful Sunday dinner with my boys in the city! Wish Violet Lewis were here!

Who was Violet? I didn't know, and I was about to find out. Kendra had tagged her in the post. Naturally, I clicked on over to Violet's profile.

She was the spitting image of Kendra. Dark hair, dark eyes, light skin, petite body. The same small nose, the same thick lips, even the same smile. She had two kids, lived a few towns over, worked as a counselor with child services, and graduated from Penn State the year I'd graduated high school. That was relevant because in the photo from her graduation, Kendra and Robert were present and smiling, but Eric wasn't there. He wasn't on her page whatsoever.

Violet's social media was not a shrine to herself the same way that Kendra's was. One of her profile pictures was Violet, her husband, and their newborn, while Violet was still sweating from giving birth. None of her posts were public aside from her profile pictures, which was the standard-setting on most social medias.

Since they were at her graduation, it stood to reason they were her parents. They weren't listed as such, which made me wonder why Eric had not been present at her college graduation. Also, why had she moved away and taken a low-paying job in public welfare when the rest of her family was upper-middle class?

When the FBI had given the profile, they said that women who were close to Eric would have horror stories to tell about him. But those stories would've never resulted in charges, because one of his parents was also a narcissist who would've never let those stories get out into the world.

Had Eric done something awful to his little sister? Was that why she'd moved away? Was that why she wasn't present at holiday or Sunday night dinners?

Her trauma, I cared about. She didn't owe me her story, but if she'd endured trauma at the hands of her brother, she'd be a telltale example of how not every hurt person went on to hurt others.

Also because, if Eric was The Country Killer, and we had to fight to prove it in court, information like that could be valuable. I always hated when things got messy in front of a jury. If it got to a point where we arrested Eric, and he convinced the jury there was some other reason his fingerprints were found at Rachel's apartment, the case could fall apart. Even I would have to get up on the stand and testify against him with my sob story. Mine might be valuable to the jury, but the story of a young woman assaulted by her big brother? They'd eat that shit up. Might even give him the death penalty.

After flicking back to Kendra's profile to do more research, it was no surprise when I learned of her death. June 2020. Only a few months before the murders began. Suggesting that her death was the trigger that started Eric's rampage.

That was the funny thing about profiling. It always made sense after catching the guy. But when they were smart like The Country Killer, when they covered all their tracks, it was a thousand times harder to put them away.

Interrupting my search into Robert Oakley, Grace's photo lit up my screen. The clock read 7:15 AM, reminding me that she was at school. Likely calling to plead one more time that I would come in and sign yearbooks. I was glad I had a good excuse to decline this time around.

"Hey, kiddo," I said. "I know you really wanted me to come in the school today, but—"

"I need your help." She sniffled, and my heart dropped through my torso. "Please just do what he—"

Chapter 39

GRACE SCREAMED.

She screamed so loud that Tempest jumped up from the backseat. Chills crept over every inch of my arms, stretching down my spine. Lifting a hand over my mouth, hearing that scream turn to an indistinguishable sob, I swore I heard Josey for a moment.

"What about this one? You gonna let her die too?"

My first thought should've been, *Start recording.* Or maybe, *Call Gayton.*

It wasn't. My first thought was to word vomit, "If you touch her—"

"Neither of us have time for this, Maddie," he said. "Are we going to talk? Or would you rather I kill her now? Because if that's what you—"

Grace screamed. She screamed just like Josey had screamed. And again, it was thoughtless.

"Don't hurt her!" I said. Grace's scream morphed into a muffled sob. "I'll do whatever you want. Just don't hurt her."

"That a girl," he said, and Grace's sob faded. Like he was moving away from her. "So this was all I had to do, huh? Threaten your little surrogate kid?"

He said it like he was disappointed. Like he wanted me to break

242

sooner. He didn't. He wanted to psychologically torture me for days. Mine and everyone else's turmoil fueled him.

But the son of a bitch wanted me to think that if I had done something differently, the harm he'd caused could have been avoided. Like if I had sought him out and immediately handed myself over to him, he wouldn't have attacked Rachel, he wouldn't have killed Amber or Josey, and Noah wouldn't be in the hospital. This was manipulation, as narcissists were known for.

"What. Do. You. Want?" I hardened my tone, knowing that the best chance Grace had was doing as he said, but also playing on his weaknesses. "Ox is going to be here any second. I don't have time for your villain monologue. *What do you want?*"

A faint laugh, and a long moment of silence. Birds chirped in the background. He was outside, or near an open window. I recognized the birds' song. It was a distinct call. I couldn't place where I knew it from, but I knew that I did.

Damn it, I didn't have my recorder, and Ox had just run off with his phone.

But I had that burner phone. Hurriedly as the silence stretched on, I clicked around, opened the voice memos, and pressed record.

"There's a phone in your closet," he said. "Bottom drawer of the plastic dresser. By the way, why didn't you get a real one? A reliable dresser, I mean. You worked that big job. You could afford it."

I didn't care about my God damn plastic dresser right now. But maybe keeping him on the phone for as long as possible was best. At least if he was on the phone with me, I knew he wasn't hurting Grace.

"Because my plastic dresser is fine," I said. "What's on the phone?"

"It's where I'll get in contact," he said. "This one's being monitored. Even if you delete a text I send you, they'll find it. We can't have that."

"And what will you contact with? Grace's location?"

He laughed again. "Doesn't your *profile* tell you how intelligent I am? You think that I'm just going to give her back to you?"

Grace was his collateral. In exchange for her, he would get me. "A girl can hope," I said under my breath. "How will we do the exchange, then? That's what you want, right? Me for Grace?"

"We'll figure out the details once you're on your way to me," he said.

"You're out of your damn mind if you think I'm going to walk into your arms without knowing Grace is safe. Let her go, and I'll—"

"You're in no place to be making demands, Madison. I don't bluff. I will kill her, just like I killed the others. She's a bit young for me, but for good measure and to make sure you received the message, I'll do the same to her that I've done to everyone else I've killed. You don't want that, do you?"

My stomach twisted and turned. I had to pull the phone away from my face to ease some calming breaths in and out.

All true. He did not bluff. This was not a game to him, not anymore. I was the mouse he'd been toying with all week, all year, and he was ready to put me out of my misery. But he would make it as painful as possible. Grace would be next.

I couldn't live with myself if Grace was next.

A stranger's death, an acquaintance's, I could deal with that blood on my hands. But I would rather die than have Grace's blood on my hands.

That wasn't to say that I would *just* lie down and die. I would fight to save us both. If it came down to one of us, though? Grace was the one who would walk out alive.

His voice sharpened. "Do you want that?"

"No. But no deal until I talk to her."

He snorted. "And yet, she continues to make demands—"

"You're a tech genius," I snapped, partially because it was true, and partially to stroke his ego. The best way to get what you wanted out of a narcissist was to stroke their ego. "If you were able to break into the national database for DNA, creating a very in-depth deepfake would be child's play to you. So let me talk to her."

But that wasn't the only reason I wanted to talk to Grace. She was a smart kid. She knew what I did for a living. She might pass along a clue. I didn't know if she would be in the mental state for it, but I could hope.

It wasn't just that either.

I was going to fight like hell to bring her home. If I couldn't, if something went wrong, I wanted Bentley to hear her voice one more time.

"You could ask nicely," he said.

"You could just *not* kill people, but here we are."

Chuckling, the sound of the birds faded. The swinging of a storm door rattled. "It amuses me how funny you think you are."

"It amuses me how you think you're such a badass for raping and murdering innocent women."

"Yes, well, I doubt the dog thinks very highly of the vet who euthanizes them either."

Like veterinarians helping dogs cross the rainbow bridge was remotely comparable to what he did. "Just put Grace on the damn phone."

"You're on speaker. Go on."

"Maddie?" Her voice shook. "You're gonna tell my dad I love him, right?"

"You're gonna tell him that yourself."

It almost sounded like she laughed. "I hope so. I really wanted to make it to eighth grade."

That made my heart skip. Just last night, Grace had made a remark about how she wasn't looking forward to next school year. *Was* this phone call a deepfake? Plenty of websites allowed any user to upload voice clips of another person and effectively clone it. Not long ago, I had heard about a scam where people used deepfakes to convince parents that their children had been kidnapped purely to coerce them into wiring the scammers a ransom.

"You will," I said. "I'm gonna get you out of there."

"Leave Tempest at home, okay?" she asked. "That way, if we die, at least Dad has her. You have that written in your will, right? If something happens to you, Dad gets Tempest?"

This wasn't a deepfake. I could confirm with Grace's school as soon as I got off this call, but the rest of this was a textbook conversation. The kind of conversation any middle schooler would have while kidnapped. But Eric *wanted* to kill Tempest. He wouldn't use Grace's voice to tell me to leave her at home.

"Yeah, you and your dad get Tempest if something happens to me," I said, seeing Ox step from O'Meinah Cyber Security. Waving quickly, I gestured for him to hurry. "But stop worrying about me. Are you okay? Are you hurt?"

"I think my wrist is sprained," she said. "This ass face grabbed me by it as soon as I walked—"

"You talked to her," he said, drowning out whatever she was about to say. "You have until noon to escape the henchmen and meet me." The driver side door swung open, and I lifted a finger over my lips at Ox. "If you don't, Grace is dead."

The call went out.

All the color drained from Ox's face.

Amazed my voice didn't crack, tears welling in my eyes, I said, "He has Bentley's daughter. He has her, and he's going to kill her if I don't give myself over to him."

Ox was already leaping into the car and dialing on his phone. "Teaching." He jammed the key into the ignition and turned the car over. "Middle school computer science. That's what Eric Oakley started doing after he quit O'Meinah Cyber Security."

Chapter 40

Ox was on the phone with Gayton, and I was fighting the urge to hyperventilate.

Did Bentley know? Would I have to tell him? Was he already at work? I thought he said he was working early today.

Her teacher. He was her God damned teacher. When she called him an ass face, when she referenced wanting to make it to the eighth grade, that was what she meant. He was the teacher who wanted so badly to meet me, the one she mentioned last night. The homeroom teacher whose class she didn't want to be in next year.

But this was good. In a manner of speaking, she proved who he was. As long as those fingerprints matched, we could get a warrant for his arrest.

Slamming the gas, Ox passed me his phone. "Look up that address. We at least have enough to question him—"

"Are you out of your mind? We can't go to his house. He'll kill her."

"Not if you and I can hold him up long enough to get a judge to sign off on the warrant," Ox said. "As long as we have him distracted at the door, she's safe. Then the second we get that warrant, which I know won't take long since we're dealing with a missing child, we can—"

"You don't understand." Grabbing my hair in fistfuls, I forced out a slow breath. "He didn't take her to his house. He wouldn't have. All his attacks have been on somebody else's turf. There's nothing this man cares about more than his reputation. He won't let it come out that he raped and murdered almost a dozen women, let alone that he kidnapped a preteen. There won't be evidence in his home. But you know what there will be? Cameras. Cameras that he's monitoring. Right now, he doesn't know that we know who he is. The moment he realizes we do, he's killing Grace. Her eyewitness testimony is going to prove who he is."

For a few heartbeats, I watched the wheels turn in Ox's brain. "So what? We don't search his house?"

"Not yet." Rubbing my forehead, I shut my eyes and tried to think. But my brain was a jumbled mess of words in a spiderweb. Grace couldn't end up like those other women had. She was a kid. She was *Bentley's* kid. I didn't want anyone to die, but I *could not* let her die. "Unless we figure out where he is."

"What?"

"We have until noon to figure out where he is. He's not gonna hurt Grace until then." I hoped. "If we can figure out where he's holding her before that, we get a warrant for that location, then I go in."

"You're not going *in* anywhere, Maddie."

"If it's my life or a child's, the child wins." I shot him the dirtiest look. "We find out where they are, and then I adhere to his demands. That's how we get Grace out, and then you guys storm the place."

"Like it or not, you're a civilian," Ox said. "No, Maddie, you're not gonna be anyone's bait."

That was rational. I wouldn't let anyone hand themselves over to a murderer either. But this was my problem to fix. Not Ox's. Ox was the detective who had investigated this case since it began. It had been his battle. When Eric had shot me, though, when I'd become the object of his fixation, this had become my war.

Ox wasn't going to listen to that. Rightfully. That meant I had to lie. I'd have to find some way to get away from him, just as Red said I would. Unless we could find where Grace was first.

"Then we need to pinpoint any location this man may have a connection to," I said. "The FBI tech, they need to search every record Eric's name has ever been on. We need to talk to his family. We need— No, we can't talk to his family. If we talk to his family, the family'll go back and tell him, and he'll kill Grace. But the sister. The sister doesn't talk to him. I think she went no contact with her entire family. That's who we have to talk to.

"Eric, he's a hunter. That's what the profile said. In the family photos, there were deer heads on the wall. And he came from an upper-middle class family. Lower-middle class hunters just go out to the woods with their guns, but upper-middle class have hunting cabins. I bet you money that's where they are. But there are so many forests around here, and they're huge. We need to zoom in. We need to talk to that sister. That's what we need to do. I bet I can find her number—"

"Maddie." Reaching over, Ox grabbed my shaking hand. "Maddie, you need to breathe. We're going to figure this out, but you need to breathe."

Normally, I might snap and tell him to worry about the case. *Don't worry about me. Do your damn job.*

But I was going to do this, with or without Ox's blessing. I wouldn't let Bentley lose another kid. I wasn't gonna let Grace's life end before it started.

I might die doing it. There was a very good chance that I wouldn't see the sun tomorrow. I didn't want Ox's last memories of me to be the two of us fighting.

"We're going to find her, Maddie." Ox's eyes were gentler than ever as he looked between me and the road. "I promise you, we are *going* to find her."

With a hard swallow and tears in my eyes, I gave a nod.

My phone rang.

Bentley's photo lit up the screen.

"He doesn't know?" Ox asked.

I struggled out, "I don't know."

"I'll handle it when we get back to your place."

This would be the hardest moment of Bentley's life. He deserved to hear it from someone he trusted. Someone who loved Grace too.

Shaking my head at Ox, I swiped the green bar. "Hey."

"Hey, do you know what's going on at the school?" His voice was worried, but not panicked. "I just got a text that they're in lockdown, but nothing on why. Does it have something to do with the killer? I guess it could be anything, but I figured I'd ask you first. Maybe you could ask Ox for me?"

So he'd taken her from school. Either someone witnessed Grace's abduction, or the bus driver confirmed Grace had been on the bus but hadn't made it to homeroom.

"That was us," Ox said, low enough that Bentley wouldn't hear. "When we found out that Eric might be the killer, we notified the school. They're lying to the teachers and saying it's about a bomb threat. He called off work today too."

Then how had he gotten Grace? Supposed the specifics didn't matter all that much. "Yeah, Ox knows what's going on. Are you home?"

"I was just about to leave for work." The worry hadn't gone anywhere, but fear tinged his voice now. "What's going on? Should I call off?"

A lump solidified in my throat. "You should call off."

"What's happening, Maddie?"

"I'll be home soon. We're only a few minutes away. I'll tell you everything when I get there."

"I need you to tell me now." His voice deepened, but not with aggression. He wasn't angry at me. He was scared. "Grace isn't answering her phone. She knows that if I call her, even if she's at school, she has to answer me. Did something happen? Is he on a spree or something?"

Swallowing, I searched for the words. None came.

"Did I lose you? Are you there?"

My voice cracked when I said, "I'm here."

"But you don't know what to say." Bentley's voice softened, like he was connecting the dots. "If it was nothing to worry about, you would tell me. But you want to tell me in person. That means it's bad."

"Everything's gonna be okay." No matter how hard I tried to sound convincing, I knew I wasn't. "I promise, everything's gonna be okay."

"That's what I say to people who aren't gonna make it to the hospital in time." Voice trembling, his breaths picked up in speed. When he spoke again, it was almost impossible to decipher each word. "Is it about Grace?"

"It's gonna be okay," was the only way I could respond. I had no idea if it was going to be okay. I prayed today wouldn't be the one Bentley looked back on as his worst tragedy, but I was terrified it would be. "I'm five minutes away, okay? Just call your supervisor, and I'll be there soon. Then we'll talk about everything. Okay?"

A deep breath muffled through the speaker. I couldn't tell if it was a sigh, a grunt of annoyance, or a quiet sob. But eventually, he said, "Okay."

Ending the call, I did everything in my power to loosen my knotted muscles. When I released my tight fists, however, my eyes burned with tears. So I locked them all back up. I needed to keep it together. Not for me, but for Grace and Bentley.

"Are you sure you don't want me to tell him?" Ox asked.

In that monotone voice with that expressionless face? "He needs to hear this from me."

"If you tell him it's you or his daughter, who do you think he's going to choose?" Ox asked. "This might not be best to hear from you, Maddie. He could get angry, or aggressive, and—"

"He won't hurt me."

"It's not gonna hurt *you* when he's livid that you're not gonna turn yourself over to save his child?"

It wouldn't. Bentley, I was going to tell the truth to. He could help me get out undetected. But even if I were to follow Ox's lead and hide while Eric murdered Grace, it wouldn't hurt me if Bentley chose Grace over me. It was the very reason I adored him.

He was the man neither of us had growing up. He was the father we had both wanted. He put his daughter above everything and everyone, and that was what made him the type of man I wanted to spend my life with. If the roles were reversed, and I had to choose between Bentley and my child, I would choose my child. In that situation, Bentley would understand.

"I'll be fine," I said. "Hurry up."

Chapter 41

Bentley was pacing outside when we made it back to the trailer. Ox began to ask, yet again, if I wanted him to do this. I jumped from the car before he could finish. Considering the look on Bentley's face, I'd be lying if I said I didn't wish I could let Ox handle it. But if my world were to stop spinning as I knew Bentley's was about to, I would want him to be the one who kept me from falling out of orbit.

Warring with the lump in my throat, I started toward him.

With eyes full of tears, Bentley started my way too. "Is she okay? Is she hurt? She isn't de—" Stopping himself with a sharp breath, his lips quivered. The tears spilled over. "Please tell me my daughter's okay."

"She's gonna be." That must not have sounded genuine because the tears dropped from his eyes like rain from the clouds in a summer storm. "I'm-I'm—We're gonna get her back. He-he took her, but we know who he is, and we're gonna get her back."

Cupping both hands before his face, backpedaling, Bentley shook his head.

"We're gonna find her, and we're going to get her back," I said again, unsure if I was trying to convince him or myself. "Everything's going to be okay. I promise, everything's gonna be okay."

"How do you know?" Wiping the tears away, his face screwed up in confusion. "I mean, how could you know? Just because the school's on lockdown doesn't mean it's about Grace, right? Maybe she just forgot to charge her phone last night. Or maybe..." No matter how hard I tried, the tears in my eyes beaded over. Bentley knew how rare of an occasion that was, and his tears came down again. "How do you know?"

"She called me," I said. "Right before you called. He took the phone from her, and then I made him put her back on the phone. I thought maybe it was a fake at first, but she said things only Grace would've said."

Shaking his head vigorously, as though that was the only bodily reaction he remembered, he lifted his trembling hands to his face. It wasn't long before his legs were quivering as well. "She's just a kid. She doesn't know what to do. She doesn't know what to say. She's a smart assed, sweet kid, and-and I don't—What am I supposed to do? What are you guys going to do? What if he kills her?" A sob quaked through him. He was already so unsteady, and I was sure he was about to hit the ground. "She must be so scared, and I'm not there, and you're here, and-and—"

"Let's sit down." Touching both of his arms, I helped him slowly to the grass. It wasn't easy with a bum knee, but the pumping adrenaline always helped numb the pain. Once we were there, I circled my arms around him as best as I could. "She's okay. He hasn't hurt her. She's okay."

"I can't lose another kid, Maddie." The pain in those big brown eyes would haunt me in the same way that Josey's scream did. "I can't lose her. I can't."

"You won't. I promise, you—"

"You don't know that!" It wasn't a yell, but a heartbreaking cry that morphed into a soft sob. "You can't know that."

Knowing that the others were close, that they were watching, I took his cheeks in my hands. Thumbing Bentley's tears away, I leaned in and rested my forehead on his. Hopefully everyone nearby was decent enough to turn away.

I just needed to get close enough to whisper, "He doesn't want

Grace. He wants me. So I'm gonna give him that. And I'm gonna need your help to do it."

Accepting my touch, holding my face in his hands, he opened his mouth to speak, but nothing came out.

That was best. He didn't know what was going on, and it was better that he was at a loss for words than furious he hadn't joined Grace in persuading me to take her to school this morning.

"As far as everyone here knows, I'm not gonna turn myself over to him," I whispered. "But that's what he wants, and if it's going to keep Grace alive, I'm going to do it. I'll explain more when we get a minute alone, but right now, I need you to pretend like you have no idea that I have a plan. I need you to pretend you have no hope that we're gonna find her. So I'm gonna kiss you, and then I'm gonna hug you, and then I'm going to hold you while you cry until somebody comes over here and says that they need to talk to either of us. Okay?"

He blinked hard for a moment, then nodded.

So I kissed him, and I hugged him, and I held him while he cried.

* * *

Every officer and agent had the same unanimous opinion. No way in hell could I turn myself over to him. Not only was he likely to kill Grace either way, but it would only fuel his ego.

They were right. Grace was his bait. I was his prey. He hadn't offered a tradeoff because we were both dead the moment he had her. Once I was gone, he'd kill Grace. Then he would kill again, and again, and again.

That didn't mean I had to sit here with my head in my hands and mourn Grace when she wasn't gone yet. That didn't mean that I could just accept that she was dead when she wasn't. She could be soon, and I understood that, but she wasn't yet.

I pretended to, though. I sat there with my head in my hands and pretended she was already dead. I even cried. Wasn't sure if that was good acting, terror, or genuine grief for what she was experiencing, but at least it looked believable.

Everyone was on the phone with someone within the hour. That gave me the opportunity to get away and speak with Bentley. He had yelled and screamed a bit when Phillips informed him of the situation. A lot of, "You're just going to let my daughter die?" And a bit of, "But Maddie was a cop! She can handle herself! You can't just keep her here. You're forcing her to kill my daughter! You're leaving the blood on her hands!"

It was believable. Maybe because it was how he really felt. But one way or the other, neither of us looked suspicious when we met on the log in my backyard. We looked like what we were. Friends, or more than friends, comforting one another through one of the worst times in our lives.

"But do they really think they found him?" Bentley asked. "Because if they did, then you don't need to give yourself over to him, do you?"

"We're waiting on the fingerprints since the first round didn't come through the fax clear enough to be processed. We ended up having to scan the paper copy and convert it to a PDF file. They've still got to upload the prints for comparison. Once they have proof that they're from the same man, Ox will get a warrant to search any properties he owns. But I already checked. The only place Eric owns is his home. Which means he's taken her somewhere else. Somewhere that could take us hours, maybe days, to find. Maybe it's an old hunting cabin, maybe it's an abandoned building." I shook my head and blew out a shaky breath. "He worked for a security company for years. He hacked into *my* cameras. I have no doubt that he has cameras at his own house, and that he's watching them. So the moment they go to search his home, Grace is dead."

Watching Bentley's lips tremble felt like a blade in my gut. But he needed to know exactly where my thoughts were heading. If he didn't, we had no chance.

"So it's a bad thing that we know who he is?" Bentley said.

"No. It's good. It gives you guys places to look when I'm gone." God damn it, I wish I could say this softer. "But that's not what I need your help with. Ox knows what I know. After I leave, he's gonna dig into Eric's family. The analysts at the FBI are probably looking into all his purchases as we speak. That might point us to where he is before the time runs out. The problem is, we need to disable his cameras before Ox gets the warrant finalized. Which is where I need your help."

Head tilting, Bentley studied me for a few heartbeats. "I can barely use social media. How can I disable his cameras?"

Swallowing, I glanced around to make sure no one was watching us too closely. "Last night, this guy tried to kill Noah."

"Noah Ward? Why?"

"Because Noah identified him to me."

Still, Bentley's puzzled eyes studied mine.

"If the police storm his house with a warrant, he'll know we found him, and this will end in a murder suicide. But if a few of Simeon's guys storm his house to get him back for shooting Noah, they're unrelated incidents. He won't know that the cops know who he is."

For a few heartbeats, Bentley only stared at me. "I don't understand."

This was the part I really didn't want to say aloud. "Okay, think about it this way. If the police go in with a warrant, they can only search the residence. They can't damage his property. If Simeon's guys went in, vandalized his house, shot out his security system, and turned off the Wi-Fi, it'd look like retaliation for the shooting. He knows Simeon will kill him. He thinks I'll put him in jail. These are two very different consequences to a narcissist."

Still, Bentley didn't seem to understand. I didn't blame him. My brain was scattered, and I was info dumping a theory. A theory that very well may blow up in our faces. "You don't think there's any risk to Grace's life by having Simeon's guys go into his house and vandalize it?"

"I think Grace's life is already on the line. I'm just trying to do as much as I can to protect her." Bentley's jaw clenched to keep from trembling, and I hated how much harder I was making this for him. "I think the act is illegal. He's going to think a bunch of drug dealers breaking into his house is revenge for trying to kill one of them. This guy isn't experienced in the drug world. All he has seen is pulp fiction about the mafia. He's going to be panicking, but he won't be panicking because he thinks the cops know anything. He knows that if Simeon is going to kill someone, Simeon isn't going to ask me for permission first. He's also not going to want the cops present when he goes to do the job. Right?"

"A distraction. Something to get his focus off Grace and the cops closing in on him."

"And a way to clear the residence so the cops can confirm they need to search elsewhere."

Slowly, the dots connected in Bentley's mind. He gave a gentle nod. "Have you talked to Simeon?"

Another hard swallow. "Like I said. This is where I need your help."

He said nothing. He just sat there, staring at me. Waiting. I imagined the brain fog was too intense for him to do much else.

"Simeon doesn't owe me anything. If he sends some of his guys to do this, there will be evidence of them committing a crime. A minor crime, but a crime he doesn't want associated with his business."

It took a few heartbeats, but eventually, his eyes softened. Shoulders slumping, he traced his tongue along his teeth. "We need to give Simeon an incentive to send his guys."

"Yeah. I don't know why he helps me when he does, but he's pissed at me for what happened to Noah. He's not gonna do me any favors. He might for someone he wants to put on his books though."

"It's worth a shot." Standing from the log, Bentley nodded toward his trailer. "I'm gonna go call him. Don't run off before I know more. Okay?"

"Maddie," Ox called, walking onto my porch and scanning the yard for me.

"Doesn't look like I'll have the chance."

Chapter 42

"Where's he going?" Ox asked, nodding toward Bentley. "He doesn't think he's leaving, does he? Because the last thing we need is for him to get himself killed too."

"No, he's just changing out of his uniform." Crossing my arms against my chest, I swallowed hard. "Any word on the fingerprints yet?"

He smiled. A big, genuine smile. Those were so rare from Ox, and I was glad I got to see it one more time before I left. If I left.

"They're a match," he said. "It was enough for a warrant. It's gonna be a crazy trial, but we've got enough to make an arrest."

That was great. But it didn't mean much for Grace. "Any idea of other properties he might be keeping her at?"

There went his smile. "Not yet. But the analysts at the FBI are looking. I'm sure we'll find something soon. Now that we know who he is, it's just a matter of time. This is the easy part."

I knew what he meant from an investigation angle. Putting a perpetrator to the crime was the hardest part. Once it was done, all that was left was the arrest, and yes, that was often the easiest part.

But Grace could die before we made it that far.

I wanted to scream that. I wanted to tell him that there was nothing easy about this situation. I wanted to yell that if it were his mom, or if it were me, he wouldn't say this was easy.

But when I opened my mouth to speak, no words came out. Instead, tears bubbled in my eyes. Because this could be the last time we saw one another.

Looking up at him, seeing all that hope in his typically blank face, it sunk in. I wanted to make it out of this alive, but I was about to surrender myself over to the man who wanted nothing more than to kill me. One of my legs didn't work as it was meant to, he was holding a young girl as collateral over me, and there was a very real chance I wouldn't make it home.

There was so much bad blood over the years between me and Ox. We'd gotten past it. We had a good relationship now. Not best friends, not boyfriend and girlfriend, certainly not husband and wife, but we were friends. The last conversation I'd had with my mom before she died was a fight. If this was the last conversation I had with Ox, I didn't want it to be the one he looked back on with regrets.

So I just nodded.

He frowned. "You okay?"

Didn't even need to pretend to sniffle. "I love that kid. She's one of my best friends, you know? That probably sounds stupid."

His frown deepened. "It doesn't."

"I'm sorry. I'm just kind of a mess right now." Letting out a huff of a laugh, I wiped the tears from the corners of my eyes. "If what happened to Josey happens to her, I don't know how I'm gonna live with myself. And Bentley's already lost a kid. I really don't think he'll survive losing another one. I just wish I could help."

"You did. You helped us get here." It was a bizarre thing to witness, but he opened his arms and hugged me. Hugging Ox usually felt like hugging a brick wall. It wasn't much different now. The wall was just a bit warmer this time. "We're gonna find her, Maddie. It's gonna be okay."

It wouldn't be. He just didn't know that yet.

Martin called, "Ox! We're gonna go interview the sister. You coming?"

Pulling back, he wiped one of my tears away. It was more like a poke than a sensual touch, but the smile he gave me was comforting. "I'll call you when I know more. Okay?"

Arms still around him, I yanked him in for another deep hug. "Please don't let him realize we know who he is."

Patting my back, he nodded against my head. "We won't execute the warrant until we've checked everywhere else. I promise."

I squeezed him tighter and tighter. There was so much I wanted to say, so much we should've said over the years, and so much that could never be spoken.

At least we weren't in love anymore. That was good. Because if I died today, it would be a lot easier for him to move forward.

"I gotta go, Maddie," he whispered.

Tugging away, I pasted on that fake smile again. "Be safe."

Returning my smile, he started walking backwards to the drive. "As soon as we get this prick, everyone's gonna be a hell of a lot safer."

It was okay. A good enough goodbye. Every word I said, he would look back on, and he would know what they truly meant.

Ox,

If you're reading this, it means I got away. And hey, maybe that means that in a few hours, I'll be on the couch with Grace. You'll be drinking beers with the guys at the station. That evil piece of shit will be locked away in a cell.

Or it could mean I'm dead. I really hope I'm not. I know you never believed me, but I didn't try to kill myself that day, and I'm not trying to kill myself now. I know I have a habit of self-destructing, usually courtesy of my subconscious, but that's not what this was.

It's about Grace. A sweet, innocent little girl. She's going to be some-

body. Maybe a detective. Maybe an author—she loves books. Maybe a doctor or a lawyer. I don't know. But I know she deserves a future.

I wish this weren't my war. I wish every day of my life that I hadn't visited my mom that night. I wish he hadn't shot me, that I hadn't lost Bear.

Most of all, I wish I hadn't lost myself. All this is kinda poetic, ya know? When the killer showed, I did. I lost myself. But recently, I found her again. The me I used to be, the me I always wanted to be. And it'll be some bullshit if fate decides that now is my time to die after I finally got on track. Poetic, but bullshit.

If that is what fate decided, though, I want you to know that I love you. I've always loved you. It's a different type of love than it used to be, but it's still love. You taught me a lot about myself, who I wanted to be, and what it's like to have a normal life. I'll always be grateful to you for that.

I'm not angry at you anymore. I forgive you. I'm sorry I held on to so much resentment for so long, but all that's gone now. Of course, now that I've done this, it's your turn to resent me. Maybe this makes us even?

Hell if I know.

I just wanted to tell you one more time that I loved you. And not to blame Bentley for this. I will haunt you for the rest of your life if you blame Bentley for this. It was always a hot topic for us, but believe it or not, I am capable of making my own decisions. The moment I realized the killer had Grace, I made this decision. It had nothing to do with Bentley.

Fingers crossed I get the two of us out. Or you guys figure out where we are. Maybe you'll get to swoop in and be my hero for once. I'm sure that would do wonders for your ego.

These probably aren't the best parting words if I'm dead. But hey, it sorta has a nostalgic vibe to it, don't you think? At least you'll read this letter in my bitchy, sarcastic voice and chuckle. Once you stop cussing out my ghost, anyway.

Love,
Maddie

Folding the envelope, I scanned the room for the best place to put it. Nightstand seemed most effective. Beneath it, there were a few more envelopes. One for Alex. One for Bentley. One for Grace, if I died, but she made it out. And one for Tempest.

Okay, it wasn't *for* Tempest. It was about her though. All her vet records, all her favorite things, and everything I knew about her family line stored on a flash drive for Bentley.

As I set the piece of paper down, I locked eyes with her in her crate. For a second, I swore she knew. I didn't know how she could, but I swore she did.

Lowering myself to the bed, I held out my hands for her and smiled. "Come here, girl."

Head slumped between her shoulders, she walked my way and rested her chin on my shoe. It was only then, reaching down to pet her, that it really sank in. She'd already lost a handler. I didn't want her to lose another one. I had a few secret weapons up my sleeve, but my priority was making sure that Grace survived. My own survival was more of a hope than a mission.

"If I don't come back," I whispered to Tempy, holding her fuzzy cheeks in my hands so we were looking at one another, "you should know that you saved my life. You gave me the best few months, Tempest. I love you more than you'll ever know. But Bentley will take good care of you. And you'll take good care of him, won't you? You'll help him just like you helped me."

"*A-woo-woo-woo,*" she whined, rolling her head toward me and pawing at my boot.

I had no idea how she knew, but somehow, she knew what I was about to do, and if she could speak, she would beg, *Don't leave, Mom. Not without me. I'll protect you. Just like I always protect you. You're my whole world.*

"I wish I could stay," I whispered, tears stinging down my cheeks. "Grace needs me. I have to help her."

Another, "*A-woo-woo-woo,*" this one ending with Tempest's head in my lap. Like she was trying to pin me in place.

Reaching down, I wrapped my arms around her neck, and I hugged her. I never encouraged people to hug dogs. They hated that. But hey, if I was gonna die anyway, would it be so bad if Tempest took a bite out of me first?

"Knock-knock," Bentley called, accompanied by a tap tap.

Swatting my tears away, I sat up. "Come in."

He did. His eyes were as red as mine. It looked like he tried to smile, but he couldn't muster one up.

I forced one and tapped the bed beside me. "Shut the door, please."

Again, he did. Bentley always kept his shoulders low. Hunch wasn't the right descriptor, not usually. He just didn't stand with that overt confidence that Ox did, for instance.

Today, though, he hunched. Like I had so many letters written, Bentley passed me one as well. One for Grace, to give to her if Eric didn't hold up his side of the bargain. Another for me, detailing his conversation with Simeon. Since the son of a bitch had put a phone in my room, bugging it was no stretch to my imagination. I didn't want him to know that Bentley and Simeon were in cahoots for obvious reasons.

The one for me read, *Simeon is sending a few guys now. He said he'll get back to me when it's done.*

After grabbing my pen off the side table, I scribbled, *What do you have to do for him?*

Bentley took the pen back and wrote, *Nothing yet. He says this one is a favor. I'm not in his debt. Each job I work, he'll pay me for.*

Frowning, I wrote, *I'm sorry you have to do this. I'm sorry for everything.*

When I passed him the pen and paper, I expected him to write something back. He didn't. Instead, he reached for my hand. Those sweet, warm brown eyes were far more sympathetic than they should have been. "There's nothing to say sorry for. None of this is your fault."

If we hadn't met one another again, Grace would be safe right now. But I didn't need him to soothe my anxiety. I just gave him a sad smile and shrugged.

My burner phone dinged with a text from Ox. Bentley craned over to read it as well. *The sister doesn't know about other properties he might own. She hasn't been in contact with him since high school. But her mom told her about a fiancé of Eric's before she died. We're going to interview her now. I'll let you know when I have more. If we don't get anything by quarter 'til, we're searching his house.*

The clock in the corner now read 11:06 AM. Meaning I had forty-four minutes to turn myself over to him. Thirty-nine, actually, if they were gonna ransack his house.

I texted back, *Okay. Thanks.*

With a careful, calming breath, I said, "Looks like it's time for Plan B."

Still teary-eyed, Bentley stayed silent.

"It'll be a nice walk, at least. Kimberly Run. That's where he wants me to go," I said. "I don't know if I'm supposed to tell you that, but he only said not to tell the cops. He didn't mention you."

Squeezing my hand, Bentley traced his thumb along the back of mine. For a few heartbeats, he said nothing. His mouth opened and shut a few times, like he was looking for the words, but none came out.

"It's okay." My voice cracked when I said it, proving how not okay all this was. "Everything's gonna be okay."

Tears flooded his eyes. Pressing his lips together to hold in the sob I was sure wanted to escape, he shook his head. "Nothing about this is okay."

"It's gonna be," I said. "It will."

Bentley let out a huff. His gaze dropped to our hands, and then to Tempest's head in my lap. With his free hand, he stroked her ear. For a while, a long while, that was all we did. We sat there holding hands and petting Tempest. The two of us were usually the chattiest people in any room. Today? There was nothing to say.

Until Bentley broke the silence with, "You don't have to do this."

I wasn't sure if he was saying it to ease his own guilt later, in case I did die, because he believed Eric would kill Grace regardless, or if it was because it was just the right thing to do. It didn't matter. "I do."

Slowly, he turned his attention away from Tempest and onto me. He spoke barely above a whisper. "I wouldn't blame you if you didn't."

Some part of him would. But that wasn't why I made this decision. It wasn't about him. "Grace isn't going to be another casualty in my war, Bentley. I'm doing this. Please don't stop me."

The tears in his eyes beaded over. "Please come back."

With a sad smile, I thumbed the tears away. "Please take care of Tempest if I don't."

"You will." Holding my cheek, he shook his head. "No ifs. You're going to come back, and you're gonna take care of Tempest until she's old and gray. That's the deal here. This is a rescue mission. It isn't suicide, Maddie."

I hoped not. But my expectations were so low, they were partying with Satan. He didn't need to worry about that, though. So I leaned in, held that strong jaw, stroked my fingers through his scruffy beard, and I kissed him. I kissed him like I should have kissed him months ago, or years ago.

It was slow, soothing, but also passionate. There was all the comfort of the time we'd spent together, pairing with the hope and excitement for what could be. Where this could go if Grace and I both walked out alive.

Like yesterday's kiss, the salty taste of tears invaded its intimacy, detracting from what it could've been. But maybe that wasn't true. Maybe true intimacy and connection came from moments like this, when hope was all but lost. When two people were at their most vulnerable. When it wasn't blue skies and butterflies, but dark clouds and emergency sirens.

For the two of us, two screwed up kids from the trailer park, maybe we needed the dark clouds and emergency sirens to feel safe. I hoped that when this was over, we could drive out of the storm and into those blue skies together, but it made sense that such gloom tinged the pinnacle of our love story.

Leaning back, I rested my forehead against his. "I guess we'll have that talk about what to call ourselves when I get back, right?"

Despite the tears rolling down his cheeks, his chuckle was genuine. "Right."

Smiling wider, I leaned in to kiss him one more time. Just a peck. We didn't have time for much more. "Help me open this window."

I started to edge Tempest off my lap and stand, but he pulled me back down. Just when I was about to ask what he was doing, he wrapped his arms around me and squeezed. He held me so tight that it hurt. It was the best hurt I'd ever felt. Hugs were nothing new for us, but this was more than that. Even though there was nothing racy about it, it didn't feel the slightest bit platonic. In fairness, though, probably because I was comparing it to that 'hugging a brick wall' sensation I got from Ox.

In my ear, voice crackling, Bentley whispered, "I love you. I'm sorry it took me so long to say it, but I love you more than just about anything. I don't want to live without you. So you come home to me, okay? Then we can start what should've started years ago, and it won't matter that it took us so long to get here. All that matters is that we're together. Me, and you, and Grace, and Tempest—we're all gonna be here together."

I still couldn't see the blue sky, but the butterflies were back.

Hugging him back with all my strength, I swallowed the lump in my throat and blinked my tears away. "I'll make it home."

Chapter 43

Getting away from the trailer wasn't too difficult. Since the others believed I agreed with them, no one was watching me closely. They thought I was napping through the stress. Since my bedroom was at the back of the house, all it took was climbing out the window instead of walking out the door. The landing would've been a lot harder if not for Bentley slowly easing me to the grass.

The hard part was sneaking through the trailer park without one of the many cops seeing me. Luckily, in my sweatpants and hoodie, I blended right in. Keeping my head down until I got to the woods did the trick.

Once I was there, I texted the number that had sent me the location. *Just got out of the trailer park. Walking through the woods. Gonna have an Uber get me to Kimberly Run.*

He texted back a thumb emoji. Seemed about right. Only assholes used the thumb emoji.

A trail connected the woods behind my trailer park to a suburb. It would've taken the average person twenty-five minutes to get to that suburb where I awaited the Uber. It took me forty. I assumed he was watching me through the GPS on the phone, however, because I didn't receive any threatening countdown messages.

The Uber driver asked me where I was going. I lied. Said just for a walk. He didn't push. Once he dropped me off, I started down the trail.

I wished I could say that the walk was pleasant. A nice way to spend my final moments. It wasn't. The sun was high in the blue sky, birds chirped all around me, and the humidity was low enough that I could enjoy the heat. But clouds still loomed off in the distance.

It was like the year I spent before I got clean. Even the prettiest of days looked dreary. No matter how lively they may have been to everyone else, a grim storm tinted my irises.

That wasn't to say I'd lost hope. I was gonna fight like hell to make it out of this alive. Guess I just wasn't naïve enough to believe that I'd get a happy ending.

Only a few minutes after I had stepped foot in Kimberly Run, the phone rang. I answered with, "You gonna drive by and have me jump into the backseat?"

He chuckled. "Not exactly."

"Then what, exactly?"

"You continue ahead for about ten minutes. On your right, there will be a trail to the hilltop. At its peak, there is a small gravel road. Are you familiar with it?"

Swatting a bug away, I said, "Can't say that I am."

"You don't need to be," he said. "On this gravel road, parked off to the shoulder, there will be an old silver car. You'll get into the passenger seat and await further instructions."

I was literally a sheep being led to her slaughter. "Awesome. So where are you leaving Grace?"

"Once you're in my custody, I will let her go."

"So once I get in the car?"

"Once I'm sure no one has followed us to my second location."

Stopping, I snorted. "That wasn't the deal. The deal was you get me, and you let Grace go."

"And I will. Once I have you here."

"So you think I'm stupid." I laughed. "No. I'm not getting in this car until you prove to me that you're going to let Grace go."

He laughed too. Mine was annoyed while his was snarky. "Do you really think you're in a position to be making demands, Madison?"

My name sounded disgusting on his tongue. "I think that if you kill Grace, I call Ox right now and this whole thing is off."

"Let's see. Grace Roycroft. Bentley Roycroft. Alex Rodrigo. Ashley Harper. Teresa Taylor. Darius. Greg. And, oh, Tempest, of course," he said. "Bentley looks tough, but he's a heavy sleeper. Alex couldn't hurt a fly. She has a wonderful security system, but I've disabled it half a dozen times in the last year, and she hasn't been notified of any of them. Ashley, I will admit, would be a bit of a hassle. She's as much of a bitch as you are. But if I try hard enough, it won't be much trouble. My God, Teresa. You would think that woman is a man the way that she walks around in the world. She doesn't even lock her windows. Did you know that? Considering who her son is, I would've expected her to be more cautious about her safety. Darius? He's alone all the time, with the hours his mother works and all. Wouldn't be too difficult to break in one night. Greg's stoned all the time, abducting him would be easy. Oh, and Duke. Come to think of it, I would probably be better off abducting Duke than Greg, wouldn't I? You care more about the dog than you do the man. Am I making myself clear, Madison?"

Clenching my hand into a fist, my jaw tightened. If I didn't turn myself over to him now, he would just continue down the list of people I cared about. Even my asshole landlord and the best friend who'd screwed my fiancé. As much as I wished I was selfish enough to be okay with losing them, I wasn't. If Harper or Greg called me begging for their lives, I would do for them just as I was doing for Grace.

"If you don't do this now, you will do it when I—"

"I get your God damn point," I snapped, stomping along the trail toward the hilltop. "Our deal is still on when I get there, isn't it?"

I could practically hear his smug smile. "Of course it is."

Meaning it wasn't. He was going to kill Grace, make me watch, and then kill me.

He would try, at least. I did have a plan. A shitty plan, but a plan.

"Great. Then I'll see you soon, asshole." I ended the call.

Hunting Grounds

When I made it to the vehicle, I considered looking at the VIN number and texting it to Bentley or Ox. Maybe it would lead them to us. Or, more than likely, the guy would see me do it and kill Grace.

So I flung open the door, dropped into the passenger seat, and pouted like a punished child. Staying on autopilot may have been better for my mental health, but fury was how I survived. And if he were watching me, at least nothing about my behavior would lead him to believe I had a plan.

Again, the phone rang. I answered with, "What now, asshole? What do you want me to do?"

"First of all, call me an asshole again, and Grace might lose a finger." Praying he could see it, I rolled my eyes. "Secondly, you're going to remove all of your weapons and throw them into the woods."

"I'm not stupid. I didn't bring weapons."

"Grace, would you rather lose a finger or a toe?"

She shouted an obscenity in the background. Part of me wanted to scream and tell her to do what he said. The other part of me was proud.

Either way. He had likely been watching me with deer cams as I walked. I thought I was sly with my thigh holster, but those were more effective for people who had more going on downstairs than I did. Also had a pocket knife tucked into my shoe that he may have gotten a glimpse of, another one in my sports bra, and one more in my hoodie pocket.

I opened the door and tossed them out. But only because I was counting on him making me do exactly that. "Alright. They're in the woods. What now?"

"Open the glove compartment. There will be a book inside. Grab it."

I did. "And what do you want me to do with the book? Is this my weapon? That how this is going to go—an academic gladiator match?"

Another chuckle. "Open it."

Again, I did.

Out of everything this man had done to me, this was the cruelest.

"Go on. Open it."

Jaw clenching, my breaths quickened. "This is stupid. It doesn't even make sense. You're a sadist. You want to see me in pain."

"I'm watching you struggle right now." Still, it was like I could see his smile. "Come on, Mad dog. You know you want to."

Part of me did. Part of me always would.

Inside the hollowed out book rested a tiny baggie of cream-colored powder and a straw. If I had to guess? Heroin. It was hard to be certain without testing it, but I doubted he would've given me cocaine or ecstasy before this.

Had to give him credit, though, because it was ingenious. It was pretty close to white, meaning it was high quality. Since I had no tolerance, moments after consuming it, I would nod off. I might even overdose. Which led me to believe that he wasn't far with a bottle of naloxone so he could revive me quickly if I did.

Of course, that didn't matter now. Not really.

After I nodded off, I would be transported to another dimension of pure euphoric bliss. Bliss that I resented. Bliss that I had worked tirelessly to never chase again. Bliss that I didn't want.

And that was his point. Forcing me to relapse was psychological torture.

The second half of it was that even when the high wore off, I would be foggy. Maybe not incapacitated but dazed. Which meant it would be a hell of a lot harder for me to enact my plan. Not impossible, but a hell of a lot harder.

"I won't fight you," I said. "When you come to get me, I'll go willingly. You want to make this hurt, make this hurt. But I won't feel a damn thing you do to me if I take this."

"We're both aware that this isn't about sedating you, Madison."

Hence why it was heroin and not Rohypnol.

"I highly recommend you do as I say before it's too late for Grace."

Squeezing my hand so tightly that blood welled around my fingernails, I cussed beneath my breath and dropped the phone to the driver's seat. There was a lump in my throat as I tore open the bag. I ignored it.

This wasn't relapsing. Even if I enjoyed this, it was not a relapse. Alex said so, and she was a doctor. This was forced. I was not willingly losing my sobriety, even if I adored the rush.

Actually, there was no if about it. I *would* enjoy this. I was an addict, and my drug of choice was oxies. Heroin was oxies on steroids. Of course I was going to like this. That was exactly why he was doing it. To make me hate myself for failing the accomplishment I was most proud of.

But Alex said it wasn't a relapse if I didn't consciously choose it. That's what I had to cling to.

As I put one end of the straw into the bag and the other end into my nostril, I told myself again, *This is not a relapse. I don't want to do this. I am not relapsing. I am being drugged.*

But holy shit, it was hard to remember that when the euphoria hit.

Chapter 44

I couldn't say what happened next. One minute, I was in the passenger seat of that old car with a straw up my nose, looking at the green trees out the window. The next, I was lost in a bliss-filled dream.

People think that opiates just make you sleep. Sometimes, that's the case. But when you take a shit-ton? The body drifts into a glorious illusion. Like a fantasy world where all my hopes had become reality.

But even the dream was a blur. Only a vague image remained, sitting on a swing suspended from the porch roof of an old farmhouse overlooking a wildflower-coated hillside. There was plenty of shade, but it felt like a layer of summer sun caressed every inch of my skin. That was always my favorite part of getting high. The warmth.

Beside me, holding me, Bentley smiled and yelled something to Tempest I couldn't decipher. She was running in that field, and Bear was at her side. Chasing after them through the field, Grace smiled at me over her shoulder. She yelled something, but I didn't know what. I didn't *care* what. It was so warm, so cozy, and all I cared about was staying in that moment forever.

Then the yell became distinct. She wasn't smiling anymore. She was crying, and the porch swing was swaying, even though Bentley and I were still.

"Damn it, wake up!"

My eyes flung open.

There she was. Grace's face, inches before mine.

She wasn't crying, but the redness of her eyes told me she had been. Her hands were on my biceps, shaking me.

Gasping, I jarred forward to wrap my arms around her. But pain soared up my wrists all the way to my neck.

"You're okay." Grace breathed the words as a sigh of relief. "Thank God, you're okay."

Everything was still foggy. All I could see were Grace's worried eyes burning into mine. It took a moment of staring into them before I realized where I was and what had led me here.

As reality set back in, I groaned, "That piece of shit."

"I said the same thing," Grace muttered. "Did he hurt you?"

"No, but he said he'd let you go when he had me." Blinking hard, trying to see through the haze, I pulled again on the restraints. Only then did I realize my arms were tied behind me. Whatever held them wasn't soft like the red ribbon he was famous for. It was cold metal. "Did that prick cuff me?"

Frowning, Grace nodded. She kept her hand on my shoulder as she gestured to a wooden table on the right. On its top sat a purple prescription box trimmed in white. "He only took the rope off me so I could give you that if you needed it."

A purple prescription box I knew well. Naloxone, as I expected.

As for the rest of the room, also what I expected.

Four log walls. A dingy light bulb hung from the center of the ceiling. My feet rested on old, decrepit wood floors. To the left, light trickled in from the corner of a boarded off window. Beneath it was a twin bed. The bed Josey had died on, I assumed. No other decor or distinguishable characteristics, aside from the door behind me with a hole where the handle should've been.

Hunting cabin, if I had to guess.

"Your heartbeat was so slow." Swallowing, Grace rubbed a hand up and down my arm. "But you're okay, right?"

I was high. Less high than I had been, but still high. If I stood up, I would probably fall back down. My knee didn't ache for the first time in months—guessed that was something. Everything had a foggy hue to the edges, but at least I wasn't nodded off. That much was for certain because there was no way in hell I would've imagined this up as a pleasant dream.

"I'm okay." Squinting her over, I struggled to keep my eyes open. "Are you okay? Are you hurt?"

Grace held up her wrist. The normally cream color of her flesh was tainted purple and blue. "I think it's broken, but it could be worse. Did he hurt you at all when he got you? Do you know what he gave you?"

"Not that I remember," I said. "And heroin, I think." Grace swallowed hard, so I forced a smile for her and segued onto what she needed to know. "I'm okay. Really. Do you like my hair?"

With knitted brows, she cocked her head to the side. "What?"

"My hair. I cut it. But ugh, my ponytail's kinda tight." Rolling my neck from one side to the other, I gave her a wide-eyed look that I prayed she understood. "Can you take it down for me?"

For a second or two, she kept giving me that confused look.

Eyes still wide, I glanced toward the top of my head in gesture. "I think I might have a knot back there. Be careful."

It took a few more seconds, but then her eyes got bigger too. Nodding slowly, she said, "Sure," then leaned in and began untying my rats' nest of a mane. She picked and picked for a moment, yanking and pulling, which may have hurt if not for the heroin. Eventually, she took in a quiet gasp.

I exclaimed a quick, "Ow," to disguise it. "I told you to be careful. It's a knotted mess."

"Sorry." Balling her hand to a fist and dropping it to her side, she tucked the hair from my face. A heartbeat or two ago, it looked like she was just about out of hope. Now there was the faintest glimmer of it in her eyes. "You're gonna need a whole bottle of conditioner to get that out."

"Eh. Better it's an ugly disaster than a pretty lock in his trophy case."

Grace let out a half laugh, understanding exactly what I had done.

When I was a cop, I'd once arrested a nineteen-year-old woman. She'd been on a lot of drugs, strung-out, combative, and all I could do was wait for backup once I got her cuffed. That was protocol for K-9 handlers—we couldn't put a criminal in the backseat with our dog.

Once he arrived, we did the usual pat down, and then my fellow officer was ready to load her into the backseat of his cruiser. But as he'd opened the rear door, I told him to slow his roll. Sure, we had patted her down, but her long black hair was unkempt. So I'd searched through it before we put her in. And thus, this idea.

Eric had a thing for women's hair. It was a fixation, maybe an obsession, but at the very least, a trophy. When I was getting ready to come here, I made it look as ugly as possible. I teased all the way from my ends to my scalp with a comb until my entire head was all but matted. In part, to make it as unappealing to him as possible. To make him less excited to run his fingers through it.

But that was more of an added benefit than an intentional repellant.

After tossing it up into a messy bun, incredibly grateful that I hadn't chopped it too short, I tucked two tiny razor blades close to my scalp with bobby pins.

A hell of a Hail Mary, but if I knew anything about men, it was that while they loved women's hair, they knew next to nothing about it. The average man would not think that a woman could hide a razor blade in her locks, but with enough attention to detail, hair made for excellent camouflage.

"Where is he?" I asked.

Squatting so she was at eye level, she gestured to the window. "He's got a laptop out there. I think it's the only place he can get a signal."

Still blinking hard, trying to see clearer, I scanned the ceiling for the glowing light of a camera. If he were searching for a signal, that meant no Wi-Fi. No Wi-Fi, nothing to hook up live camera feeds to. "So he's not watching us."

She mouthed, "But he might be listening."

Probably. He was waiting for me to come to so the show could begin.

Glancing over my shoulder, I said, "That door locked?"

"Only when he's not in here. It's a padlock on the outside, I think." She then mouthed, "He doesn't lock the main door."

Meaning he'd use physical force alone to subjugate us once he was inside. That was good. There were two of us now, one of whom was armed. If she stabbed him in the right place with that razor blade, she'd have enough time to run.

Lowering my voice, I glanced at Grace's fist. "You get the chance to hurt him, you do it, and you run."

Leaning in, she whispered, "He has a gun in the back of his pants. Should I try to—"

"No." Her wrist was injured, she wasn't trained past basic self-defense I'd taught her—which apparently hadn't worked—and she was half his size. No way in hell was she getting that gun off him. I mouthed, "Just stab him."

I'd taught her to aim for the eyes. That could kill him, or at least disable him long enough for her to get out the door.

With a hard swallow, she nodded.

"Did you notice if he has any weaknesses?" I asked.

"He has a gash on his forehead like someone hit him with something. He's stumbled a few times."

Concussion. Which put my stoned ass on an even playing field.

"Good. That's good," I murmured. "Do you know how to get back to civilization from here?"

"Dad didn't get the code." She frowned. "I guess it wasn't a good one, anyway. But yeah, I know where we are. So do you. Laurel Ridge State Forest. We walked up here with Tempest a few weeks ago."

I still wasn't sure which code she was referencing, but I knew the park well. "You know which trail?"

"Not by name. It's a little quad trail, like, a mile from the one we walked. On the quad, it took us ten minutes or so to get here from that Y. You know, the one where Dad had us go left because to the right was up the mountain? He said it'd hurt your knee?"

Relief flooded me. In that case, I knew exactly where we were, the mountain. As teens, Bentley and I used to hike up here and smoke weed at the peak. The views of the countryside were wondrous any time, but a thousand times prettier high.

"This place isn't on top of the mountain, is it?"

"No, it's at least another ten minutes to the top."

"So if you get out?"

She gave a half smile. "I tuck, roll, and use the bushes for cover."

I smiled back. Bentley and I had told her a story about how when we'd done just that after almost getting busted by the park rangers. Tucked, rolled, and used the bushes for cover. "Smart kid."

"Never thought your experience as a teenage dirtbag could save a life, huh?"

Laughing quietly, I shook my head. I could blame the drugs, but if anyone could make me smile in a situation like this, it was a Roycroft. "I love that you understand the cultural significance of that phrase."

"I love that you *showed me* the cultural significance of that phrase." Her smile stretched wider and tears gathered in her eyes. I wasn't sure if it was at the storyline of that underrated film, or because I might die, and she'd lose the best movie aficionado she'd ever met. "Thanks for teaching me not to be an uncultured swine."

"Thanks for not telling your dad what I let you watch."

The smile stayed, but her lips began to tremble and a tear fell from the corner of her eye. She swept it away. "Bet you wish you would've told him how you felt now, huh?"

"I did," I said.

Mouth dropping, even her eyes smiled. "Really? What'd he say? And why didn't you tell me!"

"We were going to." I glanced around. "But things were a little hectic, ya know?"

Gradually, all her joy dissipated. "Oh. Right."

Shit. I shouldn't have said that. I wasn't sure why I had. Maybe because I was high. Or maybe because I thought it'd be a pleasant distraction. But Grace was probably thinking, *Ah, shit, Dad finally fell for someone again, and now she's gonna die, just like Mom did. I might die too, and he's gonna be worse than he's ever been.*

Time for a subject change.

"You know what I want to do when we get home?" I asked.

The look in her eyes told me she wasn't sure she believed we would, or at least that I would, but she said, "What do you want to do?"

"I want you to teach me how to bake that lemon meringue pie." She'd made it a few weeks prior, and I gobbled up half of it in the same night. "Or, better yet, is there a way to just make meringue? Is that a thing? Because that was the best part."

Still teary-eyed, she laughed. "You can barely make cookies from a tub. I don't think you're ready for meringue."

"I think you underestimate me." Smirking, I narrowed my eyes. "I bet I can make the best meringue."

"Meringue is *not* an easy dessert."

"I saw you do it. It's just eggs."

"It is not just eggs. Eggs have to be the right temperature, and humidity in the air has to be just right, and you have to get your peaks firm without over whipping. Any bit of flavor you add can completely throw off the balance. You can't even have a drop of water in the bowl when you start."

"Well, you're the expert. Teach me how. And you didn't answer my question. Is there such a thing as just meringue? Like a meringue pie?"

"There are meringue cookies. You'd probably really like those. But it's not an easy process. And you have to be really patient. They take, like, forever."

"Do the cookies come out kind of soft, like the meringue on top of the pie? Because all you did was torch the meringue."

"No, they're completely different." The distraction was doing its job, because she dropped back onto her bum and wide-eyed focus replaced the tears. "They're sort of hard, actually. But that's what's so cool about them. They almost look like a little clay sculpture or something, but then you bite into it, and it just melts in your mouth. They taste like meringue on the pie, but they almost look chalky. And it's so weird because when you look at it, you think you're about to bite into something really hard, but then it just—"

Hinges squealed.

Grace jumped forward, placing her hands on the armrests like she was about to collapse into my chest and cover her eyes for comfort. Breaths halting, she stared past me.

"Stand up and put your hands in front of you," he said.

Chapter 45

"Sorry I'm just getting back to you," Lisa said. "I've been in meetings all morning. I keep my phone turned off while I'm working."

Lisa Morris. A forty-year-old woman. Attractive, with dark hair, dark eyes, and light skin. Successful marketing consultant for a big corporation in California.

Eric Oakley's ex-fiancé.

According to the FBI tech, Lisa had moved away almost a decade ago. She now resided in Southern California. Hence why this meeting was a video call.

"That's no problem. Thanks for meeting with me at all." Ox angled his phone so that Martin could see the screen as well. Phillips was driving, Gayton was in the passenger seat, while Ox and Martin took the back. "I'm Detective Lennox Taylor, this is agent Martin, and agents Phillips and Gayton are listening over the Bluetooth from the front seat."

Huffing, Lisa ran her fingers through her hair. "Shouldn't surprise me that the FBI calls me one Friday afternoon about Eric. Always knew that bastard would kill somebody."

"You wouldn't know it from looking at his record."

"You wouldn't know he's a misogynistic pig, either. He's just really good at hiding it." With a sigh, she propped her phone up on something and leaned closer to the screen. "But I haven't talked to him since I was thirty. I really don't know how I can help you."

Ox wanted to press. He wanted to know more. Why? What had he done? That information would help in a courtroom. But he didn't have time for that.

"We understand," Martin said. "But any input you have on him could save a young girl's life." Stiffening, Lisa stroked her hands up and down her arms, as if to self soothe. Just like Maddie and Abigail had. "Do you know of any isolated areas where he might go frequently? It would be somewhere that he has been many times, probably since his childhood."

"Like the woods?" she asked. "He loved all the local forests. He used to hunt with his dad as a kid. By the time we met, he hiked there a lot with his mom." Lisa rolled her eyes. "Eric loves his mommy."

"Any forest in particular?" Ox asked. "I'm sure you're aware, but there are hundreds upon hundreds of square miles of forests around here. We really need to narrow it down."

A text from Derek slid across the top of the screen. *Call me when you can.* Whenever he got off this call, Ox would. It was probably about Eric's home. The place had already been ransacked when they arrived.

Ox did the mental math. Maddie and Simeon. Simeon wanted revenge for what had happened to his guy, and Maddie wanted the cameras knocked out before the police arrived. Smart. Illegal, but smart. Ox was only a few minutes from the trailer park now, though. He'd discuss it with Derek and Maddie when he arrived.

"I hiked with him a couple times, but it was never my thing." Frowning, Lisa rubbed a hand over her chin in thought. "He never took me anywhere special in the woods, if that's what you're asking. But there was one forest he went to a lot... I don't remember what it's called, but it wasn't too far from his parents' house."

"I'm gonna list a few," Ox said, glancing down at his notes, "and you let me know if any sound familiar."

"Sure," Lisa said.

"Loyalhanna Lake," Ox said, hoping that was the one she referenced. It was closest to where Eric had grown up. When Lisa didn't respond, he continued. "Ohiopyle. Kooser. Linn Run. Laurel Summit. Laurel—"

"Wait, maybe that was it." Eyes creasing in focus, her head tilted slightly to the side. "Laurel something. I know it was Laurel something."

Ox stared at his notes a moment longer, letting out a harrumph.

Surely this had to be a joke.

There were four different state parks and forests in the area, spanning a few hundred square miles, all beginning with the name Laurel. Laurel Hill, Laurel Summit, Laurel Mountain, and Laurel Ridge.

Unless Lisa knew for absolute certainty, there was no reason to send search teams to four different state forests that covered hundreds, if not thousands, of miles.

Just fantastic.

"You're sure you don't remember which?" Ox asked.

"He went to all of them." She shook her head. "They all sound so similar, and I don't want to tell you for certain and send you to the wrong place when there's a little girl's life on the line."

"What about defining characteristics?" Ox asked. "Were there any particular views, or maybe waterfalls or trails that you remember? Did he rock climb? Was it something like that?"

"He hunted. And I know that some of the parks he hunted at, he wasn't supposed to. He never talked much about the hike itself. If he ranted and raved about anything when he got home, it was about the animal he killed. It wasn't about the nature. He preferred *destroying* nature."

Sounded about right for a serial killer. That was why Ox had never enjoyed hunting. He saw nothing wrong with the survival aspect, but anyone who enjoyed the act of killing another living creature made him uneasy.

Ox looked at Martin, who tightened her lips together and shook her head. It wasn't enough. A vague, incredibly rough idea, but not enough.

"Thank you for your help. Is it alright if we give you a call back if we have any more questions?"

"Of course, yeah," Lisa said. "I'm sorry I wasn't more help."

Ox said, "Don't worry about it," before ending the call. Dialing Derek's number, the trailer park now in sight, Ox said to the others, "Any ideas how we can narrow this down?"

"Not off the top of my head," Phillips said under his breath.

"Maybe that'll jog something for Maddie?" Gayton asked. "Maybe something he's said will relate back to one of these Laurel state parks?"

Ox was about to say, "Maybe," but Derek's voice coming through the speaker cut him off. "You're gonna be pissed."

"I've been pissed for the last week," Ox said. "What's going on?"

"She did it. She left."

Ox wasn't certain that he knew what Derek meant, but the possibility had his heart plummeting through his chest. "What are you talking about?"

"Maddie snuck out her bedroom window like a damn teenager," Derek said. "She left us all notes. Goodbye letters, I guess. We're close to finding this guy, aren't we?"

As quick as Derek had spoken, Ox's blood rolled to a boil. At his side, his hand trembled. To steady it, he clenched it to a fist. His stomach ached, and his chest hurt. He hated every second of it.

"What did it say? The letters. Did she give us a code? Do you have any ideas where he is?"

It took a few heartbeats before Derek responded. Terror edged his voice. "We're not close to finding this guy."

"Damn it, Derek, what did the letter say?"

"Nothing that's gonna help us find her," Derek responded in the same tone. "Bentley says she's been gone for almost two hours. We need to send guy's to his house, right the hell now, and have them search all the woods nearb—"

"What do you mean 'Bentley says?'" Ox's heart was slamming so hard against his ribs that he wouldn't be surprised if he had a heart attack. Especially now that they were on Maddie's street, and Bentley sat underneath the tree separating his driveway from hers. "Did he help her get away?"

Derek's disappointed frown was almost audible. "Maddie wasn't our perp, Ox. She was allowed to leave, and if she did, we both know Bentley isn't to blame for that. She—"

He said something else, but Ox had already jumped from the car and started toward Bentley.

Bentley had his chin in his hand, tears in his eyes, and was staring down at his phone. Ox knew he was probably looking at images of his kidnapped daughter, maybe of Maddie, but he didn't care.

"What the hell did you do?" Ox stomped towards him. "Where did she go?"

"Taylor," Derek said in an almost fathering tone, jogging over from Maddie's door. "Don't do something you'll regret."

Wiping his tears away, Bentley stood. "I already told Derek. She met him at—"

"What the hell were you thinking?" Ox shoved Bentley backwards. It wasn't enough to do any damage, but Bentley's head hit his trailer with a clunk that would make anyone cringe. Bentley was already so disoriented, he didn't have a chance to say or do anything before Ox grabbed him by his shirt and pinned him there. "If you cared about her at all, you wouldn't have let her do this!"

"I didn't *let* her do anything." The pain must have been leveling out because fire shone in Bentley's tear-soaked eyes. "There's no telling Maddie what to do. You were with her for ten God damn years and you never figured that out? I told her she didn't have to do this, but she wanted to. Because she gives a shit about my kid. Since apparently none of you do." He waved at all the cops and agents, face scrunched up in fury. "You guys couldn't catch him before. She's the closest you got. So yeah, I trust her to make it back here more than I trust any of you to do what you should've done a year and a half ago."

It was instinct. Ox didn't think as he raised his fist, not until it was at eye level.

Then he stopped. He was on the clock. Assault was a justifiable reason to terminate his employment, remove him from this case, and possibly end his career as a whole. Even if Bentley did deserve it.

"Go ahead," Bentley said, opening his arms at his sides. "Hit me. It's not gonna solve anything. It's just wasting time that you could spend looking for my daughter and the woman we love. But go ahead, man. You've been wanting to since you met me. I won't even press charges. But it'll prove exactly why she chose me over you. Because you just want to control her, and I actually give a damn about what she thinks."

Ox had never wanted to hit somebody so badly in his life. But he couldn't. Partly because it would ruin his life—his career—but mainly because Bentley was right. If Maddie came out of this alive, she would absolutely take Bentley's side. Even their friendship would end.

"If she doesn't make it home," Ox said, lowering his voice so no one else could hear, "I'll kill you. And I'll find a way to get away with it."

"If *neither* of them make it home," Bentley said, "I'll beg you to."

Giving him one more shove against the trailer—for good measure—Ox turned to Derek. "Which state park starting with the word Laurel is closest to where we are right now?"

"What?"

"State parks. State forests. The ones that start with the word Laurel. Laurel Hill, Laurel Summit, Laurel Mountain, Laurel Ridge. Which is closest?"

"Laurel Hill and Laurel Summit are about the same distance, but different directions," Derek said, face scrunching up in confusion. "Why?"

"He's got connections to one of them. We'll go to Hill." Ox started toward his car. "Send a team to Summit."

"Ox, hang on a second." Catching up to him, Derek put a hand on Ox's chest. "These forests span hundreds of miles. There's no point in running there yet. We need to narrow it down. We need to—"

"He has her!" Ox yelled. "He's had her for two God damned hours! If she's still alive, he's putting her through the worst shit imaginable. I'm not waiting around for another dead end. Either send your guys, or I'm going alone."

"Wait," Bentley called, eyes wide. "Laurel Ridge? Maybe Laurel Ridge?"

"Why?" Ox snapped. "There are four of them. Why Laurel Ridge?"

"Grace." Wiping the rest of his tears away, Bentley wet his lips. "When she called Maddie, she made a comment. She mentioned a conversation that she and I had while we were hiking at Laurel Ridge a few weeks ago. It's gotta be Laurel Ridge."

"Laurel Ridge is the farthest one away," Derek said. "So you better be right, kid."

"What was the comment?" Ox asked.

"Something about how if Maddie dies, Tempest goes to me," Bentley said. "And I know that she could have just been saying that to Maddie either way, but we had this exact conversation while we were hiking. Maddie had us hold Tempest while she went into the bushes to pee, and somebody else with a dog walked by. The dog was being super aggressive, it tried to charge at Tempest, but Tempest thought that it was charging a Grace, and she went into defense mode. By the time the other person got their dog away from us, Tempest was freaking out. She wouldn't stop licking and sniffing Grace. And Grace said, 'If Maddie dies working one of her crazy cases, we're gonna keep Tempy, right? Because she'll get put down at a shelter without us or Maddie.'"

Derek frowned at Bentley. "That ain't much, kid."

Ox agreed.

"This wasn't even a month ago. She knew that I would remember that conversation." Bentley's eyes were still wide, pleading. Ox wanted to believe him, but if it was the farthest park from where they currently were, he needed a good reason. "I love her too, man. I wouldn't suggest it if I thought it was a long shot."

"You don't think that a young girl would be concerned about Maddie, who is obsessed with her dog, bringing her dog as backup against a serial killer?" Ox asked genuinely. He wasn't being sarcastic or witty. He wanted to know why Bentley was so sure so he could feel equally assured.

"Grace knows Maddie. Grace knows that Maddie lost Bear *because* of this guy," Bentley said. His eyes were so innocent, so pleading, that for a second, Ox saw in him what Maddie did. "Grace knows that Maddie wouldn't bring Tempest. Not like this. Not when she was going off alone. Not when she knew how high the risk was. Grace only would've said that to clue me in on something. It's got to be where they are. And if Grace recognizes it, then I know where they are. I know the trails out there. I can show you exactly where we go when we hike, and we can find them. Please trust me. Please."

Ox was still livid. Pissed. The urge to punch Bentley had gone nowhere.

But it was the most they had, and Ox was not as familiar with the wilderness around here. Let alone the woods that Bentley, Grace, and Maddie had hiked together.

Ox nodded toward his car. "Will it tolerate the roads up there?"

"Not as well as my truck," Bentley said.

Ox started past him. "Where's Tempest?"

"What?" Bentley asked. "Maddie didn't want to bring her. He killed her last dog—"

"He killed *our* dog." Ox shot him the filthiest look over his shoulder. "Bear was my dog too, so I'm well-aware. But Tempest isn't just a service dog. Until recently, she was a police dog. Maddie never had you play the 'Find Mom' game with her?" Bentley's expression told Ox he had. "If I take her out into those woods, and I tell her to find Mom, she'll lead us right to her. So where the hell is Tempest?"

With a hard swallow, Bentley said, "In her crate in the living room."

Jogging to Maddie's door, Ox called, "Get one of your daughter's dirty shirts."

Chapter 46

"IT'S OKAY," I TOLD GRACE, DOING MY BEST TO SMILE. "IT'S OKAY. Do what he says."

Standing slowly, she clasped her hands together in an almost prayerlike pose before her chest. Backpedaling, her eyes didn't leave him for a second.

Once she was in the corner on my right, footsteps thumped past me. All I could see was his back as he tied her hands. To my surprise, he wasn't as big as he looked in the photos. Just above average in height, a bit thinner than he had been the night he shot me, and he catered to his left arm, tucked close to his chest. A frequent occurrence for someone with chronic pain.

Good. He deserved to be in pain after everything he had done. Also good, because while it may not have looked like it to everyone else, to a fellow chronic pain sufferer, I knew his weak spot was a thousand times weaker than even he'd realized.

"I was wondering when I would get to meet you," I said. "How ya doing, Red?"

Swiveling away from Grace, he smiled. It was exactly how I'd imagined it would be. No matter how charming his features may have been, there was a haunting edge to that level of arrogance. "Better than I have

290

been in a long time, Mad dog. How about yourself? Did you enjoy your trip?"

"You don't *trip* on opiates." My smile could never look as conniving as his, but I did my best. "But can't complain. Thanks for that. I got to get high one last time without having to carry the burden of a relapse. Really, I owe you the world."

Just the slightest twitch of his eye was enough to tell me I was getting under his skin. "I knew you'd enjoy it."

No, he didn't. He'd hoped that I would hate myself for it. "That's how it is, huh? We're doing each other favors now? And here I was thinking you hated me."

He shoved Grace to the floor. It took everything I had to appear unaffected by that. Walking toward me, he fished beneath his shirt for the hunting knife on his hip. "But we both know you're lying. No matter how high you are, I know you hate yourself right now. And you should. Josey would still be here if not for you. So would Amber."

I did hate myself for that. But Gayton had told me to be a bitch. To act unfazed. To not give him the rise he craved. "Josey would still be here if you hadn't killed her. Amber would still be here if you hadn't killed her. Audrey would still be here if you hadn't killed her. They would all still be here if *you* hadn't killed them. I didn't kill them. But I did stop you for a year." I laughed, and it wasn't fake. "So, give me credit where it's due, man. I did more than Detective Taylor and the FBI combined."

Eric still wore that snarky smirk, but his jaw clenched beneath his beard. "Well, I suppose I'll have to make up for lost time once you're gone, won't I?"

"I mean, you can try. But your whole obsession with me is sort of a weak point. You went off book. Your original MO, sure, it was hard to pinpoint. But you went from a highly organized killer to one so disorganized that you told the FBI what you do for a living." I laughed again. "A bartender knows your identity. A drug dealer knows your identity. Your comfort zone is this and the surrounding counties, meaning you probably wouldn't feel comfortable killing somewhere else for a very long time, and by then, Ox and the FBI will have figured out who you are."

The chuckle he released was entirely fake. Because he knew. He knew that by fixating on me, he had lost all the method to his madness. "You're not a profiler, Madison. Don't pretend to be."

"You're not intimidating, Eric. Don't pretend to be."

He grasped either armrest and dropped his face only inches before mine. His blue eyes were colder than Ox's, and that was saying something. But I didn't so much as jolt.

I laughed. I laughed so hard that I snorted.

He grabbed me by my throat, swinging me backward against the chair's back. I wouldn't be surprised if it threw something out in my neck. "No? Not at all?"

"If I'm talking," I said between laughs, "you're not squeezing hard enough."

He held harder, and I was still able to laugh. Which only made me laugh harder. The shot I'd hit him with must've caused nerve damage to make his grip so weak, and I found that hilarious.

Was it an act? Maybe. Or maybe it just *was* funny. He wanted me to perceive him as Jack the Ripper, or Ted Bundy, but all I saw was a computer nerd with a half-decent aesthetic. Then again, I didn't see the infamous serial killers as anything special either. They were all weak, punitive pricks who had no talent or substance outside of their egos.

Sure, last night, this entire week, I had been afraid. But now that he was in front of me, he looked just like every other criminal I'd arrested. He wasn't a boogeyman. He was hardly a man at all.

He wasn't even strong enough to choke me out. It was like the punchline of a joke. Even I could choke someone into unconsciousness. The big bad Country Killer who had wreaked havoc on all of southwestern Pennsylvania for a year and a half couldn't even strangle me?

I couldn't stop laughing.

Eric held the tip of that blade to my cheek. "Keep on."

"Or what?" Another laugh. "Are you going to kill me? I thought that was the whole point here."

Hunting Grounds

He pressed deeply into my flesh. It hurt, but only enough to make me stop cackling. Instead, I released something closer to a breathy chuckle. "Or I make her watch as I do to you what I did to all the others."

"You're just gonna use that threat all day, aren't you?" I smiled up at him. "How do you want me to behave? What do you want me to say, *Red?*" My spit smacked him in the cheek. It brought me more joy than it should've. "You want me to act like I'm scared? You want me to cry for my mommy? It's not gonna happen. I don't have the will to live that you think I do." That wasn't true. I did not want to die today. But I was pissing him off, and I was enjoying it. "My life ended when you shot me. You know. You've been sitting there with your binoculars, peeping into my curtains for the last year and a half like a pathetic prepubescent boy, so you're well aware. I don't have all that much to live for, dude. We can do this all week. All month. Hell, we can do it for another year and a half. I'll make you just as miserable as you made me."

Eric wrenched the blade straight down, leaving a burning path of warm blood from the middle of my cheek to my collarbone. I grimaced, but as he lifted the blade away, I laughed.

"You really are just like her." Straightening, a crooked smile played at his lips. "You're prettier, I will say that."

"Yeah?" I tilted my head back to look up at him. "And who's that?"

"Angela. Angela Natalie Castle." Ooh, he was gonna shit talk my mom. Much like I did on a daily basis. "A drain on society. Such a damn smartass. Self-centered. You don't even care that I'm going to kill that little girl. All you care about is getting a rise out of me before you die. Just like you, she willingly accepted her death. She wanted it. All so she could get a bit of relief. Just so she could get a quick laugh in before she took a trip six feet under. And I'm pathetic? Both you and your mother kill yourselves for fun, but I'm the pathetic one, Madison?"

"Ah, touché. I am a lot like her, aren't I? Live in the same trailer park, in her trailer, even in her bedroom." Sighing dramatically, I smiled. "But hey. I'd rather repeat the shitty cycle I was born into than obsess over sleeping *with* her." The warmth in his cheeks receded.

"That's always how it works with you guys. You're all statistics, too. Every single one of you, once we figure out who you are, we compare your mom to your ideal victim, and it's like clockwork. All any of you want is to screw your mom. All I wanted was to get away from mine, but you just wanted to climb back inside her."

"Shut your mouth." For the first time, those blue eyes were actually intimidating. "Before I make you."

That was a good joke, and it pissed me off that no one else was around to hear it.

Attempting to swallow a laugh, another snort escaped me. "Shit, you did, huh? It's okay. You don't have to tell me. But that's the first time you've looked really pissed since this conversation started, so you're telling me without telling me. You screwed your mom." It was cruel, and I wasn't proud of it. I never thought I'd see the day where I mocked someone's sexual assault, but he had me tied to a chair and was threatening to kill me. Forgive me for lacking empathy. "Aw man, and you want to convince me that I'm the messed up one here? Like screwing your mom is normal behavior?"

He stepped in again, eyes like daggers. "Keep going. You're gonna regret it."

"Okay, now, correct me if I'm wrong here, but there's usually a trigger that starts a serial killer's spree. And for the longest time, I was trying to wrap my head around why you went from older victims and gradually worked down to young girls. But you're mid-forties, right? Which would put your mom around seventy, maybe eighty, which is the average life expectancy. So if she died shortly before your spree began, maybe that would explain why you started with defenseless old women. And maybe you worked down in age because when you were reminiscing about her life, you found a photo album of your mom when she was younger." I smirked. "I'm getting warmer, aren't I?"

He glared down at me for a few long moments.

Then he turned around.

Grace's eyes were wide with terror, but her hands were steady. Like she saw the show I was putting on and decided to put on one herself.

With each step he took, I prayed. Not a religious person, but I prayed Grace had remembered the one thing I drilled into her head when we had discussed self-defense. *If they're bigger than you, don't let them get their arms around you.*

It seemed like such a small thing. Obviously, no one wanted their assailant to get their arms around them. But the moment they did, if they were larger, it was over. They then had complete control of your body and any defense you had against them.

"Please don't." Her voice was begging, her doe eyes no different, but she took the slightest step forward and widened her stance. A perfect illusion. "Please don't hurt me."

"You can thank Maddie for this." He reached out to grab her arm. "She just made this so much worse for—"

Grace lifted her hands. The tiniest glint of silver reflected at the edge of her palms as she dropped her fists toward his face.

He squealed.

Crimson sprayed, splashing Grace in the face.

She ducked beneath his arms as he fell into the wall to support his weight. Shimmying past him, she reached for the keys on his hip.

"You little bitch—" He spun toward her.

Grace rammed her fists into his back. Her hands were still tied, but that razor blade must have stuck out of the crease between her fingers. Because he screamed again and a line of red tainted his black jacket.

She did it again, slamming that razor blade into his back. As he dropped to the ground, she collapsed on top of him and stabbed him again, pinning him in place as he squealed and writhed beneath her. Again, she lifted the razor and slammed it into his wrist that held the hunting knife. He screamed, and she tried to grab it, but he twitched and writhed. She only managed to shove it from his grasp. As if for good measure, she plunged the razor into his back one more time, and his squeal morphed into a dull, quiet groan. It gave her just enough time to grab the keys off his hip, as well as the gun.

Holy shit. I had never been more proud in my life.

She slid the gun across the room, hurried to her feet, snatched the knife off the ground, and ran to me. Dropping the hunting knife to my lap, she jumped behind me and fumbled with the keys.

Moaning in pain, Eric tried his damnedest to get up. Arms trembling, breaths uneven, he made it all of two inches off the floor before dropping back to it.

"Give me the keys," I said, wiggling my fingers, "grab that gun, and run."

"I-I'm not leaving you," she said, followed by the *clink* of the keys hitting the ground. "Shit."

Gaining traction, Eric pulled his knees up beneath him. Relying on his lower body strength, he used his right arm to get himself onto all fours.

"Get your ass out of here *right now*." I grasped the keys when they touched my hand again. "Go, Grace. *Go now*."

Breaths hard and uneven, her shaking fingers grazed mine. "But I—"

"*Now!*" I shook my fingers from her grasp and found the small handcuff key. Fiddling with it, I used my thumb to find the hole on the cuffs and quickly inserted it.

She let out a sound that could have been a whimper or sob, followed by, "I'm sorry," and her feet slamming against the hardwoods. The squeak of hinges and the smacking of a screen door sounded next.

She was out.

It only took me two seconds to free my arms.

Bending to reach the rope around my ankles, I watched Eric out of the corner of my eye. With one hand on the wall, he searched for a lip to dip his fingers into. To help him upright.

The gun was on my right, only a few feet away. Closer to me than him.

Between deep, panting breaths, Eric said, "She should have kept stabbing. You might've lived if she had."

Chapter 47

Good leg first.

I needed to get my good leg out first.

Untying the rope was taking too much time. Instead, I chiseled with the hunting knife until my leg was free. Hated to say it, but I was sorta glad he'd drugged me this time because I may've been in the midst of a panic attack if he hadn't.

Just as I swung toward my bad leg, the one that was still tied, Eric made it onto his feet with a groan.

One leg was free. The one farthest from the gun.

But screw it.

Swinging all my weight toward the left, I dropped sideways toward the gun. Pain shot through my elbow when it hit the ground, chair thumping with me. Guessed the drugs were wearing off after all.

I stretched with all my might, but the gun was just out of my reach. Only a foot away. Inches, maybe.

Eric collapsed toward it, sending it flying farther from my reach.

A steel toed kick rammed into my face.

Vision blurred, aching, I closed my fingers tighter around the blade. Blinking hard through the blood pooling in my eyes, I slammed the knife in his direction. I didn't realize what I hit until he toppled to the ground. To the left. Where he'd tossed the gun.

Now they were both out of my reach.

Using all the strength I had, I shimmied toward my legs and chiseled again at the rope on my ankle. At the very least, this fight was giving Grace more time to run. I didn't know if I had any chance, but she did. Grace had a chance.

One more layer. The rope wrapped around me four times. Just one more layer.

Maybe I had a chance too.

Cord fraying, little spindles weakening with each stroke of the serrated blade, that hope grew stronger. Stronger still when it came free. My leg collapsed to the ground, free of the rope.

But a hand fisted my hair and yanked my head backward. Like a handle, he used my knotted waves to pull me to my feet.

Before I had time to process, he slammed me backward into the wall. Cold metal touched my throat. He must've had another knife in his pocket.

A slice of bloody flesh descended from his forehead halfway down his cheek. With gritted teeth, he panted hard.

I fisted my blade behind his back, but I couldn't stab him. Not when his knife was already against my throat. He'd have plenty of time to kill me, just as I killed him.

He didn't speak. Only stared at me with the coldest, darkest look I'd ever seen. It was some combination of fury, hatred, and maybe desire. Maybe because what he wanted had nothing to do with intimacy. It was about power. He got off on the struggle for it but calling it desire wasn't fair. Desire deserved better than this piece of shit.

"If I die, you die with me," I said.

"Maybe," he said, voice low. "Or maybe I kill you, and then I go find that little girl. It's getting late. She can't make it out of here on her own once it's dark."

"She knows these woods as well as you do." That was a lie, but both mine and Grace's best shot here was if I got that blade off my throat.

Even if he were chasing Grace, it'd give me an opportunity to kill him before he could kill either of us. "It's just a matter of time before Ox shows with the FBI, Eric."

That sadistic, fury filled expression dwindled. Instead, his mouth opened slightly in disbelief, confusion. "What did you just say?"

"Eric." Time for the *big* bluff. "Eric Oakley."

Face pale, either from fear or blood loss, Eric shook his head. His hand on the blade at my neck trembled. "Grace told you that."

"Eric Oakley," I repeated, giving a smile. "Born to Kendra and Robert Oakley. Sister, Violet Oakley, now Violet Lewis. Graduated top of his class from Carnegie Mellon University. Worked for a small security company in Somerset County for most of his life after graduating college, only to shift gears and teach middle school computer science about a year ago. Upper-middle class. Failed engagement to Lisa Morris. I'm sure there's a story there, and I'm sure there's a story as to why your sister doesn't have a single photo with you on her Facebook page, but I don't care to hear your side of it."

I half expected him to run, half expected him to kill me. Instead, his hands trembled and his breathing quickened.

Smiling, I brought the blade closer to his spine. "Yeah. I knew who you were well before I got here. So does Detective Taylor, and the FBI, and your sister, and your ex-fiancé. They all know. You left a fingerprint at Rachel's apartment. We got in contact with Joe O'Meinah. He still had a paper copy of your fingerprints from when you were hired. We compared them, and it was a match." Smile stretching wider, I let out a quiet laugh. "I still don't know how you did the DNA thing, but you should've thought about that fingerprint.

"Oh, and Grace told me you were at Laurel Ridge Forest on the phone. You should've known that was why I wanted to talk to her. Considering what I do for a living, considering my history with you, you don't think that Grace and I had worked out some type of code for situations like this?" Total bluff, but if I made it out of here, we were *absolutely* developing a code for situations like this. "They wanted to come in here guns blazing, but I told them that if we did that, Grace would die. Let me go in. Let me get in his head. Let me get Grace out, and then let me get him to surrender himself. Because I promised him that I would give him a punishment worse than death.

"And this? Ruining his sparkling reputation? His family name? Stories coming out about how he raped young girls, possibly his own mother, becoming the laughingstock of the state? Or the nation?" My smile stretched wide. "Well, this is the worst torture I could give a narcissist. Seeing the look on your face when you realize everyone in the world is about to know who you are and what you've done. It won't be The Country Killer, or The Red Ribbon Killer, or Red, attached to the sick, twisted murders. It'll be you. Eric Oakley. As soon as the sun goes down, Eric Oakley's life is over. You won't even be The Country Killer. You will be some pathetic, incestual creep who doesn't even get an episode on Dateline."

Eric's eyes flicked to the window, as if to check whether the sun had set.

And there was my opportunity.

I rammed my good knee into his gut with all my strength. Hot pain seared against my throat, but he stumbled to the side, and I didn't fall with him. That was my only assurance that I hadn't died.

Lunging to the gun, I fell to the hardwoods with a grunt.

But I wrapped my hand around it. Just as footsteps stomped behind me.

Whirling around, I pulled the trigger before I even aimed. Wasted a bullet, too, because all I saw was a glimmer of his back as he bolted through the door.

"No damn way," I said, struggling up off the floor.

The screen door slammed.

How grateful I was for that heroin right about now. I could actually run after him. Wasn't even limping as I chased him toward the exit. I didn't know if I would catch him, but I knew I would shoot him.

He wasn't going to leave. He wasn't going to disappear, only to reappear in two years, or five years, or ten. Eric Oakley was going to die today. If I died trying, so be it. It would be worth it if he could never kill again.

Reaching for the storm door handle, my gaze caught on the hunting rifle leaning against the doorframe. I loved pistols, but we were in the woods. Leaving it here behind an unlocked door didn't seem wise either.

Shoving the pistol into my hoodie pocket, I grabbed the rifle.

That awfully familiar sound, the crank of an engine, accompanied by a rattle and a rev, the one that still haunted my nightmares, echoed from behind the door. The engine turnover of a four-wheeler.

"Oh, hell no," I said, throwing the door open.

Just before me, only a few hundred yards ahead, Eric slammed the gas and took off up the hill.

Lining up my shot through the scope, I prayed to hell and back that Grace was nowhere nearby. In fact, that *no one* was anywhere nearby. Because this was murder. I would not get away with it in court. He was fleeing. I had no reason to shoot.

But I did. I shot.

I aimed for the center of his back, but he hit a bump that lifted him higher off the ground. The bullet slashed through his tire with a roaring *pop*!

He fell sideways.

Disguised by the brush, I lined up another shot.

Then a glint of silver swung up from the foliage.

Boom!

I ducked to the ground for cover.

Damn it, he had a gun, too. It'd help me out in the inevitable trial, but it was gonna make this a hell of a lot harder.

"*Woof! Woof!*"

My stomach dropped.

On the left, out of the corner of my eye, a ball of black fur came into view.

A wave of panic crashed over me. "Tempest, *stop!*"

She did. Then her tail wagged. She started charging toward me instead.

"Cover!" I told her.

She dropped to her belly and vanished into the foliage.

Breath of relief escaping me, I whispered, "Good girl."

On my right, only a few dozen yards from the quad, the blur of Eric's jacket disappeared around a tree.

He couldn't get away. I could not let him get away.

Jogging off the rickety stairs, my feet whacked against the soil as if it, too, were my enemy. Swatting at tree branches, ignoring the thorns that caught on my pant legs, my heart pounded against my ribs like thunder on a metal roof in a summer storm. Violent and angry, but somehow tranquil and beautiful at the same time.

For the first time in a long time, I didn't feel an ounce of physical pain. As I ran with all my might down the path Eric had disappeared onto, all I felt was hope. Hope that it was finally over. Hope that the pain that'd haunted me all this time would vanish. Hope that all those victims would get justice. Hope that I would make it to him before the cops did. "Maddie!" Two voices called out behind me, repeating on a round. Just when one finished, another began. "Maddie!"

They could wait. Ox and Bentley could wait. If Ox saw me kill Eric while he fled, I might be the one who ended up on the stand.

I had to keep running. I couldn't wait for them to catch up either way. He would disappear into the wilderness, and he would continue to torture us for years to come. This had to end. *Today.*

Following the sound of Eric's heaving breaths, he finally came into view. Half a dozen yards ahead, half tucked behind a tree. He was catching his breath. Only his shoulder was visible, most of him disguised behind the trunk. A pistol couldn't make this shot, but a rifle could.

God, I hoped the rifle could.

Holding my breath, tucked behind a tree myself, I squatted to grab a rock. Holding it and straightening, I propped the gun in place on my shoulder and lined up my shot.

I tossed the rock.

He swung around the tree.

I pulled the trigger.

Boom!

Boom!

So had he. But Eric's bullet whirred past me.

His head jarred backward.

He collapsed to the ground with a thump.

A breathy laugh of relief escaped me. It was over. He was dead.

I hoped, anyway. Still holding the gun in place, prepared to shoot again, I took a step around the tree to start that way, to make certain he was—

"Maddie," Ox said behind me.

I spun around, ready to tell him to stay quiet, but the words lodged in my throat.

Only a few strides behind me, grasping a tree, he cupped a hand beneath his armpit. The only part of his torso not covered by a bullet proof vest.

The cop killing shot.

Blinking hard, he lifted his fingers. Dark crimson pooled in his palm, dripping down his white undershirt. "It doesn't hurt this time."

He toppled.

Chapter 48

"BENTLEY!" I SCREAMED, RUNNING TO OX AS FAST AS I COULD. "Bentley! He shot him! He shot Ox!"

Collapsing to my knees beside Ox, pressing my hand into the wound, I screamed something else, something I don't remember. A lot of things, more than likely. All to the same effect. "Help me! Please help me!"

"You're bleeding," Ox made out between trembling lips, blood-soaked fingers reaching up to cup my cheek. "He hurt you."

"I'm fine," I said, glancing away for only a second to yell, "*Bentley!* Help me!"

"What did he do to you?" Ox asked, color in his face draining.

"Stop talking. Save your energy." Whipping my head around, I yelled, "Bentley! I need some God damned help—"

Rounding the bend of a large rock, he came into view, running as fast as humanly possible.

Holding my face a bit tighter, Ox brought my attention back to him. He stroked his thumb along my cheek where Eric had cut me. "Is this all?"

"That's all." Searching for the exit wound, I patted down his body. "Where does it hurt?"

Ever so slightly, Ox shook his head. "It doesn't."

No. No, no, *no*.

Pain existed for a reason. It was the body's way of telling you something was wrong. Chronic pain served no evolutionary purpose, but pain from trauma was for survival. Pain from trauma said, "Pay attention. Something's wrong here. Fix it."

If you could feel no pain...

"Is he dead?" Ox asked.

I nodded. I wasn't certain, but I nodded. "He's gone. He'll never hurt anyone again."

Ox smiled. For a decade, I had known this man, and I had never seen him smile as big as he did in this moment. "You're gonna tell everyone it was me though, right? I-I get to be the hero this time?"

"You're gonna tell everyone that yourself." I managed to smile for him, despite the tears burning across my eyes. "I'll help you write the bullshit report."

Ox laughed, blood spraying from his lips. "Ah, shit." His shaking hand lifted to wipe it away, and he murmured, "I don't think I will, Mads."

"You're fine." Furrowing my brows, I fought with everything I had to keep from crying. Ox's lips were turning blue. His face was paper white. I didn't hear sirens roaring, so I didn't know if an ambulance was nearby. I wasn't sure it would matter either way. We were miles upon miles from civilization, at least an hour's drive to the hospital. "You're gonna be fine."

Bentley dropped to his knees beside me, tearing open his medical bag. "How you doing, man?"

Ox let out something between a huff and a laugh that ended in another blood splattering cough.

"He says it doesn't hurt," I said to Bentley.

If Bentley was overtly concerned about that, he didn't show it. He didn't even look at me. He went straight into the zone, tearing off Ox's bulletproof vest and hurriedly slicing through his shirt. Was that a good thing? Did that mean he thought he would make it if he worked fast enough?

Bentley edged my hands away from Ox's wound and began packing it with gauze. "Does that hurt?"

Shaking his head, eyes drifting down to barely open slits, Ox gestured to the rifle. "You wipe that down and put it in my hands, okay?"

"Okay." Bentley managed to smile for him. "I'm gonna roll you over to look for the exit wound, alright?"

Ox nodded.

"Maddie, look at me," Bentley said. I did. I wished I hadn't, though, because that face told me everything I was most afraid of. The softness in his big brown eyes, the way his forehead wrinkled, the bob of his throat with a hard swallow. "I'm gonna roll him, and I'm gonna keep him there while I pack his wound. I just need you to support his neck, okay? Can you do that?"

It took everything I had to keep from sobbing because I knew what Bentley was thinking. I knew, and I wished I didn't. But I nodded, and I gently grasped Ox's neck on either side, holding it straight as Bentley rolled him.

There was already a pond of blood pooling beside Ox, but it gushed from his back like a fountain. It wasn't only the blood, but the location of it that made my heart stop beating. Center of his back, directly on the spine, just beneath his shoulder blades. That was where the bullet had come out.

"You going to the Steelers training camp next month?" Bentley asked Ox, wedging gauze deep into the wound.

"Hm?" Ox struggled out.

"You know. The Steelers training camp," Bentley said, voice calm, but shaking fingers telling me what I feared. So did the fact that he was trying to distract him with sports. "You're a Steelers fan, aren't you?"

Ox made a noise. Maybe it was intended to be a laugh, but it sounded more like a gurgle. "It's-it's a requirement in the city."

"Aw, man, you should've seen what happened when I was at a

306

Browns game with a Steelers jersey on," Bentley said, chuckling, packing more and more gauze into his wound. "My wife made me take it off and walk around shirtless in sixty-degree weather so we didn't get mugged on the way home."

"Better Cleveland than Baltimore," Ox murmured.

"Or Philly. Those Philadelphians love their Eagles." Bentley stuck a few more sheets of gauze onto Ox's back and taped them in place. Grabbing a hoodie from his bag, he rolled it into a ball and pressed it firmly against Ox's back. Turning my way, he said, "I'm gonna roll him back now. Keep supporting his neck."

I nodded, then did so. In those few moments that he had faced away from me, he had shapeshifted into a different man. There was no color in his cheeks, nor in his lips. His eyes were barely parted. And yet, that always chilling blue gaze was the warmest I had ever seen it.

Arm trembling as he lifted his hand to my face, he smiled. "Keep in touch with my mom, okay? Sh-she misses you."

"Stop that." Voice cracking, my lips quivered. "Don't you tell me goodbye, Lennox."

He still smiled, but there were tears in his eyes now too. "You're all she has left. Be there for her through this."

Shaking my head quickly, my tears flooded over. "Stop it."

"She'll keep in touch." Packing more gauze into the wound, Bentley kept his voice soft. "You know she will."

Ox nodded, salty water running from the corners of his eyes. "Y-you be the one to tell her. And-and tell her I was stupid. Tell her I-I just had to top you." He smiled again. I'd always wanted to see him smile more, but now, I just wanted him to be mad. I wanted him to yell and scream and stomp out of this forest, dragging me by my elbow, furious I'd done this. "I had to be the hero this time."

"You've always been a hero," I said, accompanied by a gasping snif-fle. I knew what was coming. I hated it, but I knew, and I wanted him to know how much I loved him. I spent so much time hating him, and after this, I would never forgive myself for it. "You were my hero. You know that, right? You showed me a life I didn't know existed. You were my hero."

Sniffling too, wheezing, he shook his head. "You're your own hero. You always were."

Sob quaking through me, I held his cheek tighter. "I'm sorry. I'm so sorry for everything."

"I shouldn't have—" A blood splattering cough cut him off. "Chased you. You d-didn't need me."

"I'm sorry," was all I could make out, dropping onto his chest to hug him. "I'm so sorry."

"Stop that shit." His voice was hardly audible in my ear. Stroking a hand up and down my back, he pulled me as close to him as space allowed. "S-stop blaming yourself for shit you didn't do."

All I could do was sob. Sob, and hug him closer.

"L-let Bentley in, okay?" Ox kissed the top of my head. "He's g-good for you. He-he'll give you th-the life you want."

I couldn't respond. All I could do was weep.

"Take care of her for me," he said to Bentley.

"Th-this is okay," Ox whispered. "Dying with you in my a-arms. That's wh-what I would've picked." Another one of those gurgling laughs. "Y-you remember that?"

I did, but it wasn't funny. I couldn't laugh.

A few months into our relationship, the song *Died in Your Arms* by Cutting Crew had come on the radio while we were driving to dinner. I told him to turn it up. He mocked me. As I often did, I'd embraced his teasing. Turning the volume all the way up, dancing obnoxiously in the passenger seat, I shouted the lyrics at the top of my lungs.

It'd made him laugh until we were pulling into the restaurant. When the song ended, he'd turned the volume down and said, "Guess if I gotta die, it'd be nice to go in your arms."

For the years that followed, any time that song came on the radio, I'd reenacted that moment, dancing obnoxiously, shouting the lyrics.

Hugging me a little tighter, he whispered again, "R-remember?"

Another weep tearing through me, I nodded.

"Sing it for m-me."

"Go to hell," I said, gasping with my next sob.

His chest shook with another one of those wet laughs. "C'mon."

I shook my head. Partly because it was crude and stupid. Mostly because I could barely breathe.

Ox squeezed me closer to him. "P-please?"

"My singing'll make you grab your gun and blow your brains out."

A very faint, hardly there, chuckle. "Sing i-it, Mads."

That didn't sound like Ox anymore. His voice was so muddled, so clogged from blood, that he sounded like a different person. His hug, his limp hold on me, didn't feel like Ox's infamous brick wall of a touch. It was soft. Desperate. Pleading.

His dying wish was to hear me sing a sappy eighties song, so I sang the sappy eighties song. I sang it, and I cried, and I hugged him with all my strength, tighter when he chuckled. Like if I hugged him tight enough, if I cried loud enough, maybe he'd stay with me long enough to make it to the hospital. Maybe he wouldn't die today.

When I made it to the end of the song, he kissed the top of my head one more time. "Thank you."

And his chest stopped moving.

"Ox." I sat up and grabbed his cool cheeks. His eyes were shut. His lips were as pale as his cheeks aside from the red droplets of blood. His chest was still. "Ox, stay with me." I shook his shoulders. "Don't do this. Don't die on me. Wake up. *Wake up!*"

He didn't.

"What do I do?" Panicked, I swiveled toward Bentley. "Do I— Should I start CPR?"

Crying silently, Bentley swallowed hard. "He's gone, Mads."

The tears stopped while I sang, but those three words brought them back with a vengeance. Shaking my head furiously, I turned back to Ox, half expecting him to make a crass joke about my singing, or the irony that he came to rescue me only to die, or how stupid I was for thinking he'd survive this.

But Ox was the stillest thing in this forest. The trees swayed with the wind. The clouds floated overhead. The bugs flew from every direction.

And Ox's body was still.

Another cry, the strongest one so far, echoed from my lips down the mountainside and off the surrounding ones.

"Come here," Bentley whispered, curling his arms around my waist. He caught my weight when I toppled. Soothing a hand along my hair, he held me close, whispering, "I know. I know," to every sob I released.

Staring down at him, I kept thinking he would wake. That this was some cruel joke. Like he was getting back at me for all the time I spent hating him.

I kept thinking, *This isn't natural.* Death was as natural as birth, and yet, it was the most inexplicable paradox known to man. Dying was like a cosmic joke to whomever was in charge of it all.

Witnessing it before my eyes, watching a person I had once loved so much ebb from existence, made no sense. It was entirely illogical. How could he be here one second and gone the next? How could he be cussing at me a minute ago, laughing at me, teasing me, and then just vanish? How could this be real? How could this, while the forest swayed and danced around us and the sun shined in the sky and the birds chirped in the trees, be where we all ended up?

Why wasn't it on that swing of the wraparound porch watching those we loved frolic through a field? Why wasn't that where we all ended up?

I don't know how long Bentley held me, nor how long I cried. Only that he didn't let me go until we heard sirens. Kissing my forehead, he tugged back enough to free his arms.

Once he straightened, he grabbed the hunting rifle from the ground beside me, raised it carefully, and lifted Ox's drooping hand to it. He wrapped his fingers around the barrel, the trigger, then his bloody hand as well, to smear the prints. So that it looked like Ox touched it as he went down. Not to wipe my prints away, but so that ballistics didn't prove it'd been the wrong hand on the trigger.

Then, with Ox's limp arm raised, Bentley cocked it.

Which only made me cry again. "Let him be."

Eyes full of sympathy, Bentley frowned. "There needs to be gun powder on his hands."

"I don't care," I whispered. "I don't care if I go to jail. Just let him be."

Bentley's frown deepened. "He wanted to protect you one more time. Let him."

Shaking my head, heartbroken and angry, I turned away and pinched my eyes shut.

Boom!

Chapter 49

THE NEXT FEW HOURS WERE A BLUR.

I had hurt myself somewhere. Whether it was in the fight with Eric, the trek up the mountain, or dropping beside Ox, I didn't know. I just knew that I needed Bentley's help getting up, and then walking back to the cabin.

Grace was okay. She had some nasty cuts on her hands from the razor blades and needed stitches. Bentley believed her wrist was broken as well, but nothing life-threatening.

Tempest was fine. Bentley said she was how they'd found us. Ox had told her to "Find Mom," and she took off. She found Grace first. While we'd tended to Ox, Tempest had tended to Grace.

We didn't tell Grace what happened, but she must've put two and two together. When I sat on the ground beside her and Tempest, she tucked her arms around me and hugged me with all her might. I cried. She cried. Bentley cried.

We were all sobbing by the time Derek came into view with the FBI agents not far behind. Bentley took them to Ox's and Eric's bodies. I had to walk away while they carried Ox out of the woods on a stretcher. Watching them carry Eric's body didn't bring me close to the satisfaction I'd hoped it would.

Hunting Grounds

They asked me what happened. I didn't have good answers for them. One second, I was telling them about the phone Eric had hidden in my closet, and the next, I was bawling at the memory of Ox's final moments.

Eventually, somewhere near an hour and a half later, another detective showed up. One I hadn't seen in a while, and one I wouldn't have thought I'd wanted to. Not until she was running up the hill in tears, at least.

Ashley Harper. My ex-best friend. The best friend who had ruined mine and Ox's relationship.

That all seemed so stupid now. It was stupid for her to have slept with him, it was stupid for him to have slept with her, and it was stupid for me to have hated them both for it.

We could never be best friends again. I would never trust her alone with a partner of mine again. But I wasn't sure if anyone else understood what I was going through right now. She came closest.

She took my statement as well. I told her that Ox had ripped the gun out of my hands and ran after Eric once I'd fired the first shot that blew out his quad tire, and that I then chased after Ox. I said that I saw Eric and Ox shoot simultaneously and both go down.

Harper knew Ox. She knew he wouldn't have tried to take a gun out of my hands when there was a serial killer running away. Also knew he wouldn't have succeeded. She knew Ox wouldn't have stood out in the open and waited for a shootout, either.

But she didn't call me a liar. She just said, "I bet he's glad he got to be the hero."

At that point, I started sobbing again. We hugged. She apologized for my loss, and I apologized for hers.

Right around that time, Bentley walked my way. He said that he'd given his statement, as had Grace, and that he needed to get her to the hospital so she could get stitches. I gave them both a hug before they left.

Harper said the technicians would be here for a while. That Alex would come as well to take photos of the scene, then offered to drive me home. I assumed she mentioned Alex because she figured I would prefer for Alex to drive me home. I would have if there were no other options.

At that moment, though? I didn't want to talk. I didn't want to regurgitate the story. Alex would be as much of a mess as I was. Harper would overcompensate and offer to get me something to eat or play music that the three of us had memories of like a soundtrack, or maybe even offer to buy me a drink. I wasn't sure if she knew about my addiction and sobriety, and I didn't want now to be the time I shared it with her.

I just wanted to cuddle with my dog and get the hell out of this place.

Derek was still around, so I asked if he could drive me. Of course, he agreed. He was low on gas, so we stopped at the closest station. He went in. I sat in the passenger seat hugging my nearly hundred-pound German Shepherd like she was a baby. She didn't mind.

When Derek came back out, he said nothing. Just handed me a bottle of pop and a candy bar. Like he had when I was a kid. It didn't make the pain any less intense, but it tasted good. That was something.

Then he drove me home. He helped me to my door, encouraging me to go to the hospital with every limp. Whatever I had banged up wasn't a medical emergency, and I said so, followed by, "I just need to get out of these clothes, anyway. I have somewhere else to go."

"Then I'll wait for you to get a shower, and we'll go together." I protested, and he said, "That asshole gave you heroin, Maddie. You're not getting behind the wheel, and don't you dare argue with me. I'll follow you, arrest you, and give you a DUI."

I stopped arguing, washed Ox's blood off in the shower, got dressed and got back into the passenger seat of his cruiser. The drive was long. It was 10 PM by the time we arrived. And once we did, I didn't want to get out of the car.

But I did. I had to, so I did. That was the story of my life, wasn't it? It needed to be done, so I did it, even if I didn't want to.

Hunting Grounds

Once I stood, Tempest jumped up beside me and came right beside my hip. With her harness, I used her strength for support and started up the concrete walkway.

Gazing up at the house, I had to hold my breath to retain my composure. I would never forget the first time I walked up this path and looked up at this house. A cozy suburb. A brown house that looked just like every other one on the block. Two stories. Faux glowing votive candles in each window.

It was nothing extravagant. But I'd been so naïve back then. I had gaped in awe, as though it was a castle. For someone like me, it was. To me, anything that wasn't rusted and falling apart was a fantasy.

That was how I'd ended up here in the first place. A guy who hadn't been falling apart thought I was pretty, offered to buy me dinner, and that was a fantasy I'd been overjoyed to see turn to reality.

"*This* is where you grew up?" I'd asked Ox.

Holding my hand, he'd glanced between me and the house with his face scrunched up in confusion. "Yeah? Why?"

"It just seems like something out of a sitcom."

This was no sitcom. Sitcoms made you feel good. Made you laugh, made you smile, then made you forget. Five minutes after finishing one, you had no idea what it'd been about.

Mine and Ox's story wasn't like that. There were so few laughs, so few smiles, and I could never forget the bits of good nor the abundance of bad. I would never forget the tragic ending, either.

As much as I loved Ox, I wouldn't put him on a pedestal just because he was dead. We weren't good together. We were never meant to be a couple. But we'd been repairing our platonic relationship. This couldn't have been how we were meant to end.

Me, walking up this pathway without him, knocking on the big red door, bracing to tell his mother that her baby was gone.

This couldn't have been how we were meant to end.

But it was.

After a few cricket chirps, a light flicked on inside. Her footsteps

L.T. Ryan

padded to the door. She peeked through the curtains, gave me that same confused look her son had the day I'd first met her, and pulled it open. "Hey, sweetie. What are you doing here?"

I opened my mouth to speak, but as had happened so often recently, nothing came out.

Stepping closer, glancing past me at Derek in his cruiser, Teresa put a hand on my arm. "Are you in trouble?"

"No, nothing like that." But that was as much as I could say.

Teresa had only ever been kind to me. The mother I had always dreamed of. I adored her. I idolized her. She was the woman I had always wanted to become. Smart, career-focused, successful, and still passionate about her family. Loving to her son, but not overtly so. She was so good in a world that had always looked so bad. She deserved nothing but good.

What I was about to say would be the worst thing she'd ever heard. Her entire world was about to explode, and I was the one holding the match to the fuse.

I wanted to stretch this moment out. I wanted her to have another minute, even a few seconds, before I said the words that would change her life forever.

"Maddie." She gave my arm a gentle squeeze. "Talk to me, sweetie. What's going on?"

The dam broke. I was supposed to stay strong, make this easier for her, but the dam broke, and I wept, "He's gone. I'm so sorry. Ox's gone. I'm so sorry. I'm so sorry, Teresa. I'm so sorry."

Holding a hand over her heart, she only stared at me for a few seconds. "What?"

"The Country Killer." Cupping a hand over my mouth to keep from scream crying, I made out through the gaps of my fingers, "He shot Ox just as Ox shot him. He died in my arms. I tried to help him but where the bullet hit, he bled out so fast, and he died in my arms. I'm so sorry, Teresa. I'm so sorry."

For a few heartbeats, she just stared at me in disbelief. "I just talked to him. A few hours ago, he was driving, and I talked to him."

I didn't say anything. I only kept my hands before my mouth and held my breath to trap the grief inside.

When it set in, she grabbed the doorway to keep herself standing. Her lips began to swell, and then tremble. "He's dead?"

"I'm so sorry. I'm so, *so* sorry."

"My baby." Stumbling sideways, the tears erupted from her eyes like fountains. I caught her shoulders, helping her to the ground as she cried. "My baby. My baby's dead."

* * *

I WOULDN'T HAVE BLAMED HER IF SHE DIDN'T WANT TO SEE ME anymore. But she asked me to come in. While she sat on the sofa, I brewed our tea. Then I told her the story that Ox wanted me to tell her. I didn't call him stupid, as he had asked me to, but I wouldn't tell her the truth. I would take to my grave that I had been the one to shoot The Country Killer.

Not because I cared about going to jail. That had nothing to do with it.

Ox wanted to be the hero.

After I told her what happened, we cried. We hugged. Then we talked about the good things. All our pleasant memories with him. We laughed, and we cried some more, and then we hugged some more. Not long after the tea was gone, Teresa poured herself a healthy glass of vodka. She offered me some. Teresa knew about my addiction, so I wasn't sure why. Maybe she had forgotten in the haze of it all, or maybe she figured this was an adequate reason to abandon my sobriety.

I declined. I hadn't wanted to.

Alcohol had never been my drug of choice anyway. Since the beginning of time, however, it had been an excellent analgesic. I wanted that. I wanted to be numb. I wanted oxies. I wanted heroin. I wanted relief. I wanted to rewind time and keep that damn idiot from chasing after me.

I couldn't. That put heroin and oxies next on the list of things I wanted most.

By the time Teresa was done with the bottle, she was hardly conscious. I covered her with a blanket, made sure she lay on her side, locked the door, and walked outside with Tempest. Part of me suspected that Derek had gone home, but he hadn't. Good thing, too, because I would have called Simeon to get drugs if he had.

When I got in the car, I told him he hadn't needed to wait for me. I could've gotten an Uber. He said, "Don't worry about it, kid," and handed me another pop and candy bar.

I smiled at him, thanked him, and tore it open. I was one bite in when he said, "I know it doesn't feel as good as what he gave you today, but at least this won't ruin your life. It'll just make you fat."

Was that his way of saying, *Don't do drugs, kid?* It didn't stifle the urge, but I appreciated the sentiment.

"Bentley won't care if you get fat," Derek said. "But I don't think he's gonna let Grace see any more than she's already seen, Maddie."

The craving was still there. I desperately wanted that numb peaceful dream. But not as badly as I wanted the fantasy I had lived in that dream.

That was the extent of the conversation as we drove. Derek didn't say much else aside from asking if I liked this song or that on the radio. When we got to my house, he just said, "You call me if you need me."

I forced a smile. "Yes, sir."

Derek smiled back.

As I stepped out of the car with Tempest at my side, the first thing I saw was Ox's car. Parked in my driveway. Waiting for him to return to it.

I knew it was there, but for whatever reason, it made me cry again. It made me crave that numb, peace-filled dream.

So I didn't go home.

I walked next door, stepped up the stairs, and lifted my fist to knock. I didn't though. I just stared at the door with my fist raised.

After everything today, who the hell did I think I was? His daughter was kidnapped because of me. She'd almost died because of me. He was working for a damn drug lord again because of me. I had gotten high today. No, I wouldn't have done it if I hadn't been coerced into it, but I *had* done it. I still *wanted* to do it.

I had the audacity to walk over here crying? To play the victim?

My problems were not his problems. I couldn't put them on him. That wasn't fair. Expecting him to pick me up when I fell apart wasn't—

The door swung open.

Jumping, Bentley dropped the empty pizza box that was in his hand.

"I'm sorry," I said. "It's four in the morning. I shouldn't have just walked over—"

"Don't apologize." Letting out a breathy laugh, he bent to grab the empty box. "I mean, apologize for scaring the shit out of me, but you know you're welcome here anytime."

Maybe it was the drugs, maybe the trauma or the grief, but just looking at him brought the tears back. He was so good. He wasn't perfect, but he was so good, the way Teresa was so good, and I didn't deserve them.

There was nothing I wanted more than to find somebody who would sell me a little bag of pills or white powder. Bentley deserved someone better. He deserved someone who would help him get out of this shit, not someone who would pull him deeper into it the way I had today with Simeon. He wanted better for Grace, and I was only dragging them deeper into turmoil. He was so good to me, just as he was to every broken person who stumbled into his life, to the point of his detriment. I would be his detriment this time, just as I had nearly been today.

Just as I had been to Ox.

"Hey, hey." Eyes softening, he reached out to thumb my tears away. "Are you hungry?"

I was, but I shook my head.

Wetting his lips, he tucked my hair behind my ear. "Do you just want to sit and talk? I can't sleep either. You want to drink some coffee?"

"I wanna get high." The tears fell faster. "That's not your problem. My sobriety is my problem. But I really want to get high, and coming over here seemed like a better option than going over there by myself, where I can call Simeon, or Noah, or any of the other kids we went to school with who would take my money and let me throw my life away. But I already put you through so much today, and I don't want to throw this at you too, and—"

"Maddie." Dropping the pizza box again, he took my face in his hands. His eyes were loving and firm at once. "I've been waiting for you to come home all night. I didn't want you to be alone after what happened today, either." It physically hurt to hold his gaze when I was this close to sobbing again. That kind, loving expression was a hot sun melting the walls I had always worked so hard to keep sturdy around me. "You're not a burden, okay?"

Holding his forearms, my lips quivered. "I don't want to ruin your life. Grace almost died today because of—"

"Because of a serial killer. Not because of you. You were ready to sacrifice your life for hers. You *saved* her. You didn't have to do that, but you did, and I'll never be able to explain how grateful I am. You're not *ruining* anything." Wiping my tears with one hand, he circled the other around my waist. "This wasn't your fault. It's not your fault Ox died. Stop punishing yourself. Don't isolate and crawl into that dark place again because of it. You're not taking advantage of me. You're not hurting me. I'm your friend, and I wanna be here for you. *Please* let me be here for you."

There was a small part of me that wanted to do just that. To push him away. To self sabotage as I so often did.

Then I heard Ox in my mind, whispering, *Stop blaming yourself for shit you didn't do,* followed by, *He's good for you.*

So I nodded.

Giving a barely-there smile, he leaned in and kissed me softly. Rather than pulling away when the kiss was over, he pulled me into his chest and held me close.

While the cicadas sang, and Bentley held me in the glow of the noon, a layer of warmth as cozy as the sun coasted over every inch of my skin, just like it had on that porch. The warmth was soothing, safe, but it wasn't as good as that drug-induced dream, because there, I had felt no pain. The warmth I felt now was soothing, but every breath still hurt.

No physical pain had ever compared to this. But it hurt because it had once been so good. This hurt because Ox had saved me when he took me to that house in the suburbs, when he'd shown me that everything I'd been conditioned to believe was normal wasn't, that there was more to life than getting high and living paycheck to paycheck. And I could never return the favor. I couldn't save him like he saved me.

If it had all been bad, this wouldn't have hurt. *That* was the cosmic joke posed by the universe, wasn't it? Like how I hadn't known the comfort of safety until he'd shown it to me; without knowing how it felt to hurt, there wasn't a way to appreciate the warmth of safety when its arms were around you.

With a kiss on my forehead, Bentley whispered, "I'm gonna make you something to eat whether you're hungry or not."

"Pancakes," I said, voice muffled by his chest. "With chocolate chips."

He laughed. "Pancakes with chocolate chips it is."

* * *

Maddie's story continues in **Vanished Trails**, coming soon!
https://www.amazon.com/dp/B0CDLXNSHZ

Want a free copy of the Maddie Castle prequel novella? Sign up for my newsletter and download a copy today:
https://liquidmind.media/maddie-castle-newsletter-signup-1/

Join the L.T. Ryan private reader's group on Facebook here:
https://www.facebook.com/groups/1727449564174357

Love Maddie? Jack Noble? Rachel Hatch? Get your very own L.T. Ryan merchandise today! Click the link below to find coffee mugs, t-shirts, and even signed copies of your favorite thrillers! https://tryan.ink/EvG_

The Maddie Castle Series

The Handler

Tracking Justice

Hunting Grounds

Vanished Trails (Coming Soon)

Want a free copy of the Maddie Castle prequel novella? Sign up for my newsletter and download a copy today:

https://liquidmind.media/maddie-castle-newsletter-signup-1/

Love Maddie? Jack Noble? Rachel Hatch? Get your very own L.T. Ryan merchandise today! Click the link below to find coffee mugs, t-shirts, and even signed copies of your favorite thrillers! https://ltryan.ink/EvG_

Also by L.T. Ryan

Find All of L.T. Ryan's Books on Amazon Today!

The Jack Noble Series

The Recruit (free)

The First Deception (Prequel 1)

Noble Beginnings

A Deadly Distance

Ripple Effect (Bear Logan)

Thin Line

Noble Intentions

When Dead in Greece

Noble Retribution

Noble Betrayal

Never Go Home

Beyond Betrayal (Clarissa Abbot)

Noble Judgment

Never Cry Mercy

Deadline

End Game

Noble Ultimatum

Noble Legend

Noble Revenge

Never Look Back (Coming Soon)

Bear Logan Series

Ripple Effect

Blowback

Take Down

Deep State

Bear & Mandy Logan Series

Close to Home

Under the Surface

The Last Stop

Over the Edge

Between the Lies (Coming Soon)

Rachel Hatch Series

Drift

Downburst

Fever Burn

Smoke Signal

Firewalk

Whitewater

Aftershock

Whirlwind

Tsunami

Fastrope

Sidewinder (Coming Soon)

Mitch Tanner Series

The Depth of Darkness

Into The Darkness

Deliver Us From Darkness

Cassie Quinn Series

Path of Bones

Whisper of Bones

Symphony of Bones

Etched in Shadow

Concealed in Shadow

Betrayed in Shadow

Born from Ashes

Blake Brier Series

Unmasked

Unleashed

Uncharted

Drawpoint

Contrail

Detachment

Clear

Quarry (Coming Soon)

Dalton Savage Series

Savage Grounds

Scorched Earth

Cold Sky

The Frost Killer (Coming Soon)

Maddie Castle Series

The Handler

Tracking Justice

Hunting Grounds (Coming Soon)

Affliction Z Series

Affliction Z: Patient Zero

Affliction Z: Abandoned Hope

Affliction Z: Descended in Blood

Affliction Z : Fractured Part 1

Affliction Z: Fractured Part 2 (Fall 2021)

Get your very own L.T. Ryan merchandise today! Click the link below to find coffee mugs, t-shirts, and even signed copies of your favorite thrillers! https://ltryan.ink/EvG_

Receive a free copy of The Recruit. Visit:

https://ltryan.com/jack-noble-newsletter-signup-1

About the Author

L.T. RYAN is a *Wall Street Journal, USA Today,* and Amazon best-selling author of several mysteries and thrillers, including the *Wall Street Journal* bestselling Jack Noble and Rachel Hatch series. With over eight million books sold, when he's not penning his next adventure, L.T. enjoys traveling, hiking, riding his Peloton,, and spending time with his wife, daughter and four dogs at their home in central Virginia.

* Sign up for his newsletter to hear the latest goings on and receive some free content ➜ https://ltryan.com/jack-noble-newsletter-signup-1

* Join LT's private readers' group ➜ https://www.facebook.com/groups/1727449564174357
* Follow on Instagram ➜ @ltryanauthor
* Visit the website ➜ https://ltryan.com
* Get merch ➜ https://ltryan.shop
* Send an email ➜ contact@ltryan.com
* Find on Goodreads ➜ http://www.goodreads.com/author/show/5151659.L_T_Ryan

***

C.R. GRAY goes by a lot of names, but the most know her as Charlie, a fantasy romance author who's finally diving into the genre she's always wanted to write in - mystery and thriller. She's from a small town outside of Pittsburgh and hopes she does her city justice in the books she works on!

If she isn't writing, she's chasing after her three adorable, but incredibly stubborn, puppers - who may or may not have some of the same bad behaviors as Tempest in the Maddie Castle series. When she isn't writing, she's watching Criminal Minds or binge reading a Kathy Reichs or Kelley Armstrong novel for the millionth time. (They never get old!)

Made in United States
North Haven, CT
08 August 2023

40105924R00187